B·E·L·I·S·A·R·I·V·S

L·I·B·E·R II

G·L·O·R·I·A R·O·M·A·N·O·R·V·M

BELISARIUS

Book II:
Glory of the Romans

Paolo A. Belzoni

Arx Publishing
Merchantville, New Jersey

Arx Publishing
Merchantville, New Jersey

First Edition

ISBN-10: 1-935228-00-5
ISBN-13: 978-1-935228-00-4

Library of Congress Cataloging-in-Publication Data

Belzoni, Paolo A.
Belisarius. Book II, Glory of the Romans / Paolo A. Belzoni. -- 1st ed.
p. cm.
ISBN-13: 978-1-935228-00-4
ISBN-10: 1-935228-00-5
1. Belisarius, ca. 505-565--Fiction. 2. Generals--Byzantine Empire--Fiction. 3. Byzantine Empire--History--Justinian I, 527-565--Fiction. I. Title.
PS3602.E655B46 2010
813'.6--dc22

2010043244

To Rachel, my beloved wife and the mother of my children.

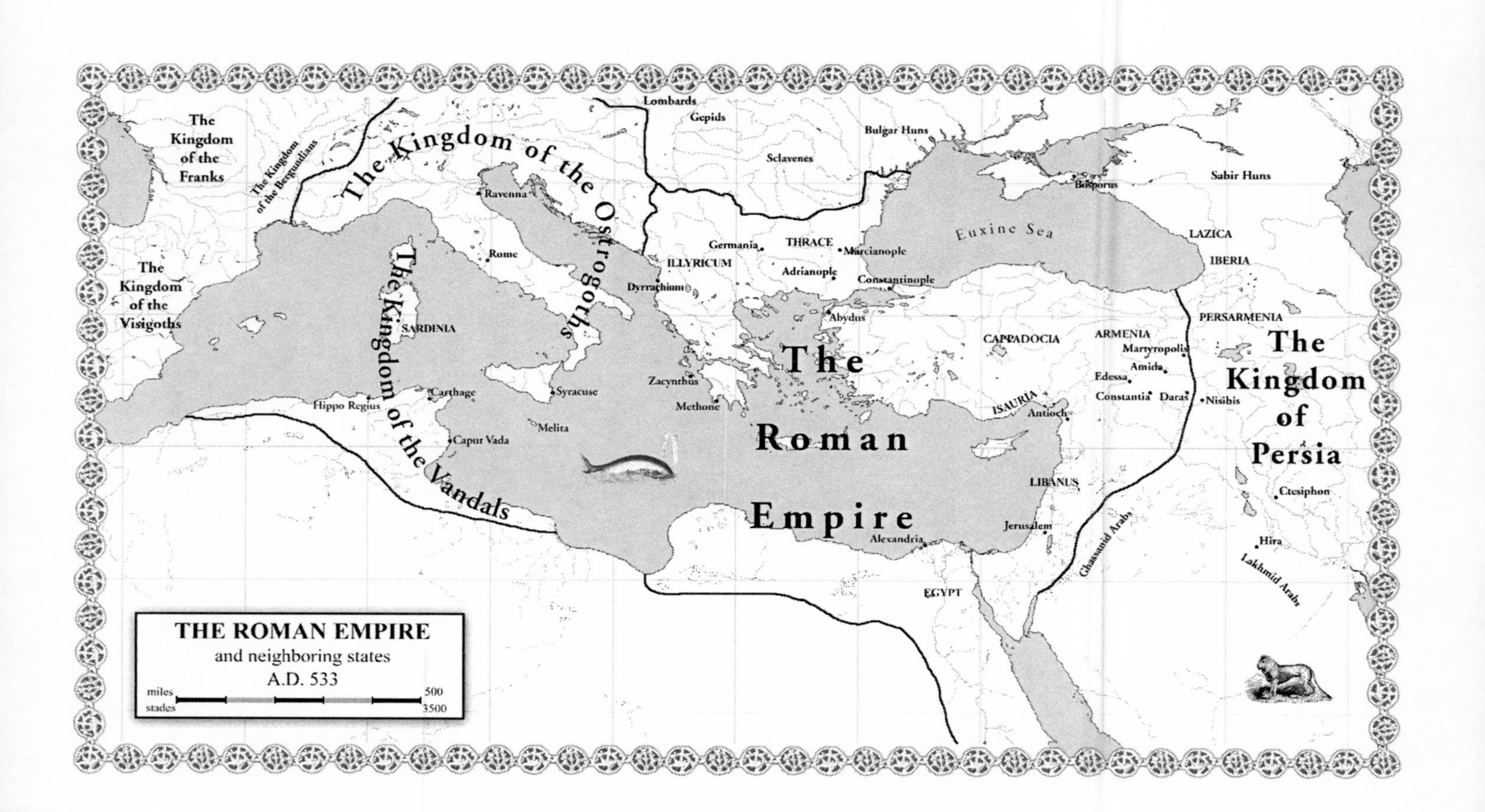
THE ROMAN EMPIRE
and neighboring states
A.D. 533
miles
stades
500
3500
The Kingdom of the Franks
The Kingdom of the Burgundians
The Kingdom of the Visigoths
The Kingdom of the Ostrogoths
The Kingdom of the Vandals
Lombards
Gepids
Bulgar Huns
Sclavenes
Sabir Huns
Bosporus
Euxine Sea
LAZICA
IBERIA
PERSARMENIA
Ravenna
Rome
SARDINIA
Germania
THRACE
Marcianople
ILLYRICUM
Adrianople
Constantinople
Dyrrachium
Abydus
CAPPADOCIA
ARMENIA
Martyropolis
Amida
Edessa
Constantia
Daras
Nisibis
The Kingdom of Persia
The Roman Empire
Zacynthus
Methone
Carthage
Hippo Regius
Syracuse
Melita
Caput Vada
ISAURIA
Antioch
LIBANUS
Ctesiphon
Jerusalem
Alexandria
Hira
Lakhmid Arabs
Ghassanid Arabs
EGYPT

Prologue

After nearly a century of weakness and decline, the mighty empire of the Romans is again on the rise under the scintillating rule of Justinian and his empress Theodora. A tireless and farsighted ruler, Justinian's great dream is to reclaim the lost provinces of the Western Empire from the barbarian nations that now dominate them. In matters of diplomacy, Justinian is a genius. He is also a master at selecting just the right men to do his bidding for him.

At the emperor's right hand is Belisarius, a brilliant general from rugged Illyricum who has risen through the ranks with unparalelled speed. With a complete mastery of cavalry tactics and an indefatigable spirit on the battlefield, Belisarius dared to face the hated armies of Persia. In the year of our Lord 530, the dashing young general won a sweeping victory over the Persians at the Battle of Daras, though outnumbered two-to-one.

With this tremendous victory, an end to the perpetual conflict on the war-ravaged eastern frontier now seems within reach, and Justinian is anxious to make peace with Persia so that he may focus his attention on the west. But while the emperor plans campaigns of glory against foreign enemies, he has neglected to secure the peace in his own capital.

NB. A glossary is provided at the back of this book for assistance with some of the obscure military and religious terms used throughout.

Additionally, a dramatis personae *is provided after the glossary to help keep track of the multitude of historical figures and fictional characters who appear in this book.*

1

AD 531, Easter Day

Fourth year of the reign of Justinian, Emperor of the Romans
Near Callinicus in Roman Mesopotamia

On the banks of the muddy Euphrates River—the edge of the fertile crescent where it is said that the earthly paradise created by Almighty God once stood—thousands of men now endured an earthly hell. For on Easter Day, rather than giving praise to Jesus Christ for his resurrection to life, the armies of two great empires sought to inflict death upon each other.

The battle need not have happened at all. The invading Persians had been brought to heel by the prowess of Belisarius, the commanding general of the Romans. His reputation was such that the Persians dared not engage with him, and upon his arrival with the Army of the East, the invaders beat a hasty retreat.

Belisarius escorted them to the border, but as the enemy host prepared to ford the Euphrates and escape back into Persia, the officers of the Roman army rebelled against their commander and questioned his courage. Belisarius, for his part, was content to let the Persians escape without bloodshed, counting it a singular blessing to defeat an enemy without losing any of his own men. But the officers under him saw in the retreating enemy a chance for earthly glory. So they raged at their general and demanded that he lead them forth into combat.

Seeing the bloodlust in their eyes and fearing the disorder of a mutiny, Belisarius grudgingly consented.

It was a decision he would subsequently regret.

✠

Belisarius raised his bow toward the enemy and loosed. Before he could draw another shaft, he sensed the hum of an incoming dart. Ducking down at the last instant, the barbed tip struck his steel helm and clanged off.

God save me! he gasped to himself, shaking off the heavy impact.

"Magister! They are taking us from the flank!" screamed Trajan, his lieutenant, pointing with his sword toward a great clamor off to the right of the Roman army.

"No!" Belisarius shouted in disbelief. He jerked his mount around to see with his own eyes and his mouth dropped open in dismay.

A messenger galloped to him, his horse in a froth. "Arethas has deserted us, O Magister! Every last Arab has fled the field!"

"The cowards couldn't even stand for one charge," Trajan raged, his fists clenched.

"Not cowards," Belisarius growled, "They are traitors! How stupid I was to entrust the right wing to them. Despite their boasts, they had no intention of fighting their brother bandits."

A great wail of despair went up from the Roman lines as the extent of the disaster was realized. Their previous swagger and order quickly dissolved into fear and chaos. In terror, thousands of mail-clad Romans threw down their arms and fled straight toward the nearby Euphrates, hoping to gain safety by swimming to the islands in midstream. Hundreds were cut down in their flight by jubilant Persians who slaughtered them with relish.

A mere thousand picked men stood by Belisarius as he fought on.

Ascan, the implacable Hunnic chieftain, along with several hundred of his best men, remained in the fight as well, forcing back the charging Persians time and again. The elite Persian Immortals, desperate to revenge themselves on the Huns for their losses at Daras the previous year, massed and flung themselves upon Ascan's men, careless of death. But the wily Hun, perched on his nimble war pony, made them pay dearly each time, dispatching some of their most valiant officers with his own deadly darts.

"We must push through and unite with Ascan's men," Belisarius commanded, drawing a javelin. *The only way to salvage the day is to recombine our remaining forces and put our backs to the river*, he thought, his mind working feverishly.

Anxious to obey their general, his stalwarts shifted front and began to move toward Ascan's surrounded contingent.

But the Persians were experienced in war and knew well that to secure the victory, it is more important to quell those forces still in the fight than to chase those who run away. Belisarius soon found his path blocked by thousands of Persians foot soldiers who, having returned from the rout, were moving in to finish the job.

"Forward!" Belisarius urged as he forced his way to the point position of his phalanx. Joining the front rank, he struck with his javelin as volleys of arrows from the men in the rear poured over his head. The lightly clad Persian footmen toppled over dead in heaps, but others took their places, their huge wicker shields presenting an impassible obstacle.

Belisarius's force was within shouting distance when an unexpected stroke from an Immortal's sword struck Ascan on the side of the face, sending a fountain of blood into the air. Seeing their hated enemy wounded, the Immortals cried out in triumph and rushed forward in a mass. Ascan's weary men melted away before the implacable Persian assault and the defenseless Hun captain was hacked to pieces—dead before he hit the ground.

With their commander slain, the remaining Huns gave up the fight and attempted to escape as best they could.

At the sight, Belisarius's remaining men let out a groan of despair.

"That's it, we're finished," cried Trajan.

"Aye," Belisarius replied, surveying a battlefied bereft of hope. "Nothing remains but to get as many of our men to safety as we can."

"Should I sound the retreat?" Trajan asked.

"Yes, we will withdraw toward Peter," Belisarius commanded, pointing to a contingent of footmen who were fighting a well-ordered rear-guard action to protect those fleeing across the river.

Commanding a moira of the Imperial household guard, the general Peter and his sturdy footmen were repelling a Saracen cavalry attack when Belisarius and his men came charging toward them. At the sight, the Saracens wheeled expertly and withdrew to regroup some distance off. The rest of the Persian cavalry also reformed nearby, preparing to deliver the *coup de grace*.

"Dismount!" Belisarius shouted to his grim-looking men. Collecting some weapons, he vaulted off of Balan, his blood-stained charger. Slapping the horse on the hindquarters, Belisarius sent him into the Euphrates to swim to safety on one of the islands. His men did likewise and soon the river was filled with a herd of war horses bobbing in the quickly reddening water.

"What happened?" Peter demanded as Belisarius and his men merged into the ranks as footmen.

"Arethas deserted us and the Persians turned our flank," Belisarius said matter-of-factly. "Ascan has been killed along with many of the Huns. The Isaurian moira has been slain almost to a man."

Peter's servile face fell. He had been one of the leaders of the faction that had demanded battle.

"Do not be downcast," Belisarius chided, sensing the man's thoughts. "Our work here today is not yet finished."

"Right. Let us acquit ourselves as true servants of the emperor should," Peter replied.

Belisarius and Peter formed the two thousand men remaining to them into a wide arc with the river at their backs. The front rank was made to crouch down with their shoulders behind their tall shields. The second rank held their shields at an angle above the heads of the first rank, creating a solid shield wall that was proof against the weakly shot Persian arrows. A third rank shored up the first two and thrust their javelins in the joints between the shields, bracing them against the ground. With the Roman rear protected by the river, the Persian and Saracen cavalry would have to charge their bristling lines head on if they wanted to complete their victory.

And charge they did.

The Saracens came first, galloping up to the Romans and discharging a swarm of arrows. Their shafts bounced harmlessly off the shield wall and the

Roman counter-volley tore through horse and man with devastating effect, dropping many of the lightly-armored Arabs to the earth.

Seeing the futility of this sort of attack, Alamoundaras, the wily and vicious Saracen kinglet, swiftly led his horsemen out of range. *Better to let the Persians bleed themselves on this stubborn shard than me*, he thought to himself, withdrawing to a small hillock nearby to watch the remainder of the battle. He would wait for the Romans to falter before re-engaging. Meanwhile, a few of his men began surreptitiously plundering the corpses of both Romans and Persians alike.

✠

Anxious to beat down the remaining Roman stalwarts, Azarethas, the Persian *chanaranges*, marshaled his cavalry. "Ride them down," he ordered the commander of the Immortals. "Leave not one standing."

"We will cave in their heads!" the commander replied zealously. Couching his lance, he launched his five thousand Persian heavy horse at the Roman shield wall like a boulder rumbling down a mountain.

✠

"They come again!" shouted Peter to Belisarius, who was busy restringing his bow.

"These are the Immortals, not wispy Saracens," Belisarius said, wedging himself into the shield wall and squinting into the approaching dust cloud. "Their aim is to ride right over and through us."

"Can we hold?" Peter asked, desperation creeping into his voice.

"Not if they hit us at full speed," Belisarius said calmly. "But let us see if their horses are awake today." Grabbing a spare shield and a sword, Belisarius began clashing them together. "Raise up a mighty noise unto the Lord, O Romans!" he urged. Concerned heads began to turn in his direction. "And let it be loud, that He might hear it above the curses of our enemies!"

Catching the idea, some of the men began to follow their commander's lead. Soon, the entire line was pounding on their shields with swords, javelins, rocks, or anything else that was handy, creating an awful, discordant din.

"Louder!" Belisarius ordered, throwing down his shield and sword and again taking up his bow.

Calling all available archers to him, he screamed his orders above the cacophony: "Up to the line and draw immediately! Watch for me to shoot. Aim for the horses in the front ranks first. Then, shoot anything that moves! Now!"

Belisarius led the archers forward to their positions behind the shield wall as the ear-splitting din rolled across the field before them like thunder. At the sound, the horses of the fast approaching Persians shook their heads in annoyance. As they closed, the noise increased until the more nervous of them began rearing and bucking in distress, fouling the line and retarding the progress of the attack. But still they came.

Belisarius picked out the heavily armored horse of an Immortal officer as his first target. He let fly his shaft and with frightful accuracy, sent it into the beast's heaving mouth—the only spot not covered with thick metal plate. The horse reared in agony and fell hard to the ground, crushing his rider and knocking another Persian off his mount.

Following their commander's lead, hundreds of Roman arrows were soon winging their way toward the Persian cavalry, striking down many. The remainder came on.

But when the point of impact arrived, only a few of the more spirited steeds could be driven into the Roman wall and impaled upon the waiting javelins. The others leaped and twisted and fought against their riders to avoid contact and escape the horrendous noise. These made easy targets for Belisarius and his archers who expertly feathered them.

From a distance, Azarethas saw his attack faltering and tore his robe in wrath. "Feckless cowards, do you fear death?" he screamed at his men. "Fear me, rather, and the punishments I will inflict upon you if you fail to ride down these Roman weaklings. You will beg for death before I'm done!"

Ashamed and enraged, the Persian horsemen reformed to charge again. This time, they coordinated their attack with massed volleys of arrows aimed at weakening one particular section of the Roman line. With fanatical fervor, they crashed their heavy mounts into the waiting Romans and enough made it through the storm of noise and darts to force the Romans to give ground or be crushed. Once contact had been made, dozens more Persians approached the line, some to push into the breech, others to discharge their arrows at the hard-pressed Romans at extreme close range.

Under intense pressure, the Romans began to fall back, slipping on the blood-saturated mud as they went.

"Hold! For God's sake, hold!" Belisarius demanded. He rushed to the threatened portion of the line with his bodyguard Unigastus following close behind. Seizing a discarded javelin and shield, he plowed into the line of straining footmen in front of him. "Push them back! Push them back! For God! For the Emperor!"

"For Belisarius!" A voice shouted from somewhere in the line. This exhortation was greeted with a hearty cheer and a renewed burst of energy.

"For Belisarius! Hero of Daras!" more voices joined. "*Nika! Victoria!*" others shouted in their particular idiom.

Infused with vigor, the backpedaling Roman line abruptly stood up and leaned forward again. Striking out powerfully with their javelins, they skewered the foremost Persians and their mounts and trampled over their bodies. With sheer power, the line muscled its way forward. Their strength swelled as they proceeded and the enemy wave slacked and ebbed away, broken upon the jagged rocks of Roman valor.

As the Persian horsemen streamed off to regroup yet again, a tremendous cheer went up from he Roman soldiery. "Belisarius, slayer of Immortals! Belisarius, master of Cabades! Belisarius, greatest of all Romans!" choruses of voices shouted, each vying to outdo the other with epithets of praise for their Magister.

✠

From an island in the Euphrates, Belisarius's steward, Solomon, scolded the refugee soldiers gathered around him and watched the continuing battle on the riverbank with alternating concern and admiration. Fitted out in a full corselet, Solomon had been given the rank of dux by his master and command of a reserve moira of cavalry. When the Persians turned the Roman flank, his inexperienced men were suddenly exposed to close combat and fled before the charging Immortals. Silently cursing this failure, Solomon's keen eyes searched earnestly for a way to make restitution.

"Our Magister remains to fight against ten times his number while you gutless creatures cower in the mud. What a shameful display," Solomon opined out loud to no one in particular. Enough of the men heard him.

A few dozen soaked and filthy soldiers came forward. "What would you have us do, O Dux?"

Solomon looked them over. The thought of ordering them to swim back across occurred to him, but he dismissed it. *Too risky and likely to be rejected by the men anyway,* he thought to himself, stroking his smooth chin. At that instant, two flat-bottomed barges loaded with cargo slowly drifted by, pushed along by stout men with polls.

"You there!" Solomon shouted, his high tenor carrying clearly across the water. "Ground here. We have need of your craft!"

The boatmen pretended not to hear and attempted to skirt the island, quickening their pace. But Solomon's men had caught the drift of his idea and were immediately in the water seizing the boats. At Solomon's command, they pitched the cargo overboard.

"I shall be flogged because of this," one of the dejected boatmen complained.

"Take it like a man, then," Solomon sniped back at him. "The value of these goods is nothing compared to the lives of our men."

In minutes, Solomon and a score of men had crowded onto one of the barges and were headed back toward the battle. "Take the other barge back to Callinicus," Solomon ordered a contingent of soldiers. "Return here with ten more boats and tell any who hesitate that they will have to answer to the Magister Belisarius himself."

✠

Belisarius had pulled back from the front line during a lull in the fighting and was refreshing himself with water when the general Peter approached.

"Your slave has arrived with twenty men from the routed reserve moira," Peter informed him.

Belisarius turned on the man with anger in his voice: "Slave he may be, but I have made him an officer in my guard, General. You will refer to him by his rank henceforth, as is proper."

"Yes, O Magister," Peter replied resentfully.

Javelin still in hand, Belisarius strode past Peter to greet Solomon. "I knew you'd turn up," he quipped, clasping arms with his steward.

"My most sincere apologies for the performance of the men under my command, O Magister. I have brought these few repentant souls to bolster your force."

"They are most welcome," Belisarius said, gesturing toward the line where each of them took up a position.

"With luck, I also bring you something else that may be of use," Solomon continued.

Belisarius shot him a quizzical look.

"You see yon barge? What could you do with a dozen such?" Solomon asked rhetorically. "I have summoned them from Callinicus, having invoked your name and called down punishments on any malingerers."

"Well done," Belisarius said, slapping his steward on the back. "Let us hope that my name inspires enough dread to light a fire under those laggardly dock monkeys."

Five more times over the course of the afternoon, the Persians hit the Roman semi-circle of steel with everything they could muster. And each time, the Romans threw them back with losses. From their protected position behind the shield-wall, Roman archers launched their lethal shafts hissing into the vulnerable Persian formations. Horses fell by the dozen, men by the score with each volley.

Soon the pace of the Persian attacks slackened.

By nightfall, it was over.

Just as dusk began to obscure the field of battle, Belisarius spied the first group of barges approaching through the foul-smelling mist which settled over the Euphrates.

"Ah, our battle fleet has arrived at last," Belisarius remarked, standing in the muddy shallows.

But Solomon was in no mood for his master's good nature. He stormed off to meet the first barge to arrive, and dressed down the men aboard. He returned to Belisarius in a snit. "Can you believe that these craven halfwits were too afraid to approach the battle during the daylight? And furthermore, they had the audacity to tell me so!"

Belisarius laughed. "Brave cowards. Who could have imagined?"

"Idiots!" Solomon seethed.

"Well, idiots or no, their tardiness meant the death of many Persians at little cost to us," Belisarius rationalized. "Now, let us get these stout fighting men to safety. They've earned their pay today."

The sun rose red over somber Callinicus the next day. Belisarius, Peter, and most of their surviving men had found refuge in the fortified city during the night, but stragglers were still wandering back all throughout the next day. The Persians, for their part, spent the morning plundering the Roman corpses left on the field and then promptly and gratefully retreated toward home.

Belisarius began his day early. He surveyed his tattered army, visited the injured, and reckoned the missing and dead.

"Do you suffer much pain?" Belisarius asked, pointing to a freshly applied bandage on the thigh of his friend Aigan. The Hunnic captain had been taken to a make-shift hospital in the Monastery of St. Zaccheus where he and hundreds of others were being treated for wounds of varying severity.

"No pain, Magister. Scratch only," Aigan replied in his awkward Greek. For effect, he stood up and hobbled around his pallet on his crooked legs, bowed from a lifetime in the saddle.

Belisarius gave a hint of a smile as the Hun winced inadvertently.

"They say Ascan slain," Aigan remarked, grimacing up into the face of his much taller commander.

"It's true," Belisarius said soberly, shaking his head. "I saw it happen."

"Take many Persians with him, eh?" Aigan rasped.

"He did. He faced death upright on his horse. None ever saw his back."

"Died like a Hun!" Aigan enthused. "We collect his body?"

"No," Belisarius admitted apologetically. "It was impossible.

Aigan exploded into a throaty laugh. "Then pity the Persian who took his steel cap—filled with fleas!"

Belisarius smiled.

Picking his way through the bustle of monks attending the wounded, Trajan entered seeking Belisarius. "Magister, there are some men back at your quarters who wish to see you," Trajan announced as he approached. There was a hint of satisfaction in his voice.

"What men?"

"Your comrades—the other commanders," Trajan smirked. "They seem in quite a humble mood this morning."

Belisarius bid farewell to Aigan and hurried back to his headquarters. There, a group of his officers were receiving a stern lecture from Solomon, who had not yet shed his armor.

"You who fought alongside him at Daras dared to question his courage? You, Marcellus, who campaigned with him in Armenia, you accused him to his face of losing his nerve, demanding that he attack a retreating enemy even on Easter Day!"

"I deny that I said that!" Marcellus protested weakly.

"You did say it!" Solomon shouted. "I marked every one of you—even the ones whose flesh now fills the gizzards of vultures."

"This is intolerable," Peter grumbled under his breath. "To be harangued by this slave."

"Then learn some humility," snapped Bouzes, who was standing next to him. He hung his head, ashamed to have been part of the cabal.

"Fools that you are, in your arrogance you thought you knew better than he did," Solomon continued. "Yet you only succeeded in staining the ground red with the blood of Romans. Almost all 2,000 of the Isaurians were slain!"

"They were among the loudest proponents of the attack," Belisarius said, having entered the courtyard unnoticed. Every head turned in his direction. "None can fault *them* for failing to match their swagger with action."

All were silent as Belisarius and Trajan made their way through them. An ornate curule chair had been set out, and Belisarius seated himself on it. "Solomon, you may return to your duties," he said, nodding.

"Yes, Magister." Solomon bowed and strode into the house.

Belisarius was silent for a long moment. "Well?" he finally barked, his annoyance getting the better of him. "I did not summon you. Why have you come?"

Shuffling forward, the officers began to form a line. Bouzes pushed his way through to be at the head. He genuflected before Belisarius, bowed his head submissively and said, "Forgive me, Magister. God knows, the fault was mine, not yours."

One by one, the others did likewise. But Peter and the other men of the imperial guard held back, scandalized. "Is this man the emperor that he receives the obeisance of his underlings in this way?" Peter grumbled. His men returned his stony gaze with grim looks. "I'll not bow my neck to him," Peter continued, leading his men abruptly toward the nearest exit. "And we'll see that the emperor hears about this shameful display."

"Do that," Solomon confronted him in the atrium. "But be sure that the emperor also hears how you imbeciles nearly mutinied because my master wouldn't engage in a pointless battle. Tell the emperor how your rash swagger cost him nearly 5,000 of his best soldiers."

"Your master aggrandizes himself…" Peter began.

"As is proper!" Solomon cut him off. "He is commander of the East, and though you have no respect for authority, be assured that my master most certainly does. He is loyal to the emperor unto death."

"Out of my way, eunuch," Peter snarled as he pushed past him into the narrow cobblestone street. "Tell Belisarius that we're leaving here at sun-up tomorrow to return to Byzantium."

"You should tell him yourself, O General," Solomon shouted after him. But Peter was finished arguing with a mere servant. "That haughty fool!" Solomon sighed out loud.

"Do not worry, O Dux. I shall make sure matters are set aright in the palace," a familiar voice piped up from behind. "I've been meaning to request a research sabbatical in the capital for some time now."

"Ah, Procopius," Solomon said, smiling, "but my master would be loath to part with you, even for a short time. As would I."

"The emperor will be looking for an independent report of the goings on here, and I'll be only too happy to provide it. With a full purse, an armed escort, and a swift horse, I may even get there before Peter and his men do."

"You bargain like a Jew rather than a Pamphylian, my friend!" Solomon laughed, clapping him on the back. "But you shall have all that you ask for, with the gratitude of the entire household."

Procopius's face broke into a sly grin. "Excellent! Now, I have had my eye on that gray filly...."

✠

Two months passed before a military tribunal from Constantinople arrived, headed by the senator Constantiolus. Presenting his credentials to Belisarius, he immediately made his purpose clear. The emperor wanted the full truth about the defeat at Callinicus and the senator had been deputized to get it.

Belisarius gave Constantiolus free and easy access to whomever he wished to interview and put no roadblocks in his way. The senator plowed through the process with a determination borne less of thoroughness than a desire to finish and depart. He saved Solomon for last, and when the dux emerged from his questioning, his face was flushed with anger all the way to his receding hairline.

"He intends to blame the entire debacle on you, Master—that much is clear," Solomon fumed.

Belisarius turned away. "You are being overly sensitive, I think. The other men tell me his methods of interrogation are accusatory and brusque, but that is the technique employed by good lawyers."

"It is more than that," Solomon groused. "Someone at the court has coated his palm with gold, I'll wager. Most likely that scoundrel Peter. Of course, if that's the case, it means there is a way we can influence the course of this investigation as well."

"Are you suggesting that we offer him a bribe?" Belisarius laughed.

"A bribe, Master?" Solomon said, false innocence permeating his voice. "Not exactly. It would just be a few nomismata to balance out the *evidence* presented by your adversaries. Not at all an uncommon practice."

Belisarius frowned. "No bribes. If he chooses to indict me to the emperor, then so be it. I erred in allowing myself to be swayed by the men. If the emperor decides to punish me for this error, I will accept it."

Solomon's mouth twisted, but he said no more.

✠

Another two months went by before an imperial courier found Belisarius exercising in the courtyard of his headquarters at Daras. The courier delivered his missive, accepted a follis for his trouble, bowed, and left.

After dismissing his sparring partners, Belisarius broke the seal and read.

"Any news, Master?" Solomon asked, his impatience getting the better of his discretion.

Belisarius simply laughed a shallow mirthless laugh. He sat down on a convenient bench and put a hand to his forehead. "Here, you read it," he said.

Solomon snatched up the note. It was written in the curt, official jargon of a military command. As he finished, his face fell. "You've been recalled."

"Yes, that's the gist of it," Belisarius snapped.

"That wretched Peter. I guess Constantiolus was in his pay after all," Solomon offered weakly.

"Look, are you just going to stand there stating the obvious all day long?"

Solomon looked thoughtfully at the letter again. "But Master, it's not as bad as it seems. Look here—it says that an embassy under Rufinus had made significant progress with the Persians. They are in the process of finalizing a peace with Cabades even now."

Belisarius laughed aloud, this time with more gusto, as if a thought had just entered his head.

"Master, there's no disgrace in this recall," Solomon rationalized. "The emperor is merely repositioning our forces in expectation of the treaty."

Belisarius leapt to his feet, his momentary melancholy replaced with a sudden burst of exuberance. "Don't play the sycophant with me, Solomon. I'm not the naïve boy I used to be. Whatever the reason, this recall is meant to take me down a peg, and indeed, I deserve it. But do you know something? I don't care."

Solomon looked at him strangely.

Belisarius approached his servant and slapped him hard on the back. "Let them demote me. When I get back to Constantinople, the first thing I am going to do is get married!"

II

AD 531, Summer

Fourth year of the reign of Justinian, Emperor of the Romans
At Antioch

Mundus, the Magister Militum of Illyricum, was named to replace Belisarius in the East, but he would not arrive for many months. Until then, Sittas was to be in nominal command of both Armenia and the East. Mundus was a Gepid—a race of semi-civilized but battle-ready barbarians from beyond the Ister River who had been brought into the Roman orbit within the last decade. As a high noble and a renowned champion among his people, Mundus brought with him a retinue of fighting men several hundred strong. Belisarius was expected to meet Mundus in Constantinople and provide him with a thorough overview of the situation in the East.

Leaving Daras in the hands of his capable lieutenant, Trajan, Belisarius departed in late June, along with a single tagma of his troops. The entire populace turned out to bid farewell to their beloved commander, showering his column with flowers, garlands, and acclamations as they rode though the streets and out the main gate.

The baking heat of summer was not the ideal season for travel, so the little army moved slowly and rested frequently, visiting several cities along the way. When the walls of magnificent Antioch came into view, the men rejoiced, knowing that their journey was half-way finished.

Antioch the Great was one of the finest cities of the empire, boasting a population of nearly a quarter-million. Largely destroyed in a tremendous earthquake five years before, the city had been rebuilt in grand style thanks to the largesse of the emperor Justin and his successor, the reigning emperor Justinian. Antioch had also received a new name at that time—Theopolis, or the City of God—in hopes that the Almighty would spare it from future catastrophes.

Approaching the city from the southeast, Belisarius was immediately struck by the poorly planned defensive works which encompassed the great metropolis. The walls were high and imposing, but they twisted and meandered haphazardly across the plain and up the side of nearby Mount Silpius. In a few spots, lofty eminences overtopped the walls. In his mind's eye, Belisarius could see enemy archers and siege engines positioned on those outcroppings, pouring missiles and fire onto the cowering defenders below. *I must bring these failings to the attention of the emperor upon my return,* he thought to himself as he approached the gates. *This city is too great to be defended so dreadfully.*

"Greetings, Strategos," an officer of the guard saluted, recognizing the insignia but not the man. "Welcome to Antioch the Great. How shall I announce your arrival to the Prefect?"

"Inform him that Belisarius and his men wish to refresh themselves in Theopolis for a night before continuing on to the capital."

"Belisarius?" the man gasped. "*You* are Belisarius?"

"Yes, I am."

The officer dropped to a knee clumsily. "Forgive me, Magister. I did not know it was you."

"No need for apologies," Belisarius replied. "And do not bow to me for I have been recalled and am no longer Magister of the East."

"With respect, sir, I bow not only for your rank, but in honor of your deeds. You are the hero of Daras."

"Rise," Belisarius commanded, chagrined by the unexpected praise. "Now show us to a place where these men may be lodged and fed for the night."

"With pleasure, Magister," the officer rose. "This way, if you please."

✠

Word quickly spread throughout Antioch that Belisarius had arrived, and every patrician and high official in the city sent his compliments and invitation to dine. But Belisarius politely refused them all. Instead, when all was dark, he made his way alone from the military barracks where he and his men had been quartered down the wide Street of Tiberius and Herod toward the center of town. Rising above all was the hemisphere of the Great Church of Antioch, a magnificent octagonal edifice built originally by Constantine two centuries before. It was toward this landmark that Belisarius pointed his steps.

"My apologies, but we're locked up for the night," a heavyset priest announced through a grille in one of the gates. "Come back in the morning."

"Forgive my intrusion, O Presbyter," Belisarius responded. "It was my hope to pray before the Sacrament of the altar tonight. It has been too long since Belisarius has set foot in Antioch's Great Church."

At the name, the priest's eyes widened. He fumbled for a large ring of keys and immediately unlocked the heavy bronze door. "Your pardon, Magister. I had no idea it was you," the priest apologized breathlessly. The door opened with a groan. "Enter, if you please."

Belisarius made his way toward the interior of the church, smiling inwardly. *Perhaps fame has its virtues after all.*

The priest led him to the altar and then quickly retired.

Belisarius knelt on the marble floor before the great slab and was bathed in a soft, smoky light reflecting from the underside of the dome which was covered with gold leaf. Damaged in the recent earthquake, the dome now inclined noticeably to the west. Great timbers and scaffolding had been set up to keep it from collapsing entirely.

Belisarius prayed silently for some moments, conjuring up first visions of Antonina, and then of his friend Florentius, who had been killed at the Battle of Satala the previous year. He began to pray for the repose of his soul, but stopped half way through. Florentius was in Heaven, he was sure of it.

Florentius, intercede with God Almighty on my behalf. Belisarius prayed in a whisper. *Ask Him to bless my coming marriage and to make me the kind of husband Antonina deserves.*

Belisarius immediately recalled words that Florentius had once spoken to him about Antonina: *My only concern for you is whether her very obvious beauty of face and form is matched by a hidden beauty of soul and spirit.*

A dull worry suddenly filled him. He knew so little of this woman he was going to marry. Their correspondence had been frequent while he was in the east and allowed for a kind of distant intimacy. But he hadn't actually seen Antonina in over six years. He had no idea what it would be like to be with her every day, and the notion now unnerved him.

Lord Jesus, bless our marriage, he continued, seeking divine strength. *Make it true and fruitful. Let us be helpmates to each other and let me be unwaveringly faithful to her for my whole life.*

Belisarius remained on his knees for some time reciting his prayers. When finished, he rose to depart. His footsteps echoed as he left the cool golden light which suffused the octagonal nave.

To his shock, about two dozen priests and monks had gathered in the narthex. At first, he wasn't sure what they were doing there, but their purpose soon became clear.

"God has blessed you, Magister," one of them said as he reached forward to touch Belisarius's arm. "You have conquered the Persians and humbled the proud Cabades."

"Verily, verily," the rest agreed as they came toward him eagerly, wanting nothing more than to put a hand on him. "May Christ continue to shower His graces upon you."

"I'm sorry for this," said the rotund priest who had first admitted him to the church. "When I told them you had come, they all wanted to see you."

"Thank you all, holy fathers," Belisarius replied, making his way slowly toward the door through the cassocked crowd. "It is an honor to serve the Roman Empire which God sustains."

"Amen," they replied. "May God give you strength through the intercession of Saint George."

"Please continue to pray for me," Belisarius asked as he prepared to exit. "And I'll continue to defend the empire for you, as God allows."

Turning from the priests, Belisarius opened the door and was about to head into the night. To his further surprise, the street outside the church was also filled with people.

"There he is!" someone shouted. The rest cheered and surged toward him.

It's going to be a long walk back to the barracks, Belisarius sighed to himself.

AD 531, Autumn
Fifth year of the reign of Justinian, Emperor of the Romans
At Constantinople

The October sky was steel gray and the sea in the Julian harbor was choppy as the ferry from Chalcedon lurched toward the dock. Waiting at the quay was a woman of great beauty, a veil of blue trimmed with gold covering her wavy black locks. Her full lips parted and a smile dawned on her lovely face as the gangplank was lowered.

Beside her stood a lad of eleven years, tall for his age and thin. His face reflected that of his mother, handsome and intelligent but at the same time anxious. His hair was dark but unkempt like that of most boys his age. His eyes, a clear amber in color, were searching and hopeful.

To the left of mother and son stood a young man of no more than thirty, his large eyes pinched into a squint above his aquiline nose. He was clean shaven and slightly built. His hands, stained black with ink, were clasped in front of him as he shuffled nervously on his feet.

Around them stood a dozen gnarled old dock hands with poles, ropes, and carts ready to begin unloading cargo.

"Look, there's Procopius!" Solomon shouted as he disembarked from the ship with his master.

Belisarius failed to reply, enchanted as he was with the vision of Antonina standing but fifty paces away. It took all his strength not to run to her like a child. Instead, he approached her slowly and stood before her, dropping a sack full of his personal effects on the ground.

Antonina had averted her face as he drew near. "You have grown a beard," she said, not meeting his eyes.

"Do you not like it?" he replied awkwardly, taken aback by the comment.

"It suits you very well," Antonina choked as she looked up into his face. She reached up to stroke his whiskers and at once tears began flowing from her eyes.

Unable to restrain himself, Belisarius embraced her.

"Welcome home, O bridegroom," she whispered and they remained locked together for several moments.

As soon as they separated, Belisarius turned his attention to the boy standing nearby. "You are Photius, are you not?"

"Yes, sir, I am," the lad replied.

Belisarius put a hand on his shoulder. "It's so good to finally meet you. Your mother has often told me what a fine lad you are."

"Sh-she has?" Photius quavered. "Oh."

"Photius, greet your new father appropriately," Antonina said, an authoritarian tone entering her voice.

The boy bowed to Belisarius and said in a forced voice which betrayed rehearsal: "Welcome, O father, to the imperial city. Long have we awaited your arrival and we are filled with joy that the day has finally come. Let no worries trouble your heart or fatigue afflict your spirit. But come with us to the house we have prepared to rest and refresh yourself."

"I can't think of anything I'd rather do," Belisarius said wearily.

"But Master, the men require quarters," Solomon interrupted from behind.

Belisarius made to respond but was preempted by his bodyguard, Unigastus.

"Magister, think nothing of us," the veteran said. "I lived in the Imperial City for many years before we headed east. Finding quarters for us will be no trouble."

"Solomon, give him gold—enough to quarter them all," Belisarius said. He approached Unigastus and clasped arms with him. "You will be at the wedding feast next week."

"Cabades himself couldn't keep me away," Unigastus laughed.

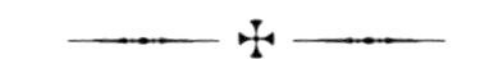

Belisarius arranged for his belongings to be hauled to the house that Antonina had prepared for them. He, Antonina and Photius then strolled slowly home, followed by Solomon and Procopius. So entranced was he with his soon-to-be wife and son that he had not so much as greeted his secretary.

At a brief lull in the conversation, Procopius piped up: "Magister, I have news from the emperor."

"News?" Belisarius said, arresting his gait. "What does he say?"

"The emperor commands that you appear before him on the morrow after your return to Byzantium," Procopius declared.

"At court or in private?" Belisarius wondered out loud.

"At court," Procopius muttered in a low voice, almost afraid of the effect this information might have.

Solomon assumed a grave expression, matched by that of Antonina.

Belisarius smiled and resumed walking. "I suppose he wants to dress me down publicly. Certainly, that is his prerogative as emperor and truly, I deserve it for allowing myself to be ruled by my officers at Callinicus. But let us leave that worry for tomorrow. Tonight, I am home. Nothing will stop me from being happy."

Belisarius and Solomon arrived at the ornate Chalke gate of the imperial palace at sunrise the next morning. There, they were joined by Unigastus and Athenodorus, two of Belisarius's chief bodyguards. The four were admitted immediately, along with a growing crowd of secretaries, lawyers, officials, clerks and other bureaucrats—the human machinery that kept the empire running.

The four men were escorted to the Delphax—the great audience hall in the imperial palace. There, the emperor Justinian sat in majesty with his consort, the empress Theodora, by his side. Belisarius had not been present at an imperial audience since Justinian had ascended to the throne, and he was struck by how magnificently both Justinian and Theodora were attired.

The emperor wore a tasseled and brocaded dalmatic, richly embroidered with golden threads. Atop this was draped a magnificent purple silk cloak, clasped at one shoulder by a golden fibula which sported a cut ruby of truly prodigious size. On his head, Justinian wore a full crown of gold topped with great round pearls. From this brilliant corona depended several more pearls on light golden chains which dangled behind his head. On his feet, Justinian wore the scarlet slippers that none but the emperor were permitted to wear.

One other aspect of the emperor's appearance struck Belisarius as he approached the throne—though Justinian appeared to be the very image of imperial grandeur, he was badly in need of a shave.

Theodora was, if possible, even more magnificently gowned than her husband. The empress was wrapped in a purple robe of the costliest silk, a lavish collar of gold cloth encrusted with pearls and gems covering her neck and shoulders. Her crown was more like a headdress complete with a sampling of every precious metal and stone the earth could yield. Long strands of pearls were strung through her thick, luxuriant hair and dangled over her shoulders, chest, and back. Belisarius wondered to himself at the strength of Theodora's neck to be able to support such a massive apparatus for more than a few moments.

Unlike her husband, Theodora's hygiene was impeccable. Coated with the finest cosmetics, her face appeared unnaturally pale and without blemish—more a mask than an actual living countenance.

"The general Belisarius, Magister Militum of the East!" a mandator announced in a loud voice. "Attended by Solomon, dux, and Unigastus and Athenodorus, tribunes."

Belisarius and his entourage prostrated themselves on the marble floor before the imperial pair.

"Rise, noble soldiers of the Roman Empire," Justinian commanded in elegant Latin. "We trust your journey was a fair one?"

"Yes, my Lord, your Piety," Belisarius replied. "The roads were clear and we met no mishaps along the way."

Solomon noticed the eyebrows of Theodora knitting in annoyance and realized that Belisarius had already committed a gaffe of some kind.

"How stands the situation on the eastern frontier?" Justinian asked curtly.

"Before my departure, your Piety, I toured the garrisons along the frontier and made certain that their men were well-trained and their officers kept them that way. The fortifications of Daras have been strengthened, as well as those of Constantia and Amida. Now, when the Persians attempt to cross the frontier, they do so only in strength and prepare with greater care. The spring and early summer saw almost no raiding activity from Persia, although Alamoundaras and his Saracen riders continue to harass our ungarrisoned frontier towns.

"Were our Ghassanid allies of no use against him?" Justinian queried.

"Your Piety, if I may be frank, Arethas and his Ghassanids are the worst type of ally. Never have I met a man who promised so much and lied so readily. They are not to be counted on by any means. Though I have no proof, it is rumored among the men that they work in tandem with Alamoundaras, playing the two empires against each other for their own mutual benefit."

Justinian furrowed his brow. "We thank you for your insights. We have heard such things from others, and indeed, for the money we have expended to ensure their allegiance, the return has been negligible."

Belisarius continued: "I should also point out to your Piety that the fortifications at Antioch the Great are in desperate need of restoration. Having seen them on our return journey, I tremble to think what would happen should the city ever be subjected to a Persian attack."

Justinian opened his mouth to respond but at that moment, a courtier came from behind the throne and whispered something hurriedly in the emperor's ear. Justinian nodded, waved the man away, and returned his attention to Belisarius. "Thank you for bringing the defenses of Antioch the Great to our attention. We will send a message to the Prefect of the East to inquire about it. Now, explain to us what happened at Callinicus."

In short, factual sentences, Belisarius recounted the battle, not leaving out his own role, having succumbed to the entreaties of his men to engage the Persians against his better judgment. "And for that, your Piety, I beg forgiveness. I should have had better control over my officers."

With a slight smile, Justinian raised his right hand as if in absolution. "You are pardoned of any wrong-doing in this matter. Let us hear no more about it."

"Your Piety is gracious beyond my worth," Belisarius replied and genuflected before Justinian. In his heart, he was jubilant.

As he rose from his knee, the empress spoke, her slightly nasal voice echoing in the cavernous space of the Delphax: "General, it has come to our attention that you are to wed within the week."

"Yes, your Grace. I am to marry the lady Antonina."

Theodora again appeared irritated, but she quickly mastered herself. "Antonina is a fine woman. You have truly done well for yourself."

"Thank you, your Grace."

"And where do you intend the ceremony to take place?"

"At the Shrine of the Hodegetria, your Grace. It is to be a small affair."

Theodora smiled. "After some consideration, we have arranged for the wedding to take place in the Great Church. Many patricians and members of the imperial court will no doubt wish to attend, among them the emperor and I."

Belisarius's jaw dropped open. "I am honored, your Grace. You are most welcome, of course."

"And then afterward, the emperor and I will host a celebration here in the palace in honor of the couple joined by God."

"Your Grace is indeed generous," Belisarius gasped, bowing deeply. "You honor us far above our rank."

"Nonsense," Theodora dismissed his comment with a wave of her hand. "Now go. The lady Antonina will no doubt wish to hear of this."

"But before you do," Justinian called out, gesturing him to come closer. He then continued in a raised whisper. "I'd like to speak to you privately. Marcellinus will show you the way to my private audience chamber. Will you come?"

"Without delay, your Piety," Belisarius replied, perplexed at the emperor's suddenly colloquial tone.

"Good. I'll see you in an hour, then, once I'm finished with all this." Belisarius followed the emperor's finger to a long line of litigants, senators, bureaucrats, ambassadors, and other petitioners awaiting their opportunity to gain the emperor's ear, if only for a moment or two.

"You must not address the emperor as 'your Piety'," Marcellinus whispered urgently to Belisarius as they made their way to the Chalke gate to bid farewell to Solomon, Unigastus and Athenodorus. "Not in private, but especially not during a public audience. And you should never address the empress as 'your Grace'. They are to be addressed always as Master and Mistress."

"Ah, I knew it!" Solomon burst out. "I saw from the empress's reaction that you were committing some breach of protocol but I couldn't figure out what it was."

"The empress introduced this innovation while you were on the frontier. She said it was necessary to humble the patricians who had become too arrogant and self-aggrandizing during the past two reigns."

"I appreciate the tip," Belisarius replied.

As they reached the Chalke, Marcellinus was momentarily called away by a clerk who had an urgent matter to discuss with him.

Solomon frowned. "Be careful when you go in there," he whispered. "Things have changed around the palace and I haven't been home long enough to discern the lay of the land. It's not a good sign that the empress expects even free men and generals to address her like slaves."

"Good advice, as usual, old friend," Belisarius responded. "I'll be careful, but I intend to be honest in all things. If this brings me ill-favor, then so be it."

Solomon smiled. *God protect this noble, naive fellow,* he thought to himself.

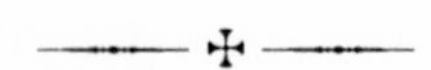

On a bench of marble polished smooth by the posteriors of many before him, Belisarius sat awaiting the emperor. After three full hours, Justinian appeared. He had shed his imperial cloak in favor of a plain tunic, and laid aside his ornate crown, wearing a simple gold diadem instead. Two slaves remained by the door, ready to serve.

"Ah, there he is!" the emperor cried in Latin upon entering the chamber. "The great general Belsarius!"

Belisarius knelt and bowed low before him. "Your servant, O Master."

Justinian snorted. "How quickly they coached you in courtly protocol. Get up, please!"

Belisarius stood and faced his emperor, a look of mild confusion on his face.

"All that nonsense is fine at an official audience. But here in private, you may address me as you addressed my uncle."

"As you wish, my Lord, your Piety."

"Come, let us sit and be at ease," Justinian gestured to a low table and couches nearby. Snapping his fingers, he called out to the slaves: "Fetch wine and fruit."

The slaves slipped behind a curtain and returned seconds later with their master's fare.

"My apologies for making you endure that foolishness about Callinicus. Your secretary, Procopius, told me everything and he is quite a keen observer of men and their motives. But for the sake of appearances, I had to say something on the subject at court. You understand, of course."

"Certainly, your Piety," Belisarius replied, sipping his wine. "So then, truly, my recall was not due to my faults at Callinicus?"

"Not at all," Justinian declared, "nor have you lost your rank." He then moved closer and spoke conspiratorially in a low voice: "Hermogenes and Rufinus are on the brink of a truly historic treaty—an Eternal Peace with the Persians. Cabades has about reached the end of his mortal chain and the miserable old wretch seeks to pass on his kingdom in peace to his youngest son, Chosroes. But there are others who will try to usurp the throne of Persia once the old man's ghost flies off to hell. The last thing Cabades wants is to bequeath his young son internal and external conflicts at the same time.

"As a result of this, we have decided to alter the alignment of our forces. You have been recalled because we believe that your exemplary skills and fearsome reputation were no longer needed in the East."

That wily Solomon was right again, Belisarius chuckled to himself. "Where may I be of service to you, then, my Lord?" he said.

Justinian smiled as if Belisarius had said exactly the right thing. "I shall have a task for you soon enough—one greater and more dangerous than any you have faced to this point. All I ask is that you be patient and enjoy the comforts of the Queen of Cities while the diplomats do their work."

"That is a command I can fulfill with pleasure," Belisarius responded jovially.

"Indeed, you deserve it more than anyone!" Justinian laughed, chewing a ripe fig.

"Your Piety, if I may, there is one matter that yet concerns me," Belisarius said, feeling more free to speak his mind in the emperor's presence.

Justinian nodded and waved his hand indulgently, his mouth too full of dates to respond without spitting them on the floor.

"There are nearly two thousand soldiers in the east who remain in my pay. I am content to continue paying them if it be your will. However, my worry is that their loyalty may not be as strong as it should be to their new commander if their paymaster is someone different."

Justinian seemed caught off guard by the question and put a finger to his pursed lips. But his quick mind did not render him silent for long: "Continue to pay them yourself," he said. "As you have proven your loyalty beyond any doubt, I give you permission to add them to your household guard. When the time comes, you may summon them to the capital. You will have need of them, I promise you."

✠

"You may enter," Theodora, Empress of the Romans, called out in her pleasant voice.

A small balding man entered the gorgeously decorated room and fell prostrate before her, his head touching the magnificent Persian carpet on the floor.

"Go, all of you," Theodora commanded and her serving maids scattered like mice from a brush fire.

"Rise, Narses," the empress intoned. "What brings you to see me this evening?"

"Information, my Mistress," Narses said, his reedy voice cracking slightly.

Theodora laughed full-throat. "Do you come bearing it or seeking it?"

"Both as always, Mistress, if you will indulge me."

"Go on," Theodora smirked, leaning on a nearby couch and compulsively picking at her fingernails.

"I have heard that the emperor not only pardoned the general Belisarius, but allowed him to retain his rank as Magister of the East."

Theodora yawned, unimpressed. "Even the lowest slave present at court this morning knows that much."

"Ah, but did you know that Justinian is also grooming him for another major command? And what's more, he has granted him the privilege of adding two-thousand men to his household guard."

Theodora's attention was now fully engaged and the first signs of annoyance showed plainly on her face. "Are you sure your source can be trusted?"

"He heard the words from the emperor's mouth," Narses piped. "And worse, Belisarius forced the emperor's hand by cleverly pretending that he wanted to turn these troops over to the new commander in the east."

"And my husband knew at once that he would have to pay them himself if Belisarius did that. Mundus could never manage it on his own resources."

"I told you Belisarius was dangerous, my Mistress," Narses whispered. "The general Peter told me that his troops were calling him 'the greatest of all Romans' at Callinicus, and that afterwards he forced them to admit their mistakes and do him homage. Have I told you this?"

"Yes, several times," Theodora hissed impatiently. Her mind was now elsewhere.

"I tell you he is a threat," Narses whispered, knitting his brows. "He is not to be trusted."

Theodora rolled her eyes, seeing through Narses's motives like a gossamer window dressing. "You know, Narses, your accusations against Belisarius smack of spite and malice," she said with the hint of a smile. "Perhaps that's why I like you so much. But you must not overstate your case. Belisarius may indeed be clever and ambitious. Yet my sources—who are much closer to him than you are, by the way—say he is noble and loyal to a fault, without a scheming bone in his body. Who am I to believe?"

Narses grimaced in frustration. "Forgive me, my Mistress. My only thought is to serve you and the Emperor."

Sensing his discomfiture, Theodora softened. "I know that your intuitions are not to be despised. I agree that Belisarius bears closer scrutiny. You'll be happy to know that I have already conceived of a way to accomplish just this."

"May I ask how, my Mistress?" Narses asked, hopefully.

Theodora smiled. "You may not. Now go."

"Yes, my Mistress," Narses sighed. He quickly bowed and made his way out.

An anxious fear gripped Antonina as she found herself in the familiar halls of the palace, a courtier leading her to an interview with the empress Theodora. It had been years since she strolled these same corridors as a lady-in-waiting to the empress Euphemia, and the external decor had changed but little. What had changed was the demeanor of the ladies who hastened here and there on various missions. They all bore a look of trepidation that mirrored Antonina's own feelings at present.

Belisarius had informed her of the changes to their wedding plans made at the behest of the imperial couple and Antonina frankly resented their meddling. *It has been years since she dismissed me from her service*, Antonina worried. *Why can't she leave us alone? What could she possibly want?*

Her questions were soon answered as she was led into the presence of the empress. She bowed low to the floor and Theodora waited a long time before commanding her to rise.

"You are to be wed to the general Belisarius," Theodora began, her voice that of a military commander. "As you have no doubt heard by now, the ceremony will be conducted in Hagia Sophia and afterwards, the emperor and I will host a banquet in honor of the event."

"You are most generous, my Mistress," Antonina replied, bowing again.

Theodora squinted, as if surveying Antonina carefully. "And after your marriage, you will return to my service."

Antonina remained silent.

"Does that not please you, my dear?" the empress asked without warmth.

"I...forgive me, Mistress, I don't know what to say," Antonina stumbled.

"Come and sit," Theodora commanded. "Relax and don't be afraid."

Antonina obliged, but her rigid posture made plain her continuing anxiety.

"I know your past," Theodora smiled, a hard edge to her voice. "You spent as much time among the filth and vermin as I did. And like me, you have now managed to snare a man well above your station. Such ambition and skill impress me, and I see fit to reward it."

"Thank you, Mistress," Antonina replied, her insides churning.

"But in your case, your past isn't so very far away, is it?"

Antonina's eyes widened.

"Don't worry," Theodora laughed. "Your many secrets are perfectly safe with me."

"Yes, my Mistress," Antonina replied subserviently.

Theodora continued: "I won't demand your presence in the palace daily. Only on occasions when I have need of a woman of your intelligence and...perceptive nature."

Antonina said nothing, barely able to catch her breath.

"I'm glad we understand each other," Theodora smiled. "Now go. When I need you, I will call you."

"Yes, my Mistress," Antonina bowed low and strode quickly for the door. Once in the hallway, she had to check her gait lest she begin running. Silent tears of frustration and confusion ran down her face as she reached the Chalke Gate.

✠

The sky was azure blue and clear on the day Belisarius wed Antonina. Only a few gray thunderheads appeared on the horizon, but they seemed distant and easily ignored.

An enormous crowd filled Hagia Sophia to witness the ceremony, much to the surprise of the joyous couple. Theodora had requested the presence of every patrician family in the city, and as much as they despised her, they knew that to reject her summons was to be cast into imperial disfavor. Scores of Belisarius's army comrades stood smartly down the center of the nave, their armor kits gleaming with fresh polish. Bulking out the crowd, hundreds of members of the palace bureaucracy and the imperial household gawked eagerly at the spectacle, along with a multitude of hippodrome and theater denizens who skulked along the side aisles claiming acquaintance with the bride.

Antonina and Belisarius stood before the patriarch, he in a beautifully patterned military tunic, beneath a long red and gold cape clasped at the right shoulder, she in a shimmering floor-length gown of ivory-colored silk and gold, with a veil of flaming red framing her shining face. On their heads, both wore the matrimonial crowns.

The couple joined hands before the altar of the Great Church and Epiphanius himself, the patriarch of Constantinople, pronounced the benediction, calling upon God to bless and protect the holy and divinely ordained union of man and woman. Belisarius gazed upon his bride and wanted nothing more that to love and cherish her for the rest of his life. Years before, he had made a solemn oath over the Holy Eucharist to serve and uphold Justinian's cause on pain of eternal damnation. As Epiphanius repeated the words of Christ regarding marriage—"What God has joined, let no man put asunder"—Belisarius understood that the bond he forged that day with Antonina was just as unbreakable as his earlier one. He vowed to himself to be loyal and faithful to her unto death.

All throughout the long liturgy that followed, Belisarius's attention remained fixed on his beautiful bride and the entire event seemed to pass in the blink of an eye. So focused was he on Antonina that he never once noticed the numerous sneers and shaking heads among the crowd coerced to attend. For many of them, Antonina was a prize of dubious value. This secret scorn continued during the festivities after the ceremony. Many congratulatory smiles only thinly disguised a haughty animus for the bride and a pitying contempt for the groom.

But Belisarius perceived none of this. For him, the entire day's events were a great and marvelous blur. He awoke the next morning wondering if it had all been a glorious dream. Glancing to his left and seeing his bride still asleep beside him, he knew that it had been no dream—his reality had changed forever.

III

AD 531, Autumn

Fifth year of the reign of Justinian, Emperor of the Romans
At Constantinople

A week after his wedding, Belisarius did something he had intended to do for some time. He granted Solomon a formal manumission, breaking the bonds of his slavery and making him a free man. This came as a shock to Solomon—and not an all together pleasant one—for Solomon had developed a deep and abiding fondness for his master and had no desire to leave his service. In the end, he graciously offered his thanks, but insisted that he remain in Belisarius's service as chamberlain. Belisarius readily agreed on condition that Solomon now draw a regular salary.

Among Solomon's first duties was to find a proper dwelling for the new family. The house they currently occupied was cramped, lacking an atrium and a proper kitchen, with no room at all for the several new slaves that were to be purchased. Plus, it was located too near a factionist tenement building that bustled with loud, raucous activity at all hours of the day and night.

In the modest peristyle, Belisarius sat enjoying the afternoon sun and reading a letter that had arrived from his family in Thrace. His widowed mother, Anna, sent her regrets that she and his six brothers and sisters had not been able to make the long journey to the capital for the wedding. It was the harvest, after all, and the crops this year had been excellent. Belisarius shook his head as he read her summary of the happenings in the provincial hamlet—his sister Marcella had gotten married at last; a kindly old tanner in town had died; his sister-in-law Priscia had given birth to another baby boy; a neighbor's cow had been struck by lightning. At the close, Anna promised that she would visit him the following spring, dragging as many of his siblings along as she could.

Belisarius smiled.

A loud shout disturbed the quiet. The gate flew open and in tumbled Photius and several of his comrades, shouting and striking at each other with sticks and wooden swords.

"Die you stinking Hun dog!" one of them cried.

"You can't hurt me! I'm invincible!" another shouted among the general tumult.

"What's this?" Belisarius stood up to his full height and glared at them.

All motion stopped and all tongues were silent.

Belisarius strode over to one of the larger boys whose mouth hung open, his wooden sword on the ground. Belisarius picked it up. "Defend yourselves!" he barked.

Several of the boys looked to Photius expectantly, and the lad raised his stick to attack. Others followed his lead, smiles cracking on a few of their faces.

After a slight feint, Belisarius lashed out with his wooden sword, striking Photius's stick with such suddenness that it snapped clean in half. With practiced dexterity and fluid quickness, he sent several other swords flying, their previous owners clutching their hands, now numb from the impact. One boy, more experienced than the others, made an ill-advised thrust and Belisarius instinctively dodged to his left. The boy missed completely and was rewarded with a stroke across his backside for his effort. The others laughed uproariously.

"Come now, pick them up! Will none of you face me?" Belisarius menaced striding forward again.

In a merry panic, the boys retreated into the street and Belisarius quickly slammed the gate behind them.

Only Photius remained in the courtyard, a wooden sword in his hand. He rushed at Belisarius, swinging his blunt weapon in a controlled arc. Belisarius blocked the stroke and slowed his counter thrust so that Photius had a chance to respond. For a few more minutes, Belisarius coached the youth, then disarmed him with a sharp swipe that sent the wooden sword clattering to the ground.

"Have you always been this good with the sword, Father?" Photius gasped, exhausted from sparring.

"No indeed," Belisarius laughed. "I took my share of beatings at your age. An old tribune named Boniface taught me and he was not nearly as gentle as I am."

Photius looked up at him, afraid to speak.

"You want to learn how to use this?" Belisarius brandished the wooden sword in his son's face. "With this tool in its true form, you can take a man's life. But there is no tool on earth that can give it back to him once you've taken it. If I teach you to use it, you will have the power to defend yourself against evil men. But you will also have the power to slay the innocent."

Photius nodded gravely.

"I must, therefore, make sure you understand the value of life before I teach you how to inflict death," Belisarius said, handing Photius the wooden sword. "And if you prove to be a good pupil, I will set up a target and teach you the bow as well, once we move to our new house. And there will also be room enough for a stable. Would you like to learn how to ride?"

Photius's eyes widened in excitement. "When, Father?"

"Soon enough."

"So our new house will be very large, then?" Photius pressed. "Like a mansion?"

"No, not quite a mansion," Belisarius corrected. "But it will be large enough to accommodate all of us in comfort."

"All of us?" Photius cried excitedly. "Even my sisters?"

"Sisters?" Belisarius shook his head. "What do you mean?"

Photius turned pale, his mouth wide open.

Before he could say another word, Antonina bustled frantically into the courtyard. "Ah, here you are, Photius!" she chirped merrily. "Go inside and get cleaned up. Fausta will have your supper ready soon."

"But mother, I was..."

"Get inside now!" Antonina screamed with barely suppressed rage.

Photius knew better than to tarry.

There was a long silence.

"You heard, then," Belisarius said calmly once the boy left. "Your step-daughters?"

"No," Antonina sobbed angrily. "They are my true daughters. Anastasia and Pulcheria are their names. I bore them before my first marriage."

"How old are they?"

"Eighteen and sixteen," Antonina croaked. She slumped down on a marble bench by a pathetic fountain that dribbled water into a basin from a bare bronze pipe. "They live with a cousin of mine who adopted them as his own. I just ... I couldn't ... raise them here. Not in the city, by myself."

Belisarius eyed her, a thousand thoughts streaming through his mind, few of them happy. Without thinking, he asked an obvious question that had strangely never come up between them: "How old are you, Antonina?"

She glared back at him, tears ringing her eyes. "I am thirty-five," she said, a trace of malice in her voice.

Belisarius was thunderstruck. By her fine appearance, he never guessed that his beloved Antonina could be eight years his senior.

"Does it matter to you to have such an elderly woman for a wife?" Antonina rejoined, seizing the initiative.

"Of course not," Belisarius stammered. "But, why ... why did you not tell me?"

"What, my age?"

"No, about your daughters," he replied. "Did you think my love so shallow that I would reject you because of them?"

Antonina scowled. In her jealous mind, she had a perfectly good reason for hiding her daughters from Belisarius before she was wedded to him—they were both young, beautiful, and of marriageable age. "No, of course not," she sighed. "I am sorry. I meant to tell you a thousand times, but it's not the kind of thing I wanted to put in a letter. And once you arrived home, I was just so happy..."

Antonina began sobbing again, and any anger Belisarius may have harbored melted out of him like wax at the sight of her tears. "Don't cry, my love," he said, comforting her.

But she continued to weep for a long time, playing him easily like a two-string lyre.

Two days later, Belisarius was again reading in the cramped peristyle when Photius slunk by, a woolen hood pulled up over his head.

"Photius!" Belisarius called out.

Pretending not to hear, the lad continued into the house.

"Photius!" Belisarius shouted louder, now rising from his seat. "Come here!"

The boy stopped and turned under the shade of the portico. "Yes, Father."

As he emerged into the sunlight, Belisarius let out a gasp. "Merciful heaven, what happened to you?"

Photius's cheeks were purple with bruises and his lower lip was split. His swollen left eye was partially shut. "Green factionists," he muttered. "They got the jump on me."

"When? Just now?" Belisarius growled and stood up, his fists balled and ready.

"No," Photius mumbled. "It was yesterday."

"What happened?" Belisarius demanded. "Who were they?"

"Must I, Father?" Photius replied, a tear running down his battered cheek. "This kind of thing happens a lot. It's not important. I'm really hungry and just want to get something to eat."

Belisarius relented. "All right. I'll be in to join you in a few minutes. I want to hear everything."

Without hesitation, Photius ran into the house.

Belisarius collected his papers and followed after a moment, but Photius was nowhere to be found. *I must teach that boy to fight sooner than I planned,* Belisarius mused naively to himself.

Hypatius spat into his hand. He picked out a flagrum from among those hanging from bronze hooks on the courtyard wall. Shaking it a few times, he gave a surly grunt of displeasure and put it back. He chose instead a thick leather strap, its wooden handle worn smooth from use. "Ah, the Serpent's Tongue," he mused out loud, fingering the twin ivory barbs at the end where the strap split in two. "Is she chained, Achates?"

"Yes, Master," his manservant responded.

A woman of middle age was sobbing softly, her face pressed against the cold stone wall, her arms manacled over her head.

"I'll apply the correction myself, if you don't mind," Hypatius declared, snapping the whip a few times.

"As you wish, Master," Achates replied. "Be not lenient with her, though, Master. She deserves all this and more."

Hypatius laughed. "Lenient? I expect her stripes to be a warning sign to the entire household. The next slave who reveals any of my family's business to those on the outside will be beaten with iron, not this soft leather."

The strap flashed in his hand and the woman cried out as it stung her back.

"Am I interrupting?" another voice said.

Hypatius turned to see his brother, Probus, standing under the portico with another man beside him.

"Ah, greetings brother!" Hypatius called out, smiling broadly. "Forgive my distraction, but I've been dealing with household business all morning. This wench was heard spreading gossip in the market which came back to my ears."

"I see," Probus said, looking disdainfully down his long nose at the woman chained to the wall. "Well, have Achates finish the job then, will you? Silvanus wishes to speak to you."

"Fine," Hypatius sighed. He tossed the lash to Achates and eyed the man sternly. "A good beating, but not to death. Do you understand?"

"Of course, Master," Achates bowed, smirking wickedly.

Hypatius swung a military cloak over his bare arms and joined the men under the portico. "Hail to you, Silvanus," he said, greeting the man standing with Probus. A gaunt, elderly senator with a full head of pure white hair, Silvanus yet retained a sharp mind and piercing grey eyes, alive and observant. He dressed in a white toga, draped in the manner of the ancient Romans—a nod to the patrician origins of his illustrious family.

"And hail to you, O most noble nephew of Anastasius Augustus of happy memory," Silvanus replied, laying his hand on Hypatius's shoulder.

"How fares your son, the most noble Rufinus?"

"Very well indeed," Silvanus laughed, coughing slightly at the same time. "Or at least as well as can be expected for one having spent the better part of a year in Persia."

"Come, let us adjourn," Probus interrupted. "There is much to discuss."

Hypatius led his guests to a private sitting room. Wine was set out in fine gold cups and the slaves were dismissed.

"Rufinus reports that peace with Persia will be achieved at last," Silvanus began, taking a long draught of wine. "With Cabades on his deathbed, his nobles are already lining up behind the principal candidates for succession."

"May that mangy old wolf rot in hell for eternity," Hypatius offered, raising his cup.

"I'll drink to that," Probus replied.

Silvanus continued: "A draining war with Justinian is the last thing the Persians want at the moment. So there will be peace in the East and very soon."

"And yet, taxes continue to rise," Probus groused. "John of Cappadocia's agents are everywhere—assessing, seizing, defrauding. In times of peace, the Praetorian Prefect is supposed to relax the tax rates, not create additional burdens."

"You called Cabades a wolf, but that miserable fat Cappadocian is the real predator," Hypatius added, scowling. "He puts levies on anything that moves, and if it stops moving, he has his ministers kick it until it yields up a few follises."

"John is a scoundrel, it's true," Silvanus replied. "But we patricians have always found ways to avoid the taxman—even one as base and unscrupulous as the Cappadocian. It is the middling landowners and the poor who suffer most acutely."

"And who swarm into the city seeking redress," Probus added. "Thousands upon thousands have been utterly ruined by John. One can sense the anger in the streets."

"I have heard that the factions are also unhappy," Hypatius said.

Probus turned to him in surprise. "I thought you despised the factions, brother."

"Since you introduced me to their leaders, I have had a change of heart," Hypatius replied, smiling. "They have been coming to me regularly with their complaints against Justinian and his ministers—particularly the Prefect of the City. It seems Eudaimon's new policy of punishing Blue troublemakers as harshly as the Greens has made no one happy."

"Indeed," Silvanus added.

All were silent for a moment, sipping their wine.

"It's now or never for us," Hypatius announced.

"What do you mean?" Probus responded, surprised. "I've told you before, the key is patience. If we await our moment, victory is assured. If we move falsely, however..."

"*This* is our moment," Hypatius barked. "We have waited long enough. The people are angry. The factions are angry. And the Senate will back us."

"You forget that the palace and the armies remain against us," Probus argued. "Indeed, Justinian has enriched the soldiers and filled the bureaucracy with his sycophants. They will fight for him."

"Am I not a general?" Hypatius fumed. "Have I not commanded the armies in Thrace and in the East? Justinian is a palace lay-about and unlike Justin his uncle, he has not a martial bone in his body. I tell you, the soldiers will rally to me."

Probus bit his lower lip. "Brother, let us be frank. Your experiences as commander were...ahem...not the stuff of epic poetry."

"What is your opinion, Silvanus?" Hypatius broke in, unwilling to sit through the usual litany of his defects as a general.

Silvanus looked gravely from one man to the other. "Hypatius is right. If we don't act soon, Justinian and that awful wife of his will never be dislodged from their thrones. I grow weary of such a low-born wretches ruling over us. The circumstances are not ideal, but we may never have a better opportunity."

Hypatius looked triumphant.

Probus opened his mouth to speak, but his shock rendered him mute.

"Not all of the palace bureaucracy supports Justinian," Silvanus continued. "And the Scholarians may be turned as well with a few solidi slipped in the right pockets."

"But we have no force at our disposal to take the palace," Probus protested. "How are we meant to overcome the soldiers who remain loyal?"

"The mob will rally to us in huge numbers," Hypatius declared. "The soldiers will see this and understand that they can not stand against the will of the people. If they do not, we will arm the people and destroy them."

"This is dangerous talk, brother," Probus sighed. "An emperor made by the mob can just as easily be unmade by the mob. It is their nature to be fickle. And the people, even armed, can not stand against the likes of Belisarius and his men."

"We will arm certain of the demes with proper kits and weapons—not too many lest they get ideas," Silvanus explained as if he'd been considering this plan for a long time. "These, together with the mass of people, should be enough to overawe Justinian's lackeys."

An exalted smile dawned on Hypatius's face.

Probus wrinkled his brow and twisted his lips in worry. "The moment isn't right. There is too much risk," he said in a low voice.

"I am an old man," Silvanus rejoined. "I have waited nearly fourteen years to see the throne returned to a proper patrician family and I intend to see it done before I die. You, Hypatius, deserved to succeed Anastasius in the first place, not Justin—a man uncouth and unmannerly in all things. I call upon you to act as your noble blood demands and seize that which is properly yours."

Hypatius set his jaw. "I have every intention of doing just that," he growled. "And my brother Pompeius will be with us as well."

Probus shook his head slightly but said nothing.

"Good," Silvanus said, standing up. "I only ask one favor of you in exchange for my help when the time comes."

"What?" Hypatius said, suspicion creeping into his voice.

"Pardon the general Belisarius for whatever role he plays resisting you. Do not have him executed after you have ascended to the throne and disposed of Justinian and his other followers."

"Why him?" Hypatius asked.

Silvanus pressed his thin lips together. His eyes shifted slightly. "You will have need of him," he hedged. "Rufinus has told me of the man's prowess in battle—more like one of the Olympians than a mere mortal. And furthermore, the soldiers respect him. With him on your side, your throne will be secure."

"Frankly, I never thought much of him," Hypatius replied. "But as a favor to you, I shall do as you ask."

"Thank you," Silvanus said, reaching out to take Hypatius by the arm. "I shall keep you apprised of what goes on in the Senate. Things will begin happening soon. Be ready."

"I've been ready for fourteen years," Hypatius boasted indignantly.

AD 531, WINTER

Forty-fourth year of the reign of Cabades, King of Persia
At Ctesiphon, capital of Persia

In a spacious and lavishly decorated bed chamber, the great king of Persia lay dying. Seven days previous, he had collapsed during a fit of rage and had been unable to rise. Now in the dead of night, with the open fires of his religion burning around him, Cabades the king was approaching his end as magian priests chanted in their atonal rhythms.

"Where...Chosroes...son," the king slurred softly, the left side of his mouth drooping.

"He is here, O King," replied Mebodes, his master of soldiers. Tears streamed down his craggy face into his black beard.

The prince took his father's hand. "Here I am, O Father," he said.

The old man looked up through cloudy eyes and struggled to focus. For an instant, he saw his son's face, dark and extremely handsome, looming over him. "The crown...the will!" he choked.

"I have it, O King. Have no fear," Mebodes whispered through his tears.

Cabades struggled to smile, but winced in agony. "I burn!" he gasped.

"Be at ease, father. Soon you will be in the bosom of Ahura Mazda," Chosroes offered in a consoling voice.

"Angra Mainyu!" the old man gasped. "Ah! No!"

The Magians in the room suddenly ceased chanting at the sound of the evil spirit's name.

A single paroxysm of pain twisted the old man's face, and his final gasping breath left his throat with a rattle.

"Great king!" Mebodes sobbed, dropping on his knees beside Cabades's bed.

A look of disdain crossed Chosroes's face. "Bring in the dog," he ordered.

A magian priest led in a fine white mastiff with two black spots painted on its forehead. After intoning the proper prayers, the assembled courtiers waited and watched as the dog sniffed the corpse. With a happy pant, the mastiff looked bemusedly at the magi as if wondering what to do next.

"No bark," one mage said to another. "The king is most assuredly dead."

A brilliant smile flashed across Chosroes's lips a split second before he collapsed into mourning. "Let all of Persia know that the sun has gone out from the world," he cried.

"Let the whole earth lament," the assembled responded. "The great king is dead!"

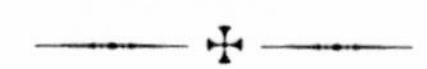

The deep murmur of a thousand men's voices filled the cavernous audience hall of the Persian royal palace. Rising a hundred feet overhead and made completely of brick, the hall's coffered vault was a graceful work of art and a marvel of engineering, As the centerpiece of the royal palace, the Persian kings had spared no expense in building this wonder of the world. Even the fire temples of the magi looked stunted and insignificant compared to the glorious palace of the king of kings.

In the center of the throng, the tall, gaunt form of Caoses could be seen, resplendent in the royal regalia of the Persian king. The eldest son of Cabades, Caoses had embraced the perverse teachings of the mad mage Mazdak who taught that men should own nothing in their own right but hold all things in common, including their wives. This vile doctrine had seduced Cabades himself as a youth and nearly cost him his throne. Seeing the error of his ways, Cabades did everything in his considerable power to eradicate the teachings of Mazdak from the earth—everything, that is, short of punishing his eldest son who surrounded himself with Mazdakites and lived happily under their sway.

Though estranged from his father, Caoses nonetheless felt that the throne was his by right. When word reached him of his father's death, Caoses immediately entered the palace and donned the royal robes. He was supported in this by many noble Persians, including his powerful brother Zames who, by virtue of an eye lost on the battlefield, could not aspire to the throne himself.

As Cabades had ruled for over forty years, there was confusion regarding the proper ceremonial for a coronation. Debate on this subject was well advanced when the imposing figure of Mebodes entered the audience hall, followed by Prince Chosroes and some especially dangerous looking officers of the Immortals.

"What is this?" Mebodes demanded, seeing Caoses in the vesture of the king. "Have you crowned a new king without first seeking the advice of the one just passed?"

"Greetings to you, illustrious Mebodes," Zames called out. "Our tradition and the laws of Persia clearly state that the eldest son shall succeed his father on the throne. Caoses, as the eldest, shall be king."

"But do our laws not also state that the king himself shall have the final say in the matter?" Mebodes rejoined.

A low murmur of voices debated the point before Caoses himself spoke: "Our excellent father made no such recommendation, Mebodes. Therefore, according to the law, I shall..."

"But you are wrong, O Prince," Mebodes shouted. Reaching into his tunic, he produced a folded piece of parchment. "This is the last will of Cabades, given to me by the hand of the king himself before his death because he knew I alone could be trusted to see it done."

Mebodes handed the document to one of the senior court officials who held it aloft so that all could see that the royal seal had not been broken.

"Read it out!" a voice shouted from the crowd. An outburst of voices added their assent.

The elderly official looked to Caoses for direction. Cowed by the vehemence of the crowd, the eldest son of Cabades foolishly nodded his acquiescence.

The courtier broke the seal and began to read in as loud a voice as he could muster: "To my most beloved servants and people, I bid you greetings from the sacred precincts of Ahura Mazda. Though I have now assumed my place in the magnificent gardens of paradise among my most mighty and distinguished ancestors, do not doubt that my spirit retains its care for you, O most cherished people of Persia. For our nation is like unto the sun, giving light and radiance to the whole world. And thus, it must be ruled by a king whose wisdom and courage shine just as brilliantly. This, therefore, is my desire for you, O most beloved Persians: that my most excellent son Chosroes be your king. And furthermore that..."

The official spoke on but his voice was drowned out in an uproar of raucous debate, accusation, and recrimination. Several men grabbed hold of Caoses and attempted to strip him of the royal garb, but they were shoved away by three burly bodyguards.

The tumult continued for some moments before Mebodes climbed the royal dais and stood towering over the crowd. In a loud voice, he began to harangue the arguing courtiers and nobles, addressing whoever would listen. Though he could barely be heard at first, heads slowly began turning in his direction. Soon there was complete silence and Mebodes's deep baritone voice echoed strongly beneath the great vault.

"...ruled over us all for more than forty years. Do you doubt his wisdom? You who followed his every command while he was still alive—will you defy the will of Cabades our king now that he is gone? A terrible shame on all of Persia to even consider it!

"This Caoses who presumed to know his father's will—how can he be king? He, a man who is led around like a camel behind the corrupt priests of Mazdak. Who among you would accept such a man as king?"

A few of Caoses's partisans voiced loud objections, but they were immediately drowned out and intimidated by the presence of Mebodes's Immortals who were fully armed and had murderous looks in their eyes.

"And Prince Zames, the most noble and courageous. All here know that he, by contrast, has every right to be king, save one—that his person bears a disfigurement."

The crowd began to grumble again, but Mebodes held out his hand to silence them.

"It is imperative that we follow the law in this matter," Mebodes continued. "And the law clearly states that the king must be whole in body if not handsome in appearance. With Prince Chosroes, the favored son of our beloved king, we see a man of sound body and splendid appearance. As most of you know, the prince is also possessed of a sharp intellect and a wisdom far beyond his years. The warlike spirit of Cabades is alive in his breast and his father predicted long ago that Chosroes would someday lead the Persians to great victories.

"At this moment, all of you have the power to decide who our next king will be. That choice may lead our nation to greater wealth, power, and glory, or else to folly and ruin. I therefore entreat you: do not forsake the final command of Cabades—the greatest king Persia has ever known. Let us, today, crown Chosroes as his successor. As for myself and the Immortals, we stand firmly behind Prince Chosroes. I urge all of you present to stand with us."

Mebodes's final words were received by the crowd as precisely the threat they were intended to be. As a result, there was a long silence beneath the great coffered vault.

Then someone from deep in the crowd shouted: "Long life to King Chosroes! We adore you, O King!"

"Hail Chosroes, king of kings!" another rang out.

There followed a mad rush of joyous exclamations as the crowd surged toward Chosroes, each noble eager to be among the first to acclaim him.

While the courtiers escorted Chosroes to the royal dais, Mebodes and several grizzled Immortals approached Caoses and his dwindling ring of supporters. "The regalia, O Prince, if you please."

Caoses scowled back at him spitefully. "Would you have me disrobe right here?"

"You may strip yourself now, or these men will do it for you," Mebodes snarled, losing patience.

In fear, Caoses tore off the royal cloak, tunic and shoes in an instant. One of his supporters threw a cape over his bare shoulders.

A servant gathered up the clothing and scurried off to the dais to bestow them upon Chosroes.

With a hard look in his eye, Mebodes rose up to his full commanding height and addressed Caoses, Zames, and their few remaining defenders. "Because you both are of the blood of Cabades the Great, you shall be granted life and allowed to remain within the king's circle of advisors and favored men. However, you must resign yourselves to this role for life and never harbor any greater ambitions. For if even the slightest trace of disloyalty to the king is discovered, you will be cast into the Prison of Oblivion forever." Mebodes shifted his glare from one man to the other. "Do you accept the benevolence of King Chosroes?"

Caoses and Zames glanced at each other bitterly and nodded, "We do."

"Then go. We will summon you tomorrow for the coronation."

Suppressing their rage, the two brothers turned and made their way out of the palace. "This shall not stand," Zames muttered as soon as they were safely out of earshot. "I have power yet to resist this usurpation and will use it. If you or I can not win the approval of the nobles, perhaps my son Cabades, our father's namesake, can."

"I am with you," Caoses whispered. "Living as slaves to our younger brother is intolerable. Let us topple him or die trying."

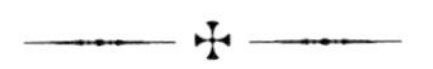

Two months later, the heads of Zames and Caoses were mounted on stakes at the tripod which stood before the royal palace. A third stake meant for the head of Zames's son, Cabades the younger, remained unoccupied—the prince had been spirited away when it became clear that the cause of his father and uncle was doomed.

The Roman ambassadors, Rufinus and Hermogenes averted their faces from the horrifying scene as they hurried into the palace to greet the new king of Persia.

Arrayed in shimmering vestments, King Chosroes made for a magnificent sight. He wore the ornate crown of the sun, the golden disk gleaming above his head with gold eagle's wings on either side. His still-scanty black beard was expertly waxed and curled, and his long black hair, oiled and shining, spilled over his shoulders like a dreadful lion's mane. From each ear dangled a cluster of three huge pearls—a white one for Sapor II, the greatest Persian king, a black one for Peroz I, who was killed in battle by the Huns, and a cream-colored one for his father, Cabades. Though Chosroes was immaculately groomed and perfectly coiffed, there was nothing effeminate about him. His face was hard and angular. His nature among his friends was naturally jocular and easily excited, but his eyes betrayed a pitiless severity with those who crossed him. And he was easily crossed.

"The Roman ambassadors, Rufinus and Hermogenes," a courtier announced as the two were ushered into the presence of the king.

Rufinus fell on his face to do homage.

Hermogenes offered a polite bow.

"Have you come, O Romans, to ratify the Eternal Peace our deceased king, Cabades, made with your king, Justinian?" Mebodes called out from his position at Chosroes's right hand.

"Yes indeed, O most excellent Chosroes, great king," Rufinus began. "And to relay salutations and brotherly affection to you from our most glorious emperor, Justinian, on your ascension to the throne of your illustrious father."

Hermogenes rolled his eyes imperceptibly.

"Read out the terms," Chosroes commanded.

A secretary stepped forward and began to read: "The Romans are to cede Pharangium and the castle of Bolum to Persia. In return, the Persians will cede all the fortresses of Lazica which were captured in the war. Furthermore, the Persians will return the general Dagaris to the Romans in exchange for the chanaranges Nabades who was captured at Daras. Finally, the Romans shall offer the annual sum of 110 centenaria of gold to Chosroes the King as tribute for the maintenance of the Caspian Gates against the inroads of the Huns."

"Not tribute, Excellency," Hermogenes corrected. "The money is a gift from one ruler to another for the mutual benefit of both."

Mebodes's eyes shifted to look upon Chosroes, but the king's jaw was set firmly and he evinced no emotion. "As our most noble father wished, we hereby ratify this Eternal Peace," Chosroes said, calling his secretary forth with the wave of his hand. A document was presented and Chosroes affixed his seal.

"When will the first payments of gold arrive?"

"Very soon, O King," Hermogenes offered. "It is our understanding that the payment in its entirety had been shipped ahead to Edessa in anticipation of the treaty.

"It is well that you did that," Chosroes replied. "We shall not consider this treaty fully in force until the gold is safely in our treasury."

"You shall have it in days, O King," Rufinus declared. "Be sure of that."

Chosroes snorted dismissively

Treaty in hand, Hermogenes and Rufinus strode forth from the palace, making sure to avoid the swarms of flies buzzing around the rotting heads of Chosroes's brothers. The empty stake was now occupied by a vulture which hissed and cackled at any who passed too close.

"Let us be gone from this place with all haste," Hermogenes muttered. "Some foreboding spirit tells me that a bit of parchment will not restrain this Chosroes for long. He is young and rash. His eyes burn with the hatred he bears for us."

"I agree," Rufinus replied. "But this war has been an open wound on both our empire and that of the Persians and they require respite every bit as much as we do. Besides, with peace in the east, it may be possible to put through some...ahem...reforms in Constantinople."

"What do you mean?"

"I have received a cryptic message from my father," Rufinus whispered, casting a suspicious glance over his shoulder. "Things are starting to happen..."

"Shhh!" Hermogenes retorted. "Do not speak of such things! Do you not imagine that the empress has ears even here?"

Rufinus nodded calmly. "When we are on the road to Nisibis, then."

"Yes," Hermogenes said, relieved. "In the desert where no one can hear."

IV

AD 532, Winter

Fifth year of the reign of Justinian, Emperor of the Romans
At Constantinople

A chill January breeze pushed the morning ferry through the whitecaps of the Golden Horn. On board, seven factionists, three Greens and four Blues, condemned to death for committing murder, were headed to the scaffolds at Sycae. Bound tightly, all of the seven snarled and cursed at their captors—particularly at Eudaimon, the Prefect of the City, who stood stoically in the bow of the boat.

A crowd had already gathered at the site of the execution, morbidly anxious to observe the spectacle. Guards frogmarched the prisoners through the unruly mob and up to the scaffold where the executioners stood at the ready.

A mandator came forth and read the sentences against each. Eudaimon nodded and the executioners set to their work with horrible precision. Three of the Blues were beheaded immediately, while two of the Greens were impaled upon poles to die slowly over several hours.

The remaining two, one Blue and one Green, were to endure the additional punishment of hanging before having their heads hacked off. A noose was slipped around their necks and two burly men hoisted them into the air, kicking and struggling. As the men flailed, however, the transom above their heads, old and warped by the sea air, began to groan and sag. To the screams of the crowd below, the heavy wooden beams swung forward and crashed to the ground, taking much of the scaffold with them.

Once order was restored, Eudaimon and his men pushed their way through the crowd. "Make way. Where are the prisoners?"

"They are here, O Prefect," a guard shouted.

"They live yet, but are injured. Touch them not!" a man cried.

"They must lose their heads today!" an executioner growled as he tried to push his way past.

But the swelling crowed blocked them. "The scaffold has collapsed. It is God's will that they be spared!"

"Nonsense!" Eudaimon barked. "Take them!"

"You will not!" a few of the men shouted back at him. "God saved them and we will not allow the devil to take them!"

By their dress, Eudaimon knew immediately that the men defending the prisoners were Green factionists who had infiltrated the crowd. To his dismay, he did not have enough of his own men present to counter their growing numbers and murderous looks. The two sides continued to bluster and threaten, but the situation became a standoff.

The noise soon attracted the attention of the monks at the nearby monastery of St. Konon, and several of them sallied forth to investigate. When the cause of the commotion was explained to them, the monks looked upon the condemned, who writhed on the ground in agony, and had pity on them. Without hesitation, they put them on a boat which they rowed to the Church of St. Lawrence and sanctuary.

Greatly angered by this turn of events, Eudaimon placed guards around the church to make sure the two men did not attempt to escape justice.

✠

That same evening, the emperor's privy council assembled in a small but well-appointed meeting room in an obscure corner of the palace. This conference after dark was unusual, and there was a sense of unease in the room.

"What's he got in store for us tonight, eh?" John the Cappadocian, the Praetorian Prefect, wondered, his loud voice carrying over the rest. He was sipping unwatered wine which dribbled down his bare chin and onto the floor.

"No idea," replied the quaestor Tribonian, obvious disgust showing on his face. "I've been at court all day and haven't heard a thing."

"He's gotten another letter from Africa," muttered Narses, the emperor's chief chamberlain. "And a group of African bishops called on him last week. Political and religious strife there."

Though he found John to be corrupt and thoroughly base in character, Narses respected the prefect's genius when it came to managing his department. His job was to fill the emperor's treasury and that is exactly what he did. No one had ever done a better job of stuffing the emperor's coffers with gold than John of Cappadocia.

"A shame, what a shame," John burped, completely without sympathy. He then grabbed a slave roughly by the collar. "Say, good fellow, is there any more of this wine?"

"Yes, O Prefect," the slave replied, struggling out of John's stubby-fingered grip. "I shall fetch you another cup."

"Make it two, so I don't have to ask you again," John barked. "You gap-toothed idiot," he remarked to himself under his breath.

The emperor arrived late, as was usually the case, and all greeted him loudly.

Justinian returned their greetings and scanned the room. "Where is Eudaimon?" he asked, missing the Prefect of the City.

"There has been a disturbance, O Master," Narses explained. "Two factionist criminals are holed up in the church of St. Lawrence. Eudaimon is there trying to coax them out."

"Can't he find someone else to do that?" Justinian responded with annoyance. "Marcellinus, send a messenger to St. Lawrence to fetch Eudaimon at once."

Narses smiled as he always did when he succeeded in putting one of his rivals in a bad light.

Justinian settled in a chair at the head of the table and the rest followed suit on either side of him. "You are all, no doubt, curious why I summoned you here this evening," the emperor began. "It is for this reason: I have decided to make war upon the Vandals and the usurper who rules over them, Gelimer by name."

Justinian let his words hang in the air. The men in the room shifted their eyes nervously from one to the other, but no one said a word.

"A year ago, some of you may remember, this Gelimer unjustly deposed our ally Hilderic, the rightful king of the Vandals. Hilderic was well disposed toward our empire and did not abuse the Romans in Africa. Nor did he persecute orthodox Catholics though an Arian heretic himself.

"As soon as we heard about this revolution, we sent a letter to Gelimer requesting that he act with prudence and release Hilderic from prison. As the second man in the kingdom, the throne would have fallen to him in due course, Hilderic being an elderly man. But Gelimer scorned our embassy, charged Hilderic with conspiracy, and threw the old man into an even deeper dungeon.

"When news of his continued intransigence reached us, we sent another letter, this time rebuking Gelimer for his actions and demanding that he release Hilderic to us to live out the rest of his life in Byzantium."

Justinian held up a scroll tied with a leather strap. "This is what that arrogant ass Gelimer sent back to us."

"Read it out, O Master, if it please you," Narses called out.

Justinian stood up and unfurled the missive. A slave carefully maneuvered a brass lampstand behind him to provide sufficient light.

Pacing slowly in annoyance, Justinian began to read:

> Gelimer, King of the Vandals and Africa to Justinian, Emperor of the Romans.
>
> You are ill informed as to the actions taken by me against Hilderic. This man was dethroned by the will of the nation of the Vandals because he was planning a revolution against the house of Gaiseric, my great-grandfather. As for me, I was advanced to the throne not of my own doing, but by the unanimous consent of the people.
>
> You and I are both kings. It is well to remember that a king ought to administer his own business and not meddle in the affairs of others, for such is unjust. But if you dare break the treaty that has kept peace between our kingdoms for seventy years and more, do not doubt that

we will resist you with all the power we can summon. And we will call to witness the oaths sworn to us by your predecessor Zeno. You would do well to remember the circumstances under which that most unfortunate emperor was forced to swear.

In disgust, Justinian tossed the letter onto the table where it curled back into its cylindrical shape. "What gall this barbarian has!" he fumed.

"Indeed, O Master," Narses replied unctuously. "His reasons for claiming the throne are clearly lies. But these could have been disregarded had he proven more tractable on other issues. But his overt claim to be sovereign in his own right and a king equal to the Roman Emperor is unpardonable. He must be dealt with."

"Well said, Narses," the emperor replied. "Roman emperors have endured this haughty tribe squatting in our Africa for too long. The time has come for action. Thus, I have deigned to close out the war with Persia and shift our forces for a great campaign against the Vandals in Africa."

"I am ever ready to serve you in this cause, O Master, as my abilities allow," Narses declared, bowing his head.

Every face at the table glared at Narses with something close to hatred in their eyes. All found his toadying utterly repulsive. But beyond that, they knew their history. Zeno's expedition against the Vandals over 70 years ago pulled men and resources from all regions of the empire, over 100,000 fighting men all told. Even the Western empire, which still clung to life at the time, contributed a share of the supplies and soldiers. It was the largest, most costly military enterprise the empire had ever attempted—and it was a complete fiasco. So great was the defeat that many blamed it for the collapse of the Western empire a mere eight years later. It bankrupted and nearly ruined the Eastern empire as well.

Everyone present knew that an attack on the rich and powerful Vandal kingdom in Africa was the height of folly. Yet none dared speak out.

Save one.

"Master, if you'll permit me," John the Cappadocian rasped in his mumbling monotone. Though his appearance was as slovenly as ever, his black eyes blazed with purpose and intellect.

"Speak, John," Justinian said.

The Cappadocian wheezed and rose awkwardly to his feet. "You, O Emperor, are great because you value reason above all other men. If someone speaks frankly and marshals his evidence well, you will pay him heed even if he should contradict your own wishes. And of necessity, I am forced to offer advice that may seem at odds with what you have proposed—at least at first. But later you will see how well it proves my loyalty to your throne.

"War is always a calamity and war with the Vandals will not come cheaply, either in treasure or in the lives of our men. Such expenditures can be made acceptable by a rapid victory which brings glory and covers up many sins. But we know that even the best-planned enterprises of men are subject to the whim of Almighty God, and given the disastrous results of previous campaigns against this foe, we should consider a new assault only with the greatest trepidation.

"Let us not forget that Carthage, the capital of the Vandal kingdom, lies 140 days journey away by land. And by ship, the journey is not much shorter for it is necessary to traverse nearly the entire sea. It should also be remembered that our soldiers have no experience in ship-board fighting. They tremble in fear at the prospect of such a fight against an enemy whose prowess is unmatched in the whole world. And even if we should manage to land our soldiers and avoid a battle by sea, all of Numidia's harbors are in the hands of the enemy. Our soldiers would be forced to encamp in a hostile land, the only haven being their own ships, against a formidable enemy host some 50,000 strong.

"But let us assume that by some miracle our forces destroy the Vandals and capture Africa. How can we hold it with Italy and Sicily in the hands of the Goths? And God forbid that defeat should be inflicted upon our forces—what will restrain the Vandals from bringing the fight to our own lands?

"In short, O Master, we will not be able to enjoy the fruits of a victory, and a defeat would surely bring harm to those regions that currently enjoy peace.

"Nevertheless, if you command me to assemble the vast sums necessary to fund such an expedition, have no doubt that I shall provide all that is needful and more. I only ask that you consider carefully the wisdom of this invasion. For when hastily made plans fail, repentance is of no account after the fact. But there is no harm in delaying or altering one's plans beforehand to avert a disaster."

John abruptly sat down with a grunt.

The rest were stupefied, wondering at the pluck and courage of the man to contradict the emperor so brazenly and effectively.

Justinian himself had no words for a long moment. Finally, he spoke: "Is there no one who can refute what the Prefect has said?"

Each man solemnly shook his head.

Justinian looked deflated. A man of decisive action, uncertainty and caution did not come easily to him.

"Master, would you like us to adjourn for the evening?" Narses broke the silence.

"Indeed," the emperor sighed. "John has provided much food for thought tonight and I'll need some time to digest it fully. You may all go."

The men filed out, each offering the emperor a silent knee as they left.

Cappadocian John caught the emperor's eye as he awkwardly genuflected. Justinian nodded sheepishly to the prefect like an overzealous school boy who had been scolded by his tutor. "Will I see you at the races tomorrow?" he whispered.

John smiled. "O Emperor, have you ever known me to miss an opportunity to take money from fools?"

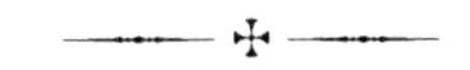

That same evening, in a large house in the Strategion section of the city, burning torches announced the meeting of some of the chief military lights of the empire. It was an informal gathering, a chance for the men of rank residing in the capital to enjoy each other's company—as well as rich food and expensive wine. The host was yet another John, this one the nephew of the rebel general Vitalian, who had come within a hair of driving the emperor Anastasius from his throne some twenty years before. John had built a fearsome reputation as a battlefield commander and had recently been promoted to strategos in recognition of his valorous deeds in defense of the empire. But John also possessed more than a trace of his uncle's rash ambition and seditious spirit.

Belisarius was present, though as a rule he disliked such functions. He preferred to remain home with his family or to dine with his own officers who called on him several times each week for that purpose. But Solomon warned him that invitations of this sort should not be spurned. Once the wine flowed freely, tongues would loosen and there would be much talk. It would be better for Belisarius to participate in such talk, rather than be the subject of it.

"Have you enjoyed Byzantium?" Belisarius asked Mundus, the Gepid general who had arrived in the city only a month ago to assume Belisarius's old post as Magister Militum of the East.

"It is the wonder of the world!" Mundus replied in his heavily accented Latin. "But enjoying it?...No, I am not."

"Truly? Why not?"

Mundus pushed close and dropped his voice to a whisper. "There are too many people here," he muttered. "The streets are too narrow. The great buildings close in around me. How I long for the open fields and meadows of my Pannonia."

"Ah, I understand," Belisarius replied. "I felt the same way when I first arrived here. You know, I'm from Thrace myself and grew up a farm boy."

"You?" Mundus marveled. "I would not have guessed it."

"My first lance was a hoe," Belisarius smiled.

Mundus laughed. "I fear I will never adapt to this life as you have. Among my people, I am a man who commands respect. People fear me because I am a mighty warrior—as is proper. But here," the Gepid ground his teeth together, "here, even the lowest scum deride me as a barbarian. Those filthy factionist dogs insult my men and throw garbage at them. My son nearly killed one of them last week."

"Fist fighting with factionists is an old sport around here," Belisarius mused. "I broke many a nose myself in my younger days."

"Good!" Mundus nodded. "Those scoundrels deserve every thrashing that comes their way."

At that moment, the Gepid spied his son by the fountain in the center of the courtyard. He was trading battle stories with John, their host, and Bessas, an old Gothic warrior who had served Justinian for many years.

"Mauricius!" Mundus called out. "Come here! There is someone I would have you meet."

A massive youth who already sported a thick brown beard, Mauricius approached with Bessas and John close behind him.

"This, my son, is Belisarius, whom the Romans call the hero of Daras," Mundus began. "Magister, may I present my son, Mauricius."

The young man seized Belisarius's arm in a grip that was more a test of strength than a greeting. "I have heard much about you, Magister. It is an honor," Mauricius declared loudly. He released his hold, duly impressed.

"The honor is mine," Belisarius replied.

"May I ask you something, Magister?" Mauricius said suddenly, stepping back a pace and drawing John into the conversation. "Is it true that this man is called 'Bloody John'?"

Belisarius laughed out loud in spite of himself.

John's mouth dropped open in horror.

"Aye, you've asked the right fellow that question, too!" Bessas interrupted with a guffaw. "It is Belisarius who got him that name."

Mauricius glanced from Bessas to Belisarius to John and then back to Bessas, somewhat confused.

Belisarius stifled his laughter and remained prudently silent.

"Ah, the good Magister is too humble to tell the tale, but not old Bessas, that's for sure," the grizzled Goth enthused in his gravelly voice.

John shifted his eyes but knew that he couldn't escape.

"Our friend John here was quite the hot head in his youthful days in the emperor's household guard. But he had the skills to back up his temperament, what being a powerful grappler. Many challenged him. Just as many fought him. But none could beat him."

Bessas paused momentarily to clear his throat. "Then, this rumor starts going around that a new ram had entered the sheepfold and none could match him at butting heads—that being our other friend here, Belisarius. Well, John heard that and just about burst his steel cap. He goes up to Belisarius and challenges him the very next day, right there in the soldier's mess. You know, our Belisarius never backed down from a fight, so outside they went to have it out."

Bessas paused again to take a long pull of wine. "Ahhh! So then, John here is so worked up, he charges right in on Belisarius to take him to the ground. John being a big fellow, I expect he thought he could wrestle Belisarius into submission. But Belisarius was lightning swift with his fists and nimble on his feet. He dodged to the left and cracked John on the bridge of his nose. Broke it with one punch. Poor John crumpled to earth like an undermined tower. Never knew what hit him!"

Bessas punched one hand with the other, mimicking the blow, and roared with laughter as he remembered the incident. His mirth was so great that Mundus and Mauricius couldn't help but join in.

"But wait, wait," Mauricius gasped, catching his breath. "That still doesn't explain how he got the name 'Bloody John'."

"Sure it does!" Bessas continued. "The blood shot out of John's nose so fast and hot that it could have been a cataract on the Ister. It drenched his whole face and shirt down to his waist. It took us near an hour to stop it. Poor fellow looked like a massacre."

The three began laughing again, failing to realize that their host was not so amused.

"Bessas, you exaggerate," Belisarius explained. "The fight was more evenly matched than that. John got in a few good blows."

John shot him an angry look and Belisarius realized that nothing he could say could retrieve the situation.

At that moment, Narses arrived and sauntered over to his friend, John. "What's so funny?" he asked.

"I'll tell you later," John replied. He then turned away abruptly and stomped off with Narses close behind.

"What's his problem?" Mundus asked, wiping a tear of jollity from his eye.

Narses led John away from his guests to a private spot behind a pillar.

"Where have you been?" John asked, still irritated.

"I've just come from a privy council meeting with the Emperor," Narses whispered. "He's thinking about invading Africa."

"Merciful God!" John choked.

"Yes, but the Cappadocian talked him out of it for now. Too risky."

"That's fortunate. What a fool's errand it would be to campaign against the Vandals," John said.

"It is especially fortunate for you," Narses replied, a deadly serious look in his eye.

"Yes? How so?"

"Because I know Justinian and just as a dog returns to his vomit, he will revisit this idea. And when he decides to proceed with it, he will need a competent general to lead the expedition. When he asks my advice on the matter, who do you think I will recommend?"

Bloody John's face turned white. "That sort of commission is suicide. Don't recommend me—unless you want me dead."

Narses smiled. "Far from dead, I want you to be the general at the emperor's right hand. But such a position is only won with brilliance on the field of battle. As it is, Sittas, Germanus and Belisarius rank ahead of you. To prove yourself, you need to accomplish something spectacular."

"But Africa?" John groaned. "It's lunacy, that's what it is. Don't recommend me. I'm serious. I'll refuse."

Narses shook his head petulantly. "Stop being such a coward. Look, were I a general, I would leap at this opportunity and grasp it with both hands."

"That's easy for you to say," John rejoined. "You're not a general and never can be."

Narses reddened with embarrassment and irritation. Though a powerful man at court and a trusted confidant of the emperor, Narses dreamed of nothing more than leading a great host into battle. Long hours had he spent studying the military campaigns of history and was certain that if given the chance, he could match Alexander, Caesar, or Constantine. But for him, such an advancement was impossible. What army would ever accept a eunuch as its commander?

"I'm sorry," John repented. "But you know full well that an invasion of Africa would be a debacle. The Vandals are too powerful. If you want to recommend anyone for it, suggest someone you want to do away with, not one of your friends."

Narses nodded slightly and twisted his lips into a sly smile. "We'll speak of this again another time," he said as he turned and headed toward the wine decanters.

AD 532, January 13
In the Hippodrome of Constantinople

The next day, chariot races were held to celebrate the advancement of those worthy men in the emperor's service to the rank of *primicerius*. It was fine weather for racing, unusually warm and dry for January, and as a result, the Hippodrome was jammed with nearly 80,000 spectators uproariously cheering for their particular color.

Justinian and Theodora occupied their usual seats in the imperial box—known as the Kathisma—before which the races began and ended. In his younger days, Justinian had been a staunch partisan of the Blue faction, but as the cares of running an empire began to occupy his every waking moment, he took less and less pleasure in the spectacles of the circus. Though he understood the utility of seeing the people and being seen by them, the idea of spending hours on end watching the races seemed like a great waste of time. To make the wasted hours more profitable, he often had work brought out to him in the Kathisma.

Theodora, for her part, remained a Green to the core and was passionately interested in the races. While she did not rise to her feet and scream as the Green charioteer rounded the spina toward the finish line like the common folk did, she yet knew every charioteer by name as well as his lifetime tally of victories and defeats.

Today, however, there was something different about the mood of the crowd and Theodora sensed it at once. "They seem uneasy today, do they not, my love?" she commented to Justinian.

"Hmm?" he replied distractedly, unwilling to lift his eyes from a letter he was reading from the Patriarch of Alexandria.

"Listen, a few are chanting," she continued, "but I can't make out what they're saying."

"They always chant, my dear," Justinian replied, his attention still fixed on the letter.

Theodora sat back, annoyed. There was no talking to him while he was so engrossed.

By the third race, the chants had become decidedly louder and clearer.

When they were not at the races, the factionists spent long hours lampooning the filthy pantomime shows in the theaters and as a result, they were experts at clever and often vicious mass heckling. The leaders of the Greens soon had hundreds crying out in unison:

Justinian Augustus, long may you reign.
Lo, I am afflicted, I can not restrain
my tongue nor my anger—Eudaimon's the cause.
That butcher, God knows, has perverted your laws.
In St. Lawrence my innocent brother doth languish,
Have mercy, O Master, and comfort our anguish."

"Do you hear what they're saying?" Theodora prodded, hoping that her husband's attention was now engaged.

"Yes, I hear them," Justinian replied. He had moved on to a detailed report from the Augustal prefect of Egypt and his eyes never left the page as he spoke. "They're referring to two murderers being held in the shrine of St. Lawrence. Eudaimon gave me the report last night. He botched the executions and because of it, the demes think the criminals should be set free."

"Well?"

"Well what?"

"Are you going to answer them?"

"No," the emperor replied casually. "Such temerity deserves no answer."

By the eighth race, the Blues had also begun chanting—not rebuking the Greens, as was their custom, but joining in the calls for clemency.

By the fifteenth race, the tenor of the chants began to change:

Thrice august Justinian have pity, we pray,
Let justice be done; let mercy hold sway.
I be not Samaritan, pagan, or Jew,
So heed my demand lest chaos ensue.
The Blues and the Greens join together to plead
That our brothers in prison be instantly freed!

Theodora looked anxiously at her husband. But Justinian had set his brow like granite as he continued to plow through his correspondence. He was a stubborn man and if the demes thought they could get an answer out of him by escalating the rhetoric, they were sorely mistaken.

By the twentieth race, however, a palpable change had come over the crowd. The normal ebb and flow of chanting no longer followed the action on the race-course, but instead merged into one tumultuous uproar of steadily increasing intensity as if a great evil spirit had taken hold of the mob. Messengers ran back and forth between the benches of the opposing factions, trading salutations for once rather than taunts and sucker punches.

By the start of the twenty-second race, something unprecedented happened—the leaders of the Blue and Green demes met in the stands and exchanged cordial greetings. At a signal, the Blues and Greens all sang out together:

> Farewell, O Justice, Justinian rules
> an empire of dunces, a palace of fools.
> We humbly beg, yet he holds us in scorn.
> Would that Sabbatius had never been born!
> God grant us this moment for venting our spleens,
> Victory to the triumphant Blue-Greens!

A tremendous roar went up and the people began shouting "Victory to the merciful Blue-Greens! Victory! *Nika!*" So loud and strange was the shouting that the charioteers themselves halted in mid-race and gazed up into the stands attempting to figure out what was happening.

Whipped into a frenzy, the mob now only required a channel for their wrath and this was eagerly provided by the leaders of the demes. Soon the people were marching out of the Hippodrome in a great mass. Their faces were filled with rage and their fists pumped the air. "*Nika!* Victory to the merciful Blue-Greens!" they continued to shout as they made their way onto the Mese.

Justinian stood up and watched them go, no longer able to ignore them.

"There, you see? Now they will riot," Theodora reproached him.

"Not in my city, they won't," Justinian muttered. "I'll set the Excubitors on them. See if I don't!" The emperor bustled out of the Kathisma and into the passage that led back to the palace, an anxious look on his face.

"Find out where they're going and what it will take to placate them," Theodora commanded Basilides, the Master of Offices, as she followed her husband out.

Many of the people dispersed immediately upon leaving the Hippodrome, anxious to protect their homes and families in the event of a riot. But some 10,000 of them marched in a great mass down the Mese to the Praetorium of the City Prefect. Eudaimon was there waiting for them. He had received warning of their coming and had massed his soldiers before the gates. But when he saw their numbers and heard their chanting, he immediately grew fearful.

One of the Greens with a particularly loud voice stepped to the fore and shouted to the soldiers: "Where is Eudaimon, that wicked spirit? Tell him to release our brothers, Phaulos and Elithios, who are trapped in Saint Lawrence. The merciful Blue-Greens command it!"

Eudaimon heard the demand and was incensed. He gathered up his courage and stepped onto the balcony of the Praetorium overlooking the mob. "Disperse! All of you disperse!" he shouted. "You dare to cause this disturbance for the sake of two murderers? You well know that this Green Phaulos killed

Sebastian the silversmith, striking him down for a few coins. And Elithios, the Blue, slew a woman and child of the Greens while drunk. For these reprobates you risk the emperor's wrath?"

But the crowd was past the point of responding to logic.

"You speak lies, most unfortunate of men!" the Green spokesman shouted back and the crowd roared along with him. "Phaulos and Elithios have been falsely accused. The fact that you could not hang them proves it! God has willed that they live!"

"God does not protect those who murder," Eudaimon angrily rebutted.

"Then He will not protect you, butcher!" a Blue factionist screamed and hurled a stone. Eudaimon ducked and it missed his head by inches. But it was followed by a shower of projectiles as the mob erupted.

Eudaimon quickly retreated back into the Praetorium and the crowed surged forward. Their numbers were such that the soldiers could only block their way for a few moments. They burst through the gate in a fury, and began ransacking the place, overturning tables, smashing furniture, and beating the prefect's staff with ferocity. Several of the more level heads made their way into the dungeons beneath the Praetorium. A few threats sufficed to obtain the keys and soon every cell was flung opened and a thousand cut-throats, thieves, brawlers, arsonists, and panderers streamed onto the streets of Constantinople.

Hopelessly outnumbered, Eudaimon and a hundred of his men continued to resist. After a few good beatings, however, he realized the situation was beyond his control and they retreated to the palace to warn the emperor.

Their work done, the factionists set fire to the Praetorium, and the mob stood in the square and cheered as the burning building lit up the night sky. A few brigades of firemen attempted to approach but were promptly driven off by a hail of stones and bricks. "Nika! Victory to the merciful Blue-Greens!" they shouted as the Praetorium collapsed in a shower of sparks and glowing embers.

The fugitives Elithios and Phaulos were soon freed from Saint Lawrence and eagerly joined the rampaging throng who greeted them with a hero's welcome.

"Now what?" a Blue cried.

Elithios raised a flaming brand over his head: "Now we take our vengeance!"

"Nika! Nika! Nika!" the throng erupted. "Vengeance for the merciful Blue-Greens!"

✠

Belisarius and his family were enjoying a quiet evening at home when the first great tongues of flame lapped the night sky. Their new house was located in the Quarter of Olybrius on rising ground toward the Church of the Holy Apostles and from the roof, they could watch the fire from a mile out. What they could not discern was the cause.

"That looks like the Praetorium of the City Prefect," Photius observed.

"Yes," Belisarius agreed. "And the fire is so large it will take the entire fire brigade to put it out."

"It gives me pause that a fire in such an important place has been allowed to burn so freely," Antonina added. "Something is amiss."

At that moment, someone began pounding at the front gate. Belisarius hurried down the narrow steps and through the peristyle. One of the slaves had already opened the gate and Solomon was standing by, an oil lamp in hand. Belisarius arrived and was surprised to see Unigastus and Athenodorus standing outside in full armor.

"Hail, O Magister," they saluted.

"Hail, good fellows," he replied. "What brings you?"

"A great riot has broken out," Athenodorus explained. "It began in the Hippodrome and has spilled out into the streets. The emperor has turned out the Excubitors, but they have been unable to quell it."

"We were tasked to bring you to the palace, O Magister, by the emperor's secretary himself," Unigastus added.

"I am ready," Belisarius replied. "Let us depart."

"Magister, I would recommend a full kit and sword," Unigastus said. "The factionists run wild and are killing and burning at random. God knows, we may need to fight our way to the palace."

"What is this?" Antonina interjected. She and Photius had now arrived and she was annoyed that their evening had been disrupted.

"A riot," Belisarius replied. "The emperor has summoned me to the palace. Photius, fetch my armor."

"Yes, Father," the lad replied and sped off into the house.

"Your family would be safer in the palace, O Magister," Athenodorus suggested. "We could escort them."

"And leave our home to those brigands?" Antonina responded angrily. "Never."

Belisarius nodded his agreement. "Solomon, get into your gear. Arm the slaves with bows and set them atop the portico above the gate. Challenge any who approach."

"May I help, Father?" Photius asked breathlessly, having run all the way carrying some sixty pounds of gear on his back.

"Yes, Solomon will give you a bow. But you are under his command. If you do not follow his orders to the letter, I will hear of it."

"Yes, Father," Photius replied eagerly.

"That goes for you, too, wife," Belisarius chided.

"I am mistress of this house and will do as I please," she said defiantly, embracing him and caressing his cheek. "But get you into your kit. It is unwise to keep the emperor waiting."

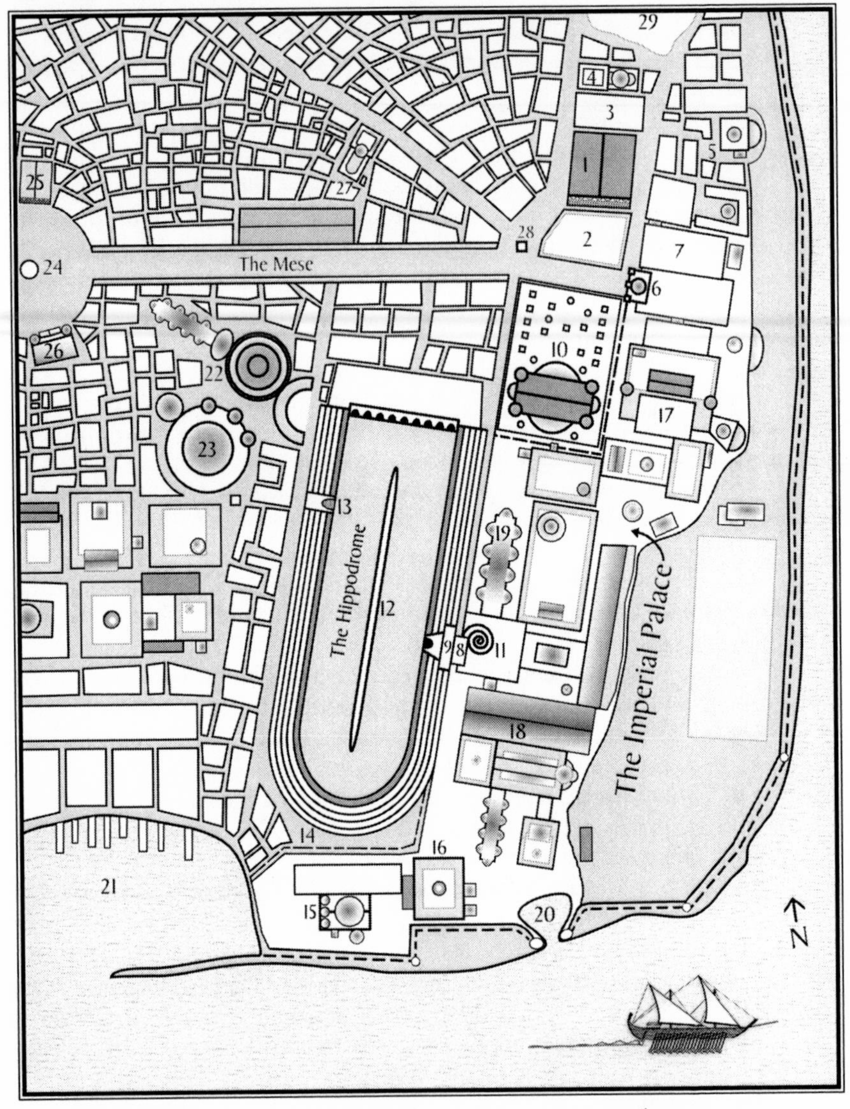

The Palace District of Constantinople, AD 532

1. Hagia Sophia
2. Augustaion
3. Hospice of Sampson
4. Hagia Irene
5. Shrine of the Hodegetria
6. Chalke Gate
7. Magnaura
8. Pulpita
9. Kathisma
10. Baths of Zeuxippos
11. Gate of the Snail
12. Spina
13. Gate of Death
14. Sphendone
15. Church of Sts. Sergius and Bacchus
16. Palace of Hormisdas
17. Delphax
18. Daphne
19. Triklinos of the Nineteen Couches
20. Boukoleon Harbor
21. Julian Harbor
22. Palace of Lausus
23. Palace of Antiochus
24. Forum of Constantine
25. Senate House
26. Praetorium of the City Prefect
27. Church of the Theotokos Chalkoprateia
28. Milion
29. Acropolis

V

AD 532, JANUARY

Fifth year of the reign of Justinian, Emperor of the Romans
At Constantinople

The soot-black night closed in around them as Belisarius and his men threaded their way through the backstreets. They arrived at palace without incident and were immediately led into the emperor's presence where dozens of senators, patricians, and other important men were already gathered. The situation was explained to Belisarius in detail but the report was only halfway given when Basilides, the Master of Offices, entered with a group of battered-looking Excubitors. They all bore expressions of dread on their faces.

"O Master, I bring grave tidings," he cried. "The Chalke Gate and the Public Colonnade are now ablaze."

The assembled senators and bureaucrats gasped in shock.

Basilides continued: "We were unable to silence them. They rage and boast that will burn the entire city to ashes."

At that moment, more ill news arrived. A group of men in ecclesiastical garb rushed into the emperor's presence, led by Marcellinus, Justinian's secretary, and Ephiphanius, the patriarch of Constantinople.

"The Great Church is aflame!" the patriarch cried. "And the mob blocked the fire brigades. If we can not get through soon, it will be destroyed!"

"Almighty God, no!" the assembled cried out.

Justinian rose up in a fury. "This has gone too far! Belisarius, assemble your men. Force a way through for the fire brigades. We can not stand by as the city is destroyed by these demons."

"As you command, O Master!" Belisarius replied, ready for action.

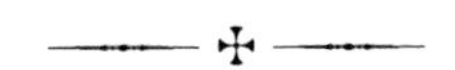

Belisarius mustered his tagma before the Chalke Gate—all picked men, experienced in battle, imbued with courage, and eager to follow their commander's lead. Joining Belisarius that evening was an old friend. Vidimundus the Goth had recently returned to Constantinople from the Armenian frontier where he had been serving under the Magister Sittas, the emperor's brother-in-law. He had been Belisarius's first commander and had recognized his talents early on. The two remained fast friends as Belisarius scaled the ranks and their paths in life diverged.

Approaching fifty, Vidimundus had begun to suffer the ailments common to men of that age, particularly those who had spent a lifetime marching from one fight to the next. A prolonged flare up of gout had caused him to be cashiered from the army once the Eternal Peace with Persia was ratified. But a month of relaxation in the capital had refreshed him, and as he knew nothing about life outside of the ranks, he soon found himself fraternizing with the men of Belisarius's tagma. When the muster was sounded, he was among the first to don his armor.

Belisarius led his men from their barracks directly to the Forum of Constantine where the main mass of rioters had clogged the streets. He could see the conflagration consuming the Great Church and realized that if the fire brigades couldn't be brought through immediately, Hagia Sophia and its magnificent columns would be lost forever. He began to run and his men followed, but upon reaching the Forum, they were met by a wall of people.

"More womanly excubes!" a Green shouted to his comrades, all of whom held stones and chunks of masonry in their hands. "Let's give them a proper salute!"

The Green was more than a little surprised when the heavy hail of projectiles did not cause an instant retreat. Instead, Belisarius and his men raised their shields and began moving forward, deflecting the missiles with ease.

"*Spathae*!" Belisarius cried.

With frightful precision, three hundred swords rang from their scabbards. Sensing a different sort of soldier had been unleashed upon them, the factionists' rain of stones began to slacken. Soon, it ended completely as the mob panicked and attempted to flee. But such uncoordinated mass movements of people are fraught with danger and so dense was the crowd in the Forum of Constantine that in seconds, hundreds of rioters were pushed to the ground and trampled by their fellows as they rushed to get away.

Belisarius and his men waded into the throng and plowed through, locking their shields together for added impetus. A few of the factionists, protected by the writhing mass of people between them and their targets, continued to fling stones and occasionally scored a hit on a helmeted head. But the tagma pushed ahead, treading roughly on those bodies unfortunate enough to fall before them.

One man who had fallen, a tall blond-haired Green with a long drooping moustache, unexpectedly leapt to his feet among the Roman ranks and buried a dirk in Vidimundus's unarmored neck.

At that, all order disintegrated. The Green fled into the crowd like a viper through high grass and a dozen of Belisarius's men raced after him in a blind fury. Worse, they no longer put up their swords, but now slew any who stood in their way.

"Saint George! What has happened?" Belisarius cried as he arrived at the spot where Vidimundus lay.

Two soldiers attended the Goth who looked forlornly up at his friend, a pool of crimson blood spreading around him. The soldiers had foolishly removed the knife and Vidimundus's life was quickly ebbing away. "I am sorry," the Goth gurgled. "Didn't see him."

"Courage, old man!" Belisarius said, kneeling down next to him. At the sight of the wound, he knew at once it was hopeless.

Vidimundus gazed vacantly into the night sky. "Pray for me," he whispered as he breathed his last.

✠

"We failed to get the fire brigades through in time, O Master, and I fear that the Great Church has suffered irreparable harm," Belisarius announced dejectedly as he entered the Delphax. His face, usually so handsome and alert, was black with ash and drawn with fatigue. His hands were caked with dried blood and his armor showed the scuffs of a dozen buffets or more. "However, we scattered the mob in the Forum of Constantine, and the brigades are now working freely throughout the city."

"Well, that's some good news," Justinian sighed. "In fact, it's the first bit of good news we've had all day."

"Perhaps that ends it then," Basilides sighed.

"Indeed, indeed," Justinian enthused optimistically. "The loss of the Great Church is a tragedy, but as a wise man once said, 'none should be reckoned great who are amazed that buildings fall and mortals die.' Have the flags hung out for the races tomorrow morning and we'll see if we can't quell any remaining anger with a little spectacle."

"As you command, O Master," Basilides replied. He then bowed and made his way out.

"General, you have done well tonight," Theodora added in a voice much less cheering than that of her husband. "We understand that you have suffered some losses. You have our leave to attend to them."

"Thank you, O Mistress," Belisarius bowed, amazed that the empress had already received a report.

"And get you some rest here in the palace, as well," Theodora continued. "I suspect we shall require your services again before long."

✠

At first light the next morning, the patricians Pompeius and Probus, escorted by several stout bodyguards, made their way to the mansion of their brother, Hypatius. He was expecting them.

"Have you been out, brother?" Pompeius asked in greeting, dispensing with formalities. "The Mese is a shambles and the Great Church is an ash heap."

"Yes, I've heard," Hypatius replied. "It's quiet now, though. I am told that Justinian's soldiers broke up the riot late last night."

"Indeed. And he's got the race flags out already this morning," Probus added.

Hypatius was about to say something in response, but thought better of it. With a jerk of his thumb, he dismissed his slaves and then motioned his brothers into a private meeting room.

"The emperor thinks this is over, but we've got to find a way to keep the momentum going," Hypatius whispered once the door was shut.

Probus smiled and pulled a folded sheaf of parchment from inside his cloak. "That, my brother, is already taken care of."

Hypatius took the parchment and read it. He reached the end and chuckled. "Silvanus thinks of everything. But while his agents among the factionists guide them in the proper course of action, what are we to do?"

"We wait," Probus declared. "Silvanus's servant—the one who delivered that letter to me this morning—also told me that the Scholarians and many within the Senate and the palace are eager for open rebellion. When the moment is right, they will cut down Justinian and Theodora and we'll never have to dirty our hands. Once the deed is done, the throne will be handed to you, brother. You need only be patient."

"Patient, you say?" Hypatius grumbled. "I was patient fourteen years ago after our uncle died and those fools in the palace handed the throne to Justin. No, I'm finished with patience. Fortune favors the bold, as the poet said, not the patient."

"Well, then what do you propose we do?" Probus snapped.

"I'm going to grab Fortune by his forelock," Hypatius replied, making a snatching gesture with his hand.

"How, exactly?"

Hypatius's ardor subsided as he sat down to think.

"Let us go to the palace," Pompeius offered.

"What, walk into the lion's den?" Probus shot back. "You can't be serious."

"I am perfectly serious" Pompeius replied.

"That is sheer lunacy."

"No, it's not," Hypatius said, supporting his brother. "In fact, I think it's a brilliant idea."

"How do you reckon?"

"Don't you see?" Pompeius explained. "We enter the palace saying that we're afraid of the mob. Once inside, we'll be closer to the center of the action and perfectly positioned to influence events."

"Yes," Hypatius agreed. "We'll be able to gather followers around us and begin suggesting to others that these riots are Justinian's fault and that he's no longer fit to occupy the throne. At the same time, we convince Justinian to throw more and more of his loyal units into the fight. Then, when he is stripped of his followers and we have turned enough of the bureaucracy to our side, we will strike."

"Yes, exactly," Pompeius nodded fiercely.

Probus shook his head. "No, it's all wrong. Even if Justinian is stupid enough to allow us into the palace, he won't give us the freedom to wander around and do as we please. We'll be watched closely. And should any inkling of our plot reach the Emperor's ears, be assured that Theodora will insist that he throw us in prison—or worse."

"Bah, it's an audacious plan," Hypatius declared. "I'm sick and tired of passively waiting for the throne to fall into my lap. It's time for action and I am ready. Are you with me, brothers?"

"I am," Pompeius answered without hesitation.

Probus remained silent in thought.

"Well?"

"I will not enter the palace with you," he said. "I admit, it's a brave plan, but the line between bravery and stupidity is often a fine one. Instead, I will remain here and support our cause as best I can from the outside. If a struggle ensues in the palace between you and Justinian's henchmen, I may be able to render some signal assistance by rallying the Senate."

Word quickly spread through Constantinople that the race banners had been set out before the Hippodrome, and with relief the common folk began flocking there in hopes that the riot had ended. On the way, many stopped to gawk at the ruins of the Great Church—now nothing but a charred pile of rubble. A few forlorn clerics picked through the debris, attempting to rescue whatever artifacts they could. Several tired-looking Excubitors formed a cordon around the building to ward off looters.

No factionists could be seen anywhere. Many assumed that they had been wiped out the previous evening, or were now in hiding from the emperor's wrath. Whatever the reason, the people eagerly filled in the lower tiers of the Hippodrome, taking the best seats that were usually occupied by the Blues and Greens.

The calm endured only a few minutes.

"Fire!" someone screamed and ten thousand heads turned.

"The Hippodrome is ablaze!"

A great groan of dread went up from the commoners as plumes of black smoke began to rise from the empty upper tiers of benches. In a mad rush, they stampeded out of the Hippodrome and scattered back to their homes.

Clearly, the riot had not ended yet.

From the palace, Justinian could see the smoke rising from the Hippodrome and soon a report was brought to him that a large mob had gathered before the partially burnt Chalke Gate chanting their demands. In frustration, the emperor sent Basilides and Constantiolus to find out what they wanted.

They returned to the Delphax after a short time, covered completely with filth. Justinian stood up at the sight of them.

"The rabble greeted us with a barrage of rotten fruit, O Master," Constantiolus said, digging a chunk of quince out of his ear. "We were able to quiet them only long enough to hear their demands."

"They want the heads of Eudaimon, Tribonian, and the Cappadocian," Basilides burst in. "They said that these two are the cause of their anger and nothing could pacify them except the expulsion of these men."

"How dare they dictate to me!" Justinian growled angrily.

"Master, the danger is great," Constantiolus whispered, drawing near the throne. "They have beaten off the Excubitors repeatedly and the Scholarians have simply refused to move against the crowds at all. They say it's not their business."

"Cowards," Justinian fumed.

"Indeed, O Master," Basilides agreed. "The rabble is gaining in boldness and it may only be a matter of time before they try to storm the palace."

Justinian took these words like a blow to the head. He slumped down dazed upon his throne. "What do you recommend, then?"

"If the mob tries to rush the palace, we will not be able to stop them," Constantiolus admitted. "Therefore, let us all board ship for Hebdomon. Seven thousand of my troops are there and are completely loyal. We can retake the city in a day or two and crush this riot."

Justinian shook his head.

"The factions are indeed audacious," Theodora replied calmly, sensing an opening. "But fleeing the palace will only show our weakness and make them bolder still."

"Then what do you suggest, my Empress?" Justinian looked up hopefully.

"Give them what they want," Theodora replied decisively. "Dismiss those three worthless rogues who have done so much to instigate this riot but so little to suppress it."

Justinian thought for a moment in silence. These men had been his loyal confederates for years. But if he had to sacrifice them to retain his throne, he would do it. "Yes," he nodded.

"Master!" Basilides gasped, open-mouthed. "Is it wise to give in to them?"

Justinian ignored him. "Inform the crowd of our decision," he commanded. "And summon Eudaimon, Tribonian, and John to us at once. We would get them on a ship to Chalcedon before any of these dogs has a chance to lay hands on them."

"I obey, O Master," Basilides bowed and left to carry out his orders.

"I want you on a ship to Hebdomon within the hour," the emperor addressed Constantiolus. "Bring your troops into the city and smash this revolt."

"Yes, O Master," Constantiolus replied, saluting.

"But before you go, summon the generals Belisarius and Mundus," Justinian ordered. "Tell them to bring all of their retainers with them as well. We will need every available man to safeguard the palace."

✠

Thursday, January 15 dawned with the factionist mobs in control of the city and Justinian and his court holed up in the palace complex. When informed that their demands had been met in full, the demes celebrated with a jubilant new outburst of plunder, arson, and random murder. And since Tribonian, Eudaimon, and John of Cappadocia had been so intensely disliked, many of the common folk also rejoiced in their downfall and increasing numbers joined the factionist cause.

But if Justinian and Theodora thought that giving the rioters what they wanted would end the strife, they could not have been more wrong. For according to human nature, when you reward a certain behavior, you are sure to get more of it.

In the Senate house near the Forum of Constantine, the factionists set up their headquarters. There met some five hundred of their leaders—a senate of wolves made up of exceedingly violent and corrupt men, most of whom had made small fortunes in gambling, prostitution, and petty thuggery. About twenty of them stood on the rostrum, alternately addressing the crowd and debating their course of action.

"The city is ours," declared Cleon, a Green originally from Egypt. "We need only take the palace and arrest that weakling Justinian and then the empire will be ours as well."

"Take the palace? Are you mad?" a Blue named Delphios rejoined. "We have no weapons and Justinian still has many soldiers loyal to him."

"What, those cowardly Excubes?" replied Phaulos, the Green who had been freed from sanctuary in St. Lawrence. "We've routed them time and again. They will not deter us."

"It is true that the Excubitors and Scholarians pose no threat to us," Delphios said. "But the emperor has veterans under Belisarius and Mundus in the palace who are not to be despised. And worse, the praesental army at Hebdomon may yet be brought against us."

"Let them come!" boasted Elithios, the Blue freed along with Phaulos. "We have fortified the Octagon with barricades and will meet them with fire and burning pitch. By the saints and all the gods, I swear they will get a taste of this they won't soon forget." In his fist, he shook a heavy iron rod that he had looted from a destroyed building.

"Quit your boasting, Elithios, you great fool," Delphios barked back at him. "With weapons like those, we stand no chance against professional soldiers. We need true weapons and we need them in vast quantities."

"Where?" Cleon asked. "The people are disarmed."

"But the patricians aren't," Phaulos said. "When we burned the palace of Lausus, we discovered a cache of swords."

"But ruined in the fire," someone chimed in from the back.

"Yes, sadly, that's true," Phaulos remarked.

"Ah, but which nobles will aid us?" Cleon asked. "Most of them have either fled the city or are hiding in the palace."

"We don't need their aid!" a random voice chimed in. "Death to the patricians! Let's burn them out and take what we need!"

A loud roar greeted this acclamation. "Nika! Nika!" they chanted, pumping their fists in the air.

Finally, Cleon called for quiet. "Brothers, it would be a pleasant thing indeed to burn out the patricians and sack their mansions. Who can argue it? But let us assume that we do this—what will we do when the last palace is looted and the last nobleman slain? Will we rule the city? The empire? No, more likely, we will be attacked by those senators and generals who have fled the city. And if, somehow, we defeat even these, then what? Will we be the cause of the downfall of the Empire of the Romans?"

A low murmur of confusion rippled through the mob gathered in the Senate house. "Heaven forbid we should do such a thing!" a lone voice called out above the others.

"Indeed, heaven forbid," Cleon continued. "Therefore, I propose to you, brothers, that instead of destroying the empire, we simply destroy Justinian's despicable regime."

The assembled roared their approval.

"And to do this, we will need to promote a candidate of our own to the throne," Cleon added.

The factionist leaders looked from one to the next, each one of them thinking the same thought. Before they could voice it, Cleon spoke again: "No, it can not be one of us. Would a Blue tolerate a Green as emperor? Would not the Greens riot if we chose a leader from the Blues? And furthermore, the candidate must be a man who may be acceptable to the patricians and the bureaucrats in the palace."

"Who then?" Delphios urged.

"The august and all-conquering house of Anastasius!" a voice called out from the back. "Let the rightful heirs take back the throne stolen by Justinian!"

There was a brief silence and then the leaders all shouted as if struck by the same epiphany simultaneously. "Let the nephews of Anastasius rule!" they chanted. "Hypatius for emperor of the Romans!"

Still chanting, they marched out into the Forum of Constantine where some twenty thousand of their confederates were waiting for them.

Cleon remained on the rostrum and heard the roar of the crowd in the forum with satisfaction. A man approached him with a wide grin on his face. Cleon returned it with a friendly salute. "Well done, Achates. Your acclamations were perfectly timed," he whispered.

"And your performance was spectacular—worthy of a scene from Eurypides," Achates, the manservant of Hypatius, declared. "Be assured you shall be paid well for it."

In his heart, however, Achates was unimpressed. *How easily led this ignorant rabble is,* he mused scornfully to himself. *Once he is on the throne, my master will put them in their place as Justinian should have done long ago.*

✠

The chant quickly spread and soon the entire mass was of one mind. The goal of their riot had now changed from pillage and plunder to revolution.

They would march to the house of Hypatius and crown him emperor.

When they arrived at the front gate of Hypatius's palatial villa, however, it was barred against them. They began to sing the songs most commonly intoned during the coronation ceremony for a new emperor and within a few moments, a woman appeared above the gate along with two servants. She was matronly if not elderly, and bore a look of consternation on her plump face.

"Woman, we have come to make the master of this house the master of all the Romans. See him out!" the Blue leader Delphios called.

"God forbid you should ever do it!" the woman called back with a loud, determined voice. "I am his wife, Mary, and my husband is a loyal servant of Justinian Augustus. In any case, you have come too late. My husband and his brother Pompeius have retired to the palace."

The leaders of the factions were momentarily at a loss. After a brief conference, Delphios emerged and was boosted up above the crowd by two burly Blues. "Hypatius and Pompieus have fled, but one brother yet remains for us—Probus for emperor of the Romans!"

"No!" Achates gasped. He grabbed Cleon by the shirt. "Stop them! They were supposed to rally for Hypatius, not Probus!"

"Who can control these people?" Cleon shrugged with a smile. "Sometimes it's better to just go along with the crowd." He then screamed at the top of his lungs: "Probus for emperor!"

"Nika!" the crowd responded. "Probus for emperor! All hail the victorious and merciful Blue-Greens!"

Achates sprinted to the house of Probus as fast as his feet could carry him. "Let me in, immediately!" he screamed to the slaves manning the front gate. Recognizing him, they did as they were commanded.

Probus met him in the courtyard. "What is it? What has happened?"

"The plan," Achates gasped, "the plan has miscarried. The mob is headed this way. They mean to make you emperor and not my master, your brother."

Probus was horrified. His face lost all color and his hands began to tremble. "No, this cannot be. If they seize me now and crown me, I'm a dead man."

"You must flee with all haste," Achates cried urgently.

"Yes, yes, you're right," Probus agreed readily. "Lysander, go down to the harbor and prepare my ship immediately. Run!"

"I obey, O Master," the slave responded and sped out the mansion's rear gate.

Probus continued shouting orders to his slaves: "Memnon, collect horses. Claudian, pack money and as many of the family treasures as you can into trunks. We're sailing for Chalcedon within the hour."

"There is no time, O Master," Memnon wailed. "There is a crowd at the gate! They are calling for you to come out!"

"God save me!" Probus gasped, his eyes darting back and forth like a trapped animal. His knees buckled as he began to swoon.

"Listen!" Achates shouted grabbing him roughly by the shoulders. "You can still get out the back to your ship. But you must leave right now!"

"What of my household? My possessions? My money?"

"We will defend the house, O Master," Claudian, his head manservant, declared bravely. "Only go now or we can do nothing to save you. Here is a horse. Ride, O Master!"

Without another thought, Probus mounted the sturdy stallion. "Defend my property, Claudian," he barked severely. Without waiting for a reply, he galloped out the back gate with Achates running after him on foot.

"Where is Probus! Bring him out!" the crowd chanted at the front gate. "Probus for emperor of the Romans! Hail to the victorious house of Anastasius!"

"Why have you come here?" Claudian demanded, shouting down from the rooftop.

"We have come for Probus!" Delphios shouted back to him. "Tell him we would make him emperor of the world if he will only give us weapons!"

"We have no weapons here," Claudian lied. "And if we did, what makes you think we'd be foolish enough to give them to you?"

"Send out Probus!" Cleon cried. "The victorious Blue-Greens have no interest in talking to a stupid slave like you!"

"My master is gone, you mongrel," Claudian replied testily, though imprudently. "When he heard you factionists were coming for him, he decided it would be better to drown in the sea than become emperor of a filthy rabble."

The mob grumbled angrily and a few well-thrown rocks caused Claudian to retreat back into the house.

"If Probus won't help us, then we'll turn his house to ash!" Phaulos cried. He backed up his threat with a flaming brand tossed onto the roof of the front portico above the gate. A dozen more followed.

"Death and fire to all who oppose the merciful Blue-Greens!" the mob chanted, their anger now rising to a fever pitch.

✠

The afternoon of Saturday, January 17 found Belisarius napping in the ornate Triclinum. Normally a formal banquet hall in the palace, its couches had been removed and hundreds of soldiers from Belisarius's household guard now reclined on carpets, some sleeping, others chatting in low voices.

Belisarius sat propped up against the wall in full armor, his eyes closed. His dreams were troubled with visions of raging infernos, helpless souls screaming for help, and the mocking, moustached faces of men with blood on their hands. Over the past two days, he and his men had engaged in scores of skirmishes with the factionists. He had been struck repeatedly by stones, clubs, and flaming brands and his lungs burned with the acrid smoke of a hundred burning buildings.

Having gotten a taste of Roman steel on the first night of the riot, the factionists now avoided confrontations with Belisarius and his troops. Instead, they gathered in small groups to burn and loot, but would disappear like the wind when well-ordered formations of soldiers arrived on the scene.

For his part, Belisarius had done well to maintain his composure and the discipline of his men in the face of such difficulties—that is, until the factionists set fire to the Hospice of Sampson. When he witnessed the great house of charity for the sick and dying go up in flames with hundreds of poor souls trapped inside, unable to escape, something inside him snapped.

"Are you awake, O General?" whispered Principius, one of his tribunes, tapping him on the shoulder.

At first, Belisarius did not respond. Finally, he opened his bloodshot eyes. "Twelve," he muttered groggily. He had only slept five hours in the past three days.

"My apologies, O General, but..."

"I killed twelve of them last night," Belisarius continued. "I'm not even sure all of them were factionists."

"No need to worry on that account," Principius reassured him. "They were counting their plunder when we burst in on them. If they weren't factionists, they were certainly in on the spoils."

"I have never killed a Roman citizen before this week, Principius," Belisarius sighed. "This is neither pleasant nor glorious duty."

"A nightmare is what it is," Principius agreed.

"And that's precisely what you woke me from."

"I only pray God forgives us for what we have done," the tribune whispered.

"Or what we still have left to do," Belisarius added.

Principius nodded wearily.

"I assume you woke me because the emperor requires my presence?"

"Indeed, O General," Principius replied, regaining his urgency. "It seems that the soldiers from Hebdomon under Constantiolus have been repulsed."

Now Belisarius was wide awake. "What? How is that possible?"

"The factionists fortified the Octagon and Constantiolus managed to get himself trapped in that confined space by flaming barricades. Then, the mob set the shops around the perimeter alight and threw flaming brands on the soldiers. Many escaped, and hundreds of the factionists were killed, but the army has withdrawn to Blachernae and has not been heard from since then."

"Has any effort been made to contact them?"

"Yes, several times," Principius said. "Their silence is ominous."

"Let us go to the emperor right now," Belisarius said, grabbing his helm and jumping to his feet.

Justinian was perched forlornly on his throne in the Delphax when Belisarius arrived. Clearly frustrated, the emperor sat with his head in his hands as his ministers argued around him.

"The situation has deteriorated badly everywhere in the city," Basilides reported, his words urgent and shaky. "Practically everything within a quarter mile of the palace is now a smoking ruin. Worse, we must assume that Constantiolus and his men are out of the fight. We have no mass of troops left in the vicinity of the city to call upon or flee to. The closest reliable moira is across the water in Chalcedon."

"And the security of the palace?" Justinian asked anxiously.

"They will not get in here, O Master," Belisarius declared emphatically, his voice steady. "Mundus and I have secured every potential entry point."

"And are you confident of the loyalty of your soldiers, General?" Theodora demanded.

"Without question, O Mistress."

"Very well," Justinian sighed. "I have one die left to throw, so let it be thrown. A similar rebellion threatened the throne of Anastasius in his day. He quelled it with a direct and humble appeal to the people in the Hippodrome. Tomorrow morning, let us attempt a similar bit of pantomime."

"As you command, O Master," his assembled ministers bowed and began filing out.

The emperor grabbed hold of Narses's sleeve before he could exit. He drew a heavy pouch of gold from beneath his purple cloak and handed it to his cubicularius. "I'd like at least part of the audience to be favorable tomorrow. Take this and distribute it among the leaders of the Blues."

"Without delay, O Master," Narses replied softly.

"If we can't defeat them by brute force without destroying the entire city, then perhaps we can divide them and have them destroy each other."

VI

AD 532, SUNDAY, JANUARY 18

Fifth year of the reign of Justinian, Emperor of the Romans
At Constantinople

The morning of the Lord's Day dawned blood red over the Bosporus. Astonishingly, the race flags could be seen hung throughout Constantinople and the bewildered populace picked their way through the charred wreckage to the partially scorched Hippodrome to figure out what was going on. What they saw there shocked them. Justinian sat alone in the Kathisma, uncrowned and unadorned, holding in his hands the Gospels, bejeweled and glittering. Word soon spread of this stark apparition and in no great time, masses of people were pouring into the Hippodrome, all eerily quiet.

When he perceived that the circus had filled to capacity, Justinian stood and looked out over them. After a brief pause, he began to speak, his grave tenor voice echoing over the crowd in the vast arena:

"Forgive, O Romans, the stubbornness and arrogance of your emperor. Had I only known the depth of your anger over the excesses of my ministers, I would have acted long ago to suppress them. But now that I have removed them from office and replaced them with better men, I beg you, cease your destruction! Much of our lovely Byzantium—mine and yours—has already been burned to the ground. Let us save what remains, I beg you.

"I swear upon these, the Sacred Scriptures, that no punishment shall be meted out for what has happened before now. By this power, I forgive you for what you have done—not one of you shall be arrested. Only be at peace, and no guilt shall be on your head. Rather, on my head shall the guilt remain for my sins made me deny your requests for clemency in the first place."

"Justinian Augustus, may you reign, forever victorious!" a Blue shouted in a loud voice. Several others followed in succession and a sizable number of partisans on the Blue benches took up the chant.

But the rest of the crowd remained silent and confused. They looked about at each other wondering what to do and a low murmur of discussion floated over them.

From his position in the doorway at the back of the Kathisma, Belisarius could see the emperor nodding and acknowledging the Blues who acclaimed him. *Amazing,* he thought. *He pulled it off after all.*

But the notion of success had barely been formed when it was obliterated.

"You can not be trusted, O scoundrel!" a voice rose from the Green benches.

"An oath from a liar is like a kiss from a harlot—easily given, signifying nothing!" another shouted.

The rest of the mob cheered their approval and rude epithets and garbage were soon winging their way toward the Imperial box.

"Cease! Cease!" Justinian appealed, holding out his hands. "Let us have no more of this, or I shall be forced to punish you!"

"Ah, you see!" Cleon cried. "You are already breaking your oath, you donkey!"

"Death to Justinian!" Phaulos screamed, spittle flying from his mouth. "Give us Hypatius!"

"Hypatius for Emperor of the Romans! Let the house of Anastasius rule!" others chanted. The idea proved instantly infectious and soon thousands were calling for the death of Justinian and the elevation of Hypatius.

At the sound of Hypatius's name, the emperor blanched. Shock momentarily immobilized him and he was pelted in the chest with an over-ripe fig. Belisarius rushed in and covered him with a shield. Together they descended from the Kathisma and entered the covered passage back to the palace.

"It is over," Justinian lamented. Tears seemed to be welling in his eyes.

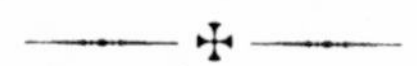

"Then it's agreed," Pompeius whispered in a voice so low as to be nearly inaudible. "When Justinian sends Belisarius and Mundus out to do battle with the factionists tonight, you and your men will arrest the emperor and empress and take them immediately by ship to Cyzicus."

The man he was addressing, a tall elderly Scholarian named Celer, smiled fiendishly. Celer had commanded the Scholarians for over two decades and had at first opposed the elevation of Justinian's uncle, Justin, during the last imperial succession crisis. He changed his tune only when Justin's ascension became inevitable. He had set aside his animus and served both Justin and his nephew reliably, if not brilliantly. But the disgust he bore for Justinian lay festering below the surface, requiring only a prick to bring it forth.

"Yes, agreed," Celer responded, patting the pouch of gold hidden in his cloak. "This is all it will take for my men to support you. As for myself, I'd do it for nothing."

"Good, good, but there's more," Pompeius continued. "Once at Cyzicus, you will hold them under guard until my brother and I have established our government and accepted the loyalty of the armies. When you have received word from us, Justinian and Theodora are to be put aboard ship for exile in Cherson—only, the ship will be poorly caulked and sink in the Euxine with all hands."

"It will be a pleasure, I assure you," Celer said, still grinning.

"Excellent. I swear to you—your loyalty to our cause will be richly rewarded, my friend," Pompeius replied nervously, shifting his eyes repeatedly over his shoulders to make sure they were unobserved. The cistern below the palace was about as private a location for an intrigue as one could wish. But still, Pompeius worried. The empress had a reputation for hearing even the deepest, darkest secrets.

Celer smiled broadly and grasped Pompeius clumsily by the arm. "By this time tomorrow, you and Hypatius will be co-emperors of the Romans," he boasted in a voice loud enough to make Pompeius jump with fright.

✣

"Tonight," Pompeius mouthed silently to his brother Hypatius as both made their way to the Delphax where they had been summoned.

Hypatius nodded in response, fully aware of the progress of the intrigue. His jaw was set and his eyes glinted with determination.

As the two entered the ornate council chamber, they were surprised to see dozens of senators and patricians in a mass before the imperial seat—practically every nobleman in the palace. Belisarius, Mundus, and a hundred of their men were also in attendance, along with Narses and thirty eunuch spathars who were the guardians of the sacred bedchamber.

Hypatius and Pompeius saluted the emperor and he acknowledged them with a silent nod.

"You are all to leave the palace immediately," the emperor announced, dispensing with formalities. "The riot has taken on dangerous proportions and the mob rages without restraint. We have determined that it would be best for you to return to your homes to defend them as best you can. You may go. Now."

"Thank you, O Master, you are most gracious," one of the senators replied.

Several others concurred, concerned as they were for the safety of their families and households. Most of the noblemen paid their respects and hurriedly departed. Within minutes, the Delphax was nearly empty.

Hypatius and Pompeius were horrified.

"My Lord, would you have my brother and I leave as well?" Hypatius asked, approaching the throne.

"Yes, and quickly," Justinian replied, his brow furrowing in annoyance.

"But my Lord, the people...." Pompeius stuttered. "They may seize us."

"Then take an armed escort if you fear them," Theodora cracked impatiently.

"No, my Mistress. Our fear is that they may seize us and... compel us to defy you," Hypatius shot back, thinking quickly.

"We are confident you would not succumb to such compulsion," Justinian declared, his voice firm. "Now go, see to your homes. If you are needed again at the palace, we shall summon you."

"Please, my Lord," Hypatius replied desperately falling down on one knee.

"It is our wish to serve beside you and render you every assistance to quell this revolt. Our homes are of no consequence to us. All that matters is the defense of the imperial house."

"Do not send us away, my Mistress," Pompeius added. "We beg you."

Justinian looked upon the two with extreme contempt as he struggled to master his tongue.

"Go now or I shall order the guards to throw you out," Theodora said in a low voice full of malice. The piercing anger in her eyes removed any doubt that the empress would follow through on her threat.

Pompeius and Hypatius glanced at each other and rose.

"As you command, O Mistress," Hypatius replied, a barely concealed sneer on his lips. The two brothers turned and strode out of the Delphax, their scheme shattered.

Once they were gone, Justinian turned to Narses who was lurking, as ever, behind a curtain to the right of the throne. "Clearly, they were planning something," the emperor declared. "Your intuitions were correct again, old friend."

The eunuch emerged and stood submissively beside the emperor. "With the people shouting for them, they have become a threat to you, O Master. Better that they are outside the palace where they can do less immediate harm."

"And their reaction left little doubt about their intentions," the emperor said, rubbing his unshaven chin. "Make sure they are watched closely."

"Yes, O Master," Narses replied. "My agents are following them even now."

Belisarius stood by amazed. He had witnessed the entire scene and was impressed with how perfectly Narses had predicted the brothers' reaction prior to their arrival. *What skill this man has in reading the ill intentions of others,* he thought to himself.

Belisarius then spoke up: "We must not forget about their brother, Probus, O Master. Has he been located, yet?"

"Probus has fled the city," Theodora replied before her husband could speak. "We are told that he is now in hiding at the estate of Silvanus near Chalcedon."

"Silvanus is another who bears watching, Master," Narses added. "My spies have marked his slaves among the leaders of demes."

Justinian sighed. "There will be many accounts to settle when this is over."

"What would you have us do now, O Master?" Basilides asked nervously.

"What can we do but wait?" Justinian replied in frustration. He had not slept in days and the weariness showed plainly on his face. "We have sent an urgent message to Germanus, my nephew, at Thessalonica and ordered him to come to the capital with his army immediately. But we may not expect him for two weeks at least. Until then, we must keep them out of the palace and prevent them, as best we can, from destroying the rest of the city."

Hypatius and Pompeius fled safely from the palace to their mansions. On the way, however, Hypatius had pulled back his hood to reveal himself momentarily to a pair of prowling of factionists. They recognized him immediately and ran off to spread the news.

"Why are you here, husband?" Hypatius's wife, Mary, cried as she embraced him. "The mob has visited our gates each of the past three days seeking you. You must flee to the suburbs. If they catch you here..."

"They will catch me here," Hypatius interrupted. "I expect them to arrive shortly."

Achates, his manservant, removed his gray cloak and clasped on one of brilliant white instead.

Mary's face became frantic. "There is still time to escape..."

"Nonsense. I do not wish to escape," Hypatius said calmly. "They will attempt to make me emperor and two times, I shall refuse them, as is proper. But at their third petition..."

"Are you mad? By the Theotokos, no!" Mary screamed.

"My Lord, the crowd has arrived outside the front gate!" a servant yelped. "They are calling for you!"

Hypatius squared his shoulders and threw back his cloak. "I shall go to them."

"No!" his wife cried, her light brown eyes flashing, her voice choked with tears of desperation. "If you embrace them, you will be embracing death." She seized his arm tightly, her feet rooted to the spot.

"Achates, take my wife inside," Hypatius ordered. "Politics of this sort is no place for women or the faint of heart."

Hypatius went out to the crowd and did exactly as he said he would. At first, he pretended to resist the urgings of the mob to accept the crown. But eventually, he gave in to their demands and the people went wild in their rapturous joy.

"Hypatius Augustus, you conquer!" they chanted. "May you reign for many years and good!"

They were about to lead him to the Forum of Constantine when Mary emerged from the house with her daughters, maids and kinswomen. They formed a cordon around Hypatius, locking their arms together. "I will not let you take him to his death!" she screamed to the mob, her gray hair flying loose. She locked her arms around her husband and would not let go.

"Release me, woman," Hypatius demanded, struggling against her.

Some of the mob began to laugh at the scene.

"It seems the Augusta would thwart us!" Cleon joked. "Let us clear her serving ladies away. We must not let our emperor fall under the sway of a woman!"

"No, not like that worthless cur Justinian!" Phaulos replied and the crowd laughed again.

With little tenderness, the factionists shoved the women aside. Hypatius consigned his wife to a male slave who restrained her and carried her back into the house as she wept bitterly.

The men of Hypatius's household and many of his kinsmen joined him as he processed to the Forum of Constantine at the head of the mob. There, they were met by an even larger crowd, some 40,000 strong who cheered when he arrived. Among them, Hypatius marked several Scholarians, Excubitors, palace eunuchs, and men of rank. At this sight, his confidence grew.

From the Placillian palace, some of the rebel eunuchs had plundered the imperial insignia and this was brought forward. At the base of the lofty column topped by a golden statue of Constantine in the center of the forum, Hypatius was raised on a shield and acclaimed as emperor.

"Hypatius Augustus, you will conquer," they cried. "Nika! Victory to the most triumphant Blue-Greens! Victory to our emperor, Hypatius Augustus!"

They lowered him to the ground and put the emperor's cloak over his shoulders. On his head, they placed a golden diadem.

Again, the people cheered: "Nika! Hypatius Augustus, long may you reign!"

Cleon approached him along with several of the other factionist leaders. "O Emperor, lead us," he said, prostrating himself. The others did likewise. "We require only weapons to dislodge that usurper Justinian from the palace. Will you provide them?"

"Indeed I shall," Hypatius replied, already adopting the mannerisms of an autocrat. He turned to his brother who had now arrived and stood by his side. "Pompeius, assemble what arms you may from my house and those of the senators present here. Justinian has little strength left in the palace. Let us go there and overawe him into surrender or take him by force."

"Hypatius Augustus, you rule!" Cleon and his cohorts cried out in their joy.

Constantiolus made his way back to the palace and stood before the emperor and empress. "My men remain at Blachernae, O Master," the general said, his head down in shame. "They will not fight. It was all I could do to keep them from joining the rebels."

"This is bad, very bad," Mundus whispered to Belisarius who stood beside him.

Belisarius nodded, concern etched on his face.

Several eunuchs, looking battered and disheveled, then entered the Delphax with Narses at their side. For the first time, the emperor's grand chamberlain looked truly afraid. "My...Master," he stammered. "The mob has...crowned Hypatius. These spathars witnessed everything. In the Forum of Constantine, the rebels raised him on a shield."

"And now they are headed here, O Master," one of the spathars cried, falling on his face. "A huge mob, amongst whom may be seen many traitors from the palace itself. We were recognized and barely escaped with our lives."

Justinian trembled. His mouth hung open and fear was plain in his eyes.

"Master, we must escape!" Basilides insisted. "We have only a few hundred men here in the palace. We can't possibly resist the mob in their tens of thousands."

Justinian shook his head. "I can't believe it has come to this. Hypatius, that treasonous wretch!"

"If we take ship, we can escape the city and meet Germanus and his army half-way," Constantiolus suggested urgently.

Justinian nodded. "How many ships have we?"

"Three," Narses replied readily. "It should be enough for all of us. Shall I have the money from the sacred treasury loaded aboard?"

"Yes, do so now," Justinian commanded grimly. "I see no alternative. We must flee if we would carry on the fight."

"As you command, O Master."

At the word, the remaining ministers of the court sprung frantically into action.

"Stop!" a woman's voice cried out.

All present turned and looked upon Theodora. Her normally pale face was crimson with anger.

"You cowards!" she raged, all pretense of courtly formality flung aside. "I have sat here and watched you fools bungle your way through this affair and have held my tongue, as a woman is expected to do," the empress slurred, her voice falling back into the rude accents of her degenerate youth. "But I shall hold it no longer, as it is clear to me that the so-called men present in this hall have no more courage than a maiden who shrieks at the sight of vermin.

"You are determined on flight and indeed, flight may bring you safety—at least for a little while. But just as it is impossible for a living man to escape death, it is equally unendurable for an emperor to exist as a fugitive. Make no mistake, O husband—once you leave this palace, you leave your empire behind as well. For my part, now that I have attained it, I shall never be separated from the purple. I have risen from nothing, lived in poverty among the filth of mankind and I swear to you I will never return to that life. Nothing but death will separate me from this throne, nor will I ever live a day when all who meet me do not call me mistress."

All present remained in total silence as Theodora turned her cold gaze on her husband. "If you are utterly lacking in courage, husband, flight will prove no difficulty. You are exceedingly wealthy and the ships await you in the sea below. You may fly to the end of the earth to find a refuge secure from all threats if you so desire. But if you do so, I promise you that a day will come—and soon—when you would happily exchange your safety for death.

"As for me, I approve of a certain ancient saying: 'Royalty is a good burial shroud.' If the squalid legions of human scum out there desire my throne, they'll have to kill me to take it for I shall never yield it willingly to anyone!"

Theodora's declaration immediately put new steel into Justinian's spine. His dejected and sleep-deprived form seemed to revivify and lamps of determination glowed anew in his eyes.

"Hypatius!" one of the spathars cried as he rushed breathlessly into the hall. "Hypatius is in the Hippodrome, and has seated himself in the Kathisma! A great crowd acclaims him!"

The look of ferocity on Justinian's face intensified.

"My Lord, an opportunity as been presented to us to destroy this rebellion completely," Belisarius spoke up in a loud voice. "Our prime difficulty to this point has been locating a group of rebels who would not scatter immediately at the sight of us. But now that the serpent has a head, if we can lop it off, the body will die and quickly. With all of them packed into the Hippodrome, their leaders in the Kathisma will not be able to escape us if we can somehow get to them."

"But we are grossly outnumbered," Basilides squawked weakly. "A hundred to one!"

All ignored him.

"Take your men and see what can be done," Justinian ordered. "In the mean time, I want every reliable man capable of bearing arms outfitted immediately. Narses, that includes you. And me."

Theodora smiled and nodded approvingly at her husband, the emperor.

✠

Belisarius gathered his three hundred mail-clad stalwarts and led them through the palace to the Gate of the Snail, so called for the grand spiral staircase there—the Cochlea—that led up to the bronze doors of the Pulpita, the antechamber to the Kathisma. They could hear the loud but indistinct acclamations of a mandator and the throaty roar of thousands chanting their responses. The great noise was unnerving to all but the most steady souls.

Sensing this, Belisarius spoke: "Fellows, we few are walking into a wasps' nest. God only knows what we will meet beyond those doors. But by the oath I swore to the emperor, I will face any peril to save his throne, even at the cost of my own life. I need not remind you of your own oaths to serve and uphold the emperor. I know well your courage and your desire to see justice done to this villainous rabble. For my part, I make this promise to you—that in my zeal to defend the emperor's cause, I shall not throw away your lives carelessly. For in truth, the life of any one of you is as precious to me as my own."

"We know, Magister," Principius said with a grim smile. "Don't worry about us. If you required us to storm the fortress of Satan himself, we'd follow you."

The men behind him cried, "*Nobiscum Deus*!" and saluted briskly.

With renewed confidence, Belisarius ascended the Cochlea. His men followed with swords drawn. He took a deep breath as he approached the heavy bronze doors and attempted to turn the latch. It was locked tight.

"Let us knock and see who answers," Athenodorus suggested.

Belisarius nodded and began rapping on the door with the hilt of his sword.

Voices could be heard on the other side. A peep-hole slid open and a pair of eyes appeared. "Who goes?"

"Open these doors by the command of the emperor!" Belisarius demanded.

"Emperor, eh? Which one?" the eyes laughed.

"Justinian Augustus, you fool," Belisarius shouted. "Open at once or be accounted a traitor!"

A voice could be heard from the Pulpita beyond the doors: "Just ignore them. We will help neither side until there is a clear victor."

Belisarius recognized the voice at once. "Celer, you timid fop, open immediately!"

"I guess there was no one there after all," the eyes taunted again. The peephole then slammed shut.

"Rotten cowards! Open!" Principius cried, pounding on the door and shaking the latch without success. "Shall we stave it in, Magister?"

"No. To burst in on them would force us to fight in tight quarters where our discipline and skill at arms would be of no benefit. It was my hope that we would find some Scholarians here willing to help us arrest the usurper. But they have clearly chosen the most craven path—that of worthless parade-ground soldiers. If even the Scholarians have turned, the situation is even more grave than we feared. The emperor must know of this at once."

Justinian took the news badly. Now in his splendid gold cuirass with a purple cape draped over his shoulders, he looked every bit the martial image that appeared in caricature on his coins. "Your men and those under Mundus are all I have left," he lamented as Belisarius finished his report.

"And Narses's spathars," Theodora added.

"What, all thirty of them?" Justinian snapped.

"At this point, every man counts," Theodora retorted. "Even half men."

"How many are left to us all together?"

"My men are four hundred," Mundus replied. "All Gepids. They won't shrink from the fight, I promise you, O Master."

"My veterans number three hundred," Belisarius added. "They are battle-hardened and loyal, my Lord, and may be counted on."

"And the general John has just arrived as well along with twenty of his retainers," said Narses, eager to enhance his friend's standing even in a moment of dire crisis.

"Bloody John? Vitalian's nephew? Who summoned him?" demanded Theodora, her eyebrows knitting in annoyance. Rumor had implicated Justinian in the death of Vitalian thirteen years before, and Theodora's suspicious intuition told her that John's sudden arrival at this moment represented a danger to her husband.

"When he heard of Hypatius's sedition, he and his men rushed to the palace of their own volition to support the rightful emperor," Narses added. "He may be counted upon, my Mistress. I swear by all that is holy."

Theodora's eyes narrowed.

"Assign John and his men to my tagma, O Master," Belisarius interrupted before Theodora could respond. "They would be of great help if loyal. If disloyal, my men and I will dispatch them."

"Let it be done as you have said," Justinian replied, his face flushed with determination. "Now go out into the Hippodrome and use whatever means necessary to crush this rebellion once and for all."

✠

With a hood over his head, Narses himself, accompanied by two spathars similarly disguised, brazenly slipped into the Hippodrome via a little-used service corridor. They wore blue cloaks and ribbons and thus attired, easily made their way into the benches of the Blue factions. Once there, Narses spotted the Blue leader, Delphios, gazing forlornly at the happenings in the Kathisma. Hypatius had surrounded himself with patricians and members of the Green faction, leaving no place for the Blues.

"They have excluded you, then?" Narses whispered as he approached.

"Who in Hades are you, midget?" Delphios snapped angrily.

"A friend," Narses smiled, pressing a leather pouch bursting with gold solidi into the man's hand.

"Merciful God!" Delphios gasped.

"Spread it around, will you? The rightful emperor will soon be asserting his authority. I wouldn't want you fellows to be on the wrong side."

"Tell the emperor he has our loyalty," Delphios muttered, clutching Narses's arm.

Narses gave a knowing smirk and slunk off the way he came.

"Fellows, I have news!" Delphios cried to his sullen partisans. "Justinian has trebled Hypatius's bid for our support!"

✠

Hypatius sat nervously on the imperial seat looking out over the vast multitude of profligates, vagabonds, swindlers, ruffians, brigands, and charlatans who acclaimed him. Justinian had not made a move against him yet, but neither had his men attempted to seize the palace. Indecision paralyzed him as his many advisors squabbled over how to proceed and none of them were able to concoct a plan of action that seemed likely to succeed without the palace being sacked by the mob like an enemy capital. His previous determination drained out of him as the situation spiraled out of his control.

His attention was drawn to the Blue benches. *What is that they are chanting?* he thought, straining to hear.

"Justinian Augustus, you conquer! Lord save the emperor Justinian and the Augusta Theodora!"

Hypatius couldn't believe his ears.

The chant became louder and soon the rest of the crowd in the Hippodrome roared angrily in response. An intense storm of stones broke over the Blue benches, killing a few outright and driving the rest from their places.

The chanting was silenced and the mob exuberantly celebrated their victory, acclaiming Hypatius all the more.

But this sedition within a sedition only swelled Hypatius's anxiety.

"Look, brother, your Excubitors have arrived," Pompeius announced joyfully. Unlike his brother, Pompeius was brimming over with confidence.

Below them, on the track of the Hippodrome, nearly three hundred youths from the Green faction paraded in ragged order. They were outfitted in oversized muscled breastplates and carried large oval shields. Each brandished a sword, some more expertly than others. Out of step, they turned to face Hypatius and cried out in unison: "We salute you, O victorious Hypatius Augustus! We will storm the palace! Command us!"

At the sight of them, Hypatius lost his nerve completely. Calling to his side Ephraim, a candidatus whom he trusted, Hypatius whispered: "Go inside and say to the emperor, 'See, I have gathered all your enemies together for you in one place.'"

Ephraim looked back at him in shock.

"Do it now!" Hypatius urged through clenched teeth.

"As you wish," Ephraim replied, stupefied. He bowed and made his way quickly out the back of the Kathisma into the Pulpita behind. There he met Celer along with several other rebel Scholarians, and Thomas, a silentary who was also Justinian's personal physician.

"What is it?" Celer demanded.

"Hypatius...He just ordered me to go to Justinian and tell him, 'I have gathered your enemies for you.'"

The news was alarming, but Celer kept his head. "You can't do that," he said.

"You must let me through! If Hypatius wavers, this rebellion can not succeed. Our only hope is to get back into Justinian's good grace now while there's still a chance."

"Well, there's no point going in there," Thomas said, casting a knowing glance at Celer. "Justinian has fled. There is no one left in the palace."

Ephraim was thunderstruck. "Fled you say?"

"Yes, fled," Celer added, taking up the lie happily. "Now get back in there and tell our emperor to sit more confidently on his throne."

"Yes...yes I shall immediately!" Ephraim replied, giddy with relief. With a rapid step, he reentered the Kathisma and whispered into Hypatius's ear: "O Master, it seems that you are preferred by God to be emperor, for Justinian has fled. The palace is empty!"

Hypatius turned, incredulous. "Truly?"

Ephraim nodded joyously, a great smile plastered on his heavily bearded face.

Hypatius slowly turned back to the crowd and looked out over them again. He heard their acclamations with new ears now—those of a man who believed he deserves them.

VII

AD 532, SUNDAY, JANUARY 18

Fifth year of the reign of Justinian, Emperor of the Romans
At Constantinople

Torches were lit around the Hippodrome as dusk settled over Constantinople.

Issuing from the ruined Chalke Gate, Belisarius, Mundus, Bloody John and their gray warriors marched sullenly past the destroyed baths of Zeuxippos. The scene was nightmarish. Small fires burned all around them, sending plumes of black smoke into the dull red sky. Broken masonry and charred timbers littered the ground, covered with putrid ash. An overpowering stench insulted the nostrils—the mingled reek of burnt wood, boiling pitch, scorched marble and roasting flesh.

Belisarius lamented silently as they passed through the Gymnasion, the vast courtyard in front of the Zeuxippos. In his younger days, he had spent many hours here, studying his tactical manuals among the multitude of statues in bronze and marble that decorated the plaza. But now the place looked like a battlefield after a terrible defeat. The heroes of old lay smashed on the ground, their limbs contorted in death.

He passed a colossal statue of the emperor Septimius Severus toppled and smashed into dust and fragments, its battered marble head and hands propped up against its base. A majestic life-size bronze of the poet Virgil lay nearly whole on the ground, his two feet alone remaining on the pedestal. A few looters could be seen poking around among the broken bodies collecting gold leaf and anything else that could be melted down for a quick profit. Belisarius felt a twinge of anger at them, but the situation was too grave to waste time chasing such petty phantoms.

The column moved on toward the Hippodrome until their way was finally blocked by a smoldering mountain of wreckage from the baths. Belisarius struggled up the tottering heap and looked over. Below him, the remains of the caldarium could be seen, its beautiful red and gold mosaic pavements glimmering in the waning sunlight. He picked out several smoking piles of rags that he immediately discerned to be the bodies of those unable to escape the collapse of the great building.

"It's impassible," Belisarius announced as he descended from the pile.

"We'll have to go around."

"More delays!" Mundus griped. "Every time we try to come to grips with this scum, something prevents us."

"Like God Himself is against us!" his son Mauricius added.

"God is not against us, you idiot!" Bloody John barked back at him, losing his temper.

"Do you think God favors those wretches inside who have burned down half the city and murdered so many innocents?" Belisarius added, also irate.

Mauricius did not reply, clearly deflated by the rebukes.

"Well then, how in hell are we meant to get at them!" Mundus roared, taking up for his offspring. "Everything around the Hippodrome is a ruin threatening to cave in and destroy us!"

"Stop trembling and be a man," John shot back.

"You bastard..." Mundus growled, curling his lip. He grabbed the hilt of his sword, looking angry enough to kill.

"Be silent, both of you! Save your fury for them," Belisarius broke in quickly, gesturing toward the glowing, menacing Hippodrome. The noise of the exultant crowd wafted heavily on the chilly breeze.

"But how..." Mundus began.

"We will head back to the Mese," Belisarius cut him off. "From there, you and your men will make your way through the Palace of Antiochus to the Gate of the Dead. When you arrive there, wait and watch."

"And what will you do?" Mauricius interrupted.

Belisarius shot him an irked look. "John and I will thread our way through to the sphendone and fight our way into the Hippodrome. When you see the commotion in that quarter, you must then launch your attack from the Gate of the Dead."

"Ah, they shall be caught between us," Mundus enthused. "It is a daring plan!"

"And one that requires proper timing," said Belisarius. "Be sure to attack only when you see my men and I fully involved in the fight, for if you attack too soon, they may overwhelm you with their numbers."

"Aye, Magister!" Mundus and Mauricius replied, saluting.

✠

So many of the side streets along the Mese were blocked with rubble that Belisarius and his men had to make a wide circuit to find a route that was open. It took them much longer than planned to reach the sphendone, and Belisarius worried that the impetuous Mundus would not be able to restrain himself from launching his attack prematurely.

"The gates are all locked and secured with heavy bolts," Principius reported after a thorough search of the area. "Some Blue factionists were loitering outside, but they ran at the sight of us."

"We'll have to bash the gates in," Belisarius answered. "Find something that will serve as a ram. And quickly!"

At that moment, a group of battered Blue factionists approached Belisarius and his men, their hands in the air as a sign of truce.

"Peace, Strategos," their leader called out. "You are Belisarius, are you not?"

"I am," he replied. "Who are you?"

"Do you serve Justinian still?"

"Yes, I serve the true emperor unto death."

"Ah, that news heartens me greatly! I am Delphios, a captain of the Blue deme. We have erred greatly in siding with the Greens, O Strategos, and seek to repent."

"You chicken-hearted filth!" cried Bloody John, raising his sword. "If not for your collusion with the Greens, none of this would have happened!"

Delphios flinched, convinced that his life was about to end.

"What penance can you offer our most pious Augustus?" Belisarius asked gravely, seizing the moment. "Can you open the gates to us?"

"Yes! Yes, immediately!" Delphios replied. "Follow us!"

The Blues took off at a run toward the sphendone, followed closely by Belisarius and his men. Soon the gates were unlocked, and the whole column climbed the narrow staircase to the floor of the great circus.

Under a charcoal sky, the track was a sea of humanity. The mob's attention was fixed on the Kathisma where Hypatius and his chief supporters sat receiving their acclamations surrounded by flaming torches. Only a few people on the edge of the crowd noticed the grim-looking soldiers emerging behind them. Assuming they were friendly Scholarians, none paid them any particular heed.

Belisarius surveyed the situation. To his relief, all was quiet near the Gate of the Dead where Mundus was supposed to emerge. "We could take a few dozen men, climb to the next level and assault the Kathisma directly," he thought out-loud.

"The way is narrow," John muttered in reply, his eyes fixed hungrily on the crowd. "Our men could be trapped in the confined space and cut down. And should we fall with the cream of our soldiers, who will be left to support the emperor?"

"You are right. It's too risky," Belisarius conceded gravely. "Through the crowd, then."

"It's our only option," Bloody John replied, a little too enthusiastically.

Belisarius sighed. *God forgive me what I am about to do,* he prayed within his heart. "*Ad Octo*!" he commanded.

Immediately, his men fell into ranks eight deep, forty across the front.

"*Scuta*!"

In unison, the front four ranks unlatched their tall oval shields from their backs and presented them at front.

"*Arcus*!"

The rear four ranks drew bows and strung arrows, taking aim but holding fire.

"*Spathae*!"

In one fluid motion, the front four ranks unsheathed their swords simultaneously.

By this point, some of the mob had taken notice of the activity behind them. "Soldiers!" someone screamed and a thousand heads turned.

"Stone them!" a commanding voice rang out and hundreds of projectiles streamed toward Belisarius and his men.

Without a command, the front ranks raised their shields and the archers ducked behind them.

Belisarius waited for the initial hail of stones to slacken, then signaled to John.

"*Parati*!" John screamed.

"*Adiuta...*" cried Belisarius in a loud voice.

"*...O Deus*!" the men responded in unison.

Instantly, the archers rose up and fired a volley directly into the crowd. The rebels were packed in so tightly that every arrow could not help but find a mark. Scores lay dead and dying in an instant.

Belisarius and his front ranks plunged into the mass, striking out with their swords as they did so. The people yielded before them in a panic, realizing that they could not hope to oppose well-armed and expertly trained veterans with their bare hands. In the crush to escape, dozens fell to the ground and were trampled underfoot.

"Now die, you treasonous wretches!" Bloody John howled as he slashed a fleeing Green across the back with his sword. He smashed another in the face with the boss of his shield, splitting the man's skull. A third he transfixed through the belly.

"To the Kathisma!" Belisarius screamed over the tumult. "Arrest the usurper Hypatius!"

✠

"O Emperor, there appears to be a disturbance in the sphendone," Ephraim whispered urgently in Hypatius's ear.

"More ungrateful Blues?" Hypatius yawned. He had been emperor but a few hours, but had already over-indulged in wine and slouched on his throne.

"No, Master, they seem to be soldiers. They are led by Belisarius himself."

Hypatius immediately perked up. Rising to his feet, he scanned over the crowd and saw the danger heading his way. "Cleon! Phaulos!" he roared. "The lackeys of Justinian have cast their final dart! Gather your men and repulse this attack. Wipe them out!"

"With pleasure, O Master," the Greens replied confidently. Looking as smart as they could in their borrowed arms, they rushed off to engage the soldiers of Belisarius.

Hypatius sat down nervously to watch the ensuing fight, well knowing that his life depended upon the outcome.

✠

A sturdy Green swung a great club at Belisarius's head. The general parried with his sword and with a dexterous twist, neatly removed the man's hand. "Forward!" he urged his men.

"Magister! Soldiers!" Principius shouted. "Straight ahead!"

Scholarians? Excubitors? Belisarius puzzled, trying to figure out who was coming against him. He turned to see but could barely believe his eyes. Undisciplined youth with murder in their eyes descended upon his men like frothing mad dogs. Clad in archaic armor, they moved with the grace of dancers, but their sword strokes were clumsy and lacked power. Nevertheless, the sheer surprise and fury of their assault caused Belisarius's front ranks to buckle and fall back. A few of his men were knocked to the ground and slain as they struggled to rise.

"*Dirige frontem*!" Belisarius shouted, rallying them to repulse the attack.

Seven Greens arrayed in antique greaves and breastplates hacked wildly at Athenodorus and his men, knocking two of them down. Belisarius immediately recognized one of the Greens who wielded a bloody sword and sported a long moustache.

The general rushed into the thick of the fighting, parrying a wild stroke from a Green swordsman as he ran. A huge Green hulk swung a broken leg from a bronze statue at Belisarius and knocked him sideways. Keeping his feet, Belisarius ducked under the next swing and sliced his attacker's hamstrings on his back-stroke. The man fell shrieking to the ground. Another Green thrust a spear at him, but Belisarius adroitly knocked the point away and slashed the man across the throat in one motion.

His shaggy blonde hair hanging loose around his face like a lion's mane, the Green with the drooping moustache saw the general coming but held his ground. An expert street-fighter and a Vandal, the young man believed himself invincible, having never met a foe he could not vanquish.

Belisarius lunged into his attack and the Green parried effectively—both men duly impressed with the strength and skill of the other. On the second exchange, however, the Green only partially blocked a powerful straight thrust, and Belisarius's sword nicked him on the left cheek as he staggered backwards awkwardly to avoid death. Belisarius pressed his attack delivering several heavy blows that the Vandal parried only with great difficulty.

His sword arm tingling with the repeated impacts and his face bleeding profusely, the Green realized he was overmatched. He retreated several steps and crouched down.

"Whoever you are, you may have the victory this night. But I will live to fight another day," the Green taunted.

"Stand up and fight," cried the general, rushing forward. "Your crimes merit you only a quick death."

The Green waited until Belisarius was but a few paces away, then threw a handful of sand into his face.

Stunned, Belisarius reeled backwards, shaking his head like an enraged bull. His eyes soon cleared enough to squint, but the Green had vanished into the vast, roiling crowd. Still doubled over, Belisarius felt himself pelted on the helm and shoulders with heavy stones and an irresistible anger welled up within him. In a rage, he flung himself upon every Green fighter who came within range of his sword. He hacked and slashed without mercy until a pile of corpses lay at his feet. But even these did not glut his wrath. He looked for more targets—but they were moving away from him in a panic.

He took a few breaths and the blinding battle fury began to subside. Looking about, he could see that his men, though hard pressed, had thrown back the Green onslaught. The fight was still intense, but the untrained Greens could not hold their ground. Belisarius and his men pressed forward slowly toward the Kathisma over ground now slick with entrails and gore.

✠

At the Gate of the Dead, Mundus and Mauricius finally arrived with their Gepid warriors. Their passage through the ruined Palace of Antiochus had been more treacherous than expected. A score of his men had fallen through a weakened floor into a muddy cistern thirty feet down and it took them no short time to rescue those who survived the plunge. They tread carefully after that and the narrow lane leading up to the Hippodrome was clogged with rubble which made the going very slow. When they finally arrived at the Gate of Death, it was shut and bolted. Strangely, however, there were no guards in sight.

Mundus ordered a pair of his more nimble men to scale the gate, climb down inside, and release the bolts. They did so and the bronze grille soon swung open with a loud metallic creak.

Mundus and Mauricius ran through the gate onto the upper causeway and beheld the awful spectacle in the circus. The mob was churning like an angry green sea. Stones flew in every direction. Knots of furious factionists chanted loud but unintelligible acclamations. Hypatius and his men screamed orders from the Kathisma but complete chaos reigned among his riotous subjects. Everywhere one looked, men tore at each other with a savage ferocity better suited to barbarian nations than the Queen City of the Roman Empire.

Looking toward the sphendone, Mundus immediately spotted a sharp battle raging. "Ach! Belisarius and his men are already in the fight!" he cried.

"Let us join them at once!" Mauricius called, unsheathing his sword. "I have many scores to settle with this stinking rabble."

"Aye! Kill them all!" Mundus screamed to his men.

At the order, the eyes of his Gepid warriors gleamed with demonic delight. Without discipline, they poured through the Gate of the Dead at a run and hit the unsuspecting mob with a blood-curdling battle cry. Nearly every rebel with any kind of weapon had rushed previously to the sphendone, so those who remained in the rear were armed only with stones and leather straps. These proved no match for Mundus's heavily armed fighters.

Abandoning all restraint, the Gepids slaughtered all in their path.

Seeing themselves now attacked from both sides, the people soon despaired of victory and began to surrender. But Mundus and Mauricius were deaf to their pleas.

"Mercy! I yield!" a Green youth cried, kneeling down and raising his hands in the air.

"Die, you filth," raged Mauricius. He brought his sword down on the boy's head, splitting it in two.

"Stop, we're Blues!" a pair of men in loose-fitting blue tunics yelled out.

Mundus stabbed the first man through the belly.

"Put up your swords! We're with you!" the second screamed. It was Elithios, one of the two criminals whose botched execution had sparked the rebellion. His face bore the confident look of a man who had once cheated death and fully expected to do so again. Stretching forth his hands toward Mundus, he proclaimed: "Long live Justinian August..."

His words were cut short by a sword stroke across the face which took off the top of his head cleanly.

"No quarter, no prisoners!" Mundus shouted to his men who responded with a frenzied cheer.

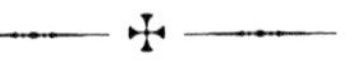

When Hypatius saw Mundus and his Gepids enter the fray, he knew the game was up. His supporters may have been able to overwhelm one contingent of soldiers by sheer numbers alone. But with two tagmas in the fight, it was hopeless. Those around him knew it too. Scholarians and Excubitors who had been celebrating near the Kathisma but moments ago were now nowhere to be found. Only a few who had gone too far to turn back remained.

"Brother, Narses and his spathars are at the door of the Pulpita," Pompeius cried urgently, fear etched on his face. "There is no place for us to escape! We can not flee into the palace and to make our way through the crowd means certain death."

"If we must be captured, let it be by Belisarius," Ephraim suggested, thinking quickly.

Seeing the man, Hypatius punched him hard in the face.

"You liar!" he screamed. "You told me Justinian had fled!"

"I was told it by his physician!" Ephraim protested, clutching his jaw.

Hypatius advanced on the man to strike him again.

"He's right, brother," Pompeius shouted, stepping in to separate the two. "Belisarius might be convinced that we arranged this as a pretense to gather all Justinian's enemies together. He could be a valuable advocate for us. If we're captured by Narses, however, there can be no such hope. And if, God forbid, we are taken by Mundus, we may be brought into Justinian's presence in chunks."

"Arrghh!" Hypatius howled in fury and despair. "To surrender to any of them....The disgrace of it!"

"Let us go," Pompeius urged. "If we can descend from the Kathisma unnoticed, we may be able to make our way to Belisarius and his men."

"I'm with you," Ephraim cried.

"As am I," added Antipater, a logothete from Antioch who had joined the rebellion.

Gesturing to his remaining guards, Hypatius and his supporters descended the narrow staircase that led from the Kathisma to the track of the Hippodrome. At the bottom, however, they were met by Cleon, Phaulos and a group of forty desperate-looking Greens who had been assigned to guard the approaches to the Imperial box.

"Out for a stroll, O Emperor?" Cleon asked, his face deadly serious.

"Get out of the way, you worthless mutts," Antipater demanded, trying to force a passage.

Phaulos erupted, smashing the man repeatedly on the head with a flaming brand. Antipater fell senseless on the ground, his garments on fire. "No one leaves!" the Green frothed. "Victory or death!"

"We made you, we will destroy you if you abandon us," Cleon barked into Hypatius's face, poking his finger into his chest.

With a trembling jaw and shifting eyes, Hypatius stumbled back up the stairs into the Kathisma followed meekly by his remaining handful of supporters.

With the opposition melting away before them, Belisarius and his men battled their way to the base of the Kathisma. Despairing of the fight, the Greens threw down their weapons and surrendered.

"Gather their swords and hold them here," Belisarius ordered his men. He then called over his three mightiest guards, Principius, Unigastus, and Athenodorus. "The few men guarding the staircase are all that stand between us and Hypatius. The space is too tight for a full assault, so the four of us will clear the way."

"I am coming as well," Bloody John interjected.

"No, stay back and bring up the tagma behind us. Be ready to cover our withdrawal should something unforeseen happen," Belisarius commanded.

"Aye," John acquiesced unhappily.

Belisarius gestured to his three stalwarts and they advanced to the attack.

As they left, Bloody John smiled, casting a hard glance at the surrendered Greens still on their knees in supplication. "Butcher these swine," he ordered coolly.

"Unigastus and I will lead," Belisarius barked. "You two, draw your bows and take down anyone who appears above us."

"Aye, Magister," Principius and Athenodorus replied.

The two men guarding the base of the stairs fell instantly to the swords of Belisarius and Unigastus. A Green on the landing above them threatened, but Principius toppled him with a swift arrow to the chest.

Reaching the dark and smoky first tier, the four were set upon by a dozen Greens who flailed at them clumsily with their rust-pitted blades. But Belisarius and his men were ready. Athenodorus and Principius drew arrows and shot in rapid succession; four victims tumbled screaming to the floor. Unigastus absorbed several heavy blows on his shield, then stabbed his assailant through the abdomen.

Raising his shield, Belisarius pushed forward against three attackers. He slew the first one with a jab to the sternum. The second he dispatched with an overhand chop to the shoulder which sheared off the man's arm and much of his torso.

The last opponent was the powerful Phaulos who struck with the insane fury of a man possessed. "Die, you slave! Why won't you die?" he shrieked, striking Belisarius with a heavy iron rod. His final vicious blow smashed Belisarius's shield to bits. "Now, I'll make an end of you," he hissed, raising his weapon.

"Come, try," Belisarius grunted, dropping the husk of his shattered shield.

Phaulos rained a dozen heavy strokes on Belisarius, but the general skillfully backpedaled and parried with his sword. Metal rang on metal and sparks flew in the smoky darkness. Then, in the instant it took for one of the glowing sparks to gleam and fade, Phaulos sensed an opening and concentrated all his strength into one brutal lunge at Belisarius's head.

"Now die!" he screamed.

He swung and missed cleanly.

Belisarius made him pay for his mistake. As Phaulos stumbled forward off balance, the general brought his sword down swiftly on the back of his neck, beheading him with a single deft stroke.

Phaulos's corpse twitched spastically on the ground, and at the sight, the remaining Greens threw down their weapons and scattered in every direction.

Wasting no time, Belisarius and his men charged up the final stairway that led to the emperor's box. At the top, Cleon and another Green rolled a huge earthenware amphora over the edge of the rail which smashed on Unigastus's helmeted head. The guard gave a little cry and fell senseless on the stairs. Undeterred, Belisarius continued ahead swiftly. The two Greens attempted the same trick again, this time with a heavy marble bench. But Athenodorus and Principius were ready for them and let fly with arrows as soon as the Greens' heads appeared above from behind the railing. One man was only nicked on the scalp, but Cleon took Principius's missile through his right eye and sprawled backwards with a horrifying shriek—dead before he hit the ground.

Exhausted and breathing hard, Belisarius reached the top and immediately spied Hypatius and his few remaining minions standing timidly near the imperial seat.

An instant later, the door to the Kathisma flew open. Narses and twenty of his spathars poured in and made directly for Hypatius and Pompeius.

"In the name of the emperor Justinian Augustus, I hereby place you under arrest for the crime of high treason," Narses announced. "Bind them and take all of them to the emperor immediately!"

"Well done, Narses!" Belisarius gasped, leaning on his sword. His tagma led by Bloody John began filing up the steps behind him.

Having gotten his prize, Narses offered only a sly smile and a haughty incline of his head before making his way back into the palace.

"See that Unigastus is taken care of," Belisarius ordered Athenodorus. "Principius, select ten men and come with me. We shall inform the emperor that the rebellion is over."

A heavy three-day beard darkened Justinian's cheeks as he paced about the Delphax, anxious for news from the Hippodrome. In his hand, he carried an ivory-hilted sword which he swung back and forth as if slashing invisible foes. Runners had been giving him regular reports about the ongoing fight, but since Narses had left with his remaining spathars, he had heard nothing.

With every moment that went by, Justinian's anxiety increased. "Perhaps they have all turned on us," he fumed out loud, feeling suddenly very weak and exposed. "Perhaps they are conspiring with Hypatius even now."

"Have courage, husband," Theodora chided, still seated upon her throne. "If this is our hour, then so be it. But I don't think so." She fondled the slim blade of a dagger.

"By the Theotokos, I pray you are right."

A loud commotion broke out at the entry to the Delphax. A dozen spathars paraded in and Justinian turned to meet them, sword at the ready. Immediately upon seeing the emperor, the spathars knelt and put their faces to the floor.

Narses followed behind, prodding ahead Hypatius and Pompeius. Both had been stripped to their tunics and were bound tightly with strong ropes.

"On your knees before your emperor, you traitors," Narses yelped in his shrill voice. "Here! Witness what they were wearing, my Master!" Narses cast the imperial gowns and diadem down on the floor at Justinian's feet in disgust as if they were the clothing of lepers.

"Master, please! Mercy!" Pompeius cried. "They forced it upon us!"

"Mercy?" Justinian raged. "How can there be mercy for villainous usurpers?"

"Lord Emperor, can you not see?" Hypatius wailed. "We did this for you! We gathered them all together so that they might be annihilated at one stroke! Ask your physician, Thomas. I tried to tell you but he said you had left the palace!"

"Pathetic!" Narses screamed. "You had the demes fight against us, tooth and claw. You acknowledged and encouraged their acclamations. Now you would add liar to your list of crimes? Odious wretch!"

Justinian's brown eyes blazed with anger. "There shall be no mercy. Even if what you say is true, the rabble obeyed you when you commanded them, yet you did nothing to stop them from destroying the city."

"But my Lord, you sent us out to them!" Pompeius begged. "In the name of God, spare us! What we did we were forced to do."

"They must die, and soon," Theodora added, her voice cold as a marble slab. "They have dared to wear the imperial insignia. That alone is reason enough to execute them. None who have donned the imperial garments in defiance of a reigning emperor can be suffered to live."

"No! Mercy!" the brothers cried.

"Clap them in irons," Justinian ordered firmly. "They shall die at first light."

Pompeius wailed at the command and threw himself flat on the ground.

"May God curse your reign," Hypatius spat. "You and your demon queen can rot in Hades."

Justinian turned away from them in disgust as several burly spathars dragged the doomed brothers from the hall.

As their last cries died away, Belisarius and his men marched smartly into the hall. "My Lord!" he saluted. "And my Lady," he bowed gracefully toward Theodora.

"General, it is so good to see you alive and unharmed by the mob," Justinian beamed, his previous wrath completely dispelled. He strode forward and embraced Belisarius who was taken aback by the unexpected show of affection.

"My Lord, by the grace of God, the rebellion is crushed," Belisarius announced. "The main force of the factionists has been destroyed. There are none left who would resist you."

"God be praised!" Justinian rejoiced, releasing a deep sigh. "Have no doubt that your loyalty will be rewarded."

After giving the emperor and empress a full report of the battle, Belisarius took his leave to attend to his men. But when he returned to the Hippodrome, the scene was much changed from when he had left a mere hour before. His tagma was gone, led out by John into the city to chase those few factionists who managed to escape. Mundus and his men were also gone, no doubt on the same kind of errand—or worse.

Belisarius stood at the blood-spattered rail of the Kathisma and looked out over a hellish vision. An awful quiet had settled over the vast expanse of the circus and the nauseating stench of death hung in the air like an evil mist. Not even the wails of the injured could be heard—because there were no injured. The bodies of the slaughtered lay piled in great twisted heaps and mounds. Their profusion was such that in only a few places could any patch of bare ground be seen.

How pleased the Evil One must be this night, Belisarius lamented to himself. *So much blood spilled, all in the name of a pointless rebellion. May Christ have mercy on these miserable souls.*

VIII

AD 532, JANUARY
Fifth year of the reign of Justinian, Emperor of the Romans
At Constantinople

The dead were gathered up into a gigantic gruesome pile over the next few days, and when the corpses were counted, it was found that over 30,000 had perished in the carnage. Hypatius and Pompeius were beheaded and their remains cast into the sea. The headless trunk of Hypatius washed up on shore a few days later and Justinian had it buried along with the other victims of the rebellion. Overtop of the site, he caused a sign to be erected which read, "Here lies the emperor of the wolves."

With the rebellion so decisively crushed, Belisarius made his way wearily home through the burned out and hauntingly quiet streets. As he approached his house, his spirits rose. To his great relief, all seemed well. Neither fires nor brigandage appeared to have affected this quarter.

"Greetings, Magister," a familiar voice sounded from the roof.

"Hail Solomon," Belisarius called back. "All is well?"

"Better than well," Solomon replied. He bounded from his position, ordered a slave to open the gate, and gestured for another to inform the lady of the house that her husband had arrived.

"No misadventures, then?"

"A few foolish souls tried to force the gate one evening, but we chased them off," Solomon smiled. "That son of yours is quite adept with the bow."

"Father!" Photius streaked out of the house. The lad embraced Belisarius tightly, his eyes flowing with tears despite his twelve years. "Thank God you're back!"

Belisarius hugged the boy, but soon his eyes caught sight of Antonina as she emerged from beneath the portico into the bright afternoon sun. She was positively radiant with joy—and something more.

Belisarius slept for an entire day and Antonina jealously guarded his bedchamber, allowing no one to disturb him, not even a courier from the palace. His dreams were dark and convoluted: random faces twisted in pain, limbs contorted in death, voices shrieking, and great fires burning all around him. He felt a mortal terror creeping up on him. His foes were too many and too mighty. They were impervious to his attacks and he felt a gnawing dread at their onset. They were coming, rank after rank in their thousands and he was alone and abandoned, his men dead around him. He glanced briefly at his sword and noticed it was broken, useless. The enemy charged with a terrifying cry and he fell to his knees before them, weak and powerless.

But the terror faded to nothingness—complete blackness and silence. A calm yellow light penetrated the darkness and brought with it a peaceful hum, like the sound of hymnody carried on an evening breeze. Within the light, he could see the form of a child—a young girl no more than ten. She led another smaller girl by the hand, an angelic creature with long hair of curly brown and eyes of shining amber. The light enfolded both girls in a soft glow, but they only smiled at him and said nothing. Belisarius felt an instant pang of recognition and rushed to embrace them. As he did so, he could perceive Antonina standing a short distance off.

"Belisarius," she called to him.

He looked down, and the two girls were gone. His eyes searched around frantically, desperate to catch sight of them again.

"Belisarius," Antonina's voice called out again, still softly but with greater urgency.

His eyes popped open.

"You must wake, my love," Antonina whispered, jostling him. "You have slept nearly an entire day and the Emperor is calling for you."

"Did I dream it?" Belisarius slurred groggily.

"Dream what?"

"About the baby."

"No, you didn't dream it," Antonina smiled, inadvertently placing her hand on her belly.

"It will be a girl," he declared.

"And how, pray tell, do you know that?"

"And we will name her Joannina."

"You *have* been dreaming," Antonina laughed. "Joannina is a fine name for a girl, but we'll need a boy's name, too, just in case."

Belisarius smiled knowingly. "The child won't be a boy. But if I'm wrong, I'll let you choose his name without any fuss."

"You may regret that. I know plenty of positively awful Isaurian names."

Belisarius rolled out of bed and stood up slowly. His stiff joints cracked at the effort. Aching waves radiated through the thick sinews of his arms, legs, and torso.

"The servants have prepared a meal for you," Antonina continued. "Bread and figs. Most of the markets are still closed so we couldn't get any meat. Only a little fish."

"It will suffice," Belisarius groaned as he stretched and inhaled deeply to clear his head.

"Shall I send in Solomon with your basin and clean clothes?" Antonina asked, throwing open the shutters to let light and fresh air into the room.

"Yes," he replied. "Did you say the Emperor had called for me?"

"Two couriers arrived last night but I sent them both away," Antonina said with a defensive edge to her voice. "I told them you were ill."

Belisarius looked irritated.

"Don't be annoyed," she snapped. "It's been nearly a week since you've had a proper sleep. You needed the rest, and as your wife, I intend to make sure that my property is correctly cared for."

Belisarius raised an amused eyebrow at her.

She rushed to embrace him. "Don't be angry. I swear Justinian never sleeps, never rests. He's always working, always planning. And he can't comprehend why all other men aren't just like him."

Belisarius returned her affection. "How could I be angry with you for taking care of me?"

"Good," Antonina declared, pushing abruptly away from him. "Now get yourself dressed and fed," she announced as she headed toward the door. Then, with a sly glance over her shoulder, she added: "You mustn't keep the Emperor waiting, lazybones."

To his surprise, Belisarius was led directly to the Daphne, the emperor's private chambers in the palace, rather than the audience hall. Justinian was dictating correspondence to his secretary Marcellinus when Belisarius arrived. The emperor was dressed informally, wearing a crimson cloak over an embroidered white tunic. His face was freshly shaven and his hair neatly trimmed and combed.

"The Magister Militum Belisarius," a mandator announced.

Justinian broke off in mid-sentence and turned with a joyous acclamation: "Hail, O most trusted friend!" The emperor rushed forward and clasped Belisarius by the right arm. "We heard you were ill. I trust you are feeling better?"

"Yes, my Lord your Piety," Belisarius replied, kneeling. "My illness was more the product of my wife's conjuring than reality, though, I must admit."

Justinian promptly raised him from the ground. "She's a good woman to give you such care. My Theodora is the same way. Always imploring me to rest and watch my health. But do you know that despite the anxious moments of the past week, I have never felt more vital in my life!"

"Yes, I can see that," Belisarius smiled.

The emperor continued without missing a beat. "At first, I was dismayed when I surveyed the destruction caused by the rebellion. So many of our precious monuments destroyed. And the loss of life—simply terrible! But now that I have had a chance to pray and consider the situation, I realize that this is a great opportunity to remake the Queen of Cities in a truly grand way. Our sainted predecessors were ambitious builders, but their masonry was of inferior quality. Who can deny it? Many of the buildings destroyed by the rebellion were already falling to ruin of their own accord. Even our beloved Hagia Sophia showed crumbling concrete and dangerous fractures in places too numerous to count.

"So now, I have summoned the most respected carpenters, artisans, and stone dressers in the empire to assist us in the task of rebuilding the city. And come see! I have commissioned Anthemius and Isodorus—our architects who are working on the church to be dedicated to Saints Sergius and Bacchus—to design a new Great Church on a size and scale the world has never seen."

Justinian shuffled through the pile of papers scattered across the large table at which Marcellinus was seated.

"The sketches are here, O Master," the secretary offered.

Snatching the papers greedily, Justinian unfolded them with immense satisfaction.

Belisarius was immediately impressed. "It is a majestic structure, beautifully proportioned, my Lord. It calls to mind the great domed church of Antioch, though seemingly much larger. Can such a structure truly be raised by men?"

"Anthemius and Isodorus are brilliant geometers, surpassed by none in the history of the world," the emperor smiled. "I have complete faith in them."

Justinian tarried over the drawings in silence for another moment, enamored with them as a young man is besmitten by a round shepherd maid. With a satisfied sigh, he refolded the papers. "Ah, but such glories must wait for the future. As for today, there is more mundane business for men like you and me."

"What is your will, my Lord?"

"Probus, the brother of the traitors, has surrendered to us," Justinian began, assuming a rigorous tone. "He has confessed everything in exchange for his life."

"Were not the rebels all slain in the Hippodrome? What of value did he have to confess?"

"Much, I'm afraid," Justinian frowned. "The conspiracy encompassed many among the patricians, in particular the family of Rufinus."

A cold chill shot up Belisarius's back. Rufinus was his family name as well. "Was the ambassador himself involved?"

"Indeed, he was involved, according to Probus," Justinian snarled, barely able to contain his anger, "though his father, Silvanus, was the true mastermind."

"And Probus himself fled to the family's estate in Chalcedon during the rebellion, isn't that right?" Belisarius recalled.

"Yes, and what's more, some slaves from the household were spotted among the leaders of the demes, urging them on. Probus claims that Silvanus provided the rebels with money and weapons as well."

"If true, their crimes are unpardonable," Belisarius admitted.

"Indeed. They must be arrested at once," Justinian declared. "And I want you to do it. Take a hundred picked men, and use caution. Their estate, the Rufinianae, is large and likely to be fortified. If they have already fled, pursue them. They must not be allowed to escape."

"Aye, my Lord your Piety," Belisarius saluted. "By your leave, I shall depart immediately."

"Yes...you may go," Justinian said with a hesitation indicating that an unspoken question remained on his lips. Belisarius was nearly out the door when it emerged: "Belisarius, your family name..."

Belisarius turned. "My Lord?"

"Your family name is Rufinus, isn't it?"

"It is, my Lord."

"Are you related...."

"No, my Lord," Belisarius chuckled. "In fact, I asked Rufinus that question once myself and he only sneered in reply. The idea of being related to a Thracian peasant family must have been offensive to him."

The emperor laughed. "Yes, quite right! Forgive me."

"Nothing to forgive, my Lord," Belisarius said. He saluted again and made his way out.

Justinian smiled after him. "Peasant stock," he chuckled to Marcellinus. "Would that all my officers were of such stock."

✠

A column of wobbly soldiers disembarked from the ferry onto the quay at Chalcedon. Their land-legs were soon under them, however, and with Belisarius at their head, they pressed on through the city and into the countryside beyond. It had been an unusually warm late January day and the men were soon sweating under their heavy armor and cloaks as they marched along the twisting road toward a beautifully landscaped villa perched upon a low hill. Funerary monuments of increasing size and grandeur studded either side of the well-maintained cobblestone lane. Belisarius marked one in particular topped by a lovely statue of Minerva embracing a young man. The inscription in particular caught his eye—Gaius Rufinus Flaccus, beloved of the gods.

The sun was beginning to set behind the red-tile-roofed mansion as the column approached. With its upper story handsomely colonnaded, and its cornices adorned with elegantly carved timbers, the house radiated luxury. A low wall of tan brick surrounded the complex, behind which a porticoed entranceway could be seen.

All seemed strangely quiet. They had met not a single soul on the road, and though smoke curled up from the roofs of various slave huts that were scattered throughout the bare fields, all were locked up tight as if bracing for a storm.

A grand fountain with two large stone geese spouting water greeted Belisarius and his men before the main entrance of the villa. The monumental bronze gate itself hung open haphazardly and no warder challenged them.

"It appears our quarry has fled, O Magister," Athenodorus opined.

"Perhaps. But let us find out for certain."

Ordering the bulk of his men to secure the grounds, Belisarius and a dozen of his veterans entered the mansion with swords drawn. Traversing the entrance corridor into the central atrium, Belisarius was thunderstruck at the opulence of the place. It was less a patrician's country mansion than a palace. Brightly patterned mosaic pavements gleamed in the torchlight, some showing figures of animals and pastoral life, others complex geometric patterns of fantastic intricacy. The portico itself was supported by tall columns of Thessalian marble, all in perfect proportion and glowing faintly green in the waning daylight. The lamp stands and brackets were of shining brass and had been affixed to the columns with the greatest care. The lamps themselves were also of brass but were festooned with acanthus leaves of silver. No one had taken the trouble to light them this night.

Every niche and alcove was occupied by a piece of sculpture representing busts of notable men and women, and numerous scenes from pagan mythology. The smooth plaster walls were covered with decorative fresco, one lengthy stretch of which was convincingly painted to resemble the shelves in a library heavy with scrolls and codices. The librarian himself could be seen in one panel, charmingly fetching a scroll that had dropped beneath a writing desk.

The open-air atrium was also opulent but looked somewhat spare by comparison. The winter cold had suppressed the luxuriant garden that thrived there in season. Water, however, still ran in tiled channels from a central fountain designed in the shape of a massive stone amphora and around it were scattered some exceedingly fine examples of portrait statuary in bronze and marble. A black life-sized bronze of a severe-looking man in Roman consular garb caught Belisarius's attention in particular. In his right hand, he clutched a scroll and his bearded face scowled out at the world as if to say, "I hold the emperor's trust. None may resist me and live."

"Looks a bit like you, Magister," Principius joked.

Belisarius grunted a laugh, though he didn't think the comment was very funny.

"Listen!" Athenodorus burst out.

All were silent and heard the noise immediately—the shrill wail of a woman.

"Upstairs!" Belisarius shouted.

Following the sound to a flight of steps, Belisarius and his men rushed up to the luxurious living quarters and into a scene of death. A bearded man lay sprawled on the floor, his face pale as newly bleached parchment, a basin filled with blood at his side. A middle-aged woman sat cradling his head, whimpering to him in unintelligible words. A blond girl, obviously a serving maid, sat petrified beside her, her face a mask of terror.

Belisarius recognized the man at once as the ambassador Rufinus. He knelt down next to the woman who didn't seem to realize he was there. "What has happened?" he asked, at a loss for what to say.

The woman looked up at him, tears and blood streaming down her torn cheeks. "He has..." she gasped, barely able to form the words. "He has opened his veins!" she moaned.

"Is he...."

"He's dead!" she screamed, clawing her cheeks again. "Dead!"

"Magister, behold!" Principius called to him and pointed to a pair of lads who had peeked into the room from another doorway. Their eyes grew wide as they spotted the soldiers and they immediately scurried off.

"Mind the women," Belisarius ordered his men. "Principius, Athenodorus, with me!"

The three tore after the boys through a dozen rooms, finally emerging onto an expansive balcony surrounded by a delicately carved marble balustrade which overlooked the valley below on one side and the atrium on the other. Unlike the rest of the house, this area was well lit with torches and the ghostly forms of the house slaves could be seen hiding behind pillars or retreating into concealed passages. Belisarius and his men held their swords at the ready.

"You are here from Justinian, no doubt," a gruff elderly voice cracked.

Belisarius and his companions wheeled to see the two boys they sought standing beside a much older man who was seated on a stone bench with a sturdy writing table beside him. Clad in a gleaming white toga with a purple border, the man positively reeked of the old Roman nobility. His full head of gray hair was curled in the style peculiar to the patricians of a more traditional flair.

Belisarius approached him, sheathing his sword. "I have been sent by our most noble emperor, Flavius Justinian, to arrest Primus Rufinus Silvanus."

"Most noble, indeed," the man said with a mocking chortle.

"Are you Silvanus?" Belisarius demanded, irked by the man's tone.

"Yes, I am," he replied. A burst of recognition caused Silvanus to start suddenly. A broad, meaningful smile spread across his face. "You are Marcus Rufinus Belisarius."

"Yes."

"You bear the likeness of your mother. Her eyes and mouth, at least. Your hair and size bespeak your father."

"How..." Belisarius stammered. "Did you know him?"

"Know him?" Silvanus laughed. "It would be strange indeed for a man not to know his own brother."

The words struck Belisarius like a thrown brick. Athenodorus and Principius who stood behind him, glanced at each other with suspicious eyes, ready for some surprise attack they felt sure was coming.

"Brother?" Belisarius finally managed.

"You mean he never told you about me? Or the rest of our family?"

"My father's family was killed when he was a youth," Belisarius replied, searching his memory.

"Is that so? What did he tell you about them?"

"Very little. It was a hard matter for him to speak about."

"Of course it was. He was never a very good liar, your father," Silvanus said. "But in truth, he wasn't really lying, was he? We were dead to him—and he was dead to us."

"Stop this nonsense," Belisarius retorted. "Why should I believe such an outlandish story as this?"

"Believe it or not, as you wish," Silvanus croaked, his voice creaking like tree branches in a gale. "But the official records will show it beyond any doubt if you take the trouble to look."

Belisarius stared at the man in silence, studying his appearance. There was no denying that he bore a resemblance to his deceased father.

Silvanus continued: "Your father, my brother, was Quintus, the fifth child of Aulus Rufinus Maximinus. He grew up right here in this house, the son of a noble Roman family of ancient lineage."

"Impossible!" Belisarius interrupted. "My father was a peasant—a free farmer from Thrace."

"Certainly, he was when you knew him," Silvanus continued, undeterred. "But he was not always so. Did you never wonder that he was literate? Could speak both Latin and Greek flawlessly? Had the diction and timing of an orator? Knew Cicero, Livy, and Horace by heart? Or in your naiveté, did you merely assume that all peasant fathers were so brilliantly educated?"

"I....just assumed...." Belisarius gasped, the awful truth dawning on him.

Silvanus continued: "He was seven years my junior, but by the time I had reached my twenty-first year, he already excelled me in all things having to do with strength and agility. And he was handsome. And graceful. And wonderfully intelligent. He was an outstanding example of Roman manhood and though I was terribly jealous of him, I loved him dearly. It grieved me when I heard he had died like a dog in Thrace."

Belisarius's head was spinning. *Can this be true?* he wondered internally. Every rational fiber of his being screamed *no*, but his heart gently assured him—*yes*.

"But why? If this is true, why did he leave here?" Belisarius demanded.

Silvanus smiled. "You have seen the inside of our house. Can you not guess?"

Belisarius opened his mouth, but Silvanus didn't wait for him to answer.

"Your father committed an unforgivable crime against our family," Silvanus grimaced, his brows knitting together in irritation. "It pains me greatly to recall it because it was partly my fault. When he was not yet twenty years old, he heard me tell of Daniel, that madman who stood upon a pillar at Anaplus for thirty years. I convinced him, along with some of our comrades, to pay a visit to this so-called holy man, fascinated as I was with such charlatans. Our aim was to deride him. Ask him ridiculous questions, mock his prophecies and perhaps see if we could trick him into coming down from his perch.

"You see, I reckoned this Daniel a fool as well as a fraud. And that was my mistake. To our astonishment, the so-called holy man deigned to see us and we were immediately shown to his column—his stand between heaven and earth as they said. Before we could say a word, he pointed down to my brother, your father, and said, 'I know why you have come, but you will not leave here as you came. You have belonged to the devil, but I hereby claim you for Christ.'

"We laughed heartily at this and attempted to insult him. But Daniel would say no more, nor would he acknowledge us any longer. He turned away and began that ludicrous sequence of exercises for which he was known, mingling chanted prayers to his crucified deity with repeated genuflections.

"We left in great cheer, but that sorcerer's magic was working upon your father's heart unbeknownst to the rest of us. It took a year to have its full effect, but to our astonishment, he embraced the despicable cross of the Galilean and even had the temerity to attempt to work a conversion on our father and mother—your grandparents—both of whom were lifelong servants of Mithras."

"You aren't Christians!" Belisarius gasped.

Silvanus laughed. "By the gods, you are slow-witted, my nephew."

"But how?" Belisarius stammered. "How did you manage to keep this a secret? If the emperor knew..."

"The emperor, that hypocrite, knows all," Silvanus laughed. "As did his predecessor and his. Our family's embrace of the old religion is tolerated because of the antiquity and prestige of our line. Certainly, a few of our ancestors have become Christians, usually to further their careers. But we have always served the Genius of Rome first. Now, at long last, we are to be suppressed."

"As you should be. You have rebelled against the rightful emperor," Belisarius declared, regaining his composure. "You foolishly sided with the rabble who burned down half of Byzantium and murdered thousands of innocents. And your side has been defeated. How can you expect to go without punishment after such treachery?"

"Rightful emperor, you say?" Silvanus chuckled in a mocking tone that Belisarius had already grown to despise. "If I have engaged in rebellion and sedition, it is only because I sought to renew the glory of our family and the empire of the Romans. I acted out of pride in my race and our Roman patrimony which is far superior to all others under heaven. And as a worshiper of the gods, I was correct to do so. For pride and the pursuit of fame and glory are no sins for those who follow the ancient traditions. Indeed, it is our greatest vocation. Compare this to the actions of your master, a so-called Christian, who has committed crimes far worse than mine in pursuit of his own earthly aggrandizement."

Belisarius glared menacingly at Silvanus.

"My nephew, I'm going to tell you something now that will wipe that self-righteous scowl right off your face. Justinian has considerably less right to the throne than the man you so stupidly helped topple, the noble Hypatius. It was a conspiracy of the most base variety that brought Justinian's uncle, Justin, to the throne—a plot hatched by your master himself and that hideous Armenian toady of his, Narses.

"For it was Narses, fifteen years ago, who helped the Grand Chamberlain Amantius steal the Emperor Anastasius's will. It was Narses who altered it, removing the declaration that Hypatius was to be Anastasius's heir. It was Narses, with the full knowledge of Justinian, who double-crossed Amantius and used his money to bribe the Excubitors to support Justin instead of Amantius's creature, Theocritus. It was Narses who locked the Ivory Gate and who would not let the imperial robes be brought out for Theocritus when he was nominated to be emperor. And it was Narses who opened the Ivory gate immediately when Justin was nominated. And finally, it was your master Justinian who insisted that Amantius and Theocritus be executed immediately after Justin became emperor. Thus the plot succeeded, the co-conspirators were eliminated, and an ignorant peasant from Illyria was placed on the throne of Julian, Diocletian, and Aurelius."

"You lie! What proof do you have of this?"

"I was there, my nephew. You were not. You were but a provincial peasant boy picking dirt from between your toes when it happened. I was told these things at the time by a slave of Theocritus and I consider his testimony unimpeachable."

"This is all hearsay..."

"You may believe that if it brings you comfort."

"Enough of your slander!" Belisarius shouted, slamming his hand down on the heavy wooden desk with enough force to make the ink bottles rattle.

Silvanus smiled placidly. "Do you see these papers here?" the old man waved his hand over the rolled scrolls and folded parchments piled next to him. "These are legal documents bearing out the truth of what I have said pertaining to our family. This one will be of particular interest to you."

Silvanus pulled a fresh scroll from the pile and handed it to Belisarius.

"What..." Belisarius stammered. He unrolled the scroll and began to read, his eyes burning with curiosity.

"It is my will," Silvanus declared. "I am a traitor to Justinian and all our family's wealth will be seized by the imperial fisc. These two boys here, your cousins Rufinus the Younger and Decius, will be stripped of everything and forced to live as paupers or confined to a monastery."

The two young men looked nervously at each other. Rufinus, the elder one, was a tall, solidly built young man showing his first beard. With his dark hair and broad chest, he bore an uncanny resemblance to Belisarius. The younger, Decius, appeared short and slight, with a cherubic face, sallow complexion, and long, thin hands.

Belisarius let the will fall from his hands to the ground.

"Ah, I see you've gotten to the meat of the matter," said Silvanus gravely.

"You've left it all to me."

"Indeed I have," Silvanus replied. "And it is natural that I do so. Upon my death, you will be the *pater familias*—the eldest male left alive in our family. And since you have proved your loyalty to Justinian beyond any shadow of doubt, though he covet the fortune, he will not confiscate it from you."

"No. This can not be," Belisarius shook his head and walked to the balustrade overlooking the fertile valley below the mansion. His thoughts were racing and he felt like a man who could not awaken from a bad dream. The night air was crystal clear and chilly and he could hear the bleating of sheep and the tinkle of a shepherd's bell a good distance off. A crescent moon provided only enough light to ascertain the outline of the hills off to the west. All else was plunged into featureless darkness.

At that moment, a contingent of Belisarius's men began filing silently onto the balcony.

Seeing them, Silvanus rose from his seat and stepped silently toward Belisarius. "It appears the final act is upon us, nephew," he whispered. "You will forgive me, but my pride is such that I can't allow a scoundrel like Justinian to determine my fate." Then, producing a long dagger from the sleeve of his cloak, Silvanus plunged it into his abdomen just below the sternum. Before Belisarius could react, the old man dropped heavily onto the tiled floor.

"What have you done? Why did you do this?" Belisarius demanded, kneeling beside him.

Silvanus smiled weakly, the color rapidly draining from his face. "Now, you will become even more powerful—perhaps the most powerful man in the empire. And Justinian will hate you."

"Why?" Belisarius repeated. Hot tears streamed down his face.

"I go now to Elysium," Silvanus gasped through lips tinged with blood, his eyes becoming vacant and glassy. "Watch over your cousins...take care of them. And if you are given the chance at empire—seize it!" With his last ounce of strength, Silvanus clutched Belisarius's hand tightly.

Belisarius looked over at Rufinus and Decius, both of whom stood petrified in their previous positions. At the glance, Rufinus rushed to his dying grandfather's side. Decius remained where he was, transfixed with fear.

"May the True God have mercy on your soul, grandfather," Belisarius whispered urgently.

"True God?" the old man slurred mockingly, the death rattle in his throat. "What is truth?"

IX

AD 532, Spring

Second year of the reign of Gelimer, King of the Vandals
At the palace at Grasse, 350 stades from Carthage

A swift stag zig-zagged through the stout cedars and dense underbrush, his eyes wide with fear. Behind him at no great distance, a hunter's horn sounded above the baying of hounds. His muscles straining, the stag accelerated and darted sharply into a meadow overgrown with tall grass. He sprinted to reach cover on the other side, but to his surprise, a line of footmen, all shouting and clashing sticks together emerged from the trees ahead and advanced upon him.

In terror, the stag doubled his course, racing back from whence he came. But there was no escape now. Three mounted men—yellow-haired giants on massive angry steeds—broke from the forest and charged at him. One launched a spear which whizzed over the stag's back. The second's missile caught him in the flank and stuck there, its barb tearing into his vitals. The third's struck him squarely in his handsome neck, knocking him to the ground in a shower of dirt, as his spindly legs flailed wildly in the air.

A moment later, he was still.

The blond giants dismounted with joyous whoops and shouts.

"Did you see that, brothers?" the eldest of them bellowed. "It was my cast that downed him!"

"You are blind, Gelimer," the tallest of the three replied mockingly. "Your spear lies yonder in the weeds."

"Come, Tzazon! The cast only appeared to be errant. In truth, my strength is such that the shaft passed clean through him!"

"It was a clear miss!" the third laughed, his large belly shaking with mirth. "It was mine that took him in the flank!"

"Aye, Ammatas, but mine was the death-blow!" Tzazon declared.

"It's a fine kill, no matter who gets the credit," Gelimer declared. As he strode forward toward the quivering carcass, the summer sun reflected brilliantly off the golden diadem on his brow. From a jeweled sheath, he drew an exquisite hunting knife with a hilt of solid gold. He deftly sawed off the stag's head, and held it aloft by its antlers, blood running down his arm.

Servants and members of his household came running to the site in great spirits.

"Who got him?" several of the youths demanded, gazing in awe on the three mighty warriors as if upon gods in human form.

"It was the king!" Tzazon cried. "His shafts are unerring!"

"A perfect cast!" Ammatas agreed. "A mighty throw that took the beast in the neck and killed him instantly."

"All glory and praise to our brave king, Gelimer!" the hunting party cried in rapture. "May you reign forever!"

Gelimer accepted their acclamations, thrusting the stag's head into the air in time with the chants. As he did so, he nodded toward his brothers with a satisfied smirk.

✠

Gelimer's summer palace at Grasse was perhaps the closest mankind had come to recreating Eden since the Fall. Fruit trees of all varieties grew in orderly rows, their bountiful branches already heavy with fruit thanks to the warm climate and long growing season. Wild flowers bloomed everywhere in a glorious array of colors and honeybees buzzed lazily from blossom to blossom, returning to well-tended apiaries laden with nectar. Slaves and draft animals too numerous to count worked the fields, which already showed a superabundant crop of the wheat for which Africa's rich soil was justly famous. Fresh water flowed from gushing springs into irrigation channels fed by waterwheels that were kept turning by the ceaseless toil of oxen.

Emerging from the wilderness, the royal hunting party followed a well-maintained Roman road through the sprawling plantation, sporting bright pennons and blaring trumpets to announce their arrival. In the train, two stags were slung on poles, along with dozens of fat partridges, three wild pigs, and a leopard that Tzazon had slain with an arrow perfectly shot. A horde of slaves met the party at some distance from the palace and immediately offered fruit and fresh water to the weary riders, the quickest ones receiving praise from their masters, the slower suffering liberal blows from riding whips.

While the slaves took charge of the meat and tended the hounds, Gelimer and his brothers rode forth into the palace together followed only by their menservants. Once inside, they entered the king's private courtyard and were met there by Gothaeus and Fuscias, two high ranking members of the Vandal court.

"Greetings, Sire," Gothaeus called out as he bowed low. "A successful hunt?"

"Indeed it was, old man," Gelimer replied with a smile. "I suppose you are looking forward to the feast tonight?"

"I'd be a liar to deny it, Sire," Gothaeus chortled, rubbing his tremendous belly for effect. "But before you enter the palace, let me warn you that a line of petitioners awaits you in the audience hall."

"In God's name, can't I get a moment's peace from these pests?" Gelimer moaned.

"My Lord, they have been waiting for you all day," Fuscias added, his voice tinged with pity. "Some have been here for several days. Their cases have all been properly vetted and referred to you as the final arbiter."

"Damn them all!" Gelimer swore as he unhitched his belt. "Pests and vermin, all of them. Why can't they solve their own problems?"

"Sire, you are their king," Gothaeus groveled. "They look to you for wisdom, but most of all for justice."

Gelimer sighed bitterly as he stripped off a soiled tunic and cast it to the ground.

"Think about it practically, brother," Ammatas advised. "The more of these cases you deal with today, the shorter the line will be tomorrow."

"Has there ever been a king so plagued with malcontents?" Gelimer growled, gritting his teeth in frustration. "You know, I have a good mind to release Hilderic from prison just to deal with this nonsense. He actually enjoyed listening to shrill old crones flinging dung on each other for hours on end."

His brothers laughed uproariously at the remark. Fuscias and Gothaeus glanced at each other, but covered their concern with nervous smiles.

Sensing their anxiety, Gelimer gave an annoyed snort, as a slave undid his bootlaces.

"What is your will regarding the petitioners. What shall we tell them?" Fuscias ventured.

His disrobing now complete, Gelimer turned away and stomped into the palace, his body covered only by a loin cloth. His manservant trailed behind him piled high with dirty linens.

"Sire?" Gothaeus called after him in a pleading tone.

"Tell them I'm going to bathe and play the lyre for a few hours," Gelimer called out without turning around. "When I'm finished, I'll hear a dozen. But no more! Choose the most worthy. I don't want to waste my time on idiotic trifles."

In the royal audience hall, the imposing figure of Gelimer sat enthroned in splendor but enveloped in boredom. Complaint after complaint was brought before him. One man complained that a stone mason had defrauded him; another that his neighbor had encroached upon his grazing land; several others complained that an aqueduct had collapsed and was turning their fields into marshland. For those cases which were particularly convoluted or required extensive review of documents, Gelimer had a simple but unjust way of ruling—regardless of the evidence presented, he always found in favor of those more closely allied to him.

By the time the final case of the day arrived before his throne, Gelimer was at the end of his patience. Three Roman merchants approached and bowed down before him.

"O King, in your infinite wisdom, show mercy to us," their leader plead. "I am Paulus and these are my partners Apollon and Timotheus. We have been unfairly accused of smuggling by the prefect in Carthage. But we did no such thing! We have always paid our taxes and have the documents to prove it."

Still on his knees, Paulus offered his evidence to Fuscias who in turn handed it over to Gelimer.

With a sigh, Gelimer took the pile of documents and leafed through them carelessly. After a few moments, he found what he was looking for.

"All three of you are followers of the creed of Athanasius and the Pope of Rome?" the king queried.

"Yes, O King...we are," Paulus replied nervously.

"Well, that complicates matters," Gelimer frowned.

A hush fell over the hall. All knew precisely what the king was driving at.

"Sire, may I make a statement?" Apollon spoke up suddenly.

"You may," Gelimer indulged with a wave of his hand. "Please proceed."

"I have given a great deal of thought to the creed of Arius. It seems to me quite reasonable that the Christ was just a man and not equal to God the Father. I feel that I could accept this teaching."

Paulus and Timotheus glanced at their partner in surprise and disgust as the words came out of his mouth.

"And have you declared this publicly before the bishop in Carthage?" the king asked.

"Not as yet, my Lord," Apollon hedged. "But I shall immediately upon my return."

"See that you do," said Gelimer. "And when you do, your debt will be forgiven and the accusation of smuggling withdrawn."

"Your wisdom is without peer, O highest of Kings," Apollon gushed, falling on his face before the king.

"And what of you two?" the King demanded. "Will you have your debts forgiven as well?"

"Have false earthly debts forgiven by incurring eternal ones?" Paulus stood on his feet, his eyes blazing. "Never!"

"You are no rightful king but a tyrant!" Timotheus cried as he also rose to his feet.

Gelimer smiled. "Have both of these criminals thrown into the Ancon prison and confiscate half of their property. Perhaps a few months in total darkness will make them more amenable to my generosity."

The mouths of Paulus and Timotheus dropped open in horror. "This is not justice!" Paulus shouted. "God will repay you tenfold for the evils you have heaped upon your subjects."

"Remove them," Gelimer yawned.

The two men were instantly seized by powerful hands and led out.

"As for you," Gelimer said, his attention returning to Apollon, "You may stay and enjoy the feast..."

"You are most kind, Sire," Apollon cut in, still on his knees.

"...in exchange for a small donative," Gelimer finished his thought. "Shall we say, a hundred solidi?"

Apollon gulped hard. "A hundred, O King?"

"Not enough? Make it two hundred, then," Gelimer decided. "It's not every day you get the opportunity to feast with your king and the royal court."

The audience hall was no sooner cleared of litigants than the tables and benches for the great feast were hurriedly set out. As the Vandal kingdom was exceedingly rich in all good things, Gelimer thought nothing of sumptuously feasting the entire court with regularity. Huge Moorish slaves shifted the heavy cedar tables into place and hefted great casks of wine up from the cellars. Roman slaves, meanwhile, bustled about here and there, spreading linen cloths over the tables, setting out the fine glass decanters and trays piled high with fresh fruits, tubers, nuts, and a dozen varieties of cheese. Place settings and goblets of silver gleamed at the high table where the king was to eat surrounded by twenty of his ministers and staunch allies. From the kitchens wafted the rich scent of baking bread mingled with that roasting meat to create an overwhelmingly tantalizing aroma capable of tempting even the most ascetic stomach.

Though the formerly barbarous Vandals had easily adapted to the luxuries of life offered by Roman civilization, they still had little patience for court ceremonial. So with little fanfare, the members of the court entered the hall haphazardly and took their seats. When Gelimer arrived, draped in a purple cloak of shimmering silk meant to approximate that of the Roman emperor, several boisterous toasts were offered and then the entire assembly set to feasting in earnest.

The Vandal nobility, like most of their race, were enormous men with prodigious appetites. Fair of face and blond of hair, many wore thick golden beards—though just as many, like the king himself, were clean-shaven. Their massive arms were equally well-suited to hefting a spear or a heavy goblet of wine. They were all powerfully built men, thick of chest and wide across the shoulders, though some of the older ones were even wider across the belly.

The Vandal women, who could be seen in profusion around the hall, were renowned for their comeliness. Tall and slender in their youth, they grew into buxom matrons nearly as large as their husbands. They wore their golden hair in long tresses or in fantastically intricate braids, the richer ones displaying a stunning array of jewelry.

A devotee of the arts, though more in the style of Nero than Maecenas, Gelimer insisted that various musical and oratorical acts accompany the feast. Of these, he preferred the most sickeningly sentimental—languid Latin love lyrics and awful odes to the lost Vandal homeland sung in the most grating Gothic. These were accompanied on the lyre by musicians whose technical skill far exceeded their ability to contrive a pleasing melody. Not infrequently, the king himself joined in, plying the strings with a dearth of ability that jangled the nerves of even his most tolerant subjects.

This night, Gelimer refrained from musical pursuits, and instead tore into a haunch of venison while tearing up over a minstrel's tale of a young warrior who hung himself after learning that his lady love had died of a serpent's bite.

Gelimer's own wife had died many years before, and though he often behaved disgracefully with the servant girls, he had never remarried.

The minstrel's song was barely finished and the applause suppressed when Fuscias approached the king with quick steps.

"Sire, my Lord, there is a visitor, a Roman," he said breathlessly with obvious fear. "He is demanding an immediate audience. I have tried to turn him away but he will not be thwarted."

Gelimer's placid melancholy flared into a hot fury. "Who?" he demanded angrily. "Who dares disturb our revelry with his pathetic trifles?"

"I dare, by God," a deep voice echoed from the hall's entrance. In stepped a churchman whom all present immediately recognized as Boniface, the Catholic archbishop of Carthage. An elderly man, Boniface had been elected to the episcopal chair of Carthage eight years before during the tolerant reign of Hilderic. But with the fall of Hilderic and the sudden ascent of Gelimer and his pro-Arian policies, Catholics had again become targets. And Boniface was the biggest, brightest target of them all.

"You?" Gelimer laughed. "I called for no jester."

The hall resounded with laughter.

"Gelimer, men may call you a king on earth, but Almighty God is King over all and he sees the wickedness you have done," Boniface declared loudly, his eyes ablaze and his voice crackling with courage. "How long will you leave your noble uncle a wretched prisoner?"

"My uncle is a traitor to the Vandal people," Gelimer retorted sharply, standing up. He wiped his greasy hands on his purple cloak. "And any who dare to stand with him are traitors as well."

All present shouted their approval.

"Have no doubt, Gelimer, that the Lord sees your iniquity," Boniface continued, ignoring the threat. "You would be wise to recall how God has humbled kings who embraced evil. Even David, who was beloved by God, was punished severely for arranging the death of Uriah the Hittite. But you, Gelimer, have contrived to pile wicked act upon wicked act. Truly you have built a great tower of evil. Beware lest it topple and crush you to earth beneath it."

Gelimer laughed. "How absurd that I must endure this lecture from a heretic here in my own court."

"Say the word and I shall slay him for you, O King!" Ammatas shouted, drawing his sword.

"What, brother? Make a martyr out of this heresiarch? Sheath your sword. I shall have him removed and we shall do what we have always done with busybodies like him—ignore them."

"You may ignore me, but God hears the cries of the innocent victims of your persecution. They rise up to Him like incense. And the terrible justice of the Almighty will not sleep forever but will fall down around your ears when you least expect it."

"Persecution, you say?" Gelimer laughed again. "You mean of those silly partners of yours in heresy? Answer me this, O bishop of fools: Why is it wickedness for me to persecute you slaves of the Pope of Rome in my kingdom and yet not wickedness for Justinian to persecute the followers of Arius within his realm?"

"In your pride, you compare yourself to the emperor of the Romans," Boniface responded, his courage unabated. "But I did not come here to discuss Justinian's faults, whatever they may be. You can not escape culpability for your sins by comparison to others who may be guilty of greater crimes. I beseech you, O King, renounce your folly. Free your uncle and his faithful men from prison and allow them to live in exile. And cease your disgraceful persecution of my flock." Dropping to his knees, the elderly cleric extended his arms toward Gelimer with tears in his eyes. "Humble yourself before the Lord now of your own volition, lest you be forcibly humbled later by some avenger sent by God."

The hall erupted in laughter and loud derision. The idea that anyone could seriously threaten the powerful Vandal kingdom was ludicrous and the warriors present showed their contempt by showering Boniface with the remnants of their meal.

But Gelimer was silent. For an instant, the words of Boniface had the desired effect, producing a tiny doubt in the king's heart. But looking around at the brash confidence of his snarling retainers, Gelimer's vanity swelled again and squashed the doubt like an insect.

"Have this jester cast into the outer darkness!" Gelimer cried over the tumult. "I have heard enough of his wagging tongue for one night!"

The king's guards immediately seized Boniface and with rough hands dragged him out. The assembled court cheered their brutality with a noise akin to a pack of baying hounds.

"And let it be known," Gelimer shouted above the din, "that henceforth, anyone else who dares to wag his tongue against the holy creed of Arius shall have it cut out!"

"Hail Gelimer! Pride of the Vandal nation! Scourge of the impious Athanasian heretics!" one of the king's men shouted out.

"Hail our mighty king!" the assembled responded.

Well satisfied, Gelimer sat back down. "Now, bring back the minstrels," he ordered, burping into a napkin. "This last act has given me indigestion."

AD 532, SUMMER

Sixth year of the reign of Justinian, Emperor of the Romans
At Constantinople

With a gasp, an elderly man sat straight up in his bed. The room was dark, and for a moment, he could not recall where he was. *Not home, certainly,* he thought to himself. *Did I cry out in my sleep as I did in my dream?* Looking out the open window, he could see the rooftops of a great city by the light of a clear gibbous moon. The sight of a tall aqueduct looming in the distance brought back his memory. He was in Constantinople, a guest of the emperor Justinian. He had come from the city of Ephesus, once a proud metropolis and home to the apostle John the Evangelist, but now a stagnant provincial backwater with a heavily silted harbor. His task was to participate in a conference between the Monophysite and Chalcedonian parties within the Church with Justinian presiding, the aim of which was to end the destructive and seemingly endless schism between the two sides.

"Your Holiness?" a young man's voice emerged from the darkness. He had heard the noise in the next room and entered bearing a flickering oil lamp. "I heard you cry out. Are you well?"

"I have had a dream," the aged bishop replied. "It was a message from God, I am certain of it."

"What did He say?"

"It is not for your ears, my son," the bishop rose, shaking his head. "It is a message for the emperor."

"The emperor?"

"Yes. And I must take it to him now," the prelate declared. He began gathering his clothing to dress.

"But it's the middle of the night!"

"Nevertheless, I must go."

"Your Holiness, surely this can wait until morning."

The old man fixed his eyes on the younger one. "My son, when you reach my age, nothing can wait until morning. And when God Himself commands you to deliver a message to the emperor, you do it. Protocol is a tool of the devil. Now hand me my cloak."

✠

Justinian was not asleep. He was pacing back and forth on a private balcony of the palace overlooking the Bosporus, pontificating about obscure points of theology. His secretary, Marcellinus, had fallen asleep on a nearby couch, as had Epiphanius, the Patriarch of Constantinople. The only one left conscious was Narses who was expertly playing a game of devil's advocate—a role that suited him exceptionally well.

"But why is it wrong to hold that Christ was from two natures before the hypostasis, but of a single nature after it?" Narses queried. "The Egyptians say it is not proper to call the one Son two. One must not part the indivisible."

"Such a position is a confusion, a comixture of the natures of Christ," Justinian retorted passionately, wholly engrossed in the debate. "There was no comixture of natures in the incarnation when Christ assumed his humanity. His Godhead derived from the Father was one nature, while his humanity derived from the Holy Theotokos was another."

Narses smirked. "The Eutychians say that formula divides the Son into two. It creates a quadrinity instead of a Trinity."

"They misrepresent the meaning of the Council Fathers at Chalcedon when they say that," Justinian shot back. "Christ is of two natures, human and divine, that are mystically joined into one single person, a single hypostasis—God the Son."

"So then if Christ was possessed of a human and divine nature during his life, which nature was it that suffered on the Cross? Why is it wrong to say, 'Holy God, Holy Mighty One, Holy Immortal One *who suffered for us*?'"

"Now we're back to the theopaschite formula," Justinian said, whirling around to face his opponent. "As I have said before, I have no debate with the notion that Christ in his divinity suffered, so long as it is not used as a proof of the monophysite position."

"But surely, it is a proof!" Narses snapped, overly anxious to make a point. "Or, so the Eutychians say..."

At that moment, the curtain leading to the interior of the palace parted and a servant emerged, bowing low before the emperor. "Forgive me, O Master, but Hypatius, bishop of Ephesus has come to the palace and seeks an immediate audience."

Justinian winced at the name as one of ill-omen, but quickly put any irrational animus aside. His enemy Hypatius was dead and gone, and this one was his ally, both theologically and politically. "By all means, show him in. We need another debater here who won't drift off."

As soon as he heard Justinian's voice, Hypatius rushed through the curtains followed by a young presbyter, his assistant. "Pardon the intrusion, O Emperor," Hypatius muttered as he prostrated himself.

"It's no intrusion at all. Indeed, I couldn't be happier to see you. But this is most unusual. Please tell us what has you up and about at this time of night?"

Hypatius rose to his feet, his lips tight beneath his white beard. "I have had a vision from God, O Emperor. And it concerns you."

Justinian's mouth opened in surprise. "Tell me," he gasped.

"Gird thy loins, O Emperor, for the Lord's message is a hard one," Hypatius bellowed, his eyes aflame.

Justinian scowled. "I would hear it immediately!"

The old man gathered his courage and spoke: "Thus sayeth the Lord to Justinian: 'Thou wretched scoundrel! I, who made thee Emperor of the Romans and saved thy throne for thee, put into thy mind the task to protect My beloved and long-suffering Christians in Africa. But thou, in fear, have ignored My command, and favored the worldly cautions of feckless advisors. And now, My servants in Africa suffer under worse tyranny and thou hast lifted not a finger to succor them.

"'And yet, if thou wilt hesitate no longer and do now as thou art commanded, know this: that I Myself will join with thee in waging war against the tyrants of Africa, and by the strength of My right arm shall make thee the lord of all Libya and Numidia.'"

Hypatius was silent. Only the waves lapping against the sea-wall fifty feet below could be heard.

"Is that all?" Justinian whispered, his eyes wide.

"Yes, O Emperor," the bishop said, bowing humbly. "Forgive my audacity, but I have spoken as bidden by the Lord."

Justinian slumped on a couch. "You have shown courage in carrying out the Lord's commands. I have shown nothing but cowardice."

"How do you know this vision was from God?" Narses interrupted, alarmed at the emperor's credulity.

"How does a man know his own face in the glass?" Hypatius replied. "I tell you, I have never had a dream like this one. I have no doubt it was the Almighty who spoke to me and ordered me to come."

"Perhaps it was some demon in disguise," Narses pressed, "offering a false command that will lead the most pious Emperor into peril. Can you assure us on this point?"

"Enough!" Justinian cried. "Hypatius is a good and humble servant of God. Do not insult him by saying he can not discern between the voice of God and that of the Enemy."

Narses was silent, unused to being rebuked so forcefully by Justinian.

"Thank you, my brother, for delivering this message," Justinian said, embracing Hypatius. "You may return to your bed having done your duty. In your prayers, tell the Lord that I have heard Him and will obey without any further delay."

"I will, O Emperor," Hypatius responded.

Alas, a catastrophe! Narses thought to himself, his brow furrowed with worry. *How easily my master has succumbed to a pious fable told by a doddering old man. This false vision will surely lead to no good.*

✠

By daybreak, it was clear that Justinian meant what he said the previous night. He ordered his morning schedule cleared and summoned his privy council to an emergency meeting. There, he announced his plans for a full-scale invasion of Africa and, with the divine authority at his back, he could not be dissuaded from this course of action.

Belisarius, too, had been summoned to this meeting of the council, but given the distance he had to travel from Chalcedon across the Bosporus to the palace, he had not yet arrived. For Silvanus's bequest had been ratified by the emperor, as the old senator had predicted, and Belisarius was acknowledged as lord of the Rufinianae. At Antonina's urging, the house in Constantinople was put out to rent and the entire household moved to the palatial estate.

"You said before that should we decide on an expedition to Africa, you could provide all the funding and more," the emperor said, addressing John of Cappadocia directly. Though dismissed during the Nika rebellion, it was only a few months before Justinian recalled John to his former position as praetorian prefect. The emperor required vast sums to rebuild Constantinople, and John's ability to extract *solidi* from an unwilling populace without scruple or pity was a talent not easily duplicated in other men.

"Yes...yes, I did, O Master," John mumbled. "But, you must understand that it will take time..."

"Get started right away. I am also putting you in charge of gathering provisions for the army and the fleet which will assemble here."

"Yes, O Master. As you wish," John acquiesced without enthusiasm. His efforts would now have to be redoubled, and though he relished the opportunity to put more tax-shirkers to torture, his inherent laziness resented this addition to his workload.

"Who will be charged with assembling this fleet, O Master?" Basilides asked.

"I have been up most of the night pondering that very subject," Justinian replied. "It must be an Alexandrian. Perhaps Calonymus? No one else known to us has ever commanded the vast number of ships which this campaign will require."

The assembled council grunted their approval with no objections.

"Let it be Calonymus, then," Justinian declared.

"As for the army, how many men will it require to complete this task?" Basilides asked.

"No fewer than sixty thousand, O Master," Narses replied. "It is said that the Vandals can field an army of fifty thousand or more first-class fighting men. As they are also fighting on their home territory, unless we can achieve numerical superiority over them, the effort is doomed from the start."

The corners of Justinian's mouth turned down as his enthusiasm sagged. "Sixty thousand, you say? That's nearly half the soldiers of the whole empire!" Justinian scribbled a few numbers on a handy waxboard. "It can't be done...." He threw the stylus down in disgust. "We would have to strip all the frontiers to do it. Or impose conscription on an immense scale. And the fleet required to transport so many men...it's unthinkable!"

"Narses is right, O Master," the general Peter added. "Sending any fewer men than the Vandals can field would be, effectively, a suicide mission."

"But where are we to get so many? Can any of you tell me? And how are we to convey them to Africa—a long and dangerous journey even under the best of conditions? There must be a way. The Lord would never have demanded this task of me if it were impossible."

Narses smiled, having achieved his aim. "Master, may I suggest a more limited expedition, then? Perhaps we could take Tripolis from the Vandals? It would require fewer soldiers and such a show of strength could overawe the Vandals into compliance. Thus you would still be fulfilling the command of God."

"Sixty thousand," Justinian sighed, stuck on the number. "How can we gather and transport so many men?"

"Who speaks of needing sixty thousand men to take Africa, O Master?" a voice replied from the doorway.

"Belisarius!" the emperor rose from his seat. Clad in a military tunic and belted with a sword, Belisarius knelt before the emperor, but Justinian immediately raised him and clapped him on the shoulder. "It is such a great pleasure to see you, my good man."

"The pleasure is mine, Master," the general replied briskly, assuming his seat at council.

Narses and John of Cappadocia both suppressed frowns at the emperor's blatant show of affection.

"I am told that it will take sixty thousand men to defeat the Vandal Kingdom," Justinian said. "Do you agree with that assessment, General?"

"Why not make it a hundred thousand?" Belisarius responded. "Or two hundred thousand? In truth, to destroy a mighty nation surely and without risk, one can never have too many soldiers. But in war, even with a tremendous host at his back, a general can be undone by a foe with discipline, courage, surprise, and dumb luck working in his favor. I need not remind anyone present of the fiasco of Basiliscus, whose massive army was defeated by little more than a favorable wind at the right moment.

"So let us deal in reality. There is no possibility that we are going to be able to gather an army of sixty thousand for this campaign. But let us see how many can be gathered and then determine what may be done."

The privy council put their heads together over a waxboard, adding together moiras and tagmas that could be spared from a variety of provinces across the empire. When the tally was complete, Justinian looked at the number with dismay.

"Thirteen thousand," the emperor sighed. "Who would be mad enough to pit so few men against so powerful a nation?"

The other generals at the table glanced at each other in trepidation, none speaking a word.

"But such an army would be sufficient to take Tripolis with ease, O Master," Narses suggested rationally. "And might I recommend the general John, the nephew of Vitalian, to command such an expedition? He is a daring and skillful commander who is perfect for the task of punishing the Vandals."

"It can be done, O Master," Belisarius said, ignoring Narses. "And if you say the word, I will be the madman who sails to Africa in command of this force. I ask only this: that you give me the freedom to summon two thousand of my own men from wherever they may be posted across the empire and to recruit and train an additional two thousand. And also, that you grant me sole command of the expedition. I have witnessed the disasters that have befallen armies where the authority is divided among several generals. Therefore, I beg you—if you would have this effort be a success, provide for it a single commander, even if you choose someone else to lead it."

Justinian stared at Belisarius for a long moment. *Is this man insane, or has God just put the instrument of victory into my hands?* the emperor thought to himself. "Do you truly think the Vandals may be defeated with a mere seventeen thousand men?"

Belisarius looked back at him soberly. "My Lord, your Piety, I will answer your question with a question. Do you intend to undertake this mission even with so few men because the Lord has commanded you? If so, then I believe you will be victorious. For sometimes it is necessary that men do the irrational so that God may achieve the impossible—or so a saintly old woman once told me."

In silence, Justinian studied the glorious mosaic map of the Roman Empire on the wall behind Belisarius. His eyes fixed on Africa. "I grant you, Belisarius, full command of this campaign," the emperor intoned gravely. "I give you my own authority to arrange all matters pertaining to this campaign and your acts no man will dare judge, as if I myself had done them."

There was a shifting of bodies in their seats, and several gasps of surprise as the emperor spoke.

Justinian rose. "As for the rest of you, I expect you to exert yourselves to the fullest in support of Belisarius and this expedition to Africa."

"We shall, O Master!" they replied in unison, some voices noticeably more eager than others.

"Excellent. This meeting is adjourned." Without farewells, the emperor strode out of the chamber toward the Delphax where he would begin his daily audiences. The rest filed out after him.

"So he means to do it, after all," Narses whispered to John of Cappadocia.

"It seems so, my little friend," John sputtered, dropping into his vernacular slurring Greek. "I'm going to have to think of new ways to squeeze the grapes for this one."

"The campaign will be a disaster," Narses continued. "It is most important, now, for us to find a way to limit the damage."

"My thoughts match yours completely," John burped. "The trick will be keeping up the appearance of doing all we can, while holding back as much as possible."

X

AD 532, Summer

Sixth year of the reign of Justinian, Emperor of the Romans
At the Rufinianae, the Estate of Belisarius

A sparkling clear azure sky reigned over the splendid pastures, rich fields, and verdant woodlands of the Rufinianae. The huge parcel of land had been well tended by the Rufinus family for generations, but the short tenure of Belisarius had already yielded several remarkable improvements. First, the new lord had caused a modest but exquisite church to be constructed adjacent to the main house. Its white dome topped by a brilliant gold cross now dominated the landscape, a beacon to all those in the vicinity that paganism had been utterly vanquished by Christ. Rustics from all the neighboring villages sojourned there to hear the Divine Liturgy and no small number of the tenant farmers living on the lands of the estate emerged, hat in hand, to request baptism.

Second, Belisarius had cleared a large field to serve as his own personal *campus martius*. Here he exercised on horseback, sometimes alone, sometimes with just his closest friends and retainers, and sometimes with several hundred of his men. On the outskirts of this field, a dozen well-appointed barracks could be seen, and a dozen more were in various stages of construction. Next to them, stables also rose, along with a mess hall and armory. Belisarius could not endure the notion of impressing the men of his household guard upon the poor citizens who lived on his land and so he decided to feed and house them at his own expense. And considering his guard was now to number nearly 4,000 strong in total, the expense would be enormous. But with the vast fortune of Silvanus at his disposal, Belisarius had few worries in this regard.

✠

"You look thoughtful, husband," Antonina mused. She grabbed Belisarius's arm and handed him an ornate brass goblet of wine. "What goes through that head of yours?"

Belisarius stared out over the festive crowd all around him. "I was just thanking God for this day," he replied. "We are truly blessed."

Antonina smiled. "And soon to be even more blessed," she said, placing his hand on her belly, now large and distended.

"Did you feel that?" he said. "She kicked me!"

"How could I not feel it?" Antonina groaned. "She kicks me all day and night." Belisarius's insistence that the child in Antonina's womb was a girl had finally won her over.

"You have suffered much for this child."

"It was a lot easier bearing children when I was 20 than it is now," Antonina sighed.

At that moment, Photius rushed up to his parents. "Father, they are calling on you to speak! You must come!"

"Yes, I've kept them waiting long enough, I suppose," Belisarius said. He took a gulp of wine and handed the goblet back to Antonina. With long strides, he parted the crowd, receiving several thumps on the back as he passed. Mounting a low circular retaining wall which surrounded the fountain in the center of the broad courtyard, he raised a hand for silence and all eyes were soon fixed on him.

"It is a varied and strange audience I see around me," he began. "And it is especially strange to be addressing all of you together. Who could have guessed that I would one day host a gathering where Unigastus, my stalwart battlefield companion, would spend an hour trading stories with my beloved mother?"

"See how he bores her with his tedious babble!" Athenodorus hooted, and the crowd laughed.

"And what madman would have suggested that my sister Eudocia would someday meet my great friend, John of Armenia?"

"He flirts with her," Principius barked. "That Armenian bears watching!"

John rose to object but his words were drowned out by the mirth of the crowd at his expense. Defeated, he shrugged his shoulders and sat back down.

Eudocia, a comely lass of seventeen, blushed furiously next to him.

Belisarius waited for the laughter to quiet and then continued more solemnly: "And who, a year ago, could have predicted that Antonina, Photius, and I would be living in such undeserved splendor and would become one family with such excellent young men as these?" He gestured to his cousins, Rufinus and Decius.

"Even the Cumean Sybil herself would have been dumbfounded," Procopius called out, stumbling slightly over his words. One too many cups of wine had passed his lips.

"On this joyful day, we have witnessed both of these youths doused with the saving waters of holy baptism. Their souls wiped clean, they now enter the Church as Christians. Let us welcome them!"

The assembled guests burst into cheers and applause. Rufinus and Decius, still in their white baptismal garments, smiled slightly and nodded their heads in acknowledgement.

"And more," Belisarius continued, "This sturdy young man, Rufinus, has consented to join with me as a comrade in arms and become one of my biscuit-eaters. As he is my cousin, I have decided to make him my personal *bandifer*."

"He is most welcome!" the soldiers present cried out with a cheer.

"As for Decius, he is not only accepting a new mode of life by embracing Christ, he has decided to take on a new name as well. Henceforth, he shall be called Theodosius—a name that combines Christian piety with Roman imperial dignity. He is a lad of scholarly mind, and his mild and compassionate disposition have endeared him to us. Because both his parents are now no longer among the living, Antonina and I have decided to embrace this most excellent youth as our son by adoption."

A surprised but approving murmur rippled over the crowd as young Photius approached Decius, now called Theodosius, and took him by the hand. With great joy, he led his new brother to stand by his mother's side. Antonina sat in a great cushioned chair, uncomfortable in the heat. But she stood up as the two boys approached and embraced them, smiling brightly.

Belisarius continued: "And today, I also celebrate the commencement of mighty labor—a campaign against the Vandals which I have been enjoined to undertake by our most pious emperor, Justinian Augustus."

"May he reign for many and good years!" the assembled responded dutifully.

"Of all the battles I have waged, I know that this one will be the greatest and most difficult. It is for this reason, that I have summoned you—all my friends. For I am under no illusions that I may accomplish so colossal an undertaking without the assistance of the best, bravest and most noble soldiers of the Roman Empire.

"It is said that the Vandals are a powerful nation and that no Roman army has ever lined up against them and survived. But it has been over sixty years since the last major battle between Romans and Vandals and much has changed since then. We Romans have repented of our past wickedness and sloughed off our weakness. We trust in Christ our Lord and know that with His aid, we cannot fail!

"For the next few months we shall exert ourselves to the utmost in the drills at arms as well as in the practice of piety. Thus, may our bodies be inured to physical hardship, and our souls chastened so that the Almighty may find us worthy instruments of His will.

Belisarius paused momentarily. To his surprise, every face remained fixed on him, and even as he laid heavy burdens on them, they met his gaze with stalwart determination in their eyes.

"I am aware that some among you think me a fool for accepting this command. But you have come nonetheless," Belisarius continued with a wry grin on his lips. "This makes me wonder whose folly is greater—that of a man who sets out on an impossible mission, or those poor gullible rubes who follow him."

The tension of the moment broken, the men laughed.

"We follow you because we trust you!" huge Uliaris cried out, standing up. "And because we love you and we would not see you face such a danger alone." Overly emotional even when stone sober, Uliaris had drunk an incredible amount of wine this day and the final few words of his declaration were drowned in his own blubbering. But he had spoken truly, and the men raised their cups toward their general.

"We love you and trust you, O Magister!" they shouted in tribute. "We are yours to command! Lead us to victory, by God!"

Anna, the mother of Belisarius, gazed out in amazement at the mass of powerful men lauding her son and tears worked their way from the corners of her eyes down her strong, toil-lined face. She knew more than any mortal was permitted about her son's future and she eyed Antonina with deepest suspicion.

"Know this," Belisarius resumed once the shouts had quieted. "I consider your trust and love the ultimate gift that soldiers may offer their commander. In return, I shall do my utmost on every occasion to make sure that you are always well-supplied and expertly led. The Vandals are indeed a dangerous foe, but I will not throw your lives away to no purpose in my zeal to see done the emperor's will. Nor will I shirk any hardship that we endure or cringe before any danger we face. With unity of purpose, and the blessing of God Almighty, I know that we will achieve a triumph the magnitude of which the empire has not enjoyed for half-a-thousand years. *Nobiscum Deus*!"

"*Nobiscum Deus!*" the assembled soldiers responded heartily with one voice.

"But today, let us celebrate!" Belisarius concluded. "Enjoy yourselves—but not too much. Tomorrow, we begin the drills in earnest."

"Hail Belisarius, beloved of God, Glory of the Romans!" the men chanted with sustained cheers.

Belisarius hopped down from his pedestal and was immediately surrounded by dozens of his friends and comrades. After nearly an hour of mingling, he made his way exhaustedly to the table where Armenian John still sat conversing earnestly with the lovely Eudocia.

"It's very rude to confine your attentions to just one person at a gathering like this, John," he chided with a mocking wag of his finger.

"Was your brother always such a stickler, Eudocia?" John said, pretending to ignore him.

"I assure you he wasn't," Eudocia said playfully. "I was only a little girl when he left for the army, but my mother shouting at him is one of my earliest memories."

Belisarius laughed and sat down across the table from them. "If you don't wish to see a repeat performance of that maternal wrath, John, I would advise you to keep your hands to yourself."

John grinned sheepishly. Beneath the table, he released Eudocia's hand and folded his own hands in his lap innocently.

"Better," Belisarius said. "Now I would speak with you on matters of business."

Eudocia wrinkled her nose in annoyance. "I shall go attend to mother," she announced, standing up.

"Perhaps I may speak to you again later?" John asked plaintively.

"Perhaps if my brother lets you," Eudocia winked, then skipped away, her curly raven locks bouncing after her.

"She is stunning," John gasped, his eyes following her.

"Business?" Belisarius said.

John turned to face him across the table. "Right, business. What is your pleasure, O Magister?"

Belisarius cut straight to the point: "Solomon has been promoted to strategos and will function as the commander of my *bucellarii*. With his new responsibilities, he will be unable to attend to the finances of either the expedition or my own household. I would like you to take on both of those burdens."

"You would trust a rogue like me with your money?" John smiled, his black beard curling smartly around his perfect teeth.

"There's no one I would trust more," Belisarius said earnestly. "You have functioned as Sittas's *optio* in Armenia and he has advised me that you can stretch a follis from Alexandria to Trebizond."

John laughed. "Sittas exaggerates. Alexandria to Damascus, maybe..."

"So you will accept?"

"Yes," John replied. "But on one condition."

"And what is that?" Belisarius said, suspicion rising in his voice.

John looked offended at his friend's tone. "Only that I don't wish to be fettered to a stool counting *nummi* once we reach Africa. Make me a tribune, at least, so I can steal some of your glory once we're on the field of battle."

"Tribune?" Belisarius laughed. "Your rank will be strategos, but you will not have a regular body of men under your command. Instead, when we are beset by the enemy in hostile territory, I will entrust you with the most critical and dangerous of missions as the need arises." The general stood up and laid a hand on his friend's shoulder. "By the time I'm finished with you, you'll be begging for your stylus and ledgers."

John gulped hard as Belisarius turned to leave. "Oh, there's one more thing," the Armenian said slyly, finding his tongue.

"What?"

"Would you give me permission to court your sister?"

Belisarius turned a cold gaze on John, his face a mask of thoughtful intensity, and for an instant John regretted his temerity. But a hint of good nature played around the corners of Belisarius's mouth. "She could do no better. Only, be careful."

"Have no fear on that account," John beamed. "My intentions are completely honorable."

"No, I meant be careful of her," Belisarius said, enjoying his friend's happiness. "I am told she has rejected eight suitors already."

John rolled his eyes. "That's because she was waiting for me," he proclaimed, thumping himself on the chest triumphantly.

✠

True to his word, Belisarius commenced training his household guard the next day. He began with a nucleus of some three hundred men—those who had been with him since his recall the previous year. But with each passing day, more men arrived, singly, in small groups, and in one case, an entire tagma two hundred strong. As the summer drew to a close, the ranks of his *bucellarii* had swelled to over three thousand, both new recruits and experienced veterans drawn from garrisons across the empire: hearty mountaineers from Armenia, swift mounted Huns under the command of the daring Aigan, powerful Heruls following their noble prince Pharas, Romanized Goths from the environs of Constantinople, energetic Isaurians from southern Asia Minor.

But the bulk of the men were sturdy horsemen from the plains of Thrace and Illyricum, the Latin-speaking countrymen of Belisarius and Justinian. They were the descendants of Roman army veterans and the remnants of Dacia, the lost province across the Ister abandoned during the reign of the emperor Aurelian 250 years before. They had intermarried with Macedonians, Goths, and native Thracians in the intervening years and though their land had been devastated by Attila and overrun repeatedly by other hostile hordes, Thrace and Illyricum still yielded the richest harvest of first-class fighting men in the whole empire.

Yet with all these men at his disposal, Belisarius scanned the horizon each evening from the wide balcony of the Rufinianae with a keen eye. Three of his oldest comrades whom he had invited to join him—Dorotheus, Constantinus, and Trajan—had not yet arrived.

✠

After a particularly hard day of drills in the mid-summer heat, Belisarius washed, ate, and then retired to his large private balcony to relax as the sun set. His mother, Anna, and Eudocia his sister were with him, enjoying the few remaining hours of his company. Having already stayed beyond their planned return date by two weeks, the two were to depart the following morning.

"Are you certain you can't stay a little longer—at least until the baby is born?" Belisarius asked.

His mother sighed. "You know we can not. The harvest will be upon us soon and I can not be absent for it."

"Come, surely someone else can manage it this season. Agricola, perhaps?"

"Your brother has his own land to concern him," Anna replied. "And you well know that even one poor harvest can ruin a small farm. The taxes levied by the emperor are truly onerous."

Belisarius waved his hand dismissively. "I'll pay your taxes, then."

"You will not," Anna snapped.

"Then sell the farm. Come live here with us. I have plenty of land. Just say the word and I'll have an exact replica of the farm built right here."

Anger flared on Anna's face for an instant. "My son, I don't want to live here."

Belisarius dropped his head like scolded child. "Have you not felt welcome here, mother?"

Anna's stern voice softened a bit. "I would not have stayed as long as I have if I had felt unwelcome. But my place is on that small farm in Germania that I built and defended with your father, may his soul rest in God's mercy. And Thrace is where my other children live with their families. Would you have me abandon them?"

"Then let them all settle here."

Anna sighed again. "No. This place is too filled with ghosts for my liking. Your father fled from here and had he not done so, I should never have met him. For me to sell off our beloved little plot and settle here—I couldn't do it. I would be betraying his spirit."

"Am I then betraying him by abiding here?"

Anna smiled, motherly pride evident on her face. "No, you are not. You are the eldest son and this is your lawful legacy. You must do with it as you see fit."

Belisarius shook his head, a crooked smile on his lips. "I'm sorry, mother, I just don't see the logic."

"You need not," Anna said. "Only accept it."

"And what about you, sister?" Belisarius said, turning toward Eudocia. "You have been uncommonly quiet this evening."

Eudocia's face reddened immediately and her mouth dropped open, but she was saved from having to respond by the appearance of Solomon in the doorway leading to the inner rooms.

"Procopius has arrived with John of Armenia, Magister," he announced. "Shall I send them up?"

"Yes, at once," Belisarius replied.

"We shall leave you men to your business, then," Anna declared, getting to her feet and smoothing out her plain brown skirts. "Eudocia and I still have many things to pack tonight, anyway."

"I'll come visit you again before you're asleep," Belisarius said, kissing her on her plump cheek.

"Please do," she smiled.

Her eyes shifting back and forth, Eudocia appeared ready to say something as her mother bustled down the stairs. Unable to muster the courage, she meekly turned and followed.

As the two women passed out of view, John and Procopius strode onto the balcony and offered their greetings.

"You just missed my sister," Belisarius said to John.

John swallowed hard. "Did she say anything to you?"

"Actually, she was unusually quiet tonight. Why do you ask?"

"No reason," John said innocently. "I...I just haven't seen her for a couple days."

"Well, you'd better get your goodbyes in tomorrow morning. They're leaving on the noon ferry."

"I know," John muttered.

Having ignored this conversation, Procopius stood thumbing through a large codex on Belisarius's side table. "I see you're making use of the histories I sent you. Have they given you any insight into how one might defeat the Vandals?"

"Yes, I have learned a great deal," Belisarius replied, turning his attention from John. "But I think I would assimilate all this knowledge more quickly if I had a learned scholar to discuss it with. Do you know such a man?"

Procopius smiled. "If you are referring to me, I must tell you that I am certainly no expert on the Vandals."

"Perhaps not. But you know more about them than any man here. And beyond that, I trust you to paint a true portrait of them. Too many of the court advisors I have spoken to are somber prophets of despair who present the Vandals as an insuperable foe. And those few who don't fit that mold go to the opposite extreme of declaring the Vandals already vanquished, as if our appearance in Africa of itself will cause the Vandal kingdom to collapse into dust".

Procopius smiled sheepishly. "Well, Magister, I must admit that until last night, I was among those whom you call prophets of despair. Indeed, it was my intention to come to you with my regrets—that due to my rigorous schedule and personal commitments, I could not possibly accompany you on this heroic mission."

"All nonsense, of course," Belisarius added.

"Yes, all nonsense," Procopius admitted. "In truth, I was terrified. One need not be a student of history to understand that this mission is fraught with perils—sea sickness, privation, storm, shipwreck, mutiny, plague—and that's before we ever set foot in Africa."

"But you've changed your mind," Belisarius surmised.

Procopius pursed his lips and sat down nervously. "I have changed my mind and I'll tell you why—I have had a dream."

John eyed Belisarius and snorted derisively.

"I'm quite serious," Procopius sniffed.

"Please let us hear this dream, then," Belisarius said with a conciliatory wave of his hand.

Procopius took a deep breath and began: "Well, in my dream, I was sitting with you right here in this house much as we are right now. Then, one of the servants entered and announced that several men had come bearing gifts for the master of the house. We went to investigate and saw them standing in the courtyard carrying great sods of earth on their shoulders with the grass and flowers still growing out of them. You bade them place the sods under the portico. Then, you and your guardsmen reclined on the grass and began eating the flowers and urged others, myself included, to partake as well."

Belisarius chuckled, now genuinely curious. "This is an uncommon dream," he said. "Did you eat of the flowers, then?"

"Ahh, but that's the point of it!" Procopius enthused. "I was reluctant to eat the flowers at first. But when I saw you and your guardsmen eating them to no perceptible ill effect, I allowed myself to try one. And the taste..." Procopius's voice trailed off.

"The taste?" Belisarius prompted.

"Sweeter than honey," Procopius said wistfully. "I can still remember it on my tongue."

"What happened next?" John asked eagerly. "Was I in this dream?"

Procopius gazed at John as if thinking. "No," he said. "You were not. The only other thing I remember about the dream is that there was a group of men who utterly refused to eat the flowers."

"Well, that's about the most ridiculous thing I've ever heard!" John exclaimed.

Procopius looked offended for a moment, but Belisarius put a hand on his shoulder. "Absurd or no, if this dream has changed your opinion of our expedition against the Vandals, then thank God for it."

Procopius squinted his narrow eyes purposefully. "Yes, it has changed my opinion. It not only dispelled my terror, but it has made me positively eager to depart. That is, if you'll have me."

Belisarius laughed, cheerfulness brightening his entire countenance. "I couldn't imagine going without you, my friend. Finding another secretary who smoothes over my blunders in dictation so effortlessly would have been a difficult prospect indeed."

✠

Belisarius, John, and Procopius were later joined by Uliaris and the four spoke long into the evening. John remained unusually pensive and downhearted, however, and as his three guests made to depart, Belisarius sensed that there was a matter weighing on his friend's conscience that he felt unable to discuss.

Following their departure, Belisarius made his way to the apartments which his mother and sister had occupied for the past two months. He was relieved to find that the lamps had not yet been snuffed. When he entered, he found the two women chatting quietly. They had completed their packing, it appeared, and the slaves had already brought some of it down to the stables. Eudocia was seated upon her trunk, and looked upon Belisarius with wide, timorous eyes. The tracks of tears were plainly visible on her cheeks.

"Your sister has something to say to you," Anna announced before Belisarius could even offer a greeting.

Eudocia dipped her eyes and said nothing.

"Well, what is it?" Belisarius prompted.

Gathering her courage, Eudocia looked at him earnestly and spoke: "May I stay with you?"

"You want to stay?" Belisarius said, incredulous. His eyes then narrowed. "Is this about John?"

Eudocia gazed at him ferociously, as if he had said something horribly improper.

"She says she's in love with him and that he has already discussed marriage with her," Anna explained.

"And what do you think of this, mother?" Belisarius asked, somewhat shocked by the revelation.

Anna sighed. "She is of marriageable age and has a level head in such matters. But what I think is less important than what you think. As *pater familias*, you will have the final say."

Feeling the weight of his responsibility, Belisarius sat next to his sister and took her hand. "Do you truly love him?" he asked.

"I do," Eudocia replied, trying but failing to hold back her tears. "He is like no other man I have ever known. He is strong but gentle. Compassionate but clear-eyed. He has seen much of the world, but retains a childlike innocence and purity of heart. And his moods are always so jolly and bright. How is it that no other woman has claimed him before now?"

"Because he has been a soldier all his life and is an honorable man," Belisarius explained. "Soldiers have little time for mingling with women on anything but the most vulgar level, and John has never done so. He is a man of great virtue and will make an excellent husband."

"Then you agree?" Eudocia burst out, her face alight with joy.

"Yes, I agree."

Eudocia threw her arms around his neck and embraced him tightly. "Thank you, good brother."

"There is one condition," Anna said sternly, having already discussed the matter with her daughter. "I am leaving in the morning as planned—it can be put off no longer. But I would like to be present to witness this marriage, so I will return next year in the early summer after the planting. And given that the groom will shortly depart on a mission fraught with peril, let the betrothal last until that mission is completed and the groom has returned safely home. A year long betrothal is not too long and if your love is true, it will only deepen over that time."

Belisarius nodded and smiled. "It will also give John extra incentive to perform his duties well. But don't fret, Eudocia. I'll watch over him. Either in victory or defeat, we'll return by this time next year."

Eudocia frowned. "You would have us wait a whole year, then?"

"A whole year, you say?" Anna laughed. "Of all the virtues, patience is always the most difficult for the young to master."

"The year will go by quickly, sister, I promise you," Belisarius said. "And you may certainly remain here until the wedding—and beyond if you so choose."

Early the next morning, Anna departed for Chalcedon where she would take ship for Constantinople. Belisarius insisted that she take several wagon-loads of goods as gifts for his family and neighbors in Germania and to ease her journey, he arranged an escort of fifty reliable porters to travel with her the entire distance.

Anna's farewell was a tearful one as she embraced in turn her eldest son and her youngest daughter, offering them a few final words of advice. She then kissed her adopted grandsons Photius and Theodosius and scolded them playfully.

Finally, Anna turned to Antonina who stood by looking glum and extremely pregnant. Antonina had tried her utmost to warm her mother-in-law, but had largely failed. Anna had been perfectly cordial throughout her stay, but remained emotionally distant. Try as she might, Antonina could not figure out what obstacle remained in the way.

Anna now looked at her severely, but softened a little when Antonina put out her arms to embrace her. "I shall miss you, mother," she said, her voice cracking.

Anna embraced her earnestly. "Be true to him," the older woman whispered starkly in her ear so that no one else could hear. As she pulled away, she gave Antonina a fierce glance which connoted a knowledge that mere words could not convey.

She knows! Antonina thought in panic. *Dear God, will my past never cease haunting me?*

Emotionally drained, Belisarius made his way to the field where his men were already drilling under the watchful eye of Solomon. He donned his armor but refrained from joining the action until the first exercises were complete.

During the break, he found John sitting by himself under a shade tree. The Armenian looked shattered—drenched in sweat, his shoulders slouched, his head in his hands. Belisarius scooped some cold water into his helmet and approached quietly. Once in range, he dumped the contents on John's head.

John didn't flinch. "Thanks. That feels good," he said stoically.

"Stand up, will you? You miserable wretch."

"I suppose they've left," John muttered without moving, unwilling to raise his eyes.

"Yes, you missed them."

John sighed bitterly.

"Well, my mother, at least. Eudocia remains."

John now tilted his head to face Belisarius, a gleam in his eye.

"It seems you are to be my brother-in-law."

John leapt to his feet. "You wouldn't jest with me about something like this, would you?"

Belisarius shook his head. "She told us everything last night. The betrothal will be one year or until we return from Africa."

John shouted for joy. He grabbed his helm and flung it in the air where it lodged in the tree branches high above.

"You'll have to retrieve that, you know," Belisarius laughed.

"I'll get it later!" John cried, his face beaming with happiness. Then, composing himself, he said: "Permission to be excused from drilling today, O Magister?"

"Granted," Belisarius replied. "Go to her."

John took off toward the main villa at a run, shedding bits of his armor as he went.

"Have one of the men collect his kit," Belisarius said to Principius who had just arrived along side him.

"What's his problem?" Principius asked.

"Love," said Belisarius, smiling.

XI

AD 532, FALL

Sixth year of the reign of Justinian, Emperor of the Romans
In Constantinople

"You're late," Narses clucked. He pushed a tray of grapes toward his friend who eagerly grabbed a handful.

"I was detained," replied Bloody John, his mouth full. "Disciplinary problems among my men."

"Which you dealt with in your usual style?"

"Certainly," John grinned. He chewed the grapes and swallowed them seeds and all. "Forty lashes, less one, just like Saint Paul. And I have a dekarch who's a moron and loses count."

Narses frowned. "If you're too hard on them, they'll grow to hate you."

"What do I care? So long as they fear me and do what I tell them to do."

"You know, it is possible to be hard on them, make them obey you, and still have them love you."

John grunted dismissively, as if found the subject infinitely boring.

Narses let the matter go. "Did you do what I asked you to do?" he said, changing the subject.

Bloody John, however, was engaged in a conversation with a tavern slave. He called for a goblet of the house wine, warmed and uncut.

Narses rapped his fingers on the table impatiently.

"I'm sorry, what did you say?" John asked, turning back to his companion.

"The letters?"

Bloody John reclined, a guileful smile on his face. "I signed and sent them three days ago."

"To whom, may I ask?"

"The three we spoke about—his friends, the ones I served with—Constantinus, Dorotheus, and Trajan," John whispered furtively. "They wanted to give Belisarius their regrets in person and they set out from the frontier at the beginning of October. The letters will be waiting for them at Antioch."

"Do you think they'll have the desired effect?"

"They were works of art, Narses," John quietly enthused. "By my sword, you could convince a man with no arms to swim the Hellespont."

"But do you think these three will be able to convince Belisarius to abandon the Africa campaign?" Narses whispered impatiently.

"I can't answer that," John muttered, accepting his wine goblet from the slave and throwing back a swallow. "But they are among his best friends. If he'd listen to anyone, it would be them. Let us hope that the arguments you put forth in that letter find a way into their mouths when the time comes."

"Agreed," Narses smiled, raising his own goblet in tribute to his friend's statement. "In the mean time, I'll continue to explore other options."

Having just emerged from her bath, Theodora detected a bustle of whispered consternation among the dozen maids charged with applying her intricate layers of salves, powders, paints, gowns and accoutrements.

"Out with it," she called to Fulvia, her chief lady-in-waiting. "What troubles them?"

The older woman frowned at her undisciplined subordinates. "Forgive us, O Mistress. The emperor's chamberlain, Narses, waits to see you outside. I thought it best not to trouble you with his presence while you were at ease."

"You did well," Theodora replied, treasuring the older woman's care and unflinching severity even toward high officials of the court. "But you may see him in now."

"Into your privy chamber, Mistress?" Fulvia replied in shock.

"Even so," Theodora reassured her.

"Yes, my Mistress," Fulvia replied, bowing her head submissively.

Narses entered cautiously and made his obeisance, his eyes darting this way and that. As he regained his feet and caught sight of the empress, his voice stuck in his throat.

Seated on a bench and clothed in a shimmering gown of ivory-colored silk, Theodora's abundant beauty was on full display. Her face, usually coated with layers of white paint, now radiated a ruddy complexion of health and freshness. Her hair, usually bound up on top of her head in an intricate mass of ribbons, pearls, and gold, now fell about her shoulders in a luxuriant honey-brown cascade reaching nearly to her waist. Only near the corners of her large brown eyes could any sign of her forty-seven years be detected.

Narses could well appreciate how Justinian, his master, had become so completely bewitched by this creature.

"What urgent business causes you to interrupt even my toilet?" Theodora snapped coldly.

"My apologies, O Mistress," Narses replied, instantly regaining his composure. "I have some news that I thought you might be interested in hearing without delay."

Theodora raised an eyebrow as two of her maids began the complex ordeal of dressing her hair. "What news?"

"Two bits, in fact," Narses said exuberantly. He gestured to a well-cushioned couch. "May I sit?"

Fulvia clucked her tongue at the eunuch's temerity.

Theodora smiled. "Take your ease."

"First..." Narses began. Then, looking around suspiciously at the maids, he stopped and frowned.

"You need not worry about your secrets here," the empress declared in a calm, stern voice loud enough to be heard by all. "These women know how to hold their tongues. For if any word of what is said in here ever reaches the outside as gossip, be assured that I'll have every last one of the possible culprits skinned alive."

The maids eyed each other nervously behind the empress's back. They all knew that Theodora did not make idle threats.

Reassured, Narses began again: "First of all, I have received word from a courier fresh from Italy that the Pope has been seriously ill."

"Good," Theodora interrupted. "I hope he dies. That Gothic rascal has been a hindrance to our purposes ever since he stole the throne from Dioscorus. Do they think he'll die?"

"They said it was a stroke. He may already be dead for all I know."

"Then we must not delay," Theodora said. "Contact our agents in Rome at once and see what may be done to put a more pliable man on the papal throne this time."

"As you wish, my Mistress," Narses said, bowing slightly. "My second bit of news concerns the preparations for the invasion of Africa. It has come to my ears that several of the most eminent officers whom Belisarius has requested to accompany him have quietly refused."

"They are cowards," the empress announced, curling her upper lip in disdain.

"Ah, but that is what makes it interesting, O Mistress," Narses gloated. "They are not cowards at all. Some of them are even friends and former comrades of Belisarius."

Theodora knitted her eyebrows in impatience. "Friends and comrades indeed. What sort of comrades would leave their friend in the lurch when he needs them?"

Narses's face assumed the benign expression that usually presaged the moment when his facts faded into calumny and then to outright slander. "I am told that these comrades of his have heard tell of his formidable new private army. They have seen the way he conducts himself, putting on airs and receiving acclamations that belong rightfully to the emperor alone. These men are afraid that Belisarius is not assembling an army for the invasion of Africa, but is creating instead an elite fighting force capable of wielding power independently in the heart of the empire. They are afraid that they will be called upon to rebel against the ..."

Theodora began to laugh and did not cease until Narses's rambling denunciation ground to a halt.

"Why do you laugh, O Mistress?"

"I see your spite against Belisarius has not cooled," the empress smiled, shaking her head.

"But Mistress, I have an informant in their very household who tells me all this," Narses protested. "It is not personal animus that compels me to bring this unnerving news to you. It is my wish to protect and defend the emperor."

"I'm certain of it," Theodora replied in a tone that indicated exactly the opposite. Then she became severe both in facial expression and voice: "Listen to me, Narses. The emperor is unshakeable in his desire to see the Vandals crushed. Therefore, you are to do everything in your power to make sure that his desire is fulfilled. Like it or not, Belisarius has been named commander of this campaign. You will assist him in any way possible, and that includes talking sense into any of his cowardly subordinates you happen to ply for information."

Narses sat smoldering as the imperial command impacted on him.

The empress then stood up and fixed him with her burning stare: "And God help you if hereafter word comes to my ear that you have been secretly undermining this mission or its commander!"

"Yes, my Mistress," Narses muttered, shame and anger boiling in his bosom. He stood up and bowed before Theodora.

"And pass word along to that fat Cappadocian friend of yours, as well," the empress snarled. "Now begone!"

Narses bowed stiffly again and then retreated. *This was a colossal mistake,* he thought to himself as he hustled out of the empress's private apartments. *The only hope to stop this ill-fated mission now rests on Bloody John's letters.*

But unbeknownst to Narses, his visit had not been a complete failure. A few minutes after his departure, Theodora summoned Fulvia to her. "Send a message to the lady Antonina," the empress cooed, perfectly at ease. "It's time we invited her to the palace for a chat."

✠

At the head of a tagma four hundred strong, Solomon galloped out with his bow at the ready. His men followed in close formation, retaining perfect order despite the high speed. At a given spot, Solomon raised his bow to launch an arrow at a row of wooden target dummies some five hundred paces ahead. Watching his movements, Rufinus, acting in the role of bandifer, dipped his tall pennant forward and the men behind immediately drew their bows. An instant after Solomon loosed his arrow, four hundred others launched over his head toward the target. Rufinus then raised the pennant again, and the entire tagma wheeled as one and beat an orderly retreat.

Belisarius was on horseback waiting for them on a grassy rise which overlooked the field. Armenian John sat beside him, acting as a second pair of eyes.

"Hail, Magister!" Solomon shouted as he reined in his mount. "One hundred forty-three hits. Are they not impressive?"

"Excellent bowmanship given the distance," Belisarius agreed. "But the withdraw was ragged. Reset them and try it again without stragglers."

"Aye, Magister," Solomon saluted. He then turned to his tagma: "To your places by eights! We'll have another go, lads, and this time, a little crisper on the turn! Hold together and follow the standard!"

"Aye, Strategos!" the men responded in unison.

"Solomon has become quite an effective drill commander," John said.

"He has indeed," Belisarius enthused. "He has a brilliant sense of how to motivate the men. But in truth, he does all things well. Every new task I give him he first masters and then excels at it."

"Some men just seem to excel at everything," John agreed. "While others..."

Belisarius raised his eyes from his waxboard and looked at John, puzzled.

John pointed toward a lone horseman approaching at a rapid clip. The man was exceedingly large and his horse seemed to labor under his weight as it approached. His armor kit was askew and showed rust in a few spots, while his helmet was pushed back in a slovenly fashion, as if it were too small for his massive head. Sweat poured down his red face as his meaty hands jerked his mount to a stop.

"Hail, Magister!" the man gasped, nearly as breathless as his spent beast.

"Hail, Uliaris," Belisarius replied. "What brings you in such haste?"

"They've come!" Uliaris burst out without ceremony. "All three together. Dorotheus, Trajan, and Constantinus. They have only just arrived. The servants are tending to them at the main house."

"Thanks be to God!" Belisarius shouted, delighted with the news. The three had tarried so long in responding to his summons that Belisarius had just about given up on them arriving at all.

"They await you, Magister," Uliaris urged. "Will you come?"

Looking out over the field, Belisarius noticed the drill about to begin again. "Go back and tell them to wait. I will be with them once the day's drills are complete."

"Are you not anxious to see them?" Uliaris questioned, his large lower lip drooping stupidly.

"Of course he is, you great ox!" John interrupted. "But those three laggards have kept him waiting six months. They can certainly wait a few hours for him."

"Go and entertain them until I arrive," Belisarius ordered. "Ask one of the slaves to bring some choice wine up from the cellar."

At the command, Uliaris licked his lips. "Aye, Magister!" he replied with enthusiasm, saluting. Without another word, he turned and galloped back toward the house.

"You certainly know what motivates *him*," John said with a smile.

Belisarius shook his head. "What are we to do with him?"

✠

The evening meal was cleared away and the sun had long since set by the time Belisarius and John finally made their way to the main house. They found their guests within the peristyle, enjoying the good company of Uliaris and several other officers who were known to them.

"Belisarius Magister!" Uliaris cried and all the men present stood up and saluted.

Unable to restrain himself further, Belisarius rushed to greet them, clasping arms with Constantinus first of all. As salutations were exchanged, Belisarius immediately perceived that his enthusiasm at seeing his friends was not fully reciprocated. "What is amiss?" he asked. "Are you bitter that I have kept you waiting so long today?"

"Nothing of the sort, Magister," Trajan said, hanging his head. "We have come... I have come..." He then sighed and turned away shaking his head.

Belisarius looked at John. "Have these men lost their tongues out on the frontier or just their wits?"

Dorotheus spoke up: "Forgive us, Magister. We have not come for the reason you expected us. We have come because we wanted to tell you, as men, face-to-face..." But even mighty Dorotheus could not bear to say the words he had prepared in his mind. He cast his eyes at the ground in shame.

"What could possibly cause you such consternation that you can't even bear to utter it?" Belisarius asked, now turning to Constantinus for an explanation.

"What these men are trying to say is that we are not going with you to Africa," Constantinus declared forcefully. "We received your summons, and though you are our comrade and friend, we simply can not support you in this folly. The campaign is doomed to failure—it can not possibly succeed. The Vandals are a powerful race and will not be defeated by the tiny army you are proposing to throw against them."

Belisarius's perplexity turned immediately to anger. "Do you two support him in this?" he asked, glancing back and forth between Trajan and Dorotheus.

"Yes, Magister," they replied almost penitently, their eyes still downcast.

"Then what did you hope to achieve by coming here to tell me this?" Belisarius fumed. "Could you not have stated your intentions just as clearly in a letter?"

Trajan mustered up his courage: "We have come to see if it were possible to turn you from this course. To abandon this hopeless cause. It is not too late. You have achieved every success in life beyond the dreams of men like us. Fame, riches, glory—why throw it all away? Why ruin your career and probably lose your life trying to do the impossible?"

"Because it is not impossible," Belisarius barked, trying in vain to suppress his anger. "The emperor has been told by God that this task must be done, and he has entrusted to me the doing of it."

"And you believe that fable?" Constantinus rejoined. "It is your responsibility, as someone who has the emperor's trust, to convince him of the ill wisdom of this enterprise. Instead, you encourage him and the result will be a great catastrophe."

"Or a great victory," Armenian John added, soberly.

"There can be no victory here!" Constantinus cried, whirling to face John. "Basiliscus failed with ten times the number of men he is proposing to embark. He will be crushed and his men slaughtered like so many helpless goats."

John and Constantinus continued to debate, but Belisarius turned away and approached Dorotheus, who sat on a couch looking glum, his face ashen. "Have you nothing to say, Dorotheus?"

"This is much more difficult, now that I face you," he said, rubbing his forehead in frustration. "I don't want to die, Belisarius. I'm not ready."

"Is it truly fear, then, that keeps you from joining me?"

Dorotheus could not look Belisarius in the face. Instead, his eyes fixed upon the hilt of Belisarius's sword and his mind was instantly carried back four years to the dusty plain of Mindouos in Mesopotamia. There he had nearly been slain by a host of Persian horsemen, their arrows bringing cruel death to many of the men around him. Indeed, if not for the timely arrival of Belisarius and his tagma, the corpse of Dorotheus would surely lie moldering away in a shallow grave by the Nymphius River. *What time I have been given, I owe to his sword alone,* Dorotheus thought ruefully. He cursed in frustration, stood up, and turned over a small decorative table, sending the goblet and fruit bowl upon it crashing to the floor. "I can't do this, do you understand?" he cried, glowering furiously at Constantinus. Raising his fist in the air, he stormed out of the courtyard with no idea where he was going, other than away from where he was.

With a shout, Uliaris followed quickly after him.

"It is hubris, that's what it is," Constantinus accused, paying no heed to Dorotheus's outburst. His attention was now focused back on Belisarius. "Do you believe you live a charmed life? That the battlefield hold no perils for you?"

"No, I believe that what God has commanded, men may achieve if only they dare," Belisarius rebutted. "But men who shrink from the challenge and only seek after their own safety will never achieve any good thing."

"You are an arrogant fool, Belisarius," Constantinus railed, his face red with anger. "But your font of good fortune will someday run dry. And when you have failed in your lunatic mission, people will say, 'He should have put aside his vanity and heeded his friends, who knew better than he did.'"

"Who is this scoundrel who insults you so, husband?" a woman's voice rang out.

All eyes turned toward a lighted doorway in which stood the round but fierce form of Antonina. Barely visible behind her, Photius could be seen peeking over her shoulder. At her appearance, Constantinus softened. He bowed and introduced himself gallantly.

But Antonina had heard too much for her fury to be assuaged. "You call yourself a friend of my husband? No friend are you, but a craven lackwit," Antonina shouted, waddling slowly toward her quarry. "If you lack the courage to accompany him, then begone and let no stench of your unmanliness linger in our house. But if you say one word more in attempt to undermine my husband's determination to do the emperor's will, I will have my servants drive you away from our door with whips like the miserable vagabond you are."

Constantinus was stung to the quick by this unexpected attack, but mastered himself before irreparable harm could be done. "You allow your woman too great liberty with her tongue, my friend," he said with a wag of his head. "But she is right. I can see you will not be moved, and therefore I will say no more. Farewell, Belisarius. May we meet again on this earth. Come, Trajan, we depart."

"Aye, farewell, Magister," Trajan muttered, shamefacedly. With quick steps, he and Constantinus reached the gate and strode out into the night toward the stables.

"It is disgraceful, what you do," Armenian John called out after them, but they deigned not to respond.

"What of Dorotheus?" Trajan whispered as they mounted.

"Let him meet us in the city," Constantinus growled through gritted teeth. "I won't spend another instant under the same roof as that ridiculous fool and his vile wife."

Belisarius was struck dumb, no less by the rapid departure of Constantinus and Trajan than by the volcanic arrival of his wife. "Woman, what have you done? Those men were my friends."

"Friends? Indeed not," Antonina interrupted. "They were enemies come to pour poison in your ear. For it is a base sort of man who abandons his friend when he needs him the most."

"The lady speaks justly," boomed the deep voice of Dorotheus. The man himself emerged with Uliaris from a hallway leading to the kitchen. Between them they had spilt of a huge loaf of fresh bread steeped in olive oil.

"You remain," said Belisarius. "Do you not wish to follow your companions?"

"They do what is best for them. I will do what my duty calls me to do," Dorotheus declared.

"Then you are with us?"

"Aye," Dorotheus replied with a great toothy smile.

"You no longer fear death?" asked Belisarius.

"Uliaris and I talked of that," Dorotheus said dismissively as he gulped down a large mouthful and licked his greasy fingers. "But if this bread is a foretaste of heaven, then I am more than ready for it."

———✠———

"The lady Antonina, wife of Belisarius, Magister Militum," the head maid Fulvia announced.

"Send her in, then shut the door," Theodora commanded. "See that we are disturbed by no one."

"Yes, O Mistress," Fulvia replied.

Antonina entered, breathing heavily. Sweat beaded on her forehead for the day was unusually humid and she had been spirited through hot back hallways to the Empress's private garden. She wore heavy veils to conceal her facial features, but there was no concealing the fact that she was nearly bursting with child. With painful, awkward movements, Antonina crashed to her knees and prostrated herself before the Empress.

"You have come alone as I commanded?" Theodora asked, allowing Antonina to remain flat on her face.

"Yes, O Mistress. I gave my servants five follises each and told them to buy whatever they liked. They'll shop for hours on the Mese."

"And your husband?"

"I told him I wanted to go into the city to purchase a gift for him," Antonina wheezed, her lips nearly touching the ground. "It was difficult to convince him to let me leave at all in my condition."

"I'm glad to see your persuasive abilities remain intact," said Theodora without emotion.

"Yes, Mistress," Antonina replied. Her swollen knees were throbbing heavily from the pressure.

Theodora paused for a moment, then took a deep breath and continued: "It is said that your husband has gathered an impressive army at your estate—that he trains them tirelessly and that they have become the most formidable fighting force the empire has seen in two hundred years."

"Yes, O Mistress," Antonina said, not without some pride. "With them, my husband will conquer the Vandals as the emperor has commanded him."

"It is also said that your husband has another, hidden motive in creating this army," Theodora continued more sternly. "That he intends to use it to win the empire for himself."

"Merciful God, no!" Antonina replied in shock. "Whoever has said such a thing is a liar and a slanderer. My husband's loyalty to Justinian is absolute and unwavering."

Theodora was silent.

"You must believe me, O Mistress!" Antonina cried. Her knees were now screaming in pain and her back ached as though a great weight had been placed upon it.

"Rise to your feet, Antonina," the empress commanded, a trace of warmth entering her voice for the first time.

With a great struggle and several grunts, Antonina finally straightened up and faced the empress.

"You will accompany your husband to Africa."

Antonina's mouth sprung open. "But..."

Theodora's expression immediately grew dark.

"The child will be but a few months old," Antonina continued, her courage rallying. "I can not take it with me on such a dangerous voyage."

"You have time yet to rid yourself of that problem," Theodora said brutally. "There are physicians known to me who will make sure that the creature is stillborn. Then you will be free."

Antonina's face reddened with anger. "Such men are not physicians but butchers," she hissed.

"Bear it, then, if you so choose," said Theodora coldly. "But you will go to Africa with or without it."

In the face of such pitiless severity, Antonina submitted. "Forgive me, O Mistress," Antonina replied, bowing her head. "I shall do as you command."

Theodora narrowed her eyes. "I shall expect regular reports from you about all facets of the campaign—the morale of the soldiers, condition of the ships, disposition of the commanding officers. But most especially, I am interested in what goes on in your husband's mind. I would know his thoughts as if they were my own. Do you understand?"

"Yes, Mistress."

"I will have my agents nearby you at all times," Theodora continued, her voice even and clear like a military commander. "They will make themselves known to you and you will prepare for them a detailed report each month. And Antonina..."

"Yes, Mistress?"

"Your husband is to know nothing of our correspondence."

"I understand, O Mistress."

"Should he find out, both you and he will suffer."

"I shall be silent, Mistress," Antonina whispered, her eyes still fixed on the ground.

"Make certain of it," Theodora said. "Now you may go. I do not envy you your task of convincing a man of Belisarius's foolish gallantry to allow a nursing mother to embark on a military campaign."

"I shall convince him, Mistress," Antonina said as she bowed and shuffled her way toward the door.

"I have no doubt," Theodora smiled, lifting a cluster of hyacinth flowers to her nose.

Belisarius clutched the hilt of his sword with ferocious intensity. He struck the target dummy high and hard, then whirled gracefully and sliced low on the backhand, chopping into the wooden post and sending shivers in every direction. Using his foot for leverage, he dislodged his weapon and spun into a fighting stance. Then with a single deft swipe, he removed the dummy's straw head. Rearing back in frustration, he hurled his sword forward with an overhand motion into a thick wooden post where it bit deeply and stuck.

"Quite a display," Solomon offered as he appeared behind him.

Belisarius whirled around. "Is there any word?" he gasped anxiously, sweat pouring down his face.

"Yes," Solomon smiled. "The babe has just arrived and the mother is faring splendidly well."

"May Christ and the Theotokos be praised!" Belisarius cried. "May I see her now?"

"For just that reason have I come to fetch you."

✠

Antonina looked pale and exhausted when Belisarius entered her bedchamber, shouldering his way through the smiling midwives and serving women who crowded the doorway. Upon seeing her husband, Antonina's features immediately brightened. "You were right!" she called to him.

"A daughter?"

"Yes, a beautiful daughter," Antonina cooed. "Would you like to hold your Joannina?"

Belisarius kissed his wife gently on the head and then looked upon the precious bundle nestled in the crook of Antonina's arm. "But won't I wake her?" he protested mildly.

"She will be awake soon anyway, husband," Antonina chuckled. "They don't sleep for long periods at this age...as you'll soon find out."

Antonina held up the tiny infant and Belisarius accepted her awkwardly. Despite her misshapen head and little pinched face, Belisarius found himself instantly smitten. "She is beautiful."

"Aye, she's an angel come down from heaven," Antonina agreed.

XII

AD 533, Spring

Sixth year of the reign of Justinian, Emperor of the Romans
In Constantinople

Antonina never once directly petitioned Belisarius to accompany him on his Africa campaign. Instead, she took a more circuitous but infinitely more clever route toward the same goal. First, after a month, she hired a wet-nurse to help her with the care of Joannina. At the same time, she drew Eudocia, her sister-in-law, into her orbit, allowing the young woman to bond with her infant niece so that she practically became a second mother.

With her time thus freed and her vigor returning, Antonina set about assisting her husband in earnest. She began by relieving Armenian John of his more tedious duties, learning all he could teach her of accounts and keeping ledgers. She soon made herself useful in a thousand different ways, procuring supplies, organizing the non-military staff, and seeing to the equipment and comfort of the fighting men. And though her meddling often rankled the senior officers, the common soldiers came to admire her as an advocate who had their best interests at heart.

But where Antonina's work proved most useful was with the fleet. As the ships began to gather in the Golden Horn in late February, Antonina acted the part of liaison between Calonymous, the Alexandrian Prefect of the Fleet, and her husband. She was particularly active with regard to her husband's flagship, a massive single-banked dromon called the Hagios Giorgios. As she fully intended to be resident on board that same ship herself, Antonina inspected every inch of it, making sure her husband's quarters were suitably spacious. She tramped the deck, tested the rigging, and purchased new sails at her own expense. She crept through the hull, ordered dried-out caulk patched, worm-eaten timbers replaced, and a fresh coat of paint applied to the exposed upperworks. She also took special care that the ship's storage hold was well-sealed and in order, going so far as to sink great glass jars in sand to better preserve the crew's supply of fresh drinking water.

Her years dealing with the scoundrels and ruffians of the circus enabled her to order about profane sailors and rude shipwrights with perfect confidence. She spoke their vernacular with shocking proficiency and though they complained bitterly of her endless demands, they respected her growing nautical knowledge and precise eye for detail.

By the time March arrived, Antonina's presence and duties had become indispensable to the mission. With little Joannina growing and thriving while primarily in the care of Eudocia, Belisarius came to the inescapable conclusion that he must have his wife with him when he sailed for Africa. So when Antonina began dropping hints about her mad desire to endure the rigors of the expedition alongside her husband, Belisarius himself asked her to join him. She readily and immediately agreed.

What caught both parents off guard, however, was the ardent desire of Photius and Theodosius to accompany them as well. Despite the danger, Belisarius was eager to have both boys with him to give them a taste of the gravity and glories of war. Antonina hated the idea and fulminated against it with all her might. But the boys carried the day with their father in the end. The massive eunuch Eugenius, a slave recently purchased, was to accompany the boys as a chaperone. For her part, Antonina would make due with only a single slave: the young maid Macedonia whom she had inherited from the household of Silvanus.

✠

On the ides of March, Belisarius and the other senior officers were summoned to the palace by Justinian for a final conference in preparation for the campaign against the Vandals. Animated with excitement, the emperor could not bring himself to sit and instead paced back and forth at the head of the long table where the rest were seated.

"You have heard, of course, that Pudentius has sparked a rebellion in Libya," said Justinian. "We secretly sent a small force under Tattimuth to aid this revolt and we have now received word that the city of Tripolis has cast off the Vandal yoke."

"Praise be to God!" Dorotheus interjected loudly. Several others also added their voices.

Their enthusiasm brought a smile to Justinian's lips. "But there is more besides," he continued. "Just yesterday, we received word that Godas, the man to whom Gelimer had entrusted the government of the island of Sardinia, has also revolted from his master. Indeed, I have the letter from him right here. Will you read it, Marcellinus?"

The emperor's secretary, who was seated at a nearby desk, unrolled a scroll and began:

> To Justinian, Emperor of the Romans, from Godas of the Vandals, Governor of Sardinia, Greetings.
>
> Think ye not that I am acting foolishly, nor that I have suffered ill-treatment from my master, King Gelimer of the Vandals. Nay, it is for a more noble cause that I raise the banner of rebellion in Sardinia, O Emperor. It is because I have witnessed the extreme brutality of Gelimer toward both his kinsmen and his people. How can a man

continue to serve such a vicious and callous master without himself incurring a share of the blame? As for me, I prefer to serve a just king than do the bidding of a cruel tyrant. Do ye, therefore, O Emperor, send soldiers to help me guard this island and ward off the inevitable attacks of our mutual enemy.

"I have already dispatched Eulogius to act as envoy to this Godas," Justinian continued. "If the situation seems stable in Sardinia, we shall embark a small force to aid this revolt as well."

"It seems God is already smiling upon this campaign, O Master," Belisarius said. "These petty disturbances will force Gelimer to focus on his periphery while we land a hammer-blow to his middle."

"Yes, but care must be taken," Justinian replied. "Even if he dispatches armies to put down the revolts simultaneously, the forces remaining to him will still be twice what you carry with you into the field."

"All well-trained and equipped," Narses added, affirming the emperor's words of caution.

Justinian continued: "For that reason, we see it as absolutely imperative that the Romans in Africa be brought over to our cause as quickly as possible. However, it is our understanding that a good bit of affinity has developed over the years between the captive Roman population in Africa and their barbarian overlords. Therefore, when your army lands in Africa you are to put forth the word that we come not to conquer, but merely to depose the tyrant Gelimer and restore our friend Hilderic to the throne. As Gelimer rules by fear and Hilderic was, by comparison, a mild ruler beloved by his subjects, this message should have the desired effect."

"So, then, our objective is to defeat Gelimer, free Hilderic and re-establish the Vandal kingdom in Africa as it stood before," Belisarius clarified.

Justinian pressed his lips into an odd smirk as he glanced at the others in the privy council chamber. "Yes, that's it precisely," he said, forming his words a little too smoothly.

After two more hours of reporting, discussion, and debate, the conference adjourned. All were dismissed except Belisarius. He and the emperor retired to a secluded balcony in the palace where they could speak privately.

"You understand," said Justinian, "that those instructions I gave you regarding the status of Hilderic and the objectives of our campaign were incomplete."

"Master?" Belisarius replied, puzzled.

The emperor sighed. It irked him that he was being forced to explain his meaning. "We are expending millions of nomismata and risking the lives of thousands of men not simply to put an old man back on a throne he doesn't deserve. The ultimate goal of this mission is to end the Vandal tyranny in Roman Africa *forever*. I want Hilderic to be the last king of the Vandals."

Belisarius knit his brows, bothered by the emperor's tone. "You want me to elevate him as a figurehead only?"

"I don't want you to elevate him at all," Justinian said, turning away to look out over the sea. "Hilderic is an elderly man and no doubt very frail from his ordeal. As much as I have enjoyed his correspondence over the years, I realize that accidents can happen and that life can not go on forever."

"I can not assassinate the man, O Master," Belisarius said bluntly.

An angry scowl twisted the emperor's features, but as he was turned away, Belisarius could not see it. "You misunderstand. I do not want you to kill him," Justinian said, measuring his words carefully. "What I want is for you to extract a promise from him that he will acknowledge his subservient status and bequeath his kingdom to me upon his demise." Justinian turned around quickly. "Can you do *that*, General?"

"Yes, O Master," Belisarius bowed.

"Good!" Justinian replied, anxious to keep his commanding general in high spirits. "Now let me hear more about that baby daughter of yours...."

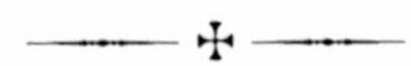

Belisarius and Justinian conversed long into the evening on a wide variety of subjects—military, personal, and theological. By the time he left the palace, Belisarius felt deeply satisfied that his mission was a just and noble one and that his master, the emperor, was a wise, pious and farsighted ruler. Indeed, that was precisely the image that Justinian had endeavored to project.

Upon the general's departure, however, Justinian immediately sought out his wife, Theodora. He didn't have to look far—the empress was waiting for him in his bedchamber, reading through a pile of ecclesiastical reports from the cities in Lydia.

"Do you have any agents among the officers of our African army that you can trust?" Justinian burst out, not even greeting his wife.

Theodora offered a sly smile.

"Fine, it's a stupid question," Justinian admitted. "Select your most trustworthy one, then..."

"And give him the task of making sure that Hilderic goes on to his eternal reward when our army reaches Africa," Theodora interrupted.

The emperor nodded, wondering how his wife had guessed his thoughts so precisely.

"Can't trust your commanding general to do it?"

"I trust that he *wouldn't* do it," Justinian snapped. "He is the sort that strives to live virtuously and, to be sure, I admire that attribute in him. But he does not understand politics. No argument of mine could have convinced him to do this deed that must be done, and indeed, should be done as punishment for a hundred years of barbarian arrogance."

"Argument? You are his emperor! Order him to do it," Theodora declared. "He has vowed to obey you—force him to take this action even if it offends his honor. Make it a test of his loyalty. Let us see which he values more—his vain desire to live with his virtue unsullied or his solemn oath to obey you in all things."

"To what end?" Justinian rejoined, relishing the debate. "Now is not the time to alienate our most able commander. Belisarius is not some craven patrician willing to do or say anything to advance himself. Nor is he a mere thuggish provincial for whom battle is a joy and killing a sport. He is something more. Something rare—a man who strives for honor and virtue in all he does."

Theodora snorted, as if her husband had said something foolish.

"And you see," Justinian continued, completely undeterred, "in order to motivate such a man, you must make him believe that your cause is right and just. For a man like Belisarius desires nothing more than to serve a master who is every bit as virtuous as he is himself."

"Does he?" Theodora asked seductively.

"Yes," the emperor said after a slight pause. "Only, it's a different type of virtue—one that operates on a higher plane."

The sea was calm with only the hint of a breeze. Constantinople was quiet. The night was far gone and not a soul stirred. From his seat in the bow of a small, four-oared ferry, Belisarius could see a single dot of light illuminating a high window in the palace. He knew it meant that Justinian had worked all through the night and was still working.

"He never sleeps," he muttered quietly to Armenian John, a trace of awe in his voice.

"Hmph," John agreed. His eyes were bleary, for Belisarius had awakened him in the middle of the night to accompany him to the city. In two days, the fleet was to depart, but Belisarius had an important obligation to complete first.

The night ferry slid silently to the quay in the Julian harbor and Belisarius flipped the ferrymaster a gold solidus for his trouble. Hooded and cloaked, he and John disembarked and strode quickly into the city.

"Thank you for coming with me," Belisarius said.

"Someone had to," John groused, mostly in jest. "Besides, I've been meaning to speak to Florentius for some time now."

The pair soon arrived at the entrance of a small monastery overlooking the Bosporus. An oil lamp was burning above the door.

"They are expecting us," Belisarius remarked.

"I alerted them when I was in the city last week," John said.

A soft rap on the door soon brought out a monk with a long beard holding a lighted taper. "Welcome to the Monastery of the Hodegetria, O Generals," he whispered. "This way, if you please."

The old monk's gait was ponderous and the two younger men had to check their pace. The halls of the monastery were cold and quiet, though Belisarius thought that he could hear feet shuffling in the darkness not far away. Their guide finally led them to a heavy decorative curtain which he pulled aside. Immediately, a chilly draft of salty air hit Belisarius and John in the face. Pulling their cloaks around them, they stepped through the arched threshold and into the open-air. With a silent gesture of blessing, the old monk departed.

The Hodegetria, an ancient icon said to have been painted by Saint Luke, occupied an enclosed niche beneath a roofed terrace, illuminated by several flickering oil lamps. Before it bubbled a fountain, far famed for the cures wrought by God through the application of its blessed waters. To give testimony to the shrine's healing power, votive offerings, rich and humble alike, crowded the multitude of alcoves surrounding the holy icon.

Belisarius fell to his knees before the icon of the Theotokos and Christ child. *I am better prepared this time, Blessed Virgin,* he began, *for I have remembered the words Antiochus the holy man enjoined me to speak in your shrine.* Dipping his hand into the font, Belisarius rubbed the frigid water over his face while praying in a whisper: "Jesus, my Savior, heal my soul and give sight unto me, that I may be able to discern Your will."

As the water ran down into his beard like icy tears, Belisarius gazed up at the icon and felt a wave of sadness wash over him. The last time he was here, his friend Florentius, now dead nearly three years, was with him. Indeed, it was Florentius who insisted that they visit the shrine in obedience to the advice Antiochus had offered.

How I miss him, Lord, Belisarius lamented, gazing at the child Jesus. *He was a great support to me and an encouragement. I feel so much weaker in spirit without him. O God, why did you take him from me?*

Belisarius's eyes shifted to the radiant icon of the Virgin. Her face was content like that of any mother holding her treasured child, but there was also a hint of sorrow in her expression. Her right hand gestured toward her Son and her eyes looked out at the world as if to say, "Do whatever He tells you to do."

Glancing to his right, Belisarius could see Armenian John on his knees in prayer before the font, his face in his hands. *But I see you have not left me friendless, O God. Though one dear friend has been taken, another now occupies his place. The Lord giveth. The Lord taketh away. The Lord giveth again. Blessed be the name of the Lord!*

The two remained in prayer for a half-hour more. Belisarius then rose and waited for John to finish. As he did, the first rays of sunlight burst over the low hills of Asia across the Bosporus, filling the shrine with a soft glow. The low, somber tones of a hundred monks chanting the Orthros infused the air like sweet incense.

"Did you speak to him?" Belisarius asked.

"Yes," John said, his face deadly serious. "I asked him to intercede with the Almighty on behalf of our campaign that it may be successful."

"Did he answer?"

"He did," John said, drooping his head. "He said, 'I'll see you soon.'"

Belisarius's jaw dropped open in disbelief for an instant, before he saw the hint of a smile form on John's face. "You lying snake. How can you jest in a place like this?"

"Sometimes laughing is the only way to keep from crying," John replied. "Besides, Florentius always loved a good jape."

"So you miss him as much as I do, then?"

"Yes," John sighed. "I do."

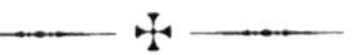

The following day was filled with feverish activity throughout Constantinople. Belisarius had devoted most of his time and energy to training his soldiers, leaving the logistical work to Solomon and Armenian John. But with so little time left before they were to depart, Belisarius wanted to see with his own eyes that everything was in a state of complete readiness. He was everywhere, moving so quickly from one inspection to the next that his secretary and bodyguards could barely keep up with him.

After spot-checking the fleet, he made himself available to the shipmasters, heard complaints and offered suggestions for a solid hour. He met with the fleet commander, Calonymous, and discussed naval tactics—a subject Belisarius had studied only in theory. His greatest fear was that the powerful Vandal fleet would ambush his armada and that all his expertly trained horsemen would drown in a watery grave before they ever drew their bows in anger. This had been the fate of Basiliscus before him and Belisarius impressed upon Calonymous his ardent desire to avoid a naval battle at all cost. This war would be won on land—or not at all.

As dusk began to settle over Constantinople, Belisarius watched the ships take on their cargo of horses, men, equipment, and foodstuffs. The emperor, it seemed, had supplied a super-abundance of everything needful. The only shortage Belisarius could perceive concerned the stock of twice-baked sea biscuits. He collared a logothete from the Praetorian Prefecture who assured him that the bushels were on their way. The prefect himself was overseeing production and he intended that the biscuits be baked at the last possible moment to ensure their freshness.

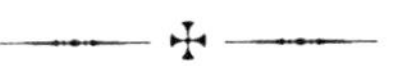

"My lord Prefect!" a man shouted as he burst into the office of Cappadocian John. His face was red and his eyes bulged with worry.

"What is it, Rufus?" John grunted angrily. "Can't you see I'm busy?" The prefect was reclining on a couch as an attractive but demure female slave freshened his wine cup.

"The biscuits, O Prefect!" cried the logothete. "Belisarius is inquiring about them. He wants them loaded immediately. I told him the situation was in hand. But I have just been to the imperial bakery and all they have is dough! They have baked nothing!"

John waved his hand and the slave girl made a hasty exit. "That's because I told them not to purchase the wood to fuel the ovens for this shipment.

Lumber is expensive and the money to bake this massive amount of bread—I put it to better use elsewhere." He stroked his flabby, clean-shaven cheeks.

"The emperor will be wroth when he finds out!" the logothete groaned.

"What a worthless coward you are, Rufus," John replied lazily. "The emperor will not find out."

"He'll have both of our heads, John," the logothete continued, growing furious at his superior's smug attitude. "You may call me a coward, but have no doubt that I will pin this malfeasance right where it belongs—on you."

John laughed, though his laugh sounded much like a man clearing his throat. He spat on the floor, then swung his feet off the couch and stood up. "I was wrong, Rufus," he rasped, getting close enough that Rufus could smell the stale wine on his breath. "You are not just a coward, you are also colossally stupid and uninventive."

Rufus stood by exasperated, his fists clenching and unclenching.

"Go down to the imperial bakeries and order those cretinous dolts to bring their dough-cakes to the Baths of Achilles."

"The baths?" Rufus screeched, tearing his hair.

"Yes, idiot, the baths," John replied, raising his voice. "Tell them to bake the biscuits using the fires that are kept burning in the basement. When they begin to turn brown, throw them into bags and take them immediately to the ships."

"Are you insane?" the logothete cried. "It's a fever swamp down there—a feculent filth pit. You want to bake bread there? And the biscuits are supposed to be twice-baked to ensure freshness for sea travel!"

Cappadocian John smiled. "Then, I guess Belisarius will have no bread at all for his campaign. And the emperor will indeed be furious. But tell me, Rufus, when I explain this situation to Justinian, who is more likely to feel the sting of his whips? His boon companion, John? Or a nobody like you?"

Rufus's face fell and his mouth twisted in confusion. He knew the answer.

"That's a good lad," John said, patting him on the shoulder. "Now get your arse over to the bakeries and get to work. You have a long night ahead of you."

With panic in his eyes, Rufus burst out the door and set off running down the street toward the bakeries.

"Besides," John said out loud, though no one was there to hear him, "all those biscuits are only going to end up at the bottom of the sea, anyway."

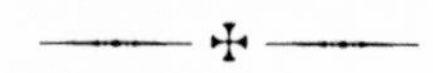

The day after the spring equinox, with men, arms, and provisions safely stowed, the great fleet emerged from the Golden Horn and rounded the promontory upon which the City of Constantine sat like a gleaming jewel. Opposite the imperial palace, Belisarius commanded his flagship, the Hagios Giorgios, to anchor at a dock where were gathered a great crowd of dignitaries in all their finery, led by the emperor himself. Theodora was by his side and Epiphanius, the patriarch of Constantinople was present as well, followed by a long train of presbyters and monks.

With blue and gold banners snapping overhead in the stiff breeze, Belisarius and his chief officers disembarked from their ship and were greeted with hearty cheers from the assembled palace denizens and government bureaucrats. The commanders saluted the emperor and empress and then dropped to their knees as Epiphanius mounted a rostrum to pronounce his blessing.

When he had concluded, a single soldier was brought forward who knelt beside the commanders. Making the sign of the cross, the patriarch uttered a prayer over the soldier: "May this man, George, newly baptized into the one, holy, Catholic and Orthodox Church of Jesus Christ, draw down additional protection from Almighty God over this great fleet which sails at His command. May he further serve as a reminder that the armies of the Roman Empire embark as believers in Christ, true God and true man. And they go forth for a just and righteous purpose, as commanded by our most pious emperor, Justinian Augustus: to defend and protect the innocent believers in the true Faith from the impious sons of heresy who would destroy them. Lord God, by Your holy mandate does this armada sail—grant unto them, O God, Your blessing, Your strength, and Your victory!"

"Amen, amen. Alleluia!" The throng responded in full voice.

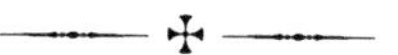

Standing on the parapet of the palace overlooking the Bosporus, Narses stared out longingly over the martial panoply below him. He sighed and shook his head.

"I feel the same way, my little friend," Cappadocian John grunted.

I doubt it, you miserable oaf, Narses stewed to himself.

"All that outlay of wealth down there," John continued. "Most of it marked for loss, never to return. How many of those men will ever see Constantinople again?"

"Probably not many," Narses agreed. In his mind, however, Narses was envisioning himself at the prow of the flagship surrounded by officers awaiting his commands.

"Ah, but you see, no matter what happens, I shall win out in the end," John gloated, slapping Narses heavily on the shoulder with his meaty hand. "In the unlikely event of a victory, the emperor will no doubt reward me for the outstanding work my prefecture did assembling the provisions and procuring the financing. However, if as is more probable, the campaign is a disaster, I shall still profit."

"How's that?" Narses turned toward him, disgust creeping into his voice.

"Well, you see," John chuckled, "I publicly placed a modest wager with the circus bookmakers, betting on the success of the mission. Once word spread, there was an immediate rush of others to do likewise, figuring that I had some sort of inside knowledge. But once the bookmakers fixed the odds to favor success, I ordered my agents to place much larger wagers in secret on the mission's failure. Clever, yes?"

"You are a cunning brute, John," Narses hissed. He then stalked away scowling ferociously.

John laughed. "So many unimaginative people out there."

Tribonian, who was standing at John's other hand, harrumphed. "Just what makes you so sure the mission will fail?"

John sidled close to him. "You are, no doubt familiar with the Sibyline books?"

Tribonian's eyes widened. "Merciful gods, man!" he whispered. "Keep your voice down!"

John chuckled. "I have consulted a very wise old fellow well-versed in the oracular wisdom of the Sibyl of Cumae. Would you like to hear what he told me?"

Nodding his head furtively, Tribonian approached as close to John as his sensitive nose would allow.

"*Africa capta Mundus cum nato peribit.*"

"When Africa is captured, the world and its offspring shall perish," Tribonian repeated slowly.

John grunted. "I don't expect the world to end any time soon, do you?"

"Such an absurdity," Tribonian huffed, exasperated. "That verse could refer to anything—any time."

"I thought of that too. So as a precaution, I have caused the haruspices to be taken."

"Are you mad?" Tribonian gasped. "If the emperor should find out..."

"Do you want to know the result?"

Tribonian's eyes darted back and forth as he tried in vain to appear calm and uninterested. "Yes."

"Bad news for our friend Belisarius," John smiled. "The haruspex said he had never seen a liver so discolored and malformed. It may even have been cancerous."

"A tragedy for the emperor," Tribonian groaned.

"But not for the empire," John added. "Perhaps after this misadventure fails, he'll be more attentive to our advice and not go off chasing insane theophanies."

✠

On the dock, the ceremony had ended and the palace bureaucrats headed back to watch the fleet depart from the terraces overlooking the sea. Justinian tarried by the dockside, walking ahead of his retinue of attendants to approach Belisarius who was giving some last minute instructions to his lieutenants.

"General, it has come to my attention that you have lost several score horses to sickness and mishaps in loading," Justinian said, his tone half-scolding.

"Nearly a hundred at last count, O Emperor," Belisarius replied. "The loss is lamentable, but we will make it good by purchasing fresh mounts in Sicily when we make landfall there."

"You need not," Justinian said, a gleam in his eye. "Sicilian horses are of inferior quality. What say you to one thousand head of the finest battle mounts from the imperial grazing lands in Thrace?"

"My Lord!" Belisarius stammered.

"You will call at Heracleia after the first day of sailing. There, the horses will be waiting for you. Have you room in the holds of those ships out there?"

"We shall make room, my Lord, your Piety!"

"Good," Justinian smiled. "You will recall that I enjoy surprising my most excellent servants with unexpected boons. Consider this your boon for this expedition."

"A more fitting and useful gift I can not imagine," Belisarius replied, genuflecting. "You are most generous, O Master."

Nervously fingering the hilt of his ceremonial sword, Justinian felt a wave of trepidation swell over him. Looking beyond his general toward the fleet extending across the water, Justinian found it exceedingly difficult to tear himself away from the men he was sending into extreme peril. He raised Belisarius and clasped his right arm tightly.

"I know you will succeed," he said, almost as if he were trying to convince himself. "You *must* succeed."

"We have done all that is humanly possible to prepare, O Emperor," the general replied. "The rest is in the hands of God."

"Right," Justinian nodded and loosened his grip. "Go then. And be assured, Belisarius, that we will be begging God every day for your victory and safe return to us."

XIII

AD 533, Spring
Third year of the reign of Gelimer, King of the Vandals
At Carthage

In the famed circular harbor of Carthage, capital of the Vandal kingdom, a great fleet packed with men-at-arms sat restlessly at anchor. Fearsome-looking soldiers stood in knots of three or four chatting along the rails. Sailors swaggered on deck as they briskly went about their duties preparing their vessels for departure. The sailors were brash and full of boasting—they knew they were the finest seamen in the world and that their warships, with their beaked prows sheathed in copper and three heavy catapults, were the most powerful on the high seas.

But their boasts paled into insignificance when compared with the outright arrogance of the Vandal soldiers who bragged continuously about their exploits in piracy, plunder, murder, and savagery. And this was no ordinary raid with limited opportunity for booty. Their king had called for the reduction of an entire island. Sardinia was their goal and Godas the rebel was their quarry. Five thousand of Gelimer's best men would crush the rebel army before any support could arrive from the Romans.

Gelimer, the Vandal king, had entrusted this mission to his brother, Tzazon. Dressed in grim gray armor the color of smoke, Gelimer and a retinue of officers arrived aboard his brother's flagship on the eve of his departure with some urgent news.

"Brother, this morning we heard word that a Roman war fleet is being assembled at Constantinople," Gelimer began, leaning over a map that was laid out on a table in the captain's quarters. "A Gothic merchant saw the ships gathering in the Golden Horn. He claims that the fleet was a large one—several hundred ships."

"That many?" Tzazon laughed. "An exaggeration, no doubt. Perhaps the merchant is poor with his numbers."

"I can vouch for him," another man called out from the king's escort. He was a tall fellow of middling build, his long, golden hair gathered up at the back of his head. His youthful face, though disfigured by the scars of battle, bore a very prominent drooping moustache.

"You know this man, Thrasamund?" Tzazon queried.

"Yes, father," the younger man replied. "I knew him when I lived in Constantinople and he visits me whenever he makes port in Carthage. He bears no love for the Romans so you may rely on him."

"Unfortunately, the man did not know when the fleet would sail or where it was headed," Gelimer added. "Did he, nephew?"

"No, and he dared not ask," Thrasamund responded. "All sorts of incredible rumors were in the air in Constantinople."

"Isn't it obvious?" said Tzazon. "They are going to attempt to reinforce Godas before we can reach him. Then, if successful, they will use Sardinia as a base from which to attack us."

"That is my belief as well," the king said. "All the more reason for you to make haste to Sardinia and annihilate this rebel. Once you have done that, you may set your fleet in ambush and take the Romans at sea where they will stand no chance against you."

"I will do so with pleasure, O King," Tzazon replied. "All is in readiness and speed is of the essence. We sail at dawn!"

✠

Standing a full head taller than ordinary men, two exceptionally large and dangerous looking Vandal guards stood on either side of a massive set of double bronze doors.

"Make way," cried Fuscias. "Throw open the doors. The king himself wishes to visit the royal treasury."

Straining their huge muscles, the guards pulled open the heavy doors which made a sonorous metallic creak as they swung on their ancient hinges. An instant later, Gelimer appeared. He and Fuscias entered the chamber followed by a train of slaves pushing carts and bearing large wicker baskets in their hands. A dozen additional guards took up their position outside the door to stare down any curious passers-by.

Inside, Fuscias lit torches and the dim light they emitted danced hypnotically on the ceiling, reflected off of the myriad gleaming objects piled high in the room. As the last torch was lit and the chamber became fully illuminated, Gelimer's eyes grew wide with greedy delight—for here was amassed the most magnificent treasure in the world.

For nearly a century, the Vandals had been a nation of corsairs, their sleek galleys preying unchallenged upon Roman merchants and stripping Roman cities of their wealth and people. With fire and sword, they had wreaked terrible destruction upon the crumbling Western Empire, and barely a single town on the Italian coast had escaped their plundering. Under their greatest king, Gaiseric, they had even dared to raid the Peloponnesus, burning venerable Greek cities and carrying off thousands into cruel slavery.

But the most infamous Vandal atrocity still resonated in the minds of men, though it occurred some eighty years before. When the Western emperor Valentinian III was assassinated, his widow Eudoxia sought an avenger to destroy Maximus who had instigated the foul deed and claimed the throne for himself. The foolish empress chose the Vandal king Gaiseric to be the instrument of her vengeance and made overtures to him that he might venture to Italy and slay the unholy usurper. Seizing the opportunity, Gaiseric advanced upon Italy with the full power of his arms and the Romans, having barely survived the ravages of Attila the previous year, were unable to resist him in any way.

Making a straight path to Rome, Gaiseric found that the people had already slain the tyrant Maximus. With no one standing in his way, he entered the city and occupied the palace. The entreaties of Pope Leo the Great prevented a general slaughter of the populace, but for two weeks, the Vandals merrily stripped the Queen of Cities of all her moveable wealth, destroying ancient buildings and impoverishing the people. His fleet bursting with the accumulated loot of an empire, Gaiseric sailed joyously for Carthage having accomplished the most audacious act of piracy in all of human history.

It was this colossal treasure that the great-grandson of Gaiseric now waded into. Pushing more insignificant antiquities aside with his feet, Gelimer browsed through his possessions with the careful eye of an old woman inspecting fresh fish on the docks.

"This one," he said, picking up a magnificent gold medallion. It showed the bust of the emperor Aurelian wearing the crown of the sun. Around the edge were engraved the words *Restitutor Orbis*.

Fuscias took it from his hands. "For the palace, O King?"

"No, have it melted down for coin," Gelimer ordered.

"Yes, O King," Fuscias replied, bowing. He dropped the medallion in one of the baskets borne by a slave.

"And this, and this," Gelimer continued, now getting into the rhythm. He passed a heavy silver decanter and a jewel-encrusted reliquary box to Fuscias. "All of these things we shall melt down or break up for sale."

"Yes, O King," Fuscias said obediently.

In the space of ten minutes, all the baskets were filled with enough treasure to pay his entire army five times over. The slaves were dispatched under heavy guard directly to the royal mint. Within a few days, it would all become coinage.

Gelimer then moved on to the statuary. "This one is disgusting," he opined, poking his finger into the chest of a large bronze of the emperor Claudius. "Look at this weakling. How the Romans managed to conquer the world, I will never know."

"Another one to be melted down?"

"For heaven's sake, yes," the king replied, a sneer on his lips.

Two slaves tilted the statue onto a cart and hauled it away.

"Now what have we here?" Gelimer said to himself as he reached a dark corner of the treasury. There stood some tattered legionary standards beside a large golden candelabrum with seven arms. Two silver trumpets leaned against the wall behind the gleaming lampstand and before them stood a heavy mahogany table inlaid with precious stones, its top a sheet of pure gold. Upon the table were placed libation bowls, jars, and censers, all made entirely of gold. "Have this melted down as well," Gelimer decided, picking up a heavy golden censer by its finely wrought chain.

"Refrain, O King, from touching those items," Fuscias objected, finally finding his courage. "These are the ornaments taken originally by Titus from the Jewish Temple in Jerusalem after the resurrection of the Christ. Thus, they are sacred."

In anger, Gelimer flung the censer at his minister. Fuscias ducked and the precious object clattered across the floor behind him. "Melt it down, damn you! The Jews are an accursed race and their baubles should be treated accordingly. I'm going to build a new fleet to launch against the Romans for their aggression on my kingdom. I will exact a terrible vengeance on them. And if I have to melt down all of this to do it, so help me I shall!"

The king turned from the Temple treasures with a swirl of his cape and advanced on Fuscias. The minister flinched as if he expected a buffet for his rash words. But Gelimer only strode by briskly, his attention fixed on another object. Relieved, Fuscias scrambled to collect the censer and surreptitiously replaced it on the golden table.

"Fuscias!" Gelimer barked.

"Yes, O King?"

"Have this installed in the palace," Gelimer said, gesturing toward a fine life-sized bronze statue of the emperor Valentinian I. In the emperor's right hand was the *globus cruciger*; his left hand was on the hilt of his sword.

"Shall I set it in the assembly hall, O king?" Fuscias asked.

"No, indeed," Gelimer growled. "It reminds me of the image of Justinian I have seen on his coinage. Set it in the practice yard. We shall use it as a target for javelin drills."

AD 533, SPRING

Sixth year of the reign of Justinian, Emperor of the Romans
At Abydus on the Hellespont

The early morning air was chilly and the choppy sea slapped against the sides of the Hagios Giorgios as she sliced through the swells pushed by a stiff north breeze. Belisarius stood at the rail near the prow wrapped in a cloak against the cold sea spray. In high spirits, his keen eyes scanned the horizon. The emperor's horses had been successfully shipped at Heracleia and the fleet had crossed the broad Propontis without incident. Now they were entering the channel of the Hellespont which led out into the azure blue Aegean Sea upon which were scattered islands with legendary names—Samos, Chios, Delos, Rhodes, Cos, Naxos, and a thousand others.

Glancing back toward the stern, Belisarius spied one of his officers leaning against the rail amidship, a heavy cloak over his head. "Hail fellow," the general called out, approaching. "Have you eaten yet this morning?"

Uliaris turned to face him, looking unshaven, grim, and just the slightest bit green. "Eaten, Magister? Surely you jest."

"Ah, the motion of the ship has made you ill," Belisarius observed.

"Me and about a dozen others in the officers' mess below," Uliaris groaned. "Though I always seem the worst off."

"You have always despised travel by sea," Belisarius noted.

"Is it any wonder?" Uliaris gagged. He then voided his gut over the rail.

Belisarius turned away. He had a strong stomach on the sea, but few were impervious when the stench of vomit is added to the rolling of the ship. "Don't worry," he said, covering his nose with his cloak. "We'll make port at Abydus this afternoon so you can get your land legs back under you—for a few hours at least."

At Abydus, the fleet took on fresh water and some additional fodder for the new contingent of horses. But when all was stored and in readiness, the order to weigh anchor and set sail was cancelled. The breeze had failed completely and the entire fleet was becalmed. There was nothing to do but wait for the wind to rise again.

Two days passed with no sign of a breeze. Belisarius drilled his men as best he could to occupy the time, but he couldn't keep them on duty constantly and many ended up in the city itself, mingling with the locals and enriching the tavern-keepers. Aware of the perils engendered when 17,000 war-bound soldiers are let loose upon a city with scarcely that many inhabitants, Belisarius set out strict orders for his men's behavior and limited the numbers who could be at liberty at any given time. He made it clear that punishments for transgressing these bounds would be swift and severe.

When the fourth day dawned and the wind remained still, frustration permeated the men and their commanders the same, and punishments for improper conduct were meted out with increasing frequency. A Thracian was demoted in rank for refusing to pay for his food and drink; a Phrygian was whipped for putting his hands on a woman; a Goth was imprisoned and fined for starting a brawl.

In the early evening just prior to the sunset, two Huns were dragged before Belisarius, obviously drunk. At the sight of them, Belisarius furrowed his brow in anger—their tunics were stained crimson with blood.

"Hail, O Magister," they said, staggering as they saluted.

"What evil have you done that you appear before me in this condition?" the general demanded.

"These men quarreled with one of their companions who was mocking them," Solomon said. "A fight broke out, and in the course of it, they drew knives and stabbed him."

"To death?" Belisarius asked.

"Yes, to death."

The two Huns stood before him grinning stupidly. "We kill Abergan, the dirty bastard," one of them boasted, swaggering unsteadily on his bowed legs.

The other concurred, made an obscene gesture then spat on the floor. He seemed proud of his bladework.

"Take these two butchers and impale them immediately atop the hill outside the city," Belisarius barked.

"But Magister..." one of the guards stammered.

"Do it now, so that all the army may see!" Belisarius shouted with a fury in his eyes that few had ever witnessed.

The Huns were dragged out shouting and protesting. But no sooner had their shouts died away than new ones were raised by a fresh cohort of Huns who arrived in the command tent. Led by Aigan, a long time friend of Belisarius and one of his cavalry commanders, the relatives of the condemned men and a dozen more Huns made a boisterous approach.

"Magister, you must to relent," Aigan spoke angrily in his broken Greek. "To serve emperor we did swear, but to live by our own laws we demand. For under law of Huns, no man may be at fault who does murder while drinking."

Belisarius scowled with an anger that surprised even Aigan. "No, I will not relent. Those men inflicted death upon a comrade, and according to the regulations which were made clear to all, the punishment for any who dare to slay their own comrade is death."

"No!" The Huns erupted in fury. "An injustice!"

"To be subject to your law, no Hun should be!" Aigan raged. "For this reason, no Hun entered into alliance with the Romans. To fight only. To be ruled by Hun laws only."

"Relent. Show justice!" the rest shouted.

"Have pity on them!" a few of the Roman officers joined in the chorus.

"They are two of the most excellent horsemen in the whole army, Magister," the dux Barbatus interjected. "Let them live, if only to inflict them upon the Vandals."

Uliaris, who was standing nearby, offered his advice: "Relent, for the sake of the army. Punish them, yes, but do not have them executed. It will show you can be merciful."

Belisarius turned a smoldering glance on him and then gestured to Solomon and Armenian John. "Proceed with the execution," he ordered. "Then, assemble all the men on the beach so that I might speak to them."

✠

The full array of soldiery was mustered on the beach, 17,000 strong, with several thousand more sailors from the fleet standing around the ranks haphazardly, curious to hear what the general had to say. Many faces among the mass of soldiers were angry but most were gray and uncertain as they cast sidelong glances at the silhouettes of the two Huns impaled on poles at the top of a nearby hill.

Belisarius mounted a low dune so he could be seen by all and better project his voice over them. Around him stood his staunchest allies—Solomon, Armenian John, Dorotheus, Uliaris, and Pharas—along with his most powerful bodyguards—his cousin Rufinus, Unigastus, Principius, Athenodorus, and Boriades. Aigan was noticeably absent. He chose to stand with the Huns in support of their outrage.

Belisarius looked out over them with a stern eye and began: "Had the lot of you been neophytes at war, your reaction to this turn of events would have been understandable. For inexperienced men often assume that triumph in the harsh struggles of war are won only through strength of arm and courage in battle. But as most of you are veterans, you know well that justice is the greatest help in gaining victory. Though it is men who trade blows with the enemy, it is God who bestows the victory in battle as it seems best to Him.

"As your commander, I have seen to your provision, equipment and training, so that you might face the enemy with every advantage that arms and physical conditioning can offer. But I consider these things of little account when compared with the things of God. For God demands justice and if we fail to demonstrate that we are just and worthy of His favor, then have no doubt that your brilliant deeds on the battlefield will come to nothing!

"The first mark of justice is the punishment of those who have committed foul and disgraceful murders, for nothing is more precious to a man than his life. And our laws wisely declare that the man who commits such a heinous act by depriving someone of life, the murderer's own life must then be forfeit.

"And let no man, be he barbarian or Roman, think to alleviate his guilt for any crime on the grounds of drunkenness. Indeed, the circumstance only aggravates his fault, especially when serving in an army. This is because, as all of you know, drunkenness itself is a misdeed worthy of the whip according to our code. And worse, in this case, these malefactors were so blind with drunken fury that they slew a man of their own nation—their very kin!"

Belisarius paused to let his words sink in. All were silent in anticipation of what he would say next.

"Let the fate of these two kin-slayers stand before you as an example so that you may see what sort of recompense such foul deeds will accord. Recall that it is your duty to refrain from laying a violent hand on anyone without just provocation. Nor may you carry off the goods of others. Before you is the proof that I will not overlook such crimes. And I will not consider any of you to be comrades of mine—no matter how terrible he is reputed to be against the enemy—if he is not able to wield his weapons with clean hands. For bravery can not be victorious unless it is allied with justice."

Belisarius descended abruptly from the dune and the men were dismissed. An uncommon hush fell over them as they considered the general's words. As many of the Huns who were Christians, including Aigan, now understood the reason for Belisarius's harsh punishment. But just as many resolved only to act with greater discretion, holding a grudge against their commander to be repaid at a later date.

"I hope your words had the desired effect," Solomon said as he walked beside Belisarius.

"As do I," Belisarius replied, his voice still agitated and his gait purposeful. "But if this be an army of wicked criminals, we can expect no aid from God. And indeed we will richly deserve the defeat that comes to us should we behave as brigands and cut-throats."

The companions of Belisarius felt a gloom creep over them to hear their general speak in such terms. Uliaris in particular was downhearted and now felt compelled to conduct himself with greater moderation, particularly when it came to indulging in drink.

The deepening twilight and an unexpected blast of the cold north wind only added to their melancholy.

But suddenly, a shout went up. Then another. Then a dozen more. Soon the entire beach was cheering as the word spread from man to man.

"Why do they cheer?" Uliaris asked. "What are they shouting?"

"The wind, you idiot!" Armenian John cried gleefully.

The men around Belisarius then joined the chorus of cheers.

"It seems the Deity was well pleased with your words, O General," Solomon remarked.

Belisarius shook his head sheepishly. "I am no saint who commands the winds," he said. "Clearly someone is praying for us who is much more holy than I am."

"It's a fair breeze!" Calonymous said, approaching at a trot with his men behind him. "What is your order, O General?"

"Break camp and get aboard ship," Belisarius shouted. "We sail at once!"

It was dawn before every man boarded and all the equipage was stowed. The stiff winds blew the fleet through the narrow strait of the Hellespont and into the open sea. A few men claimed to have spotted Porphyrius, the dreaded great whale who wrecked ships. But they took it as a fair omen that he allowed the fleet to pass without incident.

The breezes subsided somewhat during the passage across the Aegean, but it was just as well. Belisarius's greatest concern was that the fleet would be scattered on the open sea should a sudden squall assail them. So to keep order as well as possible, he commanded that the main sails of the flagships be painted red from the top corner to about a third of their breadth. He further ordered that long, upright poles be affixed to the prow of each, upon which was hung a great flaming lantern. In this way, the other vessels were able to recognize the leading ships and follow them during both day and night.

The fleet rounded the Peloponnesus without losing a single ship and touched at the town of Methone on the western coast. There waiting for them to arrive, were two tagmas of fresh troops under the duxes Martinus and Valerian that Justinian had sent ahead previously. Belisarius happily welcomed these additional forces and, as the winds had once again failed, he disembarked the entire army. Man and horse had been at sea continuously for nearly a month and Belisarius felt an urgent need to exercise them lest their vigor be sapped by the arduous journey in the cramped holds of the ships.

"Magister, something is horribly wrong," Solomon cried as he entered the command tent. "Hundreds of the men are laid low with fever—perhaps a thousand."

"A sickness?" Belisarius replied anxiously, rising to his feet.

"It was not noticed aboard ship. Most thought it was merely seasickness for it afflicts the stomach and the bowels."

"Separate out those who are sick from the rest immediately," Belisarius ordered. "If it's camp fever, we can't allow it to spread any more than it already has."

"It is not camp fever, husband," Antonina declared as she burst into the tent unannounced. The large slave Eugenius followed her carrying a sack of sea rations. "Observe what your men have been subsisting upon." Antonina snapped her fingers and Eugenius dropped the bag on the ground. Out of it poured vile-looking clumps of damp wheat flour encrusted with green mold. The stink of the stuff immediately offended the nostrils of all present.

"What is this?" Belisarius demanded. "Where are the sea biscuits?"

"Disintegrated. Crumbled back down to this rotten flour," Antonina replied. "It's clear to me that they were not properly prepared to survive a voyage by sea."

"The Cappadocian," Solomon groaned. "That worthless wretch!"

Belisarius pushed past them into the encampment where his men were bivouacked followed by his officers and domestics. Miserable soldiers gazed at him with trepidation in their faces as he passed. The stench of vomit and feces hung in the air like an evil spirit. Rumors of camp fever had spread like wildfire and with the obvious spoiling of the rations, talk of desertion was on the lips of many.

Armenian John was tending to Dorotheus when Belisarius found him. The grizzled veteran lay on a pallet, his face ashen, his beard soaked with sweat as John swabbed his forehead with damp cloth.

"Have you seen this?" John questioned as Belisarius approached. He held a moldy chunk of bread in his hand.

"Dorotheus is stricken as well?" Belisarius gasped.

"The rations have spoiled," John continued. "They're making everyone sick!"

"Have it all burned. Immediately," Belisarius ordered. "See to it yourself. Let no one else eat it!"

"Aye, Magister," John replied, standing up.

"Solomon," Belisarius said, "enter the town right away with money to purchase enough bread to feed them all."

"I go, Magister," he replied, anxious to be of use.

"I shall accompany him and explain our needs to the city fathers," Antonina offered.

"Let it be so," Belisarius replied. "Where is Procopius?"

"I am here, O Magister," the secretary replied.

"Come with me. We shall draft a letter to the emperor this very day informing him of how the malfeasance of his prefect has sickened his soldiers and left them bereft of food."

Five-hundred soldiers died miserably at Methone from the rotten bread-meal. Belisarius saw to it that the Christian rites were performed and that all were given a proper burial. Vigor and high-spirits returned with the arrival of fresh rations and Belisarius spared no effort to nurse back to health those who had been laid low. Though suffering terribly, the general Dorotheus yet clung to life, insisting that he would survive. When the wind finally picked up, however, he was still in no condition to walk and had to be carried aboard ship by his officers.

It was night when the fleet again prepared for departure. Belisarius, his officers, and domestics spent every waking hour helping to ferry the sick to their ships. Alone in the commander's cabin on the Hagios Giorgios, Antonina pored over a requisition list to make sure that the fleet would have sufficient rations for the passage across the Adriatic.

A soft knock on the door startled her.

"Come," she ordered.

"My Mistress, a lady from Methone has arrived aboard ship and insists that she must see you," Eugenius said softly, having opened the door a crack.

"Faugh! I have no time for such visits," Antonina replied.

A small middle-aged woman pushed by Eugenius and wedged herself into the room. "You will make time for me, Lady, for I come at the behest of Theodora."

Antonina's eyes widened. "Leave her be, Eugenius. Begone and shut the door behind you."

"You know why I am here?" the woman asked furtively.

"Yes," Antonina said. She turned away quickly and dug through a pile of her papers. After a moment, she produced a small scroll affixed with her seal and handed it over.

"Good," the woman said. "Someone else will contact you in Sicily and again once you reach Africa. Good evening to you."

"Tell the empress that we pray for her health and for the emperor's as well," Antonina whispered as the woman made her way out. The door closed and Antonina was overcome by a wave of guilt, knowing that she had just betrayed her husband's trust. *At least I was able to make some additional accusations against John of Cappadocia,* she rationalized. *Perhaps by acting as Theodora's informant, I can yet advance our cause if I am careful.*

Eugenius escorted the woman to the skiff which would carry her back to Methone. In the dim light, no one saw as he pressed a gold solidus and another small scroll into her hand. "Well done," he whispered. "Here is the reward for your service and another message for the empress. A man named Zeno will meet you in the agora tomorrow morning wearing a green tunic with a gold sash. Give these letters to him and he will reward you as well."

"I shall do as you say," the woman said nervously.

"See that you do. And be certain you keep these dealings quiet," Eugenius continued. "Should you fail, remember—the empress is generous to those she favors, but pitiless and vindictive on those who do her ill."

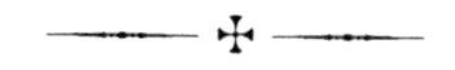

The fleet made a brief stop at the harbor of Zacynthus to take on fresh water before attempting to transit the Adriatic. There they were met by the city fathers and holy men, who processed down to the docks and pronounced a blessing over them.

"General, we know that your goal is Africa and that your arms are destined for battle with the Vandal host," an elder among the fathers declared in a loud voice. "Be assured that our prayers go with you on your mission, that you may bring to heel this wicked nation. For among us Zacynthians, the Vandal name is black and brings memories of unspeakable atrocity. That cruel tyrant Gaiseric, during his plundering of the Peloponnesus, paid a call on our undefended town after he had been repulsed at Taenarum. Without mercy, he brought down slaughter and fire upon us like a sudden storm. Out of sheer spite, he took away some five-hundred of our parents, uncles, aunts, and siblings—the best of our town..."

The old man paused, his voice choked as tears welled up in his eyes. Many of the old gray heads began to wail in grief as the memories flooded back. The younger ones joined in the chorus of the bereaved, moved to see their elders so distressed.

"Gaiseric took our people aboard his ships," the old man continued, "and in retribution for his losses at Taenarum, he slew them, chopped their bodies in pieces, and cast them uncaring into the sea."

At his words, the wails grew louder. Aboard the Hagios Giorgios, few eyes remained dry.

"For many years we have awaited an avenger from God to punish the Vandals," another of the town fathers added. "Go thou, O General, with our blessing, and do justice to this evil nation."

From the forecastle of his ship, Belisarius nodded and accepted their blessing. Beside him at the rail, Photius was troubled. "*Pater*, have we truly been sent by God to bring vengeance to the Vandals?"

"I believe our mission is ordained by the Almighty," Belisarius said softly, turning toward the boy. There was a look of grim determination in his eyes. "It is for God to decide what happens when we reach Africa, for no doubt some of the Vandals have repented of their greed and lust for blood. But for any who dare oppose us, have no doubt that I will do my utmost to bring swift retribution upon them for their crimes and those of their fathers."

It was a gentle and languid breeze which pushed the Roman fleet out of the harbor at Zacynthus and across the Adriatic. Though it made for smooth sailing, the fleet progressed so slowly that a passage normally requiring but four days with a strong wind found them still at sea after two weeks. At the dawn of the sixteenth day, though, the peak of gloomy Ætna could be clearly discerned. Spewing a thin trail of smoke and ash into the sky, the snow-capped sentinel of Sicily brought both relief and foreboding to the men. They were now out of Roman waters, and entering the domain of the Ostrogoths. Though a pact had been made with the Gothic queen to allow them safe harbor and a market at the town of Caucana on the southern coast of Sicily, no one could be sure how they would be received.

Belisarius ordered the fleet to anchor in a deserted place not far from Ætna and there discovered that even more of his soldiers had sickened on the long passage. The summer sun beat down on the fleet without remorse and the drinking water on board the ships had gone stagnant, having been stored improperly. Belisarius had remained unaware of this problem while at sea thanks to the care taken by Antonina with regard to the water jars on board the flagship. Though the general had cause to laud the foresight of his wife, the sailors and men heaped abuse upon Calonymous and blamed the water spoilage squarely on him. This unfavorable comparison to a lubberly woman so infuriated the vain prefect that his eyes now narrowed and his jaw clenched each time he set eyes on her.

Once the entire fleet was anchored, the men commenced taking on water and fitting their ships with storage jars buried in sand to keep it fresh for the passage to Africa. On the beach, Belisarius met with his officers, each of whom seemed to have a different opinion about how best to approach the landing in Africa. Dismissing them after an hour's fruitless discussion, Belisarius and Armenian John walked among the soldiers bivouaced on the beach, conversing with them and hearing their numerous complaints.

"Hail, Magister!" the men from his household guard greeted him.

"Thank God Almighty we are on land," Uliaris groaned. He sat lazily in the sand with a wineskin beside him. "Another day on that pitching tub and I may have gone mad."

"An improvement on your normal state of mind, I'd say," Athenodorus quipped and those around laughed in agreement.

"I have not seen Dorotheus on the beach. Has he rallied from his sickness?" Belisarius asked.

"No, Magister," Unigastus declared with a sigh. "When he did not disembark from his ship, I went aboard to see him. He looks awful. No color in his cheeks. And he keeps no food down at all."

"This is bad," Belisarius replied gloomily. "We can't afford to lose him."

"Pray that he'll yet rally," John advised. "It's all we can do now."

"Dorotheus will be fine!" Uliaris blurted out with a tactless laugh. "But let us discuss another subject which has troubled many of us greatly, Magister."

"And what is that?" Belisarius replied, scanning the faces of the twenty or so men seated around him. Sitting either in the sand, or on large pieces of driftwood, they looked back at the general, their eyes heavy with dread.

"We heard some of the officers discussing the possibility of a sea fight," Athenodorus said. "As you know, none of us has any experience in such a battle, and I myself am loath to learn."

"Aye, aye," the others chanted in support.

"It is said, on the other hand, that the Vandals are masters of battle at sea," Unigastus picked up the thought. "Therefore, they will attempt to take us ship-to-ship before we can make landfall."

All were silent in terrible fear, as if even the mention of such an eventuality made it inevitable.

"You can not make us fight the Vandals at sea, O Magister," Uliaris announced, his voice more of a plea than a demand. "For my part, it will be impossible for me to fight against two dread enemies at once—the Vandals on one side, and that horrible swelling sea on the other. I should just as likely give up the fight altogether and seek flight as best I can."

The rest nodded in silence, glad that Uliaris had seen fit to shame himself in their stead.

Unigastus stood up. "We promise, however, that if you manage to get us to land where we can line up against the Vandals in the usual way, we will show ourselves to be the bravest of men."

At their words, Belisarius found himself troubled, though he showed no trace of it on the outside. "I dread a sea fight no less than you do," he replied. "For that reason, we will attempt to skirt the Vandal fleet as well as we can. We'll have to put our faith in Calonymous and his sailors to see us through."

At the name, the men groaned. "Then we are as good as dead already," Principius groused.

Belisarius raised his hand impatiently. "Have trust. And do better than that—pray. Ask the Theotokos to pray for you. I am confident that by her intercession, we shall sail through the Vandal waters and make landfall in Africa without coming to harm."

The men seemed cowed by his admonition, but their anxious faces remained. Belisarius bid them farewell and turned away with John to return to his ship. He felt a profound sense of worry stealing into his heart and knew that if he stayed among them any longer, he would not be able to hide it from them.

"What do we do?" John asked in a whisper.

"I don't know," Belisarius replied. "I feel like we're blind. Like we have no idea who are enemies truly are, how strong they are, or even where they are. So many things can still go disastrously wrong."

"So if we're blind, perhaps it would be wise to find a cane," John advised.

"What do you recommend? A scouting mission?"

"Yes, but it would have to be very carefully done lest we give away our own position to the enemy."

"A spy then," Belisarius concluded, stroking his bearded chin. "Someone who is not a soldier, with an unobtrusive look about him." His eyes wandered to a skiff coming to land in which were Photius, Theodosius, Procopius, and the slave Eugenius. "I have just the man."

✠

Ill at ease and alone, Procopius poked around the bustling forum of Syracuse, the great ancient metropolis of Sicily. Though several pegs down from its former glory during the days of Archimedes, the city yet flourished under Gothic rule, largely retaining its Greek character. For that, at least, Procopius was glad. He was able to modulate his own lilt in that language with ease, so as not to call undue attention to himself. Had he needed to speak Latin, his heavy eastern accent would have given him away in a trice.

He meandered through the potters' quarter, the crowded meat market, and the foul-smelling dyers' stalls, completely at a loss for what to do. *I'm an historian, not a spy,* he muttered to himself in frustration. *This sort of research is completely alien to me and most unpleasant.* Then, a thought occurred to him.

He approached a man at random who appeared to be a Greek about his own age. "Hail, good sir. Could you direct me to the quarter of the book sellers?"

The man turned about with good nature. He was large of frame with a great black beard and a jolly twinkle in his eye. "New in Syracuse, eh? If it's the book merchants you seek, I'll wager you're a scholar."

"Indeed, I'm a writer of histories," Procopius said.

"Histories!" the man cried, louder than Procopius might have wished. "Well, come then, I'll take you to the book stalls at once. You'll find much of worth there. This city of Syracuse is truly awash in history." The man took Procopius by the hand and led him forward.

"You are from the east, yes?" Procopius said, finding something very familiar about the man's speech patterns.

"Indeed I am," the fellow replied. "Though Syracuse has been my home for many years, I was raised in the beautiful city of Caesarea in Palestine."

Procopius stopped in his tracks bringing the man to an immediate halt as well. "You are from Caesarea? I am from Caesarea!"

The man's eyes widened. "You?"

Procopius caught his breath. "You are Sergius! Your father is Simeon the merchant! It has been twenty years since I last saw you!"

A smile of recognition dawned on the man's face as Procopius dropped into his colloquial dialect. "Procopius! The beardless boy who went to Berytus to become a rhetor?" he gasped in wonder. "You are still beardless, I see."

Procopius stroked his pointed chin modestly.

The man immediately embraced him like a long lost brother. "Forget the booksellers—they will be right where they are tomorrow. You must come to my house at once!"

Offering no resistance at all, Procopius followed and within half-an-hour, found himself seated on a balcony in a beautifully appointed villa overlooking the harbor. Choice wine pressed from grapes grown in Ætna's rich volcanic soil filled his cup and a variety of delicacies, from cooked squid to sliced pears, were placed within easy reach of his fingers.

"Though my family has made a fortune in shipping, it has always been a tricky business," Sergius sighed, seating himself on a couch across from his guest. "And with the dynastic squabbles in Ravenna and Carthage, it has gotten even more difficult in recent years."

"Ah, Carthage," Procopius said wistfully, draining his cup. "A city with a long and storied history, to be sure. A fascinating history. Do you know much about Carthage? Do your ships call there with any frequency?"

"Yes, they do," Sergius said, a quizzical look on his face. His businessman's savvy detected immediately that Procopius was not telling the whole story. He then squinted and smiled broadly: "Who wants to know?"

"What do you mean?" Procopius replied coyly, arguing within his mind over how much information to divulge.

"Come now, old friend. A man like you, dressed in a fine linen tunic, does not appear in Syracuse alone without good reason. Surely you did not come all the way here just to write a history," his host said, snapping his fingers for a slave to refill Procopius's cup.

"In truth, I did not," he replied, dropping his voice and leaning in more closely. "I have spent the past decade in the service of a great man in Byzantium and I have come here on his business."

"Yes, now that's more like it," Sergius smiled, raising his eyebrows in interest. "What business is it you speak of?"

"Perhaps not the kind you are used to, my friend," Procopius nodded. "But there is certainly the opportunity to make a great sum of money in exchange for the right information."

"Now you truly are speaking my language," Sergius reclined, putting his hands behind his head. "What is it you want to know?"

Procopius waited until the slave left the balcony. "Carthage," he whispered. "Are the Vandals preparing for war?"

"Certainly," Sergius replied. "Everyone knows they have sent an expedition to Sardinia to crush the revolt there. But I have been here for the past six months, so I know only what I have heard. My steward Optatus just returned from there three days ago. He may know much."

Procopius nearly jumped out of his seat. "Three days? Sergius, by all that is holy, I would see this man immediately! Is he about?"

"He's in the house now," Sergius smiled again, his pecuniary sense aflame. "I shall have him called."

"No, let us go to him at once!"

And so they did. They found the man at a small open-air desk in the courtyard poring over inventory records and shipping manifests.

"Optatus, I would like you to meet Procopius, an old friend of mine from Caesarea," Sergius said by way of introduction. Optatus half-turned his bald head from his ledgers. He gave Procopius a harried, gap-toothed smirk and sighed the greeting of a man absorbed in his work.

"Procopius has come from the City of Constantine," Sergius continued before his underling could excuse himself. "He's in the service of a great man there. Say, you have yet to tell me the name of your master. Who is it that you work for?"

In his excitement, Procopius saw no reason to withhold the information any longer. "I serve the general, Belisarius."

At the name, both jaws dropped. "Belisarius?" they said in unison.

"The hero of Daras," Optatus stuttered.

"The one who crushed the rebellion in Constantinople," Sergius added.

Procopius nodded.

"What do you want of me?" Optatus asked, his ledgers now forgotten.

"You have returned from Carthage lately. Are the Vandals there on a war footing? Is their fleet deployed across the strait?"

"War footing? What on earth for?" Optatus responded. "Carthage is relaxed and lazy. Far from preparing for war, they are dozing at peace. And there were less Vandals to be seen in the city than usual because many of them had sailed off some time ago on an expedition against Godas in Sardinia and have not yet returned."

"And their fleet?" Procopius pressed anxiously.

"It is said that the bulk of it is in Sardinian waters. I saw only a few ships in the harbors at Carthage, but none on patrol on the sea between there and here, if that's what you mean."

"Yes, that's precisely what I mean!" Procopius said excitedly, grabbing the man's arm. "So if a man were to sail today from Sicily to Africa, would you say that he would not meet a single Vandal ship on the voyage?"

"It is unlikely he would," Optatus declared.

Procopius began pulling roughly on Optatus's muscled arm, barely moving it. "You must come with me at once to Arethousa where my boat is anchored. There are sailors aboard who would ask you more detailed questions. "Will you come?"

Optatus looked up to Sergius who gave a rapid nod of assent.

Urged along by Procopius, the three were at the quay within a few minutes. Having never let go of Optatus's hand, Procopius led him immediately aboard ship while Sergius remained dock-side wondering how he had fallen into this bizarre happenstance. While waiting, he struck up conversation with a dock hand known to him and, strangely enough, the two quickly fell to debating theology.

Distracted, Sergius did not immediately discern that Procopius's small ship had weighed anchor and raised sail.

"Procopius!" he cried when he noticed the vessel was under way. "Where are you going? What have you done with my man, Optatus?"

Procopius immediately appeared on deck. "Sergius, my friend, I beg you, do not be angry with me. I must bring your man to meet Belisarius in person."

"What?" Sergius shouted, running along the dock to keep up. "You can't just take a man's steward away like this!"

"I will bring him back," Procopius called. Optatus had now appeared beside him on the deck, his face all smiles. "A steward's job is to increase his master's fortune. When Optatus returns, he will have done that beyond your wildest reckoning. That I promise you!"

At Caucana, Belisarius had disembarked the men and horses on the beach to exercise them while waiting for Procopius to return. But in the command tent, all faces were somber and etched with worry. Stretched out on a low cot, Dorotheus was dying.

"Are you still with us?" Belisarius whispered. He had sat beside his friend for several hours, praying that he would rally, as Dorotheus drifted in and out of consciousness. But the sick man had not spoken for a long time and his breathing had become ragged and markedly more shallow. All knew the end was near.

The parched lips moved: "Water."

The camp physician, Aristo, dribbled a few drops into Dorotheus's mouth. The sick man immediately began to cough and choke weakly.

An Armenian priest stood nearby and whispered some rhythmic prayers.

Dorotheus opened his bleary eyes. "I am sorry," he croaked. "Sorry to die here so uselessly."

"You are going to live," Belisarius insisted.

Dorotheus smiled sadly. "I should like to have died in Africa with you...a hero." He grimaced in pain, overcome by his travails. "But it is not to be."

Tears began forming in the corners of Belisarius's eyes. "Don't leave us," he whispered. "I still need you here. How am I to conduct the campaign without you? Who will lead the Armenian troops? See how selfish I am? I command you to live so that you may do your duty."

Dorotheus coughed again, bringing up blood in his spittle. Aristo quickly wiped it from his lips. "A greater Master now commands me, Belisarius," he whispered. "And I dare not resist His orders." He gasped for breath and struggled to continue: "Knowing that I serve such an awesome Lord...I fear death no longer but embrace it."

Behind Belisarius, Uliaris was weeping without restraint. "It's my fault," he blubbered. "I convinced you to come with us." Uliaris dropped to his knees at Dorotheus's bedside. "Forgive me, I beg you."

"No fault of yours," the dying man mumbled haltingly. "God willed that I come, and that I die here." Then he turned his sunken black eyes back toward Belisarius. His bearded face, always so strong and vigorous, now looked wan and skull-like. "Go and conquer," he gasped. "I swear I will be your advocate in heaven...Magister...if Christ judges me worthy."

Belisarius buried his face in his hands, praying harder than before. *O Christ, can You not suffer this stalwart soul to remain with us a little longer?* His tears flowed freely down his cheeks.

"Your advocate...in heaven," Dorotheus rasped as his breath failed him.

As soon as the skiff scraped the sand, Procopius jumped out and splashed into the surf. Still holding on tightly to the hand of Optatus, he set off along the beach at a run and made immediately for the command tent. But the officers and men he discovered there were clothed in black and obviously in deep mourning. Many shed tears openly.

"What has happened?" Procopius wheezed, collaring the first person he recognized.

"Dorotheus has died," Unigastus replied, his face troubled. "They just finished the Divine Liturgy for the repose of his soul. Very sad. A great loss for us."

"The poor man," Procopius commiserated. "Killed by the bad bread after all."

"Cappadocian John murdered him as sure as if he'd driven a knife into his very back," Solomon added, having just arrived on the spot. "But you are back sooner than we reckoned. Have you brought news from Syracuse?"

"Here is your news!" Procopius shouted, dragging Optatus forward. "Take this man to see Belisarius at once."

Trusting Procopius without question, Solomon didn't waste an instant. The three men burst into the tent where Belisarius, Armenian John, and Antonina sat in silence. A single flickering lamp lit the dark interior.

At their appearance, Belisarius leapt to his feet. "Who disturbs us?" he shouted, vexed by the unannounced entrance.

"Forgive me, Magister," Solomon replied, clasping his arm. "Procopius has returned."

Belisarius's mood turned immediately. "What news of the Vandals?" he demanded, moving toward Procopius, ardor for his mission infusing his face with purpose.

"This man I have brought can tell you all you need to know, O Magister, for he was in Carthage but four days ago."

All present gasped in amazement. Belisarius began questioning Optatus and within half-an-hour, his black grief had turned to jubilation. As the other commanders heard the tale told by Optatus, they couldn't believe their luck.

"Fortune smiles upon us again, Magister!" chortled Pharas, the Herulian prince, slapping Belisarius on the back.

"Hardly fortune," Belisarius laughed. "I'll wager that Dorotheus is already pleading our case before the Throne of the Most High."

"So then we sail in the morning?" Calonymous asked.

"No. Sound the trumpets this very moment," Belasarius shouted, above the jumble of voices. "We sail for Africa now!"

XIV

AD 533, Summer
Seventh year of the reign of Justinian, Emperor of the Romans
In Vandalic North Africa

The great fleet embarked from Sicily and touched at the island of Melita where St. Paul had once been shipwrecked on the way to martyrdom in Rome. They tarried there only a day for the next morning, a strong east wind began to blow. It filled their sails and pushed the five hundred ships to within sight of Africa at a desert promontory named Caput Vada.

There, Belisarius called the fleet to halt and convoked a council of his generals aboard the flagship to discuss how best to exploit the unprepared state of the enemy. He allowed each man to speak in turn and their various opinions were made manifest. It soon became a debate between those who thought it best to disembark immediately, and those who called for the fleet to sail straight for Carthage and take the key city of Africa by storm before the Vandals could mount a defense.

Seeking the safety of his ships, the fleet prefect Calonymous was the main advocate of the latter course and though his argument at first formed the minority opinion, he depended on his eloquent friend, Archelaus, the fleet purser and the quartermaster of the army, to sway the others to his view. Archelaus rose and addressed them:

"Ill considered, in my view, is the suggestion that we disembark in this desolate region. For those of you who rushed to take this position, let me ask you: where do you propose to harbor the ships? What walled city will shelter you from the enemy? Are you insensible to the fact that not a single city in all of Africa, save Carthage itself, possesses a protecting wall thanks to that ancient decision of Gaiseric to tear them all down?

"Beyond this, it seems to me that this place is bereft of all needful things—most particularly water and food. It would be a mockery of my office were I not to point this out. For an officer who is in charge of supplying provisions to the army, when he is deprived of his means of doing so, may well be considered no more than a private citizen. And such would I become if we landed in this spot.

"Worse, let us imagine that once we have disembarked, a sudden storm blew in from the sea. One of two things would befall the ships—either they would be forced to scatter before the winds, or they would be dashed to splinters upon the rocks."

Calonymous looked on with satisfaction as Archelaus's words elicited expressions of profound dread upon the faces of the other generals. Belisarius himself heard each point with deep reflection, though his face as yet betrayed nothing of his opinion.

Archelaus continued: "Let us not make this fatal mistake, my brother officers. Nay, instead, let us sail straight for Carthage—for there is a great harbor which will protect the ships from foul winds. And given that our enemy is completely ignorant of our onset, it is my opinion that we should take the city with no difficulty at all. With Carthage as a strong base of operations, the rest of Africa will fall to us with little effort. For military strategy always dictates the taking a country's chief point, and once that is done, the enemy's will to fight will soon collapse.

"I greatly admire the virtue of our commander, who bids us speak our mind even though he himself has a wealth of experience and the supreme power over us all. I am certain, though, that having heard all these arguments, he will make a decision which will ensure both the safety of the men and the preservation of the fleet."

His speech completed, Archelaus returned to his seat where Calonymous greeted him with a nod and a smile. Among the rest of the officers, a lively general debate ensued and it now seemed that Archelaus's forceful words had swayed a clear majority to his position.

"Peace, comrades, peace!" Solomon shouted above the din, pounding his fist on the table. "Our commander speaks!" Belisarius stood and all silenced their wagging tongues, anxious to hear what he would say.

"I speak last not so that my words may be that of final decision. Having now heard what each of you thinks, I should now join my voice to yours so that you may see if my opinion on this matter holds any merit.

"While we were yet upon Sicily where brave Dorotheus was taken from us, the soldiers were heard to exclaim openly that they feared a battle by sea above all things, and if the enemy brought such a fight to them, that they would not hesitate to flee. As a consequence, we begged God to show us the land of Libya without first encountering the Vandal fleet—and lo! just such a favor has been granted us. Would we not be accounted great fools to pray for such a divine boon, only to reject it once granted?"

Calonymous stifled a scowl at Belisarius's words as he glanced around at the assembled men and noticed many heads nodding in agreement.

"And if we were to sail straight on to Carthage, what do you suppose would happen if, horrible to consider, the Vandal fleet intercepted us? Who could blame the men for flight on such an occasion? Indeed, it would be we officers who would absorb the totality of the blame because we paid no heed to the clear warnings given to us well beforehand.

"As great a risk as this would be, there is yet another more dreadful one to consider should we chose to remain aboard ship and sail for Carthage. It is said that the greatest danger is posed by storms because our ships must either be scattered or destroyed if they have no safe harbor in which to shelter. Yet what would be the greater disaster? To have our ships alone smashed, or to lose everything—ships, men, and all?"

Speaking with smooth eloquence and marshalling his points with military precision, Belisarius knew that his words were changing minds. He now prepared to utterly crush the opposing viewpoint with his final hammer blows.

"Beyond this, we must consider time to be of the essence. At the moment, the enemy is unprepared and before us is an opportunity to land uncontested in his country. Were we to land, we would immediately gain the initiative in this war and be able to dictate the course of events as we see fit.

"However, should we delay and attempt to reach Carthage, it is not unlikely that the Vandals will be made aware of our onset, and even if they are unable to muster ships to oppose us, we will certainly find them better prepared when we finally do make landfall. And God forbid that we should find ourselves forced to fight even to disembark! How much, then, would we rue our decision to forego an easy landing when it was presented to us so fortuitously.

"It is my opinion, then, that we hasten to put our men, horses, provisions and equipment on land with no further delay. Once done, we will immediately dig a trench and throw up a palisade that will guard our supplies as well as any walled city. From that initial place of security, we can carry out the war and, if we show ourselves to be courageous in the face of the enemy, we shall have no trouble obtaining additional provision. For a defeated enemy can no longer protect his wealth but is forced to yield it to those favored by victory.

"Therefore, let us land here and now and take firm grasp of this brilliant boon that Almighty God bestowed upon us."

Before the final words had been spoken, the officers were already up and out of their seats.

"Well said!" several cried.

"He is right! Who can deny it?" another shouted.

"Let us make land at once. Today!"

Only Calonymous and Archelaus remained seated and silent, their lips pursed in frustration. But when the vote was taken to see which course of action was favored by those present, it was unanimous. Whether swayed by reason, sycophancy, or politics, the officers all supported Belisarius.

The die was now cast.

By the early evening, a Roman army 17,000 strong had landed safely in Africa.

After briefly surveying his surroundings, Belisarius selected a site for the army's walled encampment and then immediately set all hands to felling trees and digging trenches. Spurred on by fear of the enemy, the soldiers and sailors needed little encouragement to work. Thanks to the exuberance of their young commander and the wise counsel of the military engineers, they completed the palisade wall and surrounding ditch in a single day.

Belisarius, Armenian John, Uliaris, and a score of his bodyguards were lending a hand with pick and shovel under the blistering sun, when Archelaus and a handful of men approached on horseback coated with dust.

"We have scoured the vicinity, O Magister," the purser announced gloomily. "There is not a drop of fresh water to be had anywhere. I have sent more riders to scout further afield, but we will need to find something soon."

"How long will the water from the ships last?" Belisarius replied, throwing aside his pick and climbing out of the trench.

"A few days. Perhaps a week if we ration it carefully."

"Under this sun, rationing the water will cause distress to both man and beast," Belisarius worried. "You will have to find a convenient water supply, Archelaus. Solomon had commerce with some shepherds this morning. If you ask them, perhaps they can tell of secret wells in the area."

Just then, a commotion arose farther up the ditch. It was a joyous din, however, as exclamations of delight mingled with shouted prayers and alleluias. The gladness seemed to spread quickly among the men, many of whom threw down their tools and ran to the spot.

Belisarius soon spied two young men rushing toward them against the flow of the crowd. They were drenched in what he assumed was sweat.

"Photius! Theodosius!" he called to them.

"Magister! Father!" they greeted him, saluting. The each carried a skin bursting with water.

"A miracle has occurred!" Photius cried. "Cyril's men struck a great rock in the earth and when they broke it in pieces, a torrent of sweet water gushed forth. A natural spring!"

"Ha ha!" Armenian John laughed, rubbing his dirty hands together. "Did I not tell you the camp was advantageously sited?"

"God is great, indeed!" Belisarius shouted. "Come, let us command the stone-dressers to build a font so that all may drink freely."

Archelaus remained rooted to the spot for a moment as Belisarius and his men rushed to the new-found spring. In amazement, he turned to a tribune on his right, shaking his head. "Who has ever heard of a commander so fortunate?" *Truck with daemons is the only way I can imagine*, he thought silently to himself. *Perhaps that wicked wife of his...*

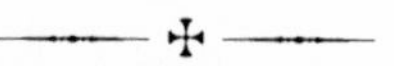

The camp soon became a hive of frenetic activity. In the center of it, the great command pavilion was soon raised. When fully erected, it was more a villa than a simple campaign tent, with spacious rooms serving both martial and domestic functions. At Antonina's insistence, the private quarters for the family and their servants were well-appointed and comfortable. Once the high poles had been set and the brocaded canvas hung, she began barking orders at soldiers and slaves as they hauled in her furniture. Every bit as disciplined, demanding, and competent as her husband, Antonina issued commands in such a way that most men were glad to do her bidding. It would be an untruth, however, to say that all men took kindly to her numerous impositions.

With her quarters readied, Antonina chased away all but her household and began organizing her various chests and linens with the help of her maid, Macedonia. A girl of fifteen and a slave since birth, Macedonia had been part of Belisarius's inheritance from Silvanus and had served Antonina for just over a year. Discreet, humble, and a hard worker, Antonina soon came to appreciate the girl's intelligence and sweet disposition. She was rumored to be of Burgundian heritage—the slave-trader who had originally sold her to Silvanus claimed she was of noble blood. But her brilliant blond hair and fine round face seemed to mark her as a native of Britain or one of the Germanic tribes of the far north.

"Mother, may I borrow Macedonia?" Photius asked, poking his head in through the curtain. "I need help hauling some baskets of clothing into our quarters."

"Get Eugenius to help you," Antonina sighed, her attention fixed on sorting the massive pile of papers on a writing desk before her.

"Rufinus sent him on an errand," Photius countered. "Please, just for a few moments?"

Antonina's eyes shifted to the girl who was busily sewing a gown. "Will Theodosius be there?" she asked suspiciously. "He has gotten a little too familiar with Macedonia of late."

The maid kept her gaze fixed on her work, but her cheeks reddened immediately.

"No, he's gone off with Eugenius as well," Photius said.

"Fine. Take her, then. But I want her back here within a quarter-hour. Is that understood?"

"Yes, my Lady," Macedonia bowed. She bustled through the curtain with a smile of thanks on her lips for Photius.

Left alone, Antonina began straightening her bedding. *It's not home, but I've slept in far worse places than this,* she muttered to herself as she arranged some silken cushions. She took a sheet from a wooden sea chest and unfurled it with a snap of her wrists to spread it out over the bed. As she did so, a small scroll dropped from it. A chill of fear ran up her spine as she picked it up and immediately recognized the seal of Theodora.

"How did this get here?" she said softly, her voice trembling. "How long has it been here?" She immediately broke the seal and read:

———✠———

The Augusta Theodora, consort of the most pious, victorious Emperor Justinian, to Antonina, wife of the Magister Militum Belisarius, Greetings.

Your previous report, collected at Methone, has been received and found unsatisfactory. The purpose of these reports is to provide me with information about your husband, his state of mind, and his dealings with the other officers in the army. On these subjects, you provided no useful information and instead went on at length about that worthless pig John of Cappadocia. I have not yet received the report you sent from Sicily. I very much hope, for your sake, that it is more complete.

Your next report will be collected on the fourth day after you land in Africa.

Antonina gasped. They had already been ashore two days, and with so much activity involved in preparing the camp, she had as yet written nothing. The letter continued:

Once in Africa, I have an urgent task that you must accomplish. Before the fleet departed, the emperor gave your husband a letter which is to be posted throughout the Vandal kingdom stating that the aim of the campaign is to put Hilderic, the deposed Vandal king, back on the throne in Carthage. By no means may this letter be posted. I command you to use whatever means seem necessary to prevent its publication. It is our will, conversely, that Hilderic never leave his prison cell. Indeed, if you can arrange it, the best outcome would be for him to be removed from among the living all together.

I cannot emphasize strongly enough how critical it is that you accomplish this task. The success of your husband's campaign may depend on it. Do not fail, for if this letter is allowed to circulate and Hilderic retakes his throne through the good offices of your husband, the consequences will be catastrophic for him and for you.

Destroy this message once you have read it. Divulge its contents to no one.

Antonina's hands were shaking as she crushed the scroll into a ball. She touched it to a flame and it quickly crumbled into glowing ashes.

She pushes my betrayal even farther, she thought, her throat tightening with dread. *Am I to suborn murder? What am I to do?*

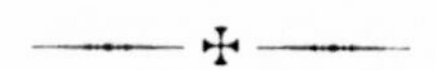

The next day started out with a brisk round of whippings. Two soldiers had been caught pilfering a nearby farmer's barn and Belisarius had each given forty lashes. He then assembled the entire army and berated them in a stern voice, deriding the folly of the two thieves, whose actions would inevitably make enemies of those naturally inclined to be friends. And worse, their theft was an offense against Almighty God, who loves and protects the poor and the just, but despises the thug and the oppressor. Such molestation and plunder of the innocent, he explained, if repeated by others, would certainly cause the miscarriage of the entire expedition.

After dismissing the men with this warning, he sent a delegation under Solomon to grant the offended farmer triple restitution for the goods that had been taken.

Once this unpleasant duty concluded, Belisarius got down to the serious business of assembling his cavalry for the push to Carthage. He was so employed when Boriades, one of his guardsmen, came thundering into the camp with twenty horsemen at his back.

"What news?" Belisarius shouted to him as he approached.

The swarthy Boriades leapt from his horse and saluted his commander. "We have captured the town of Syllectus as you commanded, O Magister. See, they have sent the keys to the city."

"Well done, Tribune."

"We have also captured the horses of the public post in the town and brought them here to the camp," Boriades continued, "and this man, who is a royal courier for the Vandal king himself."

A tall, thin Vandal was brought forward, his hands bound tightly behind his back.

"Release him at once!" Belisarius commanded. "It is not our policy to treat officers of the Vandal kingdom so harshly who have yet done us no harm. What is your name, fellow?"

"It is Gildo, my Lord," the man replied, rubbing his sore wrists. He was tall and fair, as were most of his nation, but his build was slight and fear showed plainly on his face.

"Know that you are welcome in our camp, Gildo. We have come not to conquer the Vandals but to overthrow the tyrant Gelimer. This usurper, who has imprisoned Hilderic, oppressed the people, and spoken arrogantly to the emperor, shall be cast down."

At these words, the Vandal's demeanor seemed to brighten. "Truly, my Lord?"

"Yes, you may count on it," Belisarius said, clapping the man on the shoulder. He then turned to Armenian John who was at his side. "Take this man and have him cleaned up. He dines with me tonight."

✠

Belisarius feasted Gildo sumptuously that evening and attempted to impress upon him the power and experience of the Roman army camped about him. Belisarius made it very plain that those Vandals and Roman Africans who assisted him in his campaign would be rewarded richly, while those who opposed him and supported the usurper Gelimer would be suffer all the disasters of war.

Now that he felt safe among the Romans, Gildo was free and easy with all that he knew. He revealed that Gelimer was idling in the luxuriant resort town of Hermione and had left Carthage in the care of his brother Ammatas. He admitted that the best Vandal troops had left with Tzazon for Sardinia some months ago and had not yet returned. He also reported in detail how the Vandal army was deployed throughout the country, though by this point, Belisarius had difficulty trusting the word of a man who could be turned to betrayal with such seeming ease.

Antonina was present at her husband's side, saying little, but taking in all that was said. In Gildo, her conniving mind soon saw a method to accomplish the will of the empress. And if she knew her husband as well as she thought she did, all the pieces would fall perfectly into place.

Much wine was consumed and as the repast drew to a close, Armenian John took Gildo aside. Antonina watched closely as John handed the man a sealed letter and a pouch of coins. Belisarius himself then spoke a few parting words into Gildo's ear and set the man at liberty for the evening.

Smiling broadly, Gildo wandered back to the officers couches to drink some more and to make wagers on dice with Belisarius's men.

Though her husband retired to his bed soon after this transaction was completed, Antonina remained behind with Macedonia beside her. "I have a delicate task for you, girl," Antonina said softly.

"Yes, my Lady?"

"You see that Vandal fellow? Gildo?"

"Yes, my Lady."

"Go and play the coquette with him," Antonina whispered, hiding her lips behind her upraised wine cup. "When he is good and interested, lead him around to the back of the pavilion near where the wood for the kitchen is heaped as if for a tryst."

Macedonia's eyes widened in horror. "My Lady, I...I can not. How can I?"

"You will do it because I order you to do it," Antonina growled, a dangerous edge to her voice.

Macedonia's lower lip began to quiver and her knees to tremble.

"Don't you dare cry," Antonina said sternly. "Do as I say and nothing will happen to you. Disobey, and you will be punished most severely."

Macedonia did as she was commanded, and it wasn't long before her abundant charms had the desired effect upon Gildo's lecherous appetites. He gazed upon her as a ravenous dog drools over a tender pullet. It took only the slightest suggestion from her to lead him away from his gambling and out into the night to a secluded spot behind the command tent. There, however, he was restrained by the emergence of two shadowy figures from behind the pile of firewood nearby, one much larger than the other.

"Unhand the girl, scoundrel," a woman's voice commanded, clear and menacing.

Gildo froze. "Who are you? I have done nothing. I swear!"

Antonina stepped into the dim light.

"You are Belisarius's wife," the Vandal gasped, dread entering his voice.

Macedonia struggled free of the man's grip and ran to Antonina's side.

"You may go," Antonina said.

The girl bowed low and ran off quickly into the night.

Antonina turned and fixed a deadly earnest gaze on Gildo: "As for you—my husband's steward gave you a letter this evening, did he not?"

"Yes. Yes, Lady, he did," the man whimpered. "I haven't lost it. I swear. I have it right here."

"Give it to me."

"Give...give it to you?"

"Now."

At the command, the other figure stepped into the light—it was the massive Eugenius. His hands were balled into club-like fists.

Gildo's fingers flew to his courier pouch. He whipped out the sealed parchment and presented it to Antonina.

A single glance was enough to tell Antonina what she needed to know. The seal on the document was that of Justinian himself. After looking at it, Antonina returned it to the trembling Vandal whose mouth now hung wide open in confusion.

"My husband, no doubt, told you to post this in the cities between here and Carthage."

"Yes, he did, precisely, Lady. And I am happy to do it, too."

"At least, that's what he told you to do in front of his officers."

The man's eyes shifted uncomfortably. "What do you mean?"

"What he actually wants you to do, is to take that letter straight to Gelimer himself."

"To Gelimer?"

"Yes, and to leave this very night."

"Tonight?"

"Even now," Antonina said, advancing closer.

"Now?"

By the saints, this man is thick, Antonina thought, smiling to herself.

"But..." Gildo hedged. "Why does he not tell me this himself?"

"He sends me on his behalf, fool," Antonina snarled. "Do you think my husband can be bothered to do everything himself? I am his agent as well as his spouse and my word carries as much weight as his. If you doubt this, seek him out and ask him yourself. But if he finds you still in camp on the morrow, you can believe me that your punishment will be every bit as severe as your reward tonight was generous."

"I...I..." the man stuttered.

"You have family in Syllectus, don't you?" Antonina continued, not waiting for him to answer.

"I...ah...yes I do."

"A wife, perhaps?"

The Vandal nodded. "And three small children," he added, hoping to evoke pity.

"Not much of a husband, are you?" Antonina mocked.

Gildo said nothing in reply, but cast his eyes to the ground.

"If you deliver that message to Gelimer within a week, nothing untoward will happen to your family. We will see to it that they are protected and rewarded. If, however, that letter is posted in any city or other public place, I will put your family on a slave ship to Alexandria myself. Do you understand me?"

The trembling Vandal gazed fearfully at Antonina and mustered his courage. "I will do your bidding," he declared.

"Then get on your horse and ride out this very moment," she commanded. "My servant will escort you."

Gildo made to say something more, but Antonina was deaf to him.

"Go now!" she hissed. "Heaven help your family if you fail."

Without further talk or delay, the Vandal bowed and departed, followed by Eugenius.

As the two men disappeared into the night, Antonina sighed softly with relief. *Now, I shall have something of note to put in my letter to Theodora,* she thought as she hurried back to her quarters.

✠

The next morning, the Roman army commenced the long march to Carthage in high spirits. They would travel along the coast, their left flank covered by the sea and the fleet which kept pace with them as well as it could. On the right flank at a distance of twenty stades, Belisarius positioned the warlike Huns who shouted and whooped in their eagerness for battle. In the vanguard at an equal distance from the main body of the army, he ordered Armenian John to take a tagma of picked cavalry and secure the advance.

Belisarius himself took up a position in the rear of the army with the four thousand brilliantly trained horsemen who made up his household guard. He expected Gelimer to follow them from Hermione and wanted to be absolutely certain that he had his best men around him when the Vandal king arrived to do battle.

Marching at a moderate pace, the army made nearly seventy stades each day. And the men engaged in neither drunkenness, brawling, nor plunder, thanks to the warnings and discipline of their commander. Indeed, so outstanding was the behavior of the soldiers, and so gentle did Belisarius himself appear, that the cities and towns of Africa happily provided the Roman army with markets and secure places to rest for the night.

At the town of Grasse, a mere 350 stades from Carthage, the army discovered the palatial estate of the Vandal kings, so beautiful and rich with fresh water, fruit trees and game, that every man stood gazing at it with awe.

After parlaying with several nervous-looking men in official robes, Belisarius turned back to his officers. "This estate is the property of Gelimer himself. Therefore, it is my opinion that we should relax our restrictions on the men for a day and let them encamp on the grounds and eat their fill. What say all of you?"

"Aye, it is well!" the officers responded with enthusiasm.

"But be sure they act with moderation, even here," Belisarius enjoined. "This property will soon enough devolve to the possession of Hilderic, its rightful owner, once we have deposed the tyrant."

XV

AD 533, Summer

Third year of the reign of Gelimer, King of the Vandals
At the Vandal royal palace in Hermione

Gelimer the king was shaking with rage. In his hand was crushed a bit of parchment. On the ground before him, a man lay face-down trembling.

"Get up!" Gelimer ordered.

The man complied. It was Gildo, the royal courier.

"How many did you say there were?"

"Ten thousand, O King," he replied. "Perhaps more."

"On my land? In my Africa?" Gelimer screamed, his cheeks crimson. "By all that is holy, I will make the Romans suffer for this folly! I will slaughter them until their blood runs in torrents!"

"To arms! Death to the Romans!" the hundred Vandal retainers in the courtyard cheered in response to their king's bellicose boasts.

"You will be rewarded for your loyalty to me," Gelimer fumed, addressing Gildo, but making sure his voice could be heard by everyone. "But all those who betray me, I will slay with my own hands." He took the letter which Gildo had delivered and tore it to shreds.

The assembled warriors bellowed with glee and raised their swords in the air. "To arms!" they cried again.

"You must act quickly, O King," Fuscias advised gravely. "With such a small force at their command, the Romans will depend on a general rising of your African subjects and they will try to take Carthage immediately as it is the only secure city. They will surely be on the road there by now."

"Yes, they will be," Gelimer mused, now strangely calm. He paced before his assembled men who looked upon him expectantly. "And from Syllectus, they'll reach Carthage in not less than three weeks. But they'll be moving slowly with a ponderous baggage train."

"We will overtake them!" his nephew Gibamundus added with enthusiasm. "Command us to ride!"

"Yes! To arms!" the men shouted.

"Oh, yes. We will catch them," Gelimer growled, his wrath building again. "Gibamundus, call out a general muster of every available sword-arm.

We gather here and march in three days."

"To arms!" the men thundered joyously. "A hundred years to King Gelimer! Death and slaughter to the Romans!" With that, the crowd broke up to assemble their gear and followers for the coming march.

"But first, Fuscias," Gelimer said, drawing close to his prime minister, "you will draft a letter to my brother, Ammatas."

"Yes, O King?"

"Tell him to slay at once that worthless old traitor Hilderic along with all his lackeys whom we have imprisoned," the Vandal king said with brutal relish. "And order him to collect every man who can wield a sword and see to the city's defense. The Romans can not be allowed to take Carthage."

"Immediately, O King."

"Furthermore," Gelimer continued, "tell Ammatas to have the royal treasure packed up and removed to Boula under heavy guard. Should the Romans somehow take Carthage, they shall not have my treasure as well."

"Yes, O King."

"And you, O bearer of ill news," Gelimer continued, pointing his smoldering gaze at Gildo. "You will tell us all that you know about this renegade army on our land. Then, you will carry my letter to Carthage yourself, riding day and night. Tell all that you meet that I, Gelimer the king, offer a gold solidus for the head of every Roman soldier that is brought to me."

The men remaining in the royal courtyard cheered again with delight upon hearing this pronouncement.

"I shall, O King," Gildo replied with a wicked smirk. "I leave at once!" In his mind, Gildo was already turning over ways to use his previous intimacy with the Romans to sneak into their camp and abscond with a bag of heads.

At Carthage

"O God, do Thou deliver me, for I am poor and bereft, and my heart is troubled within me."

In the dank darkness of a reeking dungeon, an old man intoned the words. He was covered with filth, wearing nothing to cover his nakedness but the ragged tatters of what had once been a fine garment. His face was mostly obscured by an unruly white beard, stained gray with dirt. What was visible of his face was little more than a hideous mask, for the man's eyes had been carved out of his head and only throbbing pustulous scars remained where his lamps used to be.

"I am taken away like the shadow when it falls: and I am cast off like a locust. My knees are weakened by the fast and my flesh melts like oil. For I am a reproach to them: they saw me and they wagged their heads."

A group of equally wretched men gathered around the old man who prayed on his knees toward the single tiny shaft of sunlight which glimmered far above them. Though he could not see it, he could sense its warmth and it comforted him.

"Help me, O Lord my God; save me according to Thy mercy. And let all know that it is by Thy hand and that Thou, O Lord, hast done it."

As if in answer to the prayer, a loud metallic creak echoed through the dungeon, as an ancient door far above them was opened. The tramp of a dozen boots could be heard descending into the darkness. After some moments, they stopped before the heavy oaken door of the old man's cell. The flickering of torches could be seen through the narrow grille—the baritone whispers of the men outside portended nothing good.

"Let's make this quick," one especially resonant voice said.

A key worked the lock and the door flew open violently with a bang.

The trembling prisoners stumbled to their feet, recoiling from the smoky torch light and the harsh red faces of the armored men illuminated by it.

"Hilderic, come forth," growled the leader of the armored men.

"Ammatas, my nephew, is it you?" the old man responded, groping forward toward the source of the familiar voice.

"The Romans have landed in Africa," Ammatas declared, ignoring the question. "They have come with an army and are on the march to Carthage even now."

"It cannot be! How is it that Gelimer allowed them to land?" the old man gasped, horrified. He leaned on the man next to him, Euagees, who was scarcely less frail than he.

"That is not your concern, you old ruin," Ammatas replied. "The Romans have come with your name on their lips. And for that reason, Gelimer the king has ordered you dead."

"No!" Euagees cried. "We did not summon them. We are their excuse, Ammatas. You must know that!"

"Nevertheless," the burly Vandal replied menacingly. He slid his sword smoothly from its sheath. The ten men behind him did likewise. "I will obey the king's command."

"Gelimer is a fool," Hilderic moaned, falling to his knees. "By killing us, you will divide and confuse our people at the moment they need to be united against the common threat."

Nevertheless..." Ammatas said again, stepping forward. There was a look of unthinking hatred in his eyes.

"For the love of Christ, we are your family! Your countrymen!" Euagees wailed, falling down prostrate before Ammatas.

Ammatas scowled. "Nevertheless." He nodded to the men on his right and they charged upon the helpless prisoners. Cries for mercy went unheeded as the ruthless Vandals ran them all through.

"Miserable traitors, die!" Ammatas declared. He raised his own weapon and dropped it heavily upon the neck of Euagees. It passed clean through sinew and bone and hit the stone floor beneath with a clang.

The last left alive was Hilderic who knelt rooted to the spot. "They will curse and Thou will bless. Let them who rise up against me be confounded, but thy servants rejoice."

"Be silent!" Ammatas screamed. He advanced on the old man and punched him full in the face with his mailed fist, shattering nose, cheekbones and teeth. The rightful king of the Vandals flew backwards and collapsed into a quivering heap. Ammatas, his nephew, rolled the bloodsoaked wreck onto his back.

"Now die!" he snarled as he rammed his sword's point through the old man's sternum.

"Let them be clothed with shame," the king gurgled his final words through his shattered mouth.

On the road to Carthage

Riding alone at the head of his column, the dux Martinus sat glumly in the saddle, suffering in the heat. He found some relief in a wet cloth he had draped over his head beneath his helmet, but this was more than offset by the incessant probing of gnats and flies around his face and eyes.

"Gahh! Get off!" he cried, swatting at a large horsefly that had landed on his nose.

"Enjoying yourself, Martinus?"

"What?" the dux turned suddenly to see the surly tribune Stotzas at his right hand. An old soldier, Stotzas had been a tribune for fifteen years, a misdeed in his past barring all consideration for advancement. His gruff manner and vulgar boasting nonetheless made him a favorite among a certain segment of the men.

"Oh, it's you," Martinus said, mildly embarrassed. "I thought you would be back with your men, riding with the baggage train."

"I have been for two days now," Stotzas grunted. "Camels stink to high heaven, do you know that? And conversation with porters and quartermasters bores me."

Martinus grimaced. The man had an annoying habit of speaking impertinently to his superiors. "So you sought me out for better conversation?"

"Well, O Dux, it was certainly not because you smell better than a camel."

Martinus shot Stotzas a menacing look, but the tribune was completely unmoved.

"The men are uneasy," Stotzas said. "Angry, even."

"You say so," Martinus replied. He turned in the saddle and glanced over the men marching behind him. "They're grim, alright. But they're solid, these fellows. Good soldiers. When you say they're angry, I think you're referring more to yourself."

"Not I, O Dux," Stotzas replied, shaking his head. "I just report to you what I've seen and heard. For your benefit, of course. The men...they chafe under the harsh rules set down for them."

"Yes, Belisarius has put the fear of God in them, I'll say that much for him."

"Fear of death is more like it," Stotzas grumbled. "Do you know the men at the rear are singing?"

"This surprises you? Soldiers often sing on the march."

"Sure, paeans to their own bravery or bawdy songs about good-time girls," Stotzas said. "But Belisarius's biscuit-eaters are singing..." he spat, "...religious hymns. And worse, he sings with them."

Martinus's sweaty face cracked into a jagged-toothed smile. "And that rankles a grizzled old pagan like you?"

Stotzas's face darkened. "No, it rankles me because of what it presages. His men know that they are marching to their deaths."

Martinus's smile evaporated. "I don't believe that's true. Belisarius is confident..."

"His confidence is a sham," Stotzas whispered. "In his heart, he knows this is a suicide mission. The Vandals know we're here. We are walking right into a trap."

Martinus remained silent, his eyes shifting. If he opened his mouth, he feared his own anxieties would spill out.

"Listen," Stotzas continued in a low voice. "I have already made arrangements with a local landowner for refuge. I would encourage you to do likewise, just in case our commander turns out to be a mere mortal on the field of battle."

"You dog! That's treason," Martinus hissed.

"It's not treason. It's a business transaction. You'll thank me for it later if it saves our hides."

Martinus looked Stotzas in the face, then looked nervously over his shoulder at his men.

"Don't worry about them. When the rout is on, they will have to fend for themselves," the old veteran said with a chuckle. "But by that time, most of them won't need for anything but a proper burial."

At Decimum, Ten Miles from Carthage

After another week on the march, the Roman army was forced to turn inland. As a result, they lost sight of the seacoast and the fleet, but before they separated, Belisarius issued a strict order to Calonymous not to approach Carthage with the fleet but to loiter along the coast until the city was safely in Roman hands.

Unbeknownst to Belisarius, however, the Vandal king's forces were now in motion and a plan was hatched to trap and annihilate the Romans in a narrow valley near a place called Decimum, the tenth mile marker from Carthage. Ammatas, the brother of Gelimer, was to ride forth from Carthage with five thousand men and block the Roman advance. At the same time, two thousand men under Gibamundus would hit the Romans on the left flank. Finally, the stymied and shaken Romans would be dealt the final crushing blow by Gelimer himself and his mighty host of twenty thousand mounted Vandal warriors. As conceived, the plan was a brilliant one which made excellent use of the Vandals' numerical superiority and their knowledge of the topography in the vicinity of their capital.

Still riding in the rear, Belisarius did not begin to appreciate the danger of the narrow passage at Decimum until the advance force under Armenian John was already passing through the valley. As his steed Balan mounted a low rise, the commander shaded his eyes and gazed over his army which marched in narrow files toward cliffs looming in the distance. A singular disturbing thought gripped him: *That is the perfect place for an ambush.*

"Principius!" he called out at once to his swift-riding tribune. "What think you of those hills which rise ahead on either side of the road?"

The guardsman likewise shielded his eyes from the oppressive brightness of the sun. "I think I would not like to be the first man through there," he replied.

"You won't be the first—John of Armenia and his men have already entered the defile. Take ten riders and tell John that the army will bivouac here for the rest of the day until we can better ascertain the disposition of the enemy forces. Tell him it is my wish that he fall back with his men and guard the entrance to the valley. The entire army will pass through together on the morrow, fully armed and prepared for battle.

"Once you have relayed this message to John, go and say the same thing to Aigan and the Huns out on the flank, ordering them to halt for the evening and be alert for the arrival of the enemy."

"I go at once, O Magister," Principius responded with a salute.

Belisarius watched him go, saying a silent prayer for the safety of John, his future brother-in-law.

"I can't wait to come to grips with these worthless Vandals," Uliaris bragged loudly at Belisarius's right hand. "They are reputed to be such fearsome warriors, but I don't believe a word of it. Two weeks now we've marched through their territory and they've not lifted a finger to stop us. The cowards." Uliaris spat on the ground in derision.

Belisarius looked at him sharply. "Just make sure to match your bravado with action once the Vandals are before you, old friend."

Uliaris seemed deflated by the rebuke and sat sullenly in the saddle as Belisarius rode forward to his cousin Rufinus, the bandifer, who was riding with the tribunes Athenodorus and Unigastus.

"Call the men to a halt," he commanded. "We camp here for the night. And distribute picks and shovels. We'll want a full palisade and ditch."

———✠———

Riding at the head of his small scouting column, Armenian John knew immediately how vulnerable he was in the narrow valley of Decimum. For that reason, he ordered his men to draw their bows and advance at a gallop and so they traversed the defile armed and with speed. When they emerged, John immediately spotted something that took his breath away—an armed contingent of Vandals about equal in strength to his own force.

What John did not discern was that this small squad was commanded by Ammatas himself who had ventured out of Carthage to scout the lay of the land ahead of his main army. He had commanded the rest of his troops to follow along behind him as soon as they could. Once they arrived, he would line them up in ranks at the mouth of the valley, dig a ditch, and thus act as an impassible obstacle to the Romans on their way to Carthage. As it was, the bulk of the Vandal army of Carthage now advanced haphazardly along the road toward Decimum with no great urgency in disordered bands of fifty or less.

As soon as Ammatas spied the Romans emerging from the valley, he moved his men to reconnoiter. Realizing that they formed a party no greater than his own, his heart became inflamed with the desire to spill their blood. "Vandals, behold! The invaders are at hand who would take all that is rightfully yours away from you!" he cried to his men. "Let us kill them all and make them regret their mad desire to challenge us!"

Wild with bloodlust, the Vandals gave a fearsome battlecry and followed their commander who charged ahead at full speed.

When John saw the enemy surging toward him, the imminent danger of battle awoke in him a strange and urgent desire to retreat. *Eudocia!* his heart screamed. *If I am killed here...*

But the instant this weakness arose, he crushed it. *Belisarius would not retreat from an equal fight,* his mind rejoined. *He would show courage and meet the enemy head-on, trusting in God's help.* Furthermore, John knew that he could not safely withdraw without causing his troops to panic and rout. For better or worse, battle was at hand and John decided to engage at once and try the enemy's strength. "Arrows!" he shouted, pulling his helm down securely on his head. "Behind me, to the flank, by fours! Eyes on the standard!"

John's superbly trained horse archers fell in behind him and all were soon galloping toward the Vandals, but at an oblique angle. Once the enemy was in range, John drew his bow and loosed. Every man behind him followed his lead.

The volley hit the Vandal line with devastating results, slaying twenty men outright and toppling another forty from their mounts. The carnage only served to further madden Ammatas, who pressed home his attack, wheeling his column about to smash into the center of the Roman line.

"Swords!" John cried. "Change front to the left!" His bandifer waved the signal and his men immediately complied.

Ammatas hit them in a frenzy, he himself spearing one of John's best fighters with his lance on the first rush. But to the Vandals' surprise, the Romans held their ground and fought back with equal vigor. Ammatas had expected the Romans to flee as soon as the first blows were struck and his anger grew white hot as he realized that the enemy were dropping many of his men to the ground.

"Will you let these worthless Greeklings stand forth against us, O Vandals?" the prince bellowed. "It would be a disgrace to our invincible heritage, for the wretched Romans have never defeated us in battle!"

His men cheered lustily, and with the added impetus, huge Ammatas slew another five Romans in rapid succession with his two-handed greatsword. "Come and taste death!" he screamed, his mount's heaving flanks now stained with the blood of his enemies. Two more Romans fought their way toward him, but before they could even aim a blow, Ammatas had slain them both.

"The men are wavering!" Boriades shouted breathlessly to John who was beside him at the end of the battle line. "Their commander cuts through us like an all-slaughtering Achilles. Behold, another three have fallen before him."

John could not respond immediately as he was engaged with a Vandal rider. With deft swordplay, he quickly unhorsed the man, and turned his attention to the center of the battle where Ammatas and his henchmen were killing all who dared challenge them. "You recall how Achilles was slain?" he asked.

Boriades nodded and both men drew their bows. With anxious energy, Boriades loosed his shaft first and though it flew with power, it clanged harmlessly off the barding of a Vandal horse.

John carefully selected a straight shaft with undamaged fletching. *O God,* he prayed as he notched it on the string, *if it be Your will, let this arrow fly true and seek out him most deserving of justice.* He pulled the bowstring back behind his ear and let fly. The dart hissed through the air and thudded home in Ammatas's chest, penetrating armor, flesh, and bone.

At first, the powerful Vandal chieftain was unaware he had been hit. He decapitated yet another Roman, though with the stroke, his right arm tingled and felt weak. His head began to spin and he became aware of a terrible burning pain in his chest.

"O Prince!" one of his henchmen groaned, his face white. "A dart..."

Ammatas couldn't respond. His sword now seemed too heavy to lift and he felt himself drifting, sagging, falling. The next thing he knew, his face was in the dust—after that, only darkness.

A tremendous cheer went up from the Romans and a simultaneous cry of dread shattered the Vandals. With their commander slain—the king's own brother—none of them thought about fighting a moment longer. All immediately disengaged and began to flee back toward Carthage.

"After them!" John cried, throwing caution to the wind. "Let none escape!"

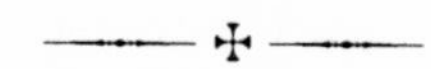

At the exact moment that Armenian John was rolling up the fleeing Vandals on the road to Carthage, the scout force of Huns protecting Belisarius's left flank detected the approach of the enemy army under Gibamundus. Though clearly outnumbered on the order of four-to-one, the Huns were in no mood to withdraw. The voyage to Africa had been tedious, painful, and completely lacking in reward to this point. For men reared in the saddle and nursed on blood, fire, and loot, this drawn out idleness was beyond bearing.

"How shall we attack, then, brothers," Aigan asked in his native tongue,

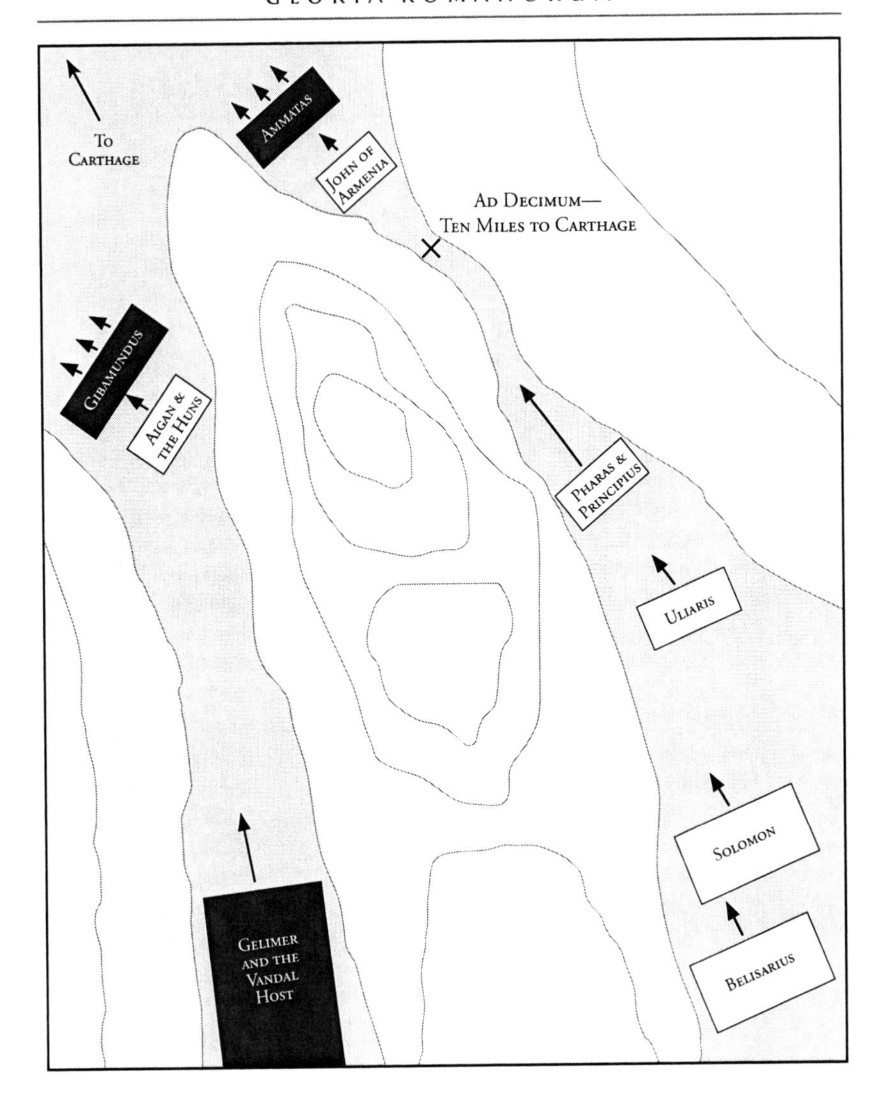

using his hands for effect "Skirmish first, or full charge?"

"Full charge," Balas opined forcefully, drawing his lance. "My hunger for battle is too great to endure this fast any longer."

"No, no!" barked Sinnion. "No battle may begin unless a member of my house strikes the first blow. I will ride out and face them alone."

"Aye," the others replied. "Well spoken."

"We will line up for battle behind you," Aigan declared. "Strike hard!"

Sinnion spurred his war pony forward and advanced toward the Vandals at a wild gallop uttering shrill war-cries as he plunged toward them. Holding a weighted iron dart over his head, he reined in a short distance from the Vandal line and shrieked out an unintelligible challenge in his own tongue. Dressed in blackened scale mail with black leather leggings, a smoke-gray steel cap, and a gruesome necklace of human bones, Sinnion was a grim specter of death on the battlefield.

"In the name of God, what is that?" Gibamundus asked Thrasamund, immediately to his right. "They can't be Romans, and I've never seen a Moor like that before."

"Huns," the man replied, twisting the end of his moustache. "Murderous, blood-thirsty creatures. Swift as demons on horseback. It was said in Constantinople that Justinian had them in his service. The old men say it was the Huns who enslaved and butchered our people when we lived in old Vandalia."

His voice was a little too loud. His ghastly words carried to those nearest and whispers of dread soon spread through the army.

His savage tirade completed, Sinnion trotted a few steps closer to the Vandal lines and cast his heavy dart at them with all his might. The missile impacted upon the shield of a Vandal horseman and dashed it to splinters, knocking the man from his horse. When no return volley was offered, Sinnion gave a haughty laugh and returned to his cheering comrades.

"These pigeons will scatter when our horses advance on them, you may be sure of that," Sinnion boasted.

Balas and Aigan smiled, their eyes glowing with battle lust.

"Let us pinion them, then, lest they escape from us," Balas growled, positioning his lance.

"Huns to the attack!" Aigan cried to the men behind them. "Full gallop! Now!"

The ranks of Huns responded with a raucous battle cry and the whole force spurred to charge, drawing their bows.

Gibamundus sat transfixed with fascination as he saw them coming. "We are more than thrice their number, yet they attack?" he mused, a quaver of fear in his voice.

"Your orders, my Lord? What are we to do?" Thrasamund asked, aware of the danger.

Gibamundus recovered from his awful reverie, his eyes snapping to focus as the first Hunnic arrows began falling among his men. "Prepare to repulse!" he cried. "Raise your shields! Counter-charge on my signal!"

The Vandal warriors braced themselves behind their shields and anxiously anticipated the order to attack. Screams of horse and man rang out as the deadly missiles found their mark, but the Vandals held fast, waiting for the signal from their commander.

"Shall we attack, my Lord?" Thrasamund asked urgently, staring at the black mass of Huns surging toward them. "My Lord?"

Gibamundus's mouth worked spastically, but no words came out. Dark blood trickled from his lips.

"My Lord!" Thrasamund screamed in horror as he noticed he fletching of a Hunnic arrow protruding from Gibamundus's neck. An instant later, the Vandal commander fell heavily from his horse.

A wail of despair went up from the Vandal host an instant before the Huns hit them at full speed.

There was no resistance. The Vandal line fractured at once under the furious attack and the entire force broke apart, each man fleeing as best he could. But if the Vandals thought that such ignominious flight across the Numidian plains could save them from the darts and javelins of the Huns, they were sorely mistaken. For the Huns enjoyed nothing more than annihilating a routed foe.

"This sport agrees with me!" Balas shouted, loosing another arrow. A hundred yards in front of him, a fleeing Vandal toppled from his horse.

"Aye, let us feast, my brothers!" Sinnion laughed, galloping along beside him. "Game is plentiful here in Africa!"

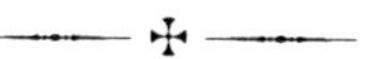

The Roman camp was already more than halfway erected by the time Principius and his scouts returned.

"Where is the magister? I must see him at once!" he bellowed, dismounting. Leaving his men behind, he picked his way through the throngs of filthy soldiers hard at work digging ditches and positioning pointed logs along the palisade wall.

"He is at the rear with his men!" Martinus cried, recognizing Principius.

"He makes us do all the work, while he takes his ease," a tribune complained. Several of the men around him grumbled their agreement.

"Be silent, Stotzas," Martinus rebuked him. "This man is one of the Magister's guards. If you're so soft that hard work disagrees with you, then lead Principius to the Magister's position, will you?"

Stotzas threw down his shovel with a clang. "I'll do it," he growled, brushing a little too close to Martinus as he walked by. "But you know better than to call me soft, O Dux."

Several of the men around him laughed as they continued working.

"Come, I will lead you to our exalted ruler," Stotzas said, drawing Principius after him. The two advanced at a rapid clip.

"You should not speak so of Belisarius," Principius said once they were out of Martinus's earshot. "The fight is about to begin and our magister remains in the rear because the Vandals are near and he wants to have his best men ready lest they surprise us from behind."

Stotzas shot him a wicked look, hot with hatred. Principius knew immediately that he had misspoken.

"His *best* men, eh?" Stotzas gave a bitter laugh.

"I meant those men he has trained himself and whom he knows best," Principius countered, "those he knows he can trust in a fight." But the conversation was beyond repair.

"There is your magister and his *best* men," Stotzas growled pointing toward a knot of officers who stood before the drawn up ranks of Belisarius's household guards. "Give him my regards." With that, the man turned and stalked back to the camp.

Belisarius was discussing the situation with Solomon and Uliaris when Principius arrived.

"What news of John?" Belisarius demanded, returning his tribune's salute.

"I did not find him at all, O Magister. But we found evidence of a fight. About twenty of ours dead along with some fifty of the enemy."

"Where?"

"As the pass opened onto the plain toward Carthage. The Vandals may have set up an ambush. I saw neither John nor Boriades among the dead, though, so it is likely they fought through it."

Anxious for John, Belisarius blanched for an instant. Whatever happened, he trusted John to act sensibly. If he did not withdraw toward the main body, there must have been a good reason for it. Perhaps the enemy had cut off his retreat. Perhaps he was leading them away to clear the road.

Belisarius set his face like flint. "It seems the battle has begun. Solomon, gather all the men together. Our moment is upon us."

XVI

AD 533, September 13
Ten miles from Carthage

Standing alone upon a craggy rock, Belisarius gazed out over his army arrayed before him in deep ranks, their colorful standards billowing in the hot wind that blew up from the desert far to the south. Directly in front of him stood the powerful men of his household guard, fully 4,000 strong and ready for combat.

They are formidable, he thought. The steely look of resolve etched upon their faces gave him comfort.

Beyond them stood the men of the regular imperial army, horse soldiers and footmen alike, with faces steadfast but betraying a hint of dread. On the right wing stood the federate allies—Pharas and his Heruls—who looked on stoically. On the left, the swarm of camp attendants, servants, porters, teamsters, and muleteers sat haphazardly in groups of five to ten, eager to hear what the commander had to say.

"Fellow soldiers!" he began. "Already, the moment of battle is at hand which will determine our fates and the fate of Africa. Our scouts have made contact with the enemy and he will soon be upon us. Now is the time when you must prove your strength and show yourselves to be brave men, for if we stand and fight, I have every confidence that we will prevail.

"But if we play the coward and falter, remember—our fleet is now a long way off. There is no fortified city we can flee to, no friend who will help us if we are put to rout. We will become hunted men in hostile land to be destroyed one-by-one by an enemy utterly lacking in mercy.

"God forbid! It is far better, then, for us to face our enemies together with courage and valor swelling in our hearts. And when we line up against the Vandals, we shall have every reason for confidence. For we trust that God will greatly aid us because we fight for a just cause. We fight to save the Africans from the bitter enslavement they have endured for nearly a century. We fight against a cruel and bloody tyrant; a usurper unloved by his subjects and countrymen alike. And as Romans, we fight for our emperor, to take back what was lost through the corruption and folly of those Romans who came before us. For unlike those who attempted to take Africa in days past and failed, we have acted in justice and displayed mercy to every African we have met. We have done right by God, and in our moment of conflict, you may engage the foe confident in the merciful good will of the Almighty One."

Here he paused, studying the faces of the men before him. Some he knew well. Others, he knew only by name. And a great many he had seen only in passing—around campfires or at the mess tent or during drills. Regardless, he loved them all for they were his comrades in arms who were to share the perils of deadly combat alongside him. *Dear God, how many will survive the coming fight?* he thought to himself. *Protect them all, O Lord!*

Not a man moved during this brief interlude.

He continued: "For those of you unable to draw confidence from the divine assistance of the Deity, know this: most of you have fought Persians and Scythians. Dangerous foes are these, who march to battle in full armor, bristling with weapons and singing songs of blood and murder. The Vandals, meanwhile, for all their fearsome reputation, have fought no one but helpless townsfolk and unclad Moors for nearly fifty years. Their idleness has made them weak and inefficient, while our continuous drills and practice have made us powerful out of all proportion to our numbers.

"And now that our camp is complete and fortified in the best possible way, we can set our minds at ease knowing that our possessions and provisions will be guarded as we venture forth to engage the enemy.

"So let every man call to mind his own valor and the prayers of those he has left behind him at home to embolden him as he embarks for glory. And let us march with contempt for our foes who will not stand against such a mighty host as march under the Roman standards this day!"

The front ranks began a cheer which rippled through the rest. The noise subsided, however, when the men noticed that their magister had dropped to his knees. At the sight, the soldiers slowly began to do the same.

Once there was silence, Belisarius cried out in a loud voice: "Witness O God, these just men who fight for a just cause! O Christ, our Savior, protect us! Holy Spirit, inspire us! Intercede for us, O most holy Theotokos!"

"Pray for us, O Mother of God!" some of the men mumbled in reply.

"Saint Michael, defend us!" Belisarius continued.

"Defend us, O Prince of the Heavenly Host!" thousands more voices responded.

"Saint George, be with us!"

"Fight beside us, Saint George, noble commander!" By this point, the entire army had joined in with a single resounding voice.

"Saints Cyprian and Augustine, holy men of Africa, protect us!"

"Bless and protect us, O Augustine and Cyprian!"

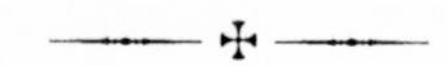

The Romans, continued to supplicate God and his saints for some time, oblivious to the two dusty figures who poked their heads above a rocky outcropping not far away. They were Vandal scouts, sent by Gelimer to locate the main Roman army—and they had succeeded.

"See how they pray!" one whispered.

"Prayer is the last refuge of the hopeless," his comrade laughed. "They are beaten already."

"Indeed, considering our king and his men are, by this time, on the highroad to Carthage."

"While these fools dig ditches and beg God for mercy."

The two men shared a knowing smile.

"Let us return to the king and let him know that the enemy awaits him, already on their knees."

Gelimer and his army were marching northwards on the double through rough hill country when his two scouts encountered him.

"Hail, O King!" they cried. "The news we bear will be like sweet music to your ears."

"Speak it, then, with haste!" Gelimer commanded.

"We have discovered the position of the Romans, O King. They have built a fort of fir trees on the main road, a short distance from Decimum, and they are no longer on the march."

"Then we are already ahead of them," Gelimer said, thinking out loud. "And they don't even know it." His face lit up with satisfaction and he clenched his fists, feeling the wild sensation of impending victory surge through him.

"We could ride on to Carthage and join hands with thy brother, Ammatas, O King," Fuscias suggested. "We could the defeat the Romans at our leisure as they surely do not have enough men to besiege the city."

"No!" Gelimer roared. "We shall leave Ammatas to his duty, which is to block the road from Decimum to Carthage. As for us, we shall take to the hills and ambush the Romans as they attempt to traverse the valley. If we ride down upon them from the high ground, there is no way they can resist us."

The retainers around Gelimer cheered their approval of his plan.

"Is it not strange to you, O King," Fuscias interjected, "that though we have gotten ahead of the Romans, we still have not encountered thy nephew, Gibamundus. For it was he and his men who were supposed to assume this road of attack upon the enemy."

"Strange. They should indeed be here by now," Gelimer said slowly, thinking. "Send out scouts at once to find them. Mayhap they have already encountered a contingent of the enemy and are giving chase."

"Aye, O King!"

"All the rest, follow me!" Gelimer cried. "To Victory! Death to our enemies!"

"Victory! Death to the Romans!" his men echoed.

At the Roman encampment, Belisarius stood facing Antonina, Photius, and Theodosius. Behind them lingered the large slave Eugenius, his square jaw jutting out, his eyes blinking nervously beneath his heavy brows. Next to him, Antonina's maid Macedonia clasped her hands tightly before her, her eyes wide with undisguised dread.

"I take my leave of you," Belisarius said, a melancholy tone entering his otherwise steady voice.

"You will be victorious, won't you, Father?" Photius asked, unembarrassed by the tears running down his face.

"Of course he will," Antonina scolded, a little too harshly. "God will protect him."

Belisarius sensed her anxiety and embraced her. "Even you doubt, O wife?" he whispered so that no one else could hear.

"No, I don't," she replied out loud, defiantly. "It's just my....damned womanhood." Though she resisted, her tears, too, were flowing freely down her stern cheeks.

"How could I have loved you, if not for your womanhood?" he smiled taking her hand.

"Go forth and conquer, most noble husband," she choked, pressing his calloused hand to her moistened cheeks.

"As God wills," Belisarius replied. "And you two," he barked, turning to Photius and Theodosius, "take care of your mother. Do you hear?"

"We will," they said in unison.

Belisarius leapt into the saddle of his waiting horse. "I go, Terentius," he said, calling to the commander of the gate guards. "Barricade the entrances to the camp and hold it. I am entrusting my cherished ones to you. Guard them well!"

"I shall, O Magister."

With final a salute to his family, Belisarius galloped off to join a large group of his officers discussing strategy with raised voices. All conversation ceased as soon as he arrived.

"What is your will, O Magister?" Solomon asked, saluting.

"The strength and disposition of our enemies is still unknown and we have not heard from our scouts. This is of great concern. Pharas, collect your Heruls and pass through the defile to the place where we know John met the enemy. Principius and his men will accompany you and show you the way."

"As you say it, O Magister," the Herulian price replied.

"Set out at once. If you find the enemy, you may skirmish with him if his numbers are not overwhelming, but send riders back immediately to inform us. Is that clear?"

"You may depend on us, O Magister," Principius declared. The two men offered hasty salutes and rode off.

"Where is Uliaris?"

"I am here, Magister."

"Take three tagmas and advance behind Pharas, but slowly. I want you to be in position to aid him should he be forced back by the enemy."

"Which ones, should I take, O Magister?"

"Are you not a dux?" Belisarius snapped angrily. "Make the decision yourself!"

"Aye, Magister," Uliaris replied glumly. *Oh, but for a drink to clear my head,* he thought to himself.

"Solomon, draw up the Imperial cavalry—all of them. Position them in ranks, but do not enter the defile until I give the order. When I do, you shall lead them."

"Aye, O Magister," Solomon said, his heart bursting with ardor for battle. Belisarius had now entrusted him with a major command and he was eager to acquit himself well.

"I will follow with my own biscuit-eaters. The infantry will remain behind to cover our rear and defend the camp. Is that clear to all?"

"Yes, O Magister," the remaining officers replied, though the commanders of the foot soldiers were noticeably unenthusiastic about the role they were expected to play. It seemed Belisarius intended to fight the battle with his cavalry alone.

The commands given, the entire Roman army sprang into action, nervous energy pulsing through every man.

Pharas kicked the battered head of the sun-scorched corpse. "Ammatas, you say?"

"That's him," a short but solidly built shepherd declared. "We saw the fight from that thicket right over there. After he fell, the rest gave up and fled back toward the city, with the whole force of Romans chasing after them."

"And you've seen nothing since then?" Pharas pressed?

"No, we've seen nothing," the shepherd confirmed. His compatriots stood behind him shaking their heads.

"My Lord! My Lord!" several Herul scouts galloped up screaming. "To the south! Come and see!"

Pharas followed them up a low incline. At the crest of the hill, he immediately spied a huge cloud of dust rising to the south not more than a few miles away. *Dust storm? Cattle stampede?* he thought to himself. But such speculation was immediately dashed.

"I see horsemen! And standards!"

"Not ours. It must be the enemy host," Pharas said in amazement. "They have gotten around us!"

"What do we do, my Lord?" one of Pharas's lieutenants asked in a panic.

"Fall back. Warn Principius. If we combine with him and gain the high-ground, perhaps we can hold them until Belisarius arrives."

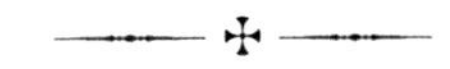

"I'm going, I said," Photius declared, rummaging around for his quiver in a pile of equipment.

"Where? The gates are locked," the maid Macedonia replied innocently.

Her blonde hair was bundled in a tight ponytail as she followed behind Photius, picking up the discarded bits of clothing he threw on the ground.

"The men like me. They will let me out."

"But why? Where will you go?" Her voice now sounded a clear note of distress.

"To join my father. I want to face danger with him."

"No! You mustn't! Your mother..."

"Won't know about it until it's too late to stop me," Photius interrupted sharply.

Macedonia's cheeks now reddened as tears began welling up in her eyes. At the sight, Photius immediately softened.

"Dear Macedonia, don't cry. I beg you." He approached as near as he dared, and put out his hand. The maid took it, her face reddening all the more. "I must do this," he declared. "I am ready."

Macedonia looked into his eyes and suddenly, the scrawny boy two years her junior seemed taller, stouter, nearly a man. A feeling unasked for and unknown suddenly burst into her heart.

"All I ask is that you wait a while before telling my mother," Photius said in a whisper. "Nothing more than that."

"How long?"

"A quarter-hour is all I will need. I have a horse and I know the man guarding the gate. By the time you tell her, I'll already be up with my father."

Macedonia nodded her assent. Her face then took on a quizzical look. "But once your father sees you, he will insist that you go back."

Photius smiled. "He will. But once I give my reason for coming, he'll let me stay with him. I'm sure of it."

She returned his smile and it took every ounce of her will to refrain from embracing him.

Photius gave Macedonia's hand a final squeeze. "Thank you. And don't worry about me. You'll see me again after the fight."

As she watched him go, a tear trickled down her cheek, but she brushed back the rest with a sniff, determined to show courage equal to that of Photius.

Unknown to her, skulking behind a curtain, the sullen Eugenius had heard and seen all. He smirked wickedly, knowing that such a courtly relationship between his mistress's son and a slave girl was a scandal—and knowledge of it could be useful for all sorts of mischief in the future.

✠

"We have sighted the enemy host!" Pharas cried. He maneuvered his horse to a position opposite Principius with his five-hundred Heruls in good order behind him.

"What? Where?" Principius replied, nonplussed.

"They have flanked us and are moving to get between us and the city."

Principius's face paled as he immediately grasped the danger. With the Vandal host between them and Carthage, any hope of taking the city by surprise was lost. Worse, even if defeated on the field of battle, the Vandals could retreat back toward Carthage and hold out indefinitely against a Roman force ill-prepared for a long siege. "We can't let them!" he stuttered, at a loss. "But how do we stop them?"

Pharas rubbed his tawny beard. "As I see things, we have but one option if we wish to keep the enemy from blocking us. Yon hillock is the greatest height for miles around. If we seize it, we will get the enemy's attention, and he may feel forced to drive us off."

Lacking any better idea, Principius nodded grimly. "Let's try," he said, slapping Pharas on the shoulder.

"Aye!" Pharas replied, eager for battle. Turning to his men, he cried out: "To the summit! Follow me!"

"*Nobiscum Deus!*" Principius and his Romans shouted.

Gelimer's scouts spotted the Roman move immediately and two thousand Vandal heavy horse were dispatched to counter it. The king watched with glee as his force and the Romans clashed on the barren hilltop and the Romans were pushed down the slope. Twice more, the Romans and Heruls massed to attack, but each time, they were repulsed with losses.

"You see!" Gelimer enthused. "These Romans can't fight. Look at them! Herded off the hilltop like sheep."

"What are your orders, O King?"

Gelimer smiled a great toothy grin beneath his beautifully wrought battle helmet which sported eagle's wings of gold on either side of an ornate crown. "Now, we crush them while they're in the valley," he growled, winding the strap beneath his thick-set chin. "Order the men forward."

The Vandal trumpets blasted out a triumphal note and the entire host began to move ahead. At their head, Gelimer rode proudly, surrounded by his stoutest champions, his heavy lance couched and ready for combat. Like a great swarm, they covered the hillock from which the Romans and Heruls had so recently been dislodged and peered down on the fleeing enemy with contempt.

"They barely withstood our first hit, O King!" a Vandal noble chortled with delight. "Fifty of the dogs killed, and only a handful of ours."

"Well done," Gelimer said offhandedly. But his mind was already on the next fight. His raptor-like eyes looked beyond the routing Romans to the line of battle he could just barely discern moving up the valley. *That's the main body blundering right towards us,* he wondered to himself. *Ha, ha! The fortune of Gaiseric yet smiles upon the Vandal nation!*

"Do we await them here, O King, and block their progress?" Fuscias asked.

"Are you insane, Fuscias?" Gelimer said. "We're going to attack them this instant and drive their vanguard right back into the main army. One charge, and this war is over!"

A great, throaty roar erupted from the Vandal host arrayed around their king.

But as the acclamations continued to ring out, a single rider tore up the hillside at a breakneck pace. He frantically reined his mount to a halt, then flung himself in the dirt before Gelimer. It was Gildo, the royal courier.

"You!" Gelimer cried, as if the man's appearance could only token some horrific catastrophe.

"Great King!" the messenger squawked. "Thy brother!"

"My brother? Which brother?"

"Prince Ammatas!"

"Ammatas?" Gelimer grunted, his eyes bulging slightly in alarm. "What of him?"

"Slain!" the man wailed. "He has been slain at Decimum! Taken by a Roman dart."

"Impossible!" Gelimer shouted, his teeth grinding together. "You lie, filthy dog!" In a rage, the king leapt from his horse, and drew his sword.

Afraid for his life, Gildo leapt to his feet. "Mercy!" he cried.

"Admit that you lied!" Gelimer shrieked, his face insane with wrath. "Admit it! Say my brother lives!"

Gildo's jaw worked wordlessly. "I....I...he is dead, my King...Mercy!"

"Graaah!" Gelimer screamed and with one brutal stroke, slashed the unfortunate man across the belly, spilling his entrails on the ground. "Bearer of ill news! Bear no more!" he cried and spat upon the bloody heap at his feet.

He then cast his sword and helm to the ground, tearing his blonde hair like a maniac. Around him, his men watched the spectacle with stunned looks of complete incomprehension. But word of Ammatas's death spread quickly through the ranks, and the murmur of concerned voices could be heard rising like foul vapors from an opened tomb.

Without warning, Gelimer strode forth with purpose and forced his way through the throng of warriors surrounding him. They dutifully made way for their distraught king, each hanging his head in sorrow as he passed. He was soon through them all and walking in the clear, alone, toward Decimum.

Fuscias and the other commanders of the army were immediately on his heels. "My King! O King, take care! The enemy awaits us."

"I must know, Fuscias," Gelimer replied without slowing his gait. "I must know if he's alive or dead."

"But the Romans!"

"They do not matter."

"But if thy brother is slain, and by a Roman shaft, what better aid can you give him than to wreak a terrible vengeance on them?"

"Think you he is slain?" Gelimer roared, turning upon Fuscias with the wide eyes and frothing lips of a lunatic. Just as suddenly, he wheeled about and continued on his path toward Decimum. "I must know!" he cried.

In shock, the entire Vandal army followed sullenly behind their stricken king, their banners drooping, their swords and lances dragging in the dust.

✠

Uliaris's scalp began to tingle with fear. Something dreadful had happened, that much was certain. The men heading toward him had obviously just seen combat—and gotten the worst of it.

Principius was the first to approach him as he sat slouching in the saddle before his force, 800 strong. "Make ready! They're coming!" he shouted, not even bothering to salute.

"Who is coming?" Uliaris replied.

"The Vandal host!"

"All of them?" Uliaris gasped. His flabby cheeks began to redden.

"We've got to check them here," Pharas joined in. "Or at least hold them for a while until Belisarius can be warned."

"If we don't, they'll drive us right into the main body," Principius gasped, wheeling about on his horse. "They charge with great power. Their horses are heavy and their lances long. We'll have to dismount and form a shield wall if we hope to stop them."

"A shield wall?" Uliaris gulped, trying to remain calm. "How many did you say there were?"

"For the love of God, man, a whole host! Thousands!" Principius shouted, his ire getting the better of him.

Uliaris immediately lost any will for battle and his hands began to tremble. The men nearest him sensed his fear like a stale odor.

Poor soldier that he was, Uliaris was equally poor when it came to choosing subordinates. One of his officers sidled up next to him and said in a low voice: "We can't check the enemy host here. We are too few. It would be suicidal to try. We need to fall back to Belisarius's position. Our only hope is to combine and fight on even terms."

"Aye, aye," two others agreed.

For Uliaris, that was enough. "Give the signal to fall back!" he cried in his bellowing voice. "Fall back! The enemy will be upon us if we don't!"

The stupidity of Uliaris's shouts stunned not only Principius and Pharas, but even those of his officers who had proffered the foolhardy advice.

"No!" Principius cried, grabbing Uliaris's horse by the bridle. "You great idiot! Send messengers back, but let us stand here! The ground is good and we have enough numbers to hold them for a long time."

"Yes! To retreat now would be a disgrace!" Pharas agreed.

"Fall back!" Uliaris continued to cry. He then gazed upon Principius and Pharas. "Mind your tongues! Do you forget my rank? It was no disgrace for you two to retreat in the face of the enemy, was it?" he blubbered. "I am doing no less than what you did."

Pharas and Principius were flabbergasted. Before their eyes, they watched as Uliaris's three tagmas dissolved into panic-stricken flight, galloping at top speed toward Solomon's meros.

"What are we to do now?" noble Pharas asked.

"We are too few to hold them alone," Principius said gravely. "We'll be swept away. We can only fall back as well and hope to do so in a more orderly fashion than Uliaris the Ox."

With that, Pharas, Principius, and their men also retreated back toward Belisarius. In their fear, no one had noticed that the enemy no longer pursued them.

Trotting forward at a steady pace at the head of his stalwart guardsmen, Belisarius had as yet heard nothing of the chaos ahead of him. In well-ordered ranks, they advanced up the valley, singing a paean to St. George, protector of soldiers. Belisarius himself prayed silently in the saddle, his eyes fixed on the hills ahead of him searching intently for any sign of ambush. To his surprise, an ambush of sorts came from the rear.

"Magister, look yonder," Unigastus warned, tapping Belisarius on the arm. He pointed to a single mounted Roman soldier who approached the army from behind on horseback. As he reached the ranks, the men began to cheer heartily, allowing him to pass through them without question.

Belisarius guessed the rider's identity at once. Turning about in irritation, he continued forward. "Have the rash young fool brought here to me at once, Rufinus."

"Aye, Magister," the bandifer replied.

Moments later, Photius was escorted to his father's side.

"Don't be angry, Father," Photius began.

"Rufinus, clap this disobedient chap in irons and send him back to the camp," Belisarius growled.

"No! Father, I did not disobey!"

Belisarius turned a withering gaze on the lad. "Then why are you here?"

"You never said I couldn't come. I want to share this danger with you!"

"I told you to defend your mother!"

"There are 3,000 footmen for that, father!"

Belisarius turned to face forward, his gaze smoldering. "Go back. Now. Count yourself fortunate if I do not have you whipped when this is over."

Photius grimaced and edged closer so that no one else could hear. "You fought at my age, father. You were younger than me, even."

Belisarius inclined his head slightly, his anger ebbing.

"And you had the privilege of being beside your father when he died—you told me as much."

Belisarius scratched his beard, saying nothing. *This whelp chews close to the bone,* he thought.

"Will you not give me the same chance?" Photius whispered, tears streaming from his eyes. "I understand the danger, father. I want to share it so that if you are stricken, I might be with you."

Keeping his face straight ahead, Belisarius nodded slightly. "Stay beside me, then," he growled. "If you lose sight of me in the fight, look for Rufinus and remain with the standard."

"Thank you, most noble father!" Photius beamed.

Belisarius was silent for several moments. "Your mother will not understand, you know," he said suddenly. "There will be hell to pay for you."

"It will be worth it," Photius muttered.

Sitting astride his armored white stallion with 3,000 imperial heavy cavalry at his back, Solomon counted himself the happiest man in the world. In his shrill yet even voice, he issued commands and they were obeyed immediately. He had specifically scuffed the shine off of his finely-wrought helm and armor so that his kit would better match the worn steel of the rest of the men. And match them he did. For he who was once scorned as a half-man, was now respected as a commander. Though he should face death in the coming fight, he would be happy nevertheless because he would die a man among men.

His first test was not long in coming.

"Riders ahead, O Strategos," the dux Barbatus said, pointing. "Do you see them?"

Solomon strained his weak eyes, shading them from the sun. "Ours or theirs?"

"Can't tell yet. But there are a lot of them, and coming in a hurry."

Solomon squinted. *Damn these eyes!*

"Your orders, Strategos?"

"Bring the men to a halt," Solomon declared. "Prepare to repulse attack. And send word immediately to Belisarius."

"Aye!" Barbatus replied and then rode off to relay the orders.

In minutes, the entire meros was braced for action, the archers in the rear ranks ready to launch a charge-breaking volley into the on-rushing attackers. Solomon sat beside the standard bearer, waiting anxiously to give the order to loose.

"Take care, they're Romans!" a voice rang out from somewhere in the front rank.

A murmur of dismay rippled through the men behind Solomon as more of them spotted the fleeing standard whipping above the disorganized mass rushing pell-mell toward them.

"Uliaris's men," Solomon muttered anxiously. "The enemy must be right on their heels." He looked behind him, then screamed to the standard bearer: "Divide ranks! Divide! Let them pass through!"

The order was relayed, and two dozen tribunes echoed it down the line. In a moment, several large gaps were opened in the ranks. With little time to spare, Uliaris's panicked men galloped through to safety, followed by Principius's tagma and the Heruls under Pharas in somewhat better order. Once they were through, Solomon ordered the lines re-formed and waited to catch sight of the enemy bearing down on him. But as the dust settled and the valley ahead of him became eerily quiet, it soon became obvious that Uliarius had fled from no one.

Belisarius caught sight of Uliaris's routed column charging toward the rear just as Barbatus had arrived to explain what was happening. Cutting off the man in mid-sentence, Belisarius spurred forward— followed by Athenodorus, Unigastus, and a dozen more of his guardsmen—into the empty space between Solomon's force and his own to confront the refugees.

"Halt!" he bellowed. "Halt!"

Despite their terror, Uliaris and his men recognized their commander and reined in.

"Magister," Uliaris gasped. "The Vandal host...thousands of them. Tens of thousands. Too many for us to resist."

"Turn your men around, you disgrace!" Belisarius rebuked him. "Where is this host? Turn around and show them to me!"

Still white with fear, Uliaris and his officers slowly turned their horses about and to their amazement, saw that the men of Solomon's meros remained in formation, ready for action but not engaged in any way.

"Where are they, cowards, who chase you?"

"But Magister," Uliaris stammered. "I saw them...well, Principius and Pharas...they saw them."

"And where are those two? Have they turned craven as well?" Belisarius scanned the field and caught sight of them, their forces drawn up in ranks behind Solomon's men.

"Stay here and reform your moira," Belisarius barked. "If they're not ready for battle by the time I return, I'll have you demoted to a common soldier. Is that understood?"

He did not wait for Uliaris to respond. He spurred Balan forward to meet Principius who was already riding toward him.

"What news?" he cried, in a tone more cordial than the one he had used with Uliaris.

"Forgive us, O Magister," he said, saluting. "We have engaged the enemy but were not able to withstand his charge. They may descend upon us at any time in full force. Alas, they have somehow gotten between us and Carthage!"

"What of John? And Aigan?" Belisarius demanded.

"Of John and his men, we saw nothing but their handiwork, O Magister," said Pharas who had just arrived. "He has slain Ammatas, brother of the Vandal king, and driven off his army which was blocking the pass."

"We saw nothing of Aigan," Principius added. "But based on where we left the enemy host, our Huns must have been overrun or turned traitor."

Belisarius's eyes widened in distress. He felt the massive weight of fortune pressing upon him and knew that the time for decisive action was now. The lives of thousands, the fate of a kingdom—and possibly an empire—rested on what he would do next.

Spurring Balan forward again, he rode on toward the front lines, his eyes alternately scanning the field for Solomon and for any sign of the enemy host.

"Magister, wait!" Principius cried forlornly, spurring forward to give chase along with Pharas. "What would you have us do?"

Belisarius did not turn to face them. "You have seen battle. Your men are no doubt weary. Merge them with those of Uliaris..."

"Magister, please," Principius interrupted. "I beg you—do not set us alongside those men, under his command..."

"It is true, we were beaten in the fight," Pharas added in support, "But you know that we are able warriors. Let us prove our bravery."

Belisarius now turned and gave both of them a hard look. "Let it be so, then. Take your men and position them on the right wing. Go!"

"Aye, Magister!" both men said simultaneously in reply. They saluted and rode off toward the front lines, their men following behind them in columns.

Solomon spotted Belisarius approaching him and rode out to meet him.

"Any sign of the enemy?" Belisarius asked.

"Nothing!" Solomon cried, half in amusement, half in disgust. "Uliaris fled from an army of ghosts."

"Truly, that news troubles me as greatly as if the Vandals were arrayed before us about to charge. It means they are on the road to Carthage right now and will reach there first unless we ride hard to catch them and then bring them to battle."

"Do you command it, then?" Solomon asked breathlessly.

"I do command it. Give the signal to move out. With speed, but hold formation!"

"Forward!" Solomon cried to the bandifer. "With speed! Hold formation!"

"I shall not return to the rear," Belisarius declared as the entire line lurched forward and picked up speed. "Athenodorus, go back and tell Rufinus to lead my biscuit-eaters forward. Be sure they keep pace."

"Aye, Magister!" the trusty tribune replied.

"And send that son of mine forward to me at once!"

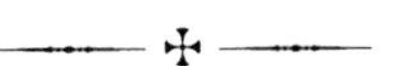

At Decimum, a somber scene unfolded. The bloody corpse of Ammatas lay spread-eagle on the ground. Sprawled atop it, the Vandal king Gelimer wept bitter tears without restraint. Around him, his chief henchmen and lieutenants gave vent to their sorrow as well, wailing aloud so that a terrible din of mourning filled the air. Beyond these, the rest of the Vandal host, some 20,000 men in all, stood bewildered and shocked, completely baffled by the tragic turn of events and uncertain as to what it betokened.

"O King!" Fuscias cried through his tears. Gelimer had lain in place sobbing for nearly half an hour and the counselor rightly feared that the initiative in battle was passing out of their hands. "Let us take thy brother back to Carthage where his body might receive the proper attention."

Some of the men nearby groaned their assent.

But Gelimer made no sound, nor did his attitude change a bit. Every few minutes his great frame convulsed with sobs and a terrible muffled wail escaped his lips.

"We can not remain here," an officer whispered in Fuscias's ear.

"I know it. But what would you have me do?" Fuscias growled.

At that moment, Fuscias sensed extreme danger. The very ground seemed to shake in anticipation of something truly dreadful approaching. He looked this way and that but could see nothing outside of the ring of tall, distraught Vandal warriors arrayed haphazardly around him.

Suddenly, the roll of distant thunder could be heard. But this thunder came not from the clear, cloudless sky—it seemed to emanate from below like an earthquake. Steadily it built until its source was unmistakable.

✠

"*Nobiscum Deus!*" Belisarius cried in a bellow as loud as he could muster.

His battle shout was immediately echoed by the on-rushing men behind him in rippling waves as they surged ahead, punctuated by regular blasts of cavalry trumpets.

Having emerged from the pass, Belisarius was amazed to see the Vandal host before him—not ready for battle, but spread haphazardly across the plain. He could barely believe his eyes when he saw them. They had neither advanced to attack him, nor made for Carthage—two courses of action that would have almost certainly resulted in the defeat of the Roman cause. Instead, they seemed lost and dazed as they milled about the plain in small groups.

Not stopping to wonder at what could have brought them to such an impasse, Belisarius instead sent his entire army careening headlong into them at a full charge.

"*Nobiscum Deus!*" they cried again as they crashed through the feeble last-instant resistance the Vandals attempted to muster.

Looking now with terror upon the very enemy they scorned not three hours before, the mighty Vandal host broke and ran, scattering in every direction. Huge warriors threw down their weapons and fled, each man seeking only his own safety. Those fortunate enough to have horses retained some hope of escape. But those on foot were mowed down by the advancing Romans as they trampled over each other in a panic to escape. Many simply surrendered or feigned death in hopes of surviving the disaster that had suddenly fallen upon them.

✠

"My Lord King! The Romans!" Fuscias cried. "They are upon us!"

Even now, however, Gelimer remained motionless upon the body of his brother.

Fuscias and several other officers looked at each other, their eyes filled with fear and purpose. In unison, they leapt off of their horses and advanced on the king. Two brawny warriors grabbed him under each arm and wrenched him to his feet.

Dazed, Gelimer stared at them. His cheeks were clawed and bleeding; his eyes were swollen, red and running with tears. He had torn out great fistfulls of his yellow hair, the rest of which lay matted to his bloody scalp.

"You dare touch me!" he squawked in a voice choked with wrath. He swung his mailed fist wildly at Fuscias but missed and tumbled to the ground again. Several more men lifted him, restraining him at the same time.

Fuscias approached him. "My King! Thy brother is dead. Dead! If you wish to avoid his fate, you must take horse and fly! Now!"

Fraught with grief, Gelimer whimpered a few unintelligible syllables, and then went limp. His men held him up, and then heaved him roughly into the saddle of his waiting stallion.

"Defend the king!" Fuscias ordered. "Make straight for Boula where we might find a place of safety to regroup! I will take the king's guard and hold the enemy here as long as possible. Fly, damn you!"

Surrounded by his hearty biscuit eaters, Belisarius and his men cheered their dazzling and incomprehensible victory in the waning light of the setting sun.

"Glory be to God, the most high!" they chanted, their swords and lances raised high above their heads. "Who but He could deliver such a victory into the hands of his servants? For He hath shown the might of his arm, and scattered the proud in the arrogance of their hearts."

As they cheered, they were joined by Armenian John and Boriades, looking haggard but exuberant. Catching sight of them, Belisarius leapt from his horse. John did likewise, and in their joy, the two men met and clasped right arms like brothers.

"Where have you been, reprobate?" Belisarius chided.

"Forgive me, O Magister," John replied, offering a salute. "I was off doing your bidding. My single tagma has destroyed the entire army of Carthage. You may see their remains scattered all the way along the road to the city. And now that you have routed the Vandal host, the city lies open to us!"

At the news, the men within earshot began to cheer afresh. "Praise be to God! All hail John, conqueror of the Vandals! All hail Belisarius, glory of the Romans!"

"Can it be true?" Belisarius wondered. "Barely three hours ago, I dared to think that you were dead and that our cause was practically lost."

"But there is more good news, O Magister!" Boriades said. "We have met up with some of Aigan's Huns—they have destroyed a force of Vandals as well. So that makes three victories in one day."

"A right and holy number, to be sure," John added, laughing.

"Aye!" the men around him concurred.

"But alas, Gelimer has slipped through our fingers. This war cannot end until he has surrendered and accepted the rightful rule of his uncle." With Photius holding his stirrup, Belisarius remounted. "Solomon!" he cried, "recall the men and set them in order. Send out messengers to bring up the infantry and the rest of the army. We march for Carthage in the morning!"

It took an entire day for the Roman army to assemble and march in good order to Carthage. Arriving there as dusk was settling, scouts announced that the gates were open—and that the citizens were urging them to enter the city at once. Wary of ambush in the dark alley-ways of a strange city, and the temptation of his own soldiers to loot in the obscurity of night, Belisarius decided to camp before the gates and await the morning to enter. Giddy with joy, the Carthaginians greeted their cautious liberators by lighting lamps and torches everywhere throughout the city, creating a brilliant illumination that nearly banished the darkness of night.

In the meantime, the fleet had rounded the headland and made anchor in safety at a place called Stagnum which was only a few miles from Carthage. Calonymus and Archaelaus soon received word of the stunning victory of Belisarius at Decimum and the sailors exploded in jubilation. Yet while they celebrated, the grasping Calonymus sailed with three ships under the cover of night into the harbor of Carthage itself and proceeded to plunder the warehouses of the rich merchants which lined the harborfront.

XVII

AD 533, SEPTEMBER 15
Seventh year of the reign of Justinian, Emperor of the Romans
At Carthage

First thing the next morning, Belisarius drew up his entire army in ranks and took his place at their head. Standing up on the back of his horse, with two men supporting his legs, he addressed his soldiers:

"You see before you fabled Carthage, a city which once battled our forefathers for supremacy of the world and came within a deuce of snuffing out the Roman race forever. Let us not forget, however, that most of the inhabitants of this city are Romans and were conquered through the nonfeasance of emperors and generals who failed utterly to protect them. As such, these people have suffered under the cruel yoke of barbarian rule for many decades.

"But now that the shifting waves of fortune have dashed the Vandals upon the rocks, the city has been left to our mercy. Let us be mindful, then, of the extraordinary blessings this campaign has enjoyed thus far, thanks in no small part to the mercy and kindness we have shown to the Libyans. If you wish such blessings to continue to flow, then it behooves all of you to shrink from doing them any harm whatsoever, either in their persons or their possessions. Should tales of such outrages reach my ears, be assured that I will look with anger and disdain upon the perpetrators and they will not be let off without severe punishment.

"I know for most of you, a reminder is more than sufficient," Belisarius said with good humor.

The men laughed, though some a bit nervously.

"Now, let us ride with our heads held high and in perfect order, as befits a triumphant army entering a great city. And be assured that if you maintain your dignity, a portion of the spoils will be yours!"

"*Gloria tibi, Domine!*" the men cried with one voice.

✠

The reception the Roman army received at the gates of Carthage exceeded even Belisarius's wildest hopes. The jubilant populace lined the walls and cheered, waving palm branches and throwing down garlands of flowers upon the soldiers as they passed by in their ranks. Once inside the city, the troops were met with a press of joyous faces, singing their praises and shouting fair blessings to them in the lovely lilting accented Latin of North Africa.

In particular, the people gasped in awe at the magnificent marital appearance of Belisarius and his retinue of bodyguards. Their sturdy chargers trotted spiritedly at the head of the army, snorting as the powerful men on their backs kept a firm grip on the reins. Belisarius led the procession, his black hair unkempt, his beard bristling. The staring throngs marveled at his muscled arms, piercing eyes, and easy grace in the saddle. But far from a cruel or distant conqueror, Belisarius acknowledged the acclamations of the people with nods of his head and the slightest of smiles, reserved mainly for the children and young boys who seemed to look upon him as some sort of god come down to earth.

The procession made its way through the cheering masses to the palace of the Vandal kings. There, Belisarius bade the army bivouac in the wide central forum. Surrounded by his principal officers and guardsmen, he briskly entered the palace without ceremony. Marching directly to the audience hall, Belisarius seated himself upon Gelimer's throne, to the astonishment of the servants and courtiers who were accustomed to wait upon the Vandal king.

"What is your pleasure, O General?" a court official asked, approaching Belisarius.

"Where is Hilderic, your king? I would have him freed at once. It is for this reason that I have come and defeated the usurper."

"Hilderic is dead," the official replied. "He was struck down in prison by his nephew Ammatas but days ago."

There was a low murmur of confused voices at the announcement. Then, a servant came forth with a box which was opened before Belisarius. Inside the box was the rotting, mutilated head of an old man.

"Here is what remains of our one-time king."

A hush settled over the room as Belisarius ordered the gruesome relic taken away. "Hilderic was the last legitimate king of the Vandals," he announced. "As he is dead, and the surviving members of his line are wicked usurpers, I declare his kingdom dissolved and ceded back to Justinian, the Emperor of the Romans."

A prolonged throaty cheer went up from the soldiers and the African Romans gathered in the hall. "Hail Justinian!" they cried. "Hail the mighty Augustus! May he reign for many and good years!"

When the acclamations subsided, Belisarius continued: "I have come here in the name of our most pious Augustus, Justinian, not as a conqueror, but as a liberator. And now that the arrogant Vandals have been humbled, our benevolent emperor wishes that the men of Africa be once more free citizens of the God-protected empire of the Romans. For it is only among the Romans, in the wide world, that justice and civilization exist, untrammeled by the rough and capricious boots of barbarian warlords."

"You say that, O General, but your words ring hollow!" a great voice bellowed. A tumult of additional voices joined in the chorus as an outraged knot of twenty men surged angrily toward the throne where they were checked by the guardsmen of Belisarius.

"Hold, fellow Romans!" Belisarius shouted above their furious din. "Hold! If you have complaints, I will hear them in reasonable voices!"

The aggrieved men settled themselves and their leader stepped forward—a bearded little man in costly attire which betrayed him at once as a wealthy merchant. "You claim that you come to bring justice to Africa, Belisarius? And yet during the night, pirates from your fleet ransacked my warehouse!"

"And mine! And mine!" shouted several of the other merchants.

"Took an entire shipment of choice wine!" one screamed, waving his fist.

"And my chest of coins!" another moaned.

"And my daughter!" yet another wailed, as the chaos of angry voices broke out afresh.

Belisarius was flummoxed. He looked to either side as if searching for information, but both Solomon on his left and John on his right were equally perplexed. *Calonymous!* Belisarius muttered through clenched teeth.

"Quiet, good men, let us have peace!" Solomon cried. But his reedy voice could not be heard over the din.

"Be silent, all of you!" John of Armenia bellowed finally, and with such authority that every wagging tongue gave pause and every head turned in his direction.

Belisarius seized the moment immediately. "If it is true that men under my command perpetrated this dastardly raid upon your warehouses, I promise you they will be punished for it. And I am in earnest when I say that we have come not to conquer and plunder our African brothers, for I have strictly forbidden my men to do any such thing. But if this injunction has been broken, I will see to it personally that you are compensated for all your losses. Now go, and in a short time, I will visit the harbor myself to inspect the damage."

At this, the aggrieved men nodded suspiciously and made their way out. "We shall see if his actions match his words," they grumbled to each other.

Belisarius spent the remainder of the day settling his army into Carthage. This proved to be a considerably easier task than he had anticipated. He had the men quartered in the very barracks where but days before Vandal warriors had resided. For lunch, they were cheerfully served the very food that was commonly distributed to the Vandals, and by the very same servants.

Those Vandals and Arian clergy who remained in Carthage took sanctuary in the churches. But Belisarius held no animus toward them. Offering pledges of safety, Belisarius gained their trust and though he had them imprisoned until the war could be concluded, he made sure they were well-fed and treated with dignity.

He toured the city's fortifications, and to his shock, discovered that they were in an advanced state of dilapidation. Wasting no time, he set work details in motion to make immediate repairs, and within a day the entire city was a hive of building activity.

As for the plundered warehouses, Belisarius soon discovered that Calonymous and his men had indeed been the perpetrators. He extracted from the prefect a public pledge that all the stolen merchandise would be returned. But the haughty Alexandrian had absolutely no intention of honoring his pledge and instead set about undermining Belisarius's authority among the other commanders whenever he could.

Scrubbing with a purpose, the maid Macedonia worked feverishly to tidy her mistress's quarters in the Vandal palace. Her tender cheek still stung from the blow that Antonina had dealt her, and a nasty red welt had swelled up under her right eye. To hide the mark, she had bundled a shawl over her head.

"Macedonia! There you are!" Photius cried as he bounded into the room. "I wanted to tell you that my mother made to punish me for sneaking off during the battle, but my father would not hear of it!"

"I'm glad of that, Photius, but I'm very busy," Macedonia rejoined. "Please leave me be for now."

"Aren't you glad to see me?" the boy asked, moving closer. "You haven't set eyes on me since I left, and now you're too busy?"

Macedonia remained hunched over on her hand and knees, her bare feet sticking out from under her long skirt. "Please, Photius. If I don't finish soon, there will be trouble."

In a single bound, Photius was in front of her. "Oh come now, you can spare a few minutes for your old friend..."

His words were cut off. Macedonia tried to hide her face in her soapy hands, but Photius saw.

"Macedonia! Who?"

"Please, just go!" the girl whimpered.

"My mother?"

Macedonia wept softly and gave no answer.

"She couldn't thrash me, so she thrashed you, instead." The realization hit Photius like a punch in the stomach. He slumped down on the marble floor next to the weeping girl. Grabbing her hands, he pulled them gently away from her face and saw the angry discolored mark on her cheek. His brows began to knit and tears soon welled up in his own eyes.

"My mistress said I should have taken better care to keep you from leaving," Macedonia whispered, sniffling. "That is why I was punished."

"Can you ever forgive me, dear Macedonia?" Photius said, his voice cracking awkwardly.

The girl smiled bravely, wiping her eyes. "For you, I would endure a thousand beatings."

Photius glanced toward the door, and seeing no one, he embraced her.

She dared not embrace him back.

"I promise you, Macedonia. There will come a day when I will repay you for this. When I am older, I will protect you."

AD 533, OCTOBER
At Boula, the Vandal Encampment

The Vandal king Gelimer stood arrayed in his armor before a large pile of heads. He paced back and forth, waving his heavy steel blade before him, as Boniface, his steward, doled out gold pieces to waiting henchmen.

"There, six," Boniface grunted. "Who's next?"

A crusty old Vandal warrior with a cunning look in his eye moved to the front. From his back, he unslung a heavy sack and dumped its contents on the ground. "Seventeen, unless I miss my count," he chortled.

Boniface poked each head with a stick and confirmed the tally.

"Just a moment!" Gelimer barked, approaching the scene. "The bounty is for the heads of Roman soldiers. Are you telling me that you managed to deprive seventeen Roman soldiers of their heads all by yourself?"

"O King," the man replied, comporting himself humbly. "My ways are wily. I did not engage these men in combat, but took them unaware, as they were foraging or hunting. But you may be sure, every last one of them is a Roman."

Gelimer fixed the man with a suspicious eye. "Romans perhaps, but soldiers? I somehow doubt it." He swung his sword briskly, and sliced through the air with purpose. "But no matter. Pay the man. If some of my citizens end up with their heads in the pile, it is their own fault for failing to resist the enemy forcefully enough."

"Indeed, Sire," Boniface agreed. "And though I am a Roman myself, I understand that this tactic will eventually force Belisarius to emerge from behind the walls of Carthage where he now sits in security."

"Yes, yes," the King enthused. "Just how did he manage to repair the walls so quickly? That's what I would like to know. It was a great failing of mine to let them fall into such disrepair. I own that. But no matter. Once he is again out in the open, we will have the opportunity to avenge our previous defeat where a single lucky blow turned the entire battle against us."

"Aye, aye!" the courtiers and warriors around him muttered in assent.

Once he had finished paying head bounties, Boniface approached his king, seeking a private audience. "My King," he began, "I have paid all your bounties this day and your pile of gold coin is barely diminished. We shall have no problem maintaining this war forever with the money at our disposal, so long as you have men to fight for you."

"We will not need to carry it on forever, for victory shall soon be ours!" Gelimer said aloud with an air of supreme confidence. He then turned and pulled Boniface aside, his eyes shifting rapidly like those of a madman. "Listen," he said quietly so no one else could hear, "if for some reason, fortune should not smile upon us in the coming fight, I want you to take all the coin we have and put it on board a ship at Hippo Regius. If you receive word that we have suffered another reverse, take the money and sail immediately for Spain. There, you will bestow it upon King Theudis of the Visigoths, so that he might receive us if we become fugitives."

"I understand, my Lord," Boniface replied gravely.

"I shall keep the royal treasure and a small quantity of coin with me," Gelimer continued. "For if I left it all with you, the nobles would grow suspicious." Gelimer frowned. "But I would prefer the bulk of our money go to Theudis, rather than fall into the filthy clutches of Justinian."

"I agree, my Lord," Boniface whispered. "I will do as you propose, and do it quietly so that no one is aware."

"Good," Gelimer muttered, patting the man on the arm. He then amplified his voice again, so that all those nearby could hear: "But have no worries, Boniface. The Romans are but clay soldiers whom we shall shatter!"

"My Lord King!" a rider shouted as he galloped into the waiting throng. He leapt from his mount and genuflected before Gelimer. "Word has arrived from the coast!"

"Tzazon?" Gelimer cried, sheathing his sword. "Give me word of my brother!"

"Tzazon has landed safely in Africa with all of his men, O King!" the courier announced. "They are already on the march and will join with you on the morrow. He charged me to say that he longs to see you and share in your grief—and to exact a bloody vengeance on these Roman pigs."

The fire that had been largely extinguished in Gelimer's eyes since the death of his brother Ammatas, now rekindled with a sudden new burst of flame.

"Yes, now that Tzazon has arrived, we shall have our vengeance! For he has returned with the flower of our armies and when combined with the white-hot hatred that the Vandal race shall forever bear toward those who seek to deprive us of our kingdom, there is no army on earth that could stand against us!"

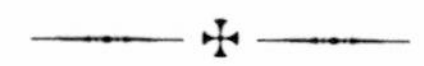

Tzazon, the conqueror of Sardinia, rode into the Vandal camp on a white horse, followed in good order by five-thousand stout warriors, all snarling with rage and ready to spill Roman blood. Stopping to greet no one, Tzazon went immediately to Gelimer's pavilion and, upon catching sight of his brother, leapt off his horse and embraced him. The two gave vent to their tears, wailing aloud but saying no word to each other.

Tzazon's Vandal warriors—gigantic rough men with hard eyes and stern faces—seeing their leaders in such a state, dissolved into pathetic lamentations. For by now, many realized that their wives and children remained in Carthage, held by the Romans. And witnessing the state of their king and his shabby encampment, they wondered aloud how such a disaster could have befallen their mighty nation.

After a long time, Tzazon released his brother and the two traded knowing looks of grim menace.

"You know what must be done, brother," Gelimer growled fiercely.

Tzazon grit his teeth with a gleam in his eye. "We must kill every last invader, tear them to pieces, and throw the bits into the sea from whence they came."

"Yes!" Gelimer hissed savagely. "We will cut down every last one of them. And when we have conquered them, we will send the right hand of Belisarius back to Justinian in a sack bearing a note that says, 'We come for you.'"

AD 533, NOVEMBER

At Carthage, in a dry cistern at the Vandal Palace

"Mother, I don't understand why you need me here with you," Theodosius whispered. Though his voice was low, it echoed nonetheless in the vaulted underground chamber made from massive cut stones. Two torches sputtered in a draft which circulated through some unseen crevice.

"Because I needed someone to come with me, Theodosius," Antonina replied. "And I trust you." She did not look at him as she said the words. "Whatever happens here, whatever you hear or see, you must keep it in the strictest confidence. Can you do that?"

"Yes, mother," he replied. Though only seventeen, Theodosius assumed the look of a mature and serious man. "You may trust me to remain silent. I will do anything to help you and Belisarius."

"You must trust me as well," Antonina said. "And know that whatever is said here, even if it sounds odd or suspicious, it is all for Belisarius's benefit."

"I will be silent," Theodosius replied.

"You may not even tell Belisarius—do you understand?"

The young man nodded gravely. "You may count on me, mother."

"Good," Antonina grimaced. Her eyes searched the darkness impatiently. Her contact was late.

Then, she heard footsteps. After a short space of time, a flickering light appeared in the distance and a large man holding an oil lamp before him materialized out of the darkness like a spirit.

"My Lady," he bowed, greeting Antonina in a menacing voice. "You know why I am here?"

His face was partially covered by his cloak and his huge frame was enough to make Antonina feel a tingle of fear. "I do. Here is my report." She handed the man a parcel tied with string.

The man took it, then seemed to notice Theodosius for the first time. "You were to come alone. Who is this?"

"You expect a woman to come to a place like this by herself?" Antonina shot back. "He is my adopted son."

The man looked from Theodosius to Antonina with suspicion in his eyes.

"I don't like it. The empress won't like it."

"I am confident she will understand," Antonina said bravely. "The boy is completely trustworthy."

"He had better be," the man growled. "Or he will lose his head."

"Have you not gotten what you came for?" Antonina snapped. "May we go now?" She was tiring of Theodora's games and now that Belisarius had won a great victory, she felt more confident in her position.

"Not yet. The empress wants to know about the Vandal treasure and when it will be shipped to Constantinople."

"We don't know, in truth," Antonina replied. "We have only discovered a small part of it. We think that it may have been put on board ship and spirited away before...."

"That is unsatisfactory," The man interrupted. "The empress is very concerned about the treasure and wants it secured and sent to Constantinople immediately. You will encourage your husband to do so at once. And you will discourage him in the strongest possible terms from distributing any of it to the soldiers. Is that clear?"

"But those men fought! How dare you...."

A loud creak was heard above them as a bronze grate swung open. Soon the voices and footfalls of men could be heard as they descended the iron rungs down to the bottom.

The cloaked man quickly retreated the way he came.

Antonina and Theodosius could only turn anxiously to face whatever was headed toward them.

"You see, it's dry. And enormous. I'll bet it extends all the way beyond the walls."

"Aye, it would be the perfect place for the enemy to enter the city secretly, assuming they know about it."

Antonina immediately recognized the voices of Uliaris and Belisarius. Her heart leapt into her throat.

It was too late to hide. The two men reached the bottom along with two soldiers bearing torches.

"Look, there is someone here!" Uliaris cried.

"Husband?" Antonina said aloud, seizing the initiative.

Belisarius was dumbfounded. "Antonina? And Theodosius? By heaven, what are you doing down here?"

"I only heard about this cistern this morning, husband, and I am here for two reasons," Antonina said with perfect composure. "I wanted to make sure that it is secure and that no enemy may take us unawares. And also, the thought occurred to me that the Vandals may have hoarded some of their treasure down here."

"But to come by yourself, with only Theodosius?" Belisarius chided, incredulous. "Are you mad?"

"I did not want to disturb you with a matter that could be a trifle until I saw it for myself," Antonina said brashly. "As you can see, there is no treasure here. But it will need to be walled up to properly secure the city."

Belisarius smiled. "An intrepid lady I have married, that much is certain. But not overcautious either."

"I never have been," Antonina sniffed.

"Well, then, your work here is done, wife. Return to the palace. No doubt you will have other adventures to busy you there."

Antonina smiled and kissed him. Then she and Theodosius climbed to the surface with alacrity and were gone.

Uliaris chortled inappropriately once she had disappeared from sight.

"What?" Belisarius asked, turning on him.

"Oh, nothing," Uliaris snickered. "Just that a lesser man than you might have been highly discomfited to find his wife alone in such a place with a handsome young lad like that."

Belisarius's upper lip curled in anger. "You truly are a complete lackwit, Uliaris, do you know that?" He then turned and forcefully grabbed a torch from the wall, sending a shower of burning embers onto the floor. He proceeded ahead into the darkened cistern alone.

"What did I say?" Uliaris muttered in confusion to one of the soldiers.

The man knew better than to respond.

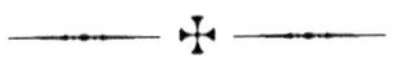

The crass comment made by Uliaris soured Belisarius's mood for the rest of that day. He remained agitated even when he arrived back at his quarters in the Vandal palace after a full day of touring, inspecting, drilling, taking reports, and giving orders.

Antonina noticed his state immediately and sought to make him comfortable, dismissing his personal attendant, bringing him wine and fruit, and helping him off with his armor kit. Her gentle attention greatly assuaged his mind.

But her soft voice is what set him most at ease. "What is it that troubles you, husband?" she asked.

"It is nothing of import, dear Antonina. Have no care about it."

"You must know by now that it is impossible for me to see you troubled and not feel the same way," Antonina replied.

Belisarius sighed. "It is that great ass Uliaris. No matter how many opportunities I give him, he always manages to demonstrate his incompetence. He is a bungler and a rash braggart who has no control over his tongue. Plus, he is overly fond of wine and carousing."

"Then why do you not simply dismiss him?" Antonina said, as though stating the obvious.

"Solomon has suggested as much. But it is not so simple as that," Belisarius grunted. "The man is one of my oldest friends from when we were children. He's practically kin. Though he can be a fool, I've got a certain loyalty toward him."

"The man is a complete buffoon," Antonina rejoined coldly. "If you continue to coddle him, it will be to your detriment someday. If I were you,

I would dismiss him now. Or demote him at the very least so that he can do less harm."

Belisarius was surprised at Antonina's vehemence. "No, that I can not do," Belisarius replied, now feeling defensive toward his old friend. "At heart, he is a good soldier and has potential as a leader. What he lacks is confidence and self-discipline."

"And you mean to give that to him? He is nearly thirty years-old. If he doesn't have those things by now, he is unlikely to acquire them in the future."

Belisarius conceded the point, nodding. "He is like a younger brother to me, Antonina."

"Yes, an idiot younger brother who could get you killed if you're not careful."

"I can't just cast him adrift," Belisarius said decisively. He stood up. "But I can limit the trouble he causes."

"How?"

"I will put him under Armenian John's direct command."

Antonina's eyes narrowed and she nodded very slightly. "Yes. That will keep him in line. John won't abide any of his nonsense. And what's more, Uliaris loves John. So he will work harder to impress him."

"Precisely what I was thinking," Belisarius smiled.

The two sat there in silence for a moment, basking in their consensus.

"You look pensive, my dear," Belisarius offered, putting a finger to her chin to move her eyes up to his.

Antonina's brows knit and her lips pinched together. *Dare I say it?* she thought within her heart. A notion had been growing in her mind every day since they had arrived in Carthage. Perhaps now was the time…

"Come now, out with it," Belisarius chided playfully.

I shall say it! she decided. She moved in close to her husband until she whispered in his ear. "Every day, you enter the Vandal palace and sit on the throne to administer Carthage. And every day, I see you and think to myself: *what a magnificent king he would make.*"

His eyes wide with horror, Belisarius pulled away from Antonina with a jerk as if she had touched his face with a red-hot iron poker.

"Antonina," he finally gasped. "I will forget that such words ever escaped your lips."

Undaunted, she closed with him and put her mouth again close to his ear. "Why not? You are a hero in this place. You have a mighty army and a fleet. And Africa is rich! No one could touch us. We would be free!"

"Free," he stammered, holding her away from him. "Free you say? You would make me a king while I live, but upon my death, I shall be a slave chained in the lowest depths of hell. Is that the fate you wish for me?"

Now it was Antonina's turn to be surprised by Belisarius's vehemence.

"I took an oath, wife!" he growled, keeping his voice down lest anyone hear. "Without my oath, what good am I to anyone? An oath-breaker is the most despicable of all men. A betrayer I would be, no better than Judas. And worse, to break an oath made before God? It is unthinkable! May I be struck dead before I ever do such a thing!"

Antonina stood back aghast. She had gravely miscalculated.

"Justinian is my lord here on earth, Antonina. I will never betray him. Never! Even if he stripped me of all rank, title, and wealth. Even if he deprived me of my very life! He is the God-protected emperor. Any authority I have comes through him. Were I to defy my emperor, what right would I have to claim the loyalty of the men under me?"

"Forgive me, husband," Antonina muttered, ashamed.

Belisarius continued as if he hadn't heard her: "I would have no claim on their loyalty. They would defy me as I defied my lord. And they would be right to do so for I would have shown myself to be a contemptible scoundrel and worse—a liar, a betrayer, and a murderer of the truth."

"I understand," Antonina said softly, as she seated herself gloomily on a fur-trimmed chair. "I am sorry."

Exhausted, Belisarius said no more and the two remained together in silence for a long time.

✠

Belisarius held court in the audience hall of the Vandal kings the next day as usual. But now he did so without his usual relish. In his heart, he had felt a certain exuberance at administering a realm and helping litigants settle their quarrels peacefully. And indeed, he had shown himself quite adept at both tasks. *In my heart, I even felt pride in my ability*, he mused to himself. *Did I not even say within myself that I would make a good king?*

It wasn't until Antonina gave voice to these thoughts that Belisarius discerned their ugliness and their diabolical inspiration. As a result, he turned on them with a vengeance when they rang in his ears.

Now, he perched upon Gelimer's throne as if it were a warm bench in hell's antechamber. Sitting upon it became a torment.

Loitering beneath a pleasant portico nearby, Uliaris chewed absent-mindedly on a piece of warm bread. In his left hand, a half-filled wine-skin drooped lazily.

"Have you heard?" a voice rang out behind him.

"Heard what, Armenian?" he replied, knowing the voice at once without having to turn around.

"You and your moira have been placed under my command."

Uliaris wheeled around excitedly. "Truly?"

"Yes," John scowled. "Belisarius told me first thing this morning."

"That is tremendous news!" Uliaris beamed. He clumsily threw his arms around John's neck.

John smiled in spite of himself. "Let go, you great ape," he commanded. He struggled free of Uliaris's grip and looked the man up and down. "Now you and I have been friends for many years," he began.

"Indeed, indeed! It will please me to serve with you again!"

"To serve *under* me, you mean," John said sternly. "You have been placed under my command and I expect you to act like a subordinate. Is that clear?"

"Why of course, John!" Uliaris replied.

"Not John to you anymore. Address me as *strategos*, as is proper. And furthermore," John snatched the wine-skin out of Uliaris's hand, "no more of this outside of meals. Do you understand me?"

"Perfectly," Uliaris replied, a little glumly. He watched in dismay as John poured the contents onto the ground.

"If I catch you, I'll have you thrown in prison. I promise you that."

"As you wish," Uliaris said, his head down.

"But only listen to me and show yourself to be a brave soldier," John said, feeling a twinge of remorse for his friend, "and you will enjoy my complete confidence. And my friendship."

The bright smile returned to Uliaris's face at once. "Ah, to fight along side a friend like you is my fondest wish!"

Before he could say any more, a troop of ragged, road-weary soldiers marched into the audience hall to present themselves.

Belisarius recognized their leader at once as his bodyguard, Diogenes, a man whom he had entrusted with spying on the Vandals and ascertaining their state and position. "What has happened?" Belisarius cried, standing up in distress, for blood ran freely from an open wound on the man's face.

"Magister, the enemy is closer than you thought," he gasped, saluting. The nineteen men behind him did likewise.

"A physician," Belisarius said under his breath.

"Aye," Solomon nodded and hurried off.

"We had advanced no more than two day's journey from the city," Diogenes continued. "We lodged in an abandoned villa, but the peasants in that area are still loyal to the enemy though we did not know it. They sent word of us to Gelimer and his men…surprised us."

Those assembled in the audience hall gasped.

Diogenes continued: "Three hundred of them. Caught us in the house in the middle of the night. If Gregorius hadn't heard them whispering outside his window, we'd all be dead men right now."

"How did you escape?" Belisarius asked, holding the man's eyes. He now descended from the raised dais.

"They did not attack at once but hesitated. We mounted up in silence in the courtyard of the house and at a signal, we all burst out." Diogenes winced in pain.

"We plowed right through them, Magister," Gregorius took up the tale. "Covered ourselves with our shields and rode all the way back here fast as we could."

"Only lost two, Magister," Diogenes said sadly. He then groaned and swayed on his feet so badly that one of his subordinates had to catch him lest he topple over.

At that moment, the physician arrived.

"Aristo, take him out and bind his wounds," Belisarius ordered. "And tend to these others as well."

"As you say," the physician replied, bowing. The injured then hobbled out in a line.

"There is more, Magister," Gregorius continued. "The Vandals from Sardinia have now arrived and joined with Gelimer—some five thousand of them or more. It is said they are the most powerful of all the Vandal warriors."

Furious conversation broke out at once in the hall as the officers and city fathers struggled to digest this alarming news.

Adding to the disorder, a pair of Carthaginian couriers burst into the audience hall shouting: "Alas we are lost! A great disaster has happened! The aqueduct! The aqueduct!"

All eyes turned to them and the tumult of confused voices grew louder and more urgent.

"Silence!" Solomon cried over them, to little avail.

"Speak!" Belisarius shouted forcefully above the din. "Tell me what happened?"

At the sound of his voice, the noise subsided enough for the couriers to be heard.

"The Vandals have broken it down," one of them wailed, his chest heaving as he struggled to catch his breath. "Thirty stades from the city. It is completely dry. Not a drop is getting through."

At this news, complete chaos erupted as men threw their hands in the air, cursing Gelimer and debating the meaning of this dreadful turn of events.

Belisarius paced back to the dais, his mind working as chaotic debate raged around him.

"Magister, what are we to do?" Solomon asked, leaning in close.

"Gelimer has been reinforced and is now taking the initiative," Belisarius replied in a low voice. "But neither have we been inactive. The walls of Carthage are strong and will not be breached and we can be resupplied by sea if need be. But we can not remain here idle. To win Africa and complete our mission, the power of the Vandals must be completely broken. And to do that, we must defeat them in open battle."

"I agree, completely," Solomon said.

"Good, then assemble John and the other officers. We have tarried here long enough."

XVIII

AD 533, December
Seventh year of the reign of Justinian, Emperor of the Romans
At Carthage

The Roman army burst out of Carthage with the first light on December 3. In the vanguard, Belisarius placed the 3,000 imperial heavy horse with Justinian's glittering banner hoisted before them. These were followed immediately by the mighty household guard of Belisarius, 3,000 strong, mounted and fully armed. All these forces he placed under the command of Armenian John.

Behind these rode Belisarius himself with 500 of his most stalwart bodyguards. The federated Huns and Heruls came next, followed at last by 5,000 footmen who advanced behind the cavalry units at a slow march.

The remainder of the infantry, under Solomon's command, was left to defend Carthage. With Procopius beside him on the battlements above the city gate, Solomon watched Belisarius and the army march off as the sun began to climb into the azure sky.

"Off he goes into history," Procopius sighed softly, a tinge of melancholy in his voice. "I have a feeling of dread..."

"What's that?" Solomon replied turning abruptly toward his friend. "You doubt him even now after knowing him for so long?"

"No one can predict what fortune has in store," Procopius said glumly. "Greater men than he have been undone by a single dart, clumsily shot, that the unseen hand directs to its mark."

"Perhaps," Solomon said thoughtfully. "But we have no choice except to trust in God to protect him. The bishop will be leading prayers for victory later this morning. I am going. Will you come?"

"You, a Jew, attending Christian prayers?" Procopius said in surprise.

Solomon scowled. "The Lord is God to all men and He hears the prayers of Jews as well as Christians."

"Well then you go pray for him," Procopius said as he turned away. "I choose to serve Belisarius's cause in my own way this morning—by working through the pile of dispatches he left me."

✠

Further down the wall, Antonina watched her husband depart with no less anxiety. On her left was Macedonia, her blond hair swirling about her face as she mouthed a silent prayer. Photius stood on her right, a petulant pout twisting his lips. Antonina had not let the lad out of her sight for the past two days—there would be no repeat of his previous tricks.

The position of the Vandals was not difficult to discern, for as soon as word went out that the Romans were on the march, Gelimer moved to intercept them. He had gathered all the remaining Vandalic strength in Africa and his army, now reinforced with Tzazon's elite warriors, again numbered over 20,000—more than enough, he reckoned, to crush the smaller Roman force in open combat. Eager for the fight, the Vandals advertised their presence outside the town of Tricamarum, some 140 stades from Carthage and dared Belisarius to come and fight them there.

For his part, Belisarius was anxious to accommodate them. Leaving his footmen to march along slowly behind them, Belisarius hurried his cavalry moiras ahead at a rapid trot. Arriving in the vicinity of Tricamarum, he made camp on a well-suited spot and studied the topography. What he saw pleased him greatly.

"Our enemy believes that his previous defeat was a mere quirk of fate," he opined to his chief officers who had gathered in the command tent. "The field he has selected says as much, for it is well suited for a clash of heavy horse and offers him little in the way of strategic advantage. However, it is even better suited for Hunnic cavalry tactics."

"Huns!" growled Barbatus, the surly dux who commanded a moira of imperial horse. "The name of that nation burns in my ears, Magister. Have you heard? They are disgruntled again. They say that we have played foul with them; that they were promised they could return to their own country long ago."

"They rage, O Magister," Aigan added in his Hunnic accent. "They call me traitor to people because I stand with your guardsmen and do not join them in their anger against the Romans. And it come to my ear that certain Vandals have crept among them, offering gold in return for treachery."

"Aye, it's true," Belisarius admitted. "I have tried to assuage them, but I fear they may not be counted on during the coming battle. But we must not allow their delinquency to hinder or delay us. And I was not referring to them when I spoke of tactics. My guardsmen are as proficient as any Hun in the art of hit-and-withdraw. Since our enemy has no mounted bowmen, but rather depends on the sword and the spear when on horseback, we will not permit him to close with us until it suits us to do so."

Belisarius looked gravely into the faces of his officers. "I want every man ready for battle first thing tomorrow morning. We will line up with John and my guardsmen in the center. Barbatus and Pappas will hold the right. Martinus and Valerian will hold the left. I have told the Huns to station themselves in readiness on the far left flank to charge the enemy at an opportune moment."

Remembering the treachery of Arethas and his Arabs at Callinicus, Belisarius turned his eyes upon Pharas. "I want your Heruls beside the Huns. Should they show any sign of treason, destroy them."

"Aye," Pharas said fiercely, showing his yellow teeth.

"But Magister, what of the infantry?" Uliaris objected. "At the rate they march, they will not arrive until tomorrow evening."

"We will engage the Vandals without the infantry," Belisarius said bluntly.

"Magister, is that wise? Our scouts say there are nearly three Vandals to every one of us!" Barbatus added. "If we are bested, where shall we find safety? At least wait for the infantry to come up and build a proper fortified camp."

Belisarius frowned. "We will not be bested," he said, meeting the eyes of each man. "Remove from your minds any thoughts of defeat. If we remain in good order, remember our training, and trust in God the Almighty, we can not be defeated by this foe."

The officers reluctantly grunted their concurrence with anxious nods and downcast eyes.

"And we must make sure this victory is decisive," John added. "We see before us the entire Vandal camp, containing their families, possessions and all. If we can but capture it, this war will be over. And I for one, am ready for it to be over."

"For it to end, we must be sure to capture the king as well," Pharas interjected.

"Ideally, yes," John smiled. "But a king without subjects and a kingdom is no longer a king—merely a vagrant."

"This is our moment," Belisarius declared, standing. "God has placed the enemy before us and his situation is well-suited to our advantage. Let us not postpone this fight for another time, seeking an even greater advantage later. For if we allow this fortunate moment to run past us, we may waste all our breath trying to catch it again."

"Aye!" the men responded with bellicose fervor, some slamming their fists on the wooden table.

The meeting adjourned, and the cavalry commanders filed out of the tent into the smoky darkness of the Roman camp. The certainty of impending battle sent a wave of electricity through the air. Every man among them felt it. And a select few saw it. For standing upright in bound bundles outside the men's tents, the javelins of the Roman horsemen glowed bright red, as if their tips had been heated in fire.

"What strange prodigy is this?" Belisarius asked, his eyes wide in wonder.

"I don't know," gaped his cousin Rufinus, who had been standing guard. "It began just as you and the others came out."

Belisarius advanced to touch one of the burning spears, but as soon as he got near, the strange vision evaporated and was seen no more.

"What do you suppose that was about?" John whispered to Uliaris.

"A good omen, if you ask me," Uliaris replied aloud, a toothy grin splitting his wide face. "Our weapons have been purified by the hand of God for the daunting task we face on the morrow."

"Not bad, you great oaf," John nodded, surprised by his friend's unusually inspired insight. He pounded Uliaris heartily on his meaty back. "We may make a philosopher of you yet!"

At dawn the next morning, the Vandalic host sallied forth from their camp. They were astonished to see the Romans already lined up, waiting for them.

The Vandals quickly formed their own battle line with Tzazon's fearsome warriors in the center. On either flank, Gelimer ranged his men in five divisions of a thousand each. All mounted except the archers, the unruly Vandal host clashed their spears and shields together, screaming their derision at the Romans over the horrible din.

Gelimer, the king, rode back and forth along the line, shouting at his men and feeding their frenzy. When he had stirred them to a climax of wrath, Gelimer stopped before them and sat stolidly on his mount, waiting for them to quiet.

"Men of the Vandal nation," he bellowed once their eyes were on him. "You see before you the wretched filth who have so treacherously invaded our land. Many of you have already suffered losses to these dogs, who have taken our possessions and even our brothers, wives and children. All know the loss that I, your king, have suffered. For our beloved prince, Ammatas, was slain by their perfidious hands.

"But now, we have a chance to avenge all. Before us they stand, arrogant and deceitful as always, thinking to break us once and for all. But their conceit will be their undoing, for their previous victory was not due to any cowardice on our part or any great bravery on their part, but was the result of a cruel trick of fate. You all know well that it is not the nature of fortune to favor one side always over the other. So be mindful of this, O Vandals, and have every confidence that victory will be ours this day!

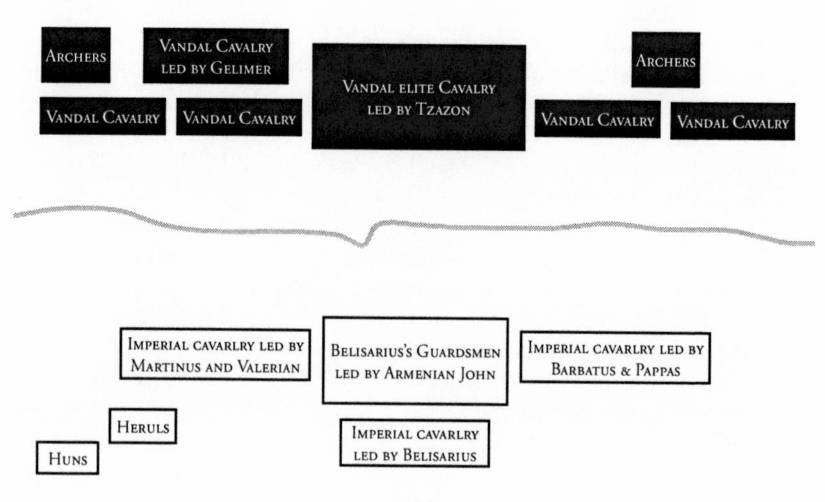

"And who can doubt that we favor the enemy greatly in number, in manliness, and in the strength of our right arms? The Romans, as everyone knows, are a pathetic and grasping race, prone to cowardice and weakness of body. I urge you, Vandals, to despise them as our forefathers did. Fear not their weapons and plunge into their ranks knowing yourselves to be warriors of invincible might!"

At this, Gelimer slung his shield over his back and drew his sword which he raised over his head.

"Mark what I do, O Vandals! To show my contempt for the Romans, I shall bear no shield against them. I shall cast no javelin or spear at them. Instead, this day, the Romans will taste my sword. Let them rue the day that they ever dared to set foot upon our Africa!"

"Romans to the vultures!" one of the Vandals cried out from the ranks.

A tremendous cheer went up from their host as the men clashed their spears and shields together to create a deafening din. Then, following their king's lead, they hung their shields on their backs and drew their swords.

"A hundred years to our mighty king!" they chanted.

"May our enemies be slain to a man!"

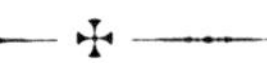

From the center of the Roman formation, John and Uliaris watched the Vandals working themselves into a frenzy. Uliaris's helm was pushed back on his head, revealing his sweaty forelocks. But his heavy jowls were clean-shaven and he stared intently at the enemy across the field, no trace of fear on his face.

"Are you ready?" John asked.

"Aye."

"You know, I want this war to end today," John declared. "Right now."

Uliaris turned his head slightly. "Yes?"

"My betrothed awaits me at home. But standing between us are twenty-thousand Vandals."

"I see," Uliaris replied.

At that moment, a messenger arrived from Belisarius. A signal would be raised in a few moments and John was to take his best tagma of five-hundred men and harass the Vandal center.

"You needn't worry," Uliaris said as the messenger rode off. "For today, you will see a new Uliaris on the battlefield."

"Is that so?" John turned, a quizzical smile on his face.

"Yes," Uliaris said slowly, still staring straight ahead. "I have caused trouble on this campaign. But now I will redeem myself. If my actions on the field of battle may speed you on your way to your beloved, then know that I will make myself a second Hercules and a terror to these barbarians. After today, none shall ever doubt the fighting prowess of Uliaris again."

John nodded, well satisfied. "It will be an honor to fight beside you."

"The honor will be mine, O Strategos," Uliaris said soberly, pulling his helmet down firmly over his brow.

Belisarius gave the signal and John rode forth with five-hundred men of the First tagma to probe the center of the Vandal line. Advancing in perfect order at a trot, they forded a small stream. Once on the other side, they increased their speed to full charge.

Tzazon saw them coming and turned to address his men with a gleam in his eye. "See! Our enemies approach. Let us emulate the king and show our disdain for them!" The Vandal prince handed his shield and lance to a servant and unsheathed his sword. "Swords only! Thus we shall show our manliness and our utter contempt for their arms!" The men behind him all followed his example.

"Let these Romans taste Vandal steel!" he screamed. "Kill them all!"

Tzazon spurred his huge mottled stallion forward and all his Vandals followed in irregular order, bellowing their ferocious battle cry.

As soon as he saw the Vandal center move forward, John had his men draw their bows. Once the enemy was in range, the Romans let fly their arrows in unison, at the same time moving off to the flank with the easy grace of practiced precision.

The volley hit Tzazon's on-charging riders with devastating results, dropping dozens of men and horses to the ground. Several missiles even struck Tzazon himself, but his stout armor and heavy helm turned them easily.

"Fear not their cowardly darts, O Vandals!" Tzazon cried, his confidence growing. "Close with them!"

"Victory or death!" the Vandals behind him shouted.

John was astonished when he saw the Vandals continue forward without losing momentum. "Another volley!" he commanded.

The men complied, taking careful aim. A swarm of Roman missiles again tore into the Vandal host. Uliaris, drawing his bowstring with all his strength, sent an arrow hissing toward Tzazon. But the deadly dart flew over the Vandal prince's head to transfix of one of his bodyguards, killing the man instantly.

"Draw back! Retreat!" John cried as it became clear that the Vandal assault could not be slowed by archery. The men complied in perfect order and without the least trace of fear.

But Tzazon would not be denied. He and his swiftest riders swarmed the Roman rearguard cutting them off, and a sharp fight ensued with Armenian John at the center of it. With brute physical strength and valor driven by rage, Tzazon and his men beat down the Roman horsemen arrayed against them, killing many.

Belisarius watched the skirmish from a distance with dread. With the rest of the Tzazon's warriors coming up quickly, John would be surrounded without immediate action.

"Magister?" Rufinus prodded. "Shall I …"

"No!" Belisarius barked. "We can't send any more to save him. It will disrupt the line and force a hand-to-hand fight with their best warriors. And that cedes the advantage to the enemy."

"He'll be killed," Rufinus whispered, stating the obvious.

Belisarius betrayed no emotion. "I can not risk the whole army for one man."

Rufinus gazed at his cousin with a mixture of awe and horror, knowing how much Belisarius loved John. But he said not another word.

God save him, Belisarius prayed. *For I can not.*

As soon as Uliaris realized the danger to John, he did not delay. Turning back with twenty men, he charged directly into Tzazon's bodyguards with a fury that scattered them. A huge Vandal champion immediately rode forward to challenge him. Uliaris was ready, blocking the heavy sword strokes with his shield. Taking his javelin in his right hand, Uliaris stabbed his foe in his unprotected armpit. With a scream, the man tumbled off his horse.

Seeing the danger to their prince, the Vandals who were pressing John changed front to repel the sudden Roman thrust. This gave John and his beleaguered men just enough space to escape and gallop back over the stream to the Roman lines. Once they were away, Uliaris and his men disengaged and with nimble horsemanship, got clear of the Vandal host without any loss.

Tzazon and his men shrieked curses at their retreating enemies and chased them as far as the stream that separated the two armies. But realizing the danger posed by the waiting Roman cavalry archers on the other side, they dared not approach any closer. After a prolonged taunt, they trotted back to their position at the center of the Vandal line. As they went, Tzazon could not help but feel dismay at the number of Vandal dead already scattered on the field, slain by Roman arrows.

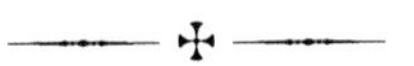

"You gave us quite a scare, John of Armenia," Belisarius said imperiously when John presented himself. His armor was dented and his face was ruddy and drenched with sweat, but John's spirit remained undampened.

"Not my intention, of course, O Magister," he replied with a salute. "But thanks to the aid of Uliaris, we escaped without much harm."

"That is well," Belisarius said, allowing his eyes to tarry on his friend's face.

John misread his expression for one of disappointment. "My apologies if I have failed you, O Magister."

"Failed?" Belisarius replied, coming to himself. "Not so. But you must exercise greater caution," Belisarius lectured. "You are now aware of the enemy's desire for battle. Be certain that on the next attack, you keep your distance from him, using archery only and not allowing him to close with you."

"Next attack?"

"Yes. Take two fresh tagmas of my guardsmen, the Second and Third, and assault the Vandal center again in the same way as you just did. Only this time, do not allow them to come to close quarters with you."

"Aye Magister!" John cried.

"And John," Belisarius added. "Make sure you keep Uliaris by your side. God seems to have tasked him as your guardian angel this day."

✠

Without delay, John and Uliaris set out again toward Tzazon's men, this time with nearly eight hundred of Belisarius's biscuit-eaters at their back.

Tzazon led his men out again, but their charge was less spirited this time. Using the same tactic as before, the Roman horsemen peppered the approaching Vandal line with darts, and the shrieks of the wounded and dying rose into the air like the foul cries of dreadful birds. At the sight, Tzazon raged at his men, urging them forward to clash with the Romans.

But John followed the advice of his commander, and his brilliantly trained cavalry archers danced away from the lumbering Vandal host, launching a final volley before sprinting swiftly back to the waiting Roman lines.

✠

"Hail Magister!" John cried as he and Uliaris presented themselves before Belisarius after the second skirmish. "What is your pleasure?"

"The enemy's charge seemed less ferocious this time," Belisarius observed.

"They have developed a distaste for Roman archery, I think," John replied. "Shall we give them another mouthful?"

"Oh yes," Belisarius said, nodding. "And a big mouthful it will be, for I want you to lead out all my guardsmen against them under my standard."

"All?" John gasped. Those around him likewise stood in amazement.

"Yes, take them all," Belisarius declared. "And after a volley or two of archery, close and take the fight to the enemy with javelin and sword. They are already dispirited, having engaged with only small numbers of our men. When they see us coming against them without fear in greater and greater numbers, their remaining courage will melt away like beeswax."

"And if we can rout the best men in their center..." John began.

"We win this war," Belisarius finished for him.

"Right! Let's win it, now!" John cried aloud to the cheers of those nearby.

✠

Gelimer witnessed this second skirmish with growing alarm. Twice now the Romans had probed his army, and twice they had escaped with barely any losses. Meanwhile, several hundred of his bravest warriors lay dead on the field. It would not happen a third time.

"The king says, 'Do not charge the Romans if they come out to do battle again,'" a messenger said to Tzazon. "He also says that if the Romans come out, hold your ground against them. He will set a chiliarchy from each wing in motion to surround them and cut off their retreat. When those men are in motion, then quickly charge the Romans who harass you."

"Good," Tzazon said, fiercely. "I'm sick of chasing these rabbits all over the battlefield. Let us set a snare for them."

Even the fiery heart of Tzazon trembled slightly at the sight of John leading a full meros of Roman cavalry out against him, all in perfect order. And his warriors, dismayed as they were by the sight, quailed all the more when they received the order not to advance but hold fast as the Romans moved toward them.

John's men surged ahead at a rapid clip and began discharging arrows as soon as they were in range. In response, Tzazon ordered his men to cover themselves with their shields. A few Vandals were felled but the vast majority of the Roman darts were shot in vain.

"They have changed tactics," Uliaris observed.

"Indeed," John replied. "Hold fire," he commanded, turning to the standard bearer.

The order was relayed and the rain of arrows brought to a halt.

"Time to hit them, then," Uliaris declared.

"Aye," John replied, stowing his own bow. "*Cursores*, javelins!"

"Javelins, *cursores*!" a dozen tribunes echoed the command throughout the meros.

"Aye!" the men of the front ranks shouted in unison as they complied.

"Good order, now fellows!" Uliaris called out. "Follow the standard and at them!"

"Aye!" three thousand throats replied as one.

"*Nobiscum Deus*!" John cried.

"*Nobiscum Deus*!" the rest replied as they launched themselves into the Vandal line.

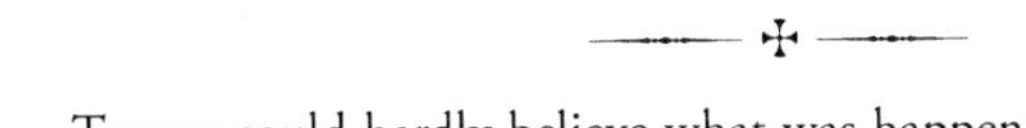

Tzazon could hardly believe what was happening. The cringing Romans, who had been so loath to come to close combat with the Vandals, were now advancing directly into him. His eyes gleamed like those of a lone wolf who had unexpectedly brought a snorting stag to bay.

"They want to fight like men? Let's fight like men!" he screamed.

His men bellowed and the whole Vandal center charged out to meet the Romans.

The initial impact was ferocious. The disorganized ranks of Vandal horsemen plowed into the Roman formations, expecting them to give way easily before them. But the biscuit-eaters of Belisarius held firm, meeting the attack with courage and strength.

Riding a sturdy Roman war horse instead of his usual swift prairie pony, Aigan the Hun ranged among the Romans, having forsaken his unreliable countrymen. Hurling heavy darts, he crippled Vandals twice his size. Then, closing with them, he effortlessly switched weapons with fluid, practiced movements, alternately slashing with his sword and stabbing with his javelin, all the while, dodging the heavy, clumsy strokes of his opponents.

Not far off, huge Unigastus clashed with Vandals of equal size, trading blow for blow until the barbarians crumbled under his superior skill at arms.

Beside him, Athenodorus, tall in the saddle and swift with the blade, took on three Vandals at once, stabbing one through the chest and breaking his sword on the helm of the second. The third, however, slashed his mount across the eyes, causing the steed to rear and topple over. Athenodorus jumped clear with the agility of a circus rider and landed on his feet weaponless. A dozen Vandal warriors moved to surround and slay him, each jostling the others to get there first.

Principius saw his comrade's plight but was powerless to help, a wall of powerful Vandals interposed between them. "Uliaris! John!" he screamed, deflecting a sword stroke with his shield. "Athenodorus has lost both horse and sword!"

From his position beside John among the horse archers in the rear ranks, Uliaris heard the cry and without order or hesitation, plunged directly into the heaving sea of battle. Squeezing into the Roman fighters at the front, he spurred his horse forward with a loud "Heya!" The animal sensed his urgency and responded with a snort and a lunge, fearlessly plowing into the Vandal ranks.

Wielding his oversized javelin like a club, Uliaris knocked Vandals from their horses to his left and right. His immense strength was such that none could withstand the crushing blows he landed on their heads and shoulders. "Come to me, cowards!" he bellowed like an angry bull. "You prefer to attack a defenseless man, eh? You are right to fear Uliaris! Come my way and I shall send you to hell!"

Vandals melted before him has he careened ahead, reckless of his own safety. He caught sight of Athenodorus as the swordless man was grappling desperately with a Vandal giant on horseback. Recklessly heaving his javelin with all his strength, Uliaris transfixed the enemy warrior through the back and he crashed heavily to the ground.

Athenodorus, drenched in sweat and blood, seized the opportunity at once. He wrenched the sword out of his stricken enemy's hand and vaulted upon his horse just as Uliaris arrived at his side. "Thanks," he gasped. "I thought that was the end of me."

"No indeed," Uliaris smiled. "It will be the end of them if I have anything to say about it!"

Several Romans nearby cheered Uliaris's bravado. "Hail Uliaris! You conquer!"

"Rally to me, then, O Romans, and let us put these Vandal dogs to flight once and for all!" Uliaris cried.

"*Nobiscum Deus*!" the Romans replied, pressing forward and scattering the Vandals who dared to oppose them.

✠

With shock, Tzazon realized that his unconquerable warriors made no headway against the Roman formations. Worse, the Romans were cutting down his men in great numbers, both hand-to-hand in the front ranks and with deadly precision archery from the rear. The king, his brother, was waiting for the Romans to become fully involved before moving to surround them from the flanks. But as Tzazon witnessed his noble warriors being slain one after another, he could no longer restrain himself. He was going to lead the Vandal host to victory right now.

"Have my Vandals become cowering women?" he roared. "You allow these scrawny Roman goats to push you back? We Vandals know no way but forward! Have you forgotten?" He raised his sword and pointed it into the Roman ranks. "We will hack our way through them like a rotten log! Who is with me?"

"Lead us, O Prince! We follow!" the two hundred massive mighty nobles of his personal bodyguard replied with a cheer.

Tzazon led his men into the thick of the fight where a ferocious melee was in progress with many Vandals falling under Roman swords. But with the weight of the greatest Vandal warriors thrown into the mix, the balance immediately tipped in their favor. Their valiant comrades falling around them, even the vaunted biscuit-eaters of Belisarius began to waver, dread showing plainly on their faces as they shrank from the enemy.

John saw the danger at once and commanded his archers to concentrate on the standard of Tzazon which was making steady progress against his men. To his dismay, the arrows which rained upon them bounced harmlessly off the stout steel plates and ornate helmets of the Vandal elites and their heavily armored chargers. The enemy continued to advance steadily. In ones and twos, bloodied Roman soldiers began to stagger back from the fight, looking for safety wherever it could be found.

No! John thought to himself. His mind reeled as he witnessed the fight slipping away from him. *Blessed Theotokos, pray for us. This day must belong to the Romans!*

"Archers, put down your bows!" John cried out, standing tall in his stirrups so all could see. "Swords, javelins at your pleasure!"

The men complied and John led them forward directly into the frightful path of Tzazon and his all-slaughtering armored giants. The two sides slammed together and clashed like great cliffs thrown up from the depths of the earth, propelled forward by some hideous impetus that made them careless of life. Slowly, the raucous cheers and hearty battle cries transformed into the piteous shrieks of men mangled, maimed and pierced.

As the clang and clash of steel on steel echoed over the field, John realized that despite his best efforts, Tzazon and his men still cut down every Roman in their path, still pushed their way forward, still advanced irresistibly. At the rate they moved ahead, they would soon cleave the Roman vanguard in half and with their superior numbers, there could be no doubt that the Vandals would then completely overwhelm John and put his men to rout.

For the first time, John looked over his shoulder at Belisarius and the rest of the army waiting a short distance away. The fire of determination in the Armenian's eyes had dimmed, replaced by a silent tremor of doubt and the agony of desperation.

✠

From the right wing, Gelimer witnessed his brother's assault with a mixture of admiration and anger. "He was supposed to hold them, not advance!" the king fumed.

"But behold, O King, he withstands them bravely and still charges ahead!" Fuscias said at Gelimer's right hand.

"What do you think of your father's rash disobedience, Thrasamund?" Gelimer glowered, turning to his other side.

"Did you order him to lose the battle, O King?" Thrasamund responded gamely, his drooping blond moustache arching over his large toothy smile. "If he is victorious, it is you who will get the glory. How can that be accounted disobedience?"

The Vandal king scowled. "I will not let him steal this victory from me," he muttered under his breath. "Fuscias!"

"Yes, O King?"

"We are moving out. Now! Signal the chiliarchs on the left to attack the Roman flank at once!"

"Yes, O King."

"Vandals! Follow your king to victory!"

"Victory! Victory!" the Vandal host echoed in the highest of spirits.

✠

The instant Belisarius spotted movement on the right and left wings of the Vandal army, he sprung into action. "Rufinus!" he barked, "Full advance!"

"Yes, O Magister!" the standard-bearer replied excitedly.

Blasts of the brass cavalry trumpets resounded up and down the Roman line as the imperial horse moved forward in perfect order. Dividing into three as it approached the open field, the right wing advanced briskly under the leadership of the stalwart duxes Barbatus and Pappas. On the left, cautious Martinus and rash Valerian led their men to battle against Gelimer and the host of bodyguards surrounding him. Belisarius commanded the center himself, determined to check Tzazon's advance and support John should the latter's men falter.

Only one worry disturbed Belisarius's mind as he surged ahead to battle. Looking off to his left, the ominous formation of five hundred federate Huns stood darkly upon a low rise. They had not bestirred themselves since the battle had commenced. *Should they hit us in the rear, it will be our demise,* Belisarius mused grimly to himself, knowing the fullness of the danger.

His eyes then shifted to the knot of four hundred Herulians standing not far off from the Huns. They too had not moved from their position. And their prince, Pharas, stood stoically keeping vigil, watching every movement of their erstwhile allies for the first sign of treachery.

Lord God, let them all keep faith, Belisarius prayed in his heart.

✠

The fight in the center had now grown desperate for Armenian John. Like invulnerable titans, Tzazon and his men crushed to the earth all who dared stand against them. Now, they had slashed, hacked, and clubbed a path all the way through the center of the Roman meros until only John and fifty of the bravest Romans stood between them and victory.

Realizing what was at stake, John grit his teeth and prepared to sell his life dearly. "With me, O Romans!" he cried. "Victory or death this day!"

Hearkening to the challenge, Tzazon and his men exploded forward, engaging the Roman's last line of defense with wrath and ferocity.

It was all John could do to keep his horse from bolting in fright from the Vandal onslaught. As he struggled, Tzazon himself charged in on him, slashing his mount across the throat. The stricken animal crumpled to the ground. Shaken, John rose up, sword in hand, expecting death from every direction. Dust swirled around him, blinding his eyes and choking him.

"Now die, treacherous dog!" a huge voice rang out. There was a clash of metal and the horrible squeal of steel scraping against steel. Then, a most hideous scream erupted, like the sound of a bull bellowing as it is slaughtered. The earth shook as a huge form crashed to the ground. A moan escaped its lips and then it moved no more.

Clearing his eyes as best he could, John stumbled toward the armored form on the ground. To his utter astonishment, it was Tzazon, the Vandal prince. The corpse's eyes were wide open with wonder, as if surprised beyond belief that so powerful a body as his could be slain at all.

Now on his guard with his sword raised, John looked about him in all directions to determine how such a mighty warrior had been laid low.

"Give me your hand!" a familiar voice called out.

"Uliaris! Is it you?" John gasped as the image of his friend emerged from the dustcloud.

The man nodded. With the sun behind his head, Uliaris looked to John exactly like an angel.

"Come, O Strategos," Uliaris said, hoisting John up onto the saddle behind him. "There is still much to do. And you need a fresh mount."

✠

The instant Tzazon's lifeless body hit the ground, all the fight drained out of the Vandals like wine from a smashed amphora. With the arrival of Belisarius and his men, the rout in the Vandal center became urgent and immediate. The panic soon spread to the wings, and try as he might, Gelimer was unable to stem the tide. He sat there in the saddle agog, screaming at his terrified men to turn around and fight. They did not heed him.

Soon, every last Vandal had fled back to their fortified camp, ceding the battlefield to the Romans. As they rushed to escape, black-fletched arrows began hissing through them, thudding into their unprotected backs. These were followed by awful war whoops and the thunder of hooves as the tardy Huns swooped down upon them in their desperate flight, eager to prey upon the defeated now that the battle was already decided.

Belisarius soon caught sight of John and Uliaris as they issued orders, trying urgently to restrain their men. He greeted them heartily and they saluted him in return.

"Brilliantly done, both of you!" Belisarius lauded.

"The credit belongs to the men," John replied humbly. "And to this fellow. He is the one who killed Tzazon."

"Uliaris?" Belisarius beamed, impressed beyond words.

"Aye," the man replied, smiling sheepishly like an overgrown child.

"You will get a gold torque for this from the emperor's own hand," Belisarius declared. "I want to hear all the details once this is over."

"You will," John promised. "Your biscuit-eaters will talk of nothing else, I assure you!"

"Well, no tales of valor until we have finished reducing that," Belisarius said, pointing to the Vandal camp that stood before them, teeming with a confused mass of beaten men. It was surrounded by an earthen rampart, studded with sharpened stakes and topped by a palisade wall of heavy logs.

"We can not attack the camp with cavalry," John observed. "We will need to hem them in for now, and keep them from escaping."

Uliaris nodded. "Yes, but before we can do that, we'll need to reform the ranks. The men are too busy plundering to take notice of anything else."

"Use the hope of better plunder to get them back in line if you have to," Belisarius said. "Once we've taken control of the situation, we'll have them dismount to take the camp."

"Aye!" John and Uliaris replied in unison.

"But it must be done quickly! Our enemies are broken now, but they may not remain so."

At that moment, a scout galloped up to Belisarius.

"Hail, Magister! I have been instructed to tell you that the infantry has arrived and awaits your orders."

Belisarius smiled broadly. Their timing could not have been better. "You will ride back and tell them to advance here on the double," Belisarius barked. "Is that clear?"

"Aye, Magister!" the man replied. "I go!"

"Fortune smiles on us again!" Uliaris chortled.

"Smiles?" John quipped. "Fortune follows our commander like a well-trained hound."

XIX

AD 533, December
Seventh year of the reign of Justinian, Emperor of the Romans
At Tricamarum

Inside the Vandal camp was a scene of despair and misery. The wounded were scattered everywhere, while those still healthy enough to walk or ride argued in panicked shouts over what course of action to take. By late afternoon, word began to spread that a fresh army of Roman footmen was approaching. Visions of a fiery death danced before the eyes of the shattered Vandals.

Distraught, Gelimer sat in his pavilion in a dazed fog. His remaining nobles stood around him in utter consternation, none daring to offer advice or even say a word. Weeping quietly, the women and children of the extended royal family sat nearby consoling each other as best they could.

"Tzazon," Gelimer muttered.

Fuscias shifted his eyes to Gothaeus. Gothaeus shifted his own eyes quickly away. Neither would respond.

"Tzazon," Gelimer said again, a bit more clearly.

"He is dead, uncle," Thrasamund said, his voice breaking. "My father has been slain by the Romans." Tears poured down the man's scarred face, mixing with the grime and blood already there.

Gelimer began to convulse silently. His trembling hands grabbed great handfuls of his newly-grown beard and tore it out by the roots. "Why!" he screamed, raising his eyes to heaven. "Why have You done this to me!"

Thrasamund had seen enough. "Listen to me, O King," he said resolutely through his tears. "Do not let my father's death go unavenged. You still have many warriors at your command. Let us draw together all who wish to fight on and make a sudden sally against the Romans, now while they are disorganized."

Gelimer only continued to sob, his face in his hands. But slowly, the men present could detect a change. The sobs became louder and more regular. Soon it became obvious that Gelimer wasn't weeping at all—he was laughing. But far from a healthy, joyous laugh, this was the disturbed laugh of a maniac.

"A sally, Thrasamund?" he chortled. "Yes, I think that's a fine idea. In fact, you lead it."

"My Lord?" Thrasamund replied, perplexed.

"As for me, I am leaving. Goodbye." Gelimer stood serenely and tossed one side of his royal cloak over his shoulder. He then strode calmly out of the pavilion and mounted his horse.

"O King! You mustn't!" Fuscias pleaded.

"Goodbye, Fuscias. You were remarkably inept most of the time. But you had your moments." Gelimer blew him a kiss, reined in his horse, and rode for the nearest gate leading out of the camp.

"Merciful God, he's really leaving!" Thrasamund gasped.

"What do we do?" Gothaeus asked in a panic.

"We follow him!" Thrasamund cried. "Who is with me?"

"Take us with you, Thrasamund!" the royal nieces, nephews and cousins begged. "We would stay with the King! Don't leave us to the Romans!"

Thrasamund twisted the end of his moustache nervously. "Whoever can ride, come with me!" he cried. "But I leave now!"

The Vandal royal family scrambled to mount any horse they could find, leaving behind everything except that which they had in their hands at the moment. Within minutes, all of them had followed Gelimer out the gate and into the quickly dying twilight.

"What now?" Gothaeus squawked.

"Do as you please," the wiser Fuscias replied. "But I am going out to salute my new masters."

✠

Night was well advanced by the time Belisarius was able to line up his footmen before the Vandal camp, ready for the assault. Illuminated only by torchlight, the ranks of dour Roman soldiers glowed red, as if already drenched in blood. A night attack meant that much wickedness could be concealed under cover of darkness. But Belisarius knew that the longer he waited, the more likely it was that the Vandal host would reconstitute itself and counterattack.

"Roman soldiers!" he shouted, as if reminding them of their identity. "We advance to take this camp and put an end to the war. All of us know what lies within—a fearsome enemy, but also defenseless women, children, the aged, and the derelict. The rules of war are clear: fight those who resist you and strike them dead if you must. However, you will give quarter and mercy to any who surrender. And you will not harm the innocents and the defenseless. For to commit such an atrocity would be to call the wrath of God down upon us all.

"There will no doubt be a wealth of slaves and plunder for the taking once we have captured this camp. But I promise you: any man who brings shame upon this army by massacring the innocent will get no share of this wealth. Instead, he will receive the just recompense for his crime, impaled on a stake outside of Carthage. Is that understood by all of you?"

"Aye," the men replied grimly in unison.

"Then let us conquer this camp and seal our victory. Tonight all of Africa belongs to the Romans again! For the emperor and for God!"

"For the emperor and for God!" the men cheered in response.

"Hail, Belisarius! You conquer!" one of the men from the rear ranks shouted.

"Victory by your sword, O Magister!" another cried out.

"Belisarius, greatest soldier of the Roman empire!" a third offered.

"Hail, Belisarius!" the rest of the army bellowed in unison. "Glory of the Romans!"

The acclamations continued on in this vein with growing intensity and enthusiasm, and Belisarius soon became deeply embarrassed by their increasingly laudatory tenor. He also noticed that Barbatus, Pappas, Valerian, Martinus and several of the other high ranking imperial officers remained silent, glowering at their men with looks of intense disapproval.

To resolve this troublesome situation, Belisarius did the most logical thing he could think of—he gave the command to begin the attack. Immediately the men fell silent and turned their attention to their officers. Once the orders were relayed, the Roman infantry began their advance on the Vandal camp.

Had Gelimer remained to encourage his remaining warriors to fight, there is little doubt they could have made the Romans pay a heavy price for their victory. As it was, when the abandoned Vandals saw Belisarius advancing upon them with a fresh army of infantrymen, every one of them who was still of sound body ran away into the night as best he could. Such was their rush to escape that they secured for themselves neither their possessions nor even their wives and children.

The command given, the imperial infantrymen charged the palisade wall with a yell. As soon as the Romans realized there would be no resistance, the well ordered ranks dissolved into a pell-mell rush, each man desperate to get his pick of the plunder and slaves.

Fuscias, Gothaeus, and a few other members of the Vandal court were immediately captured and hurried out through the chaos of the rapidly disintegrating camp. They were taken to the place where Belisarius was shouting orders to little avail.

"Mercy!" they cried, their hands raised in gestures of supplication.

"Peace be to you, O General!" Fuscias declared, taking the lead. "We surrender and beg your mercy!"

"Where is the usurper, Gelimer?" Belisarius demanded.

"He has fled, O General, along with his family. I am Fuscias, one-time prime minister of Gelimer. As the highest court official present, I hereby surrender the Vandal kingdom to you—and to Justinian whom we recognize as Augustus and our liege."

"Hail Justinian, noble Augustus of the Romans!" the men behind him added in support.

"You have spoken well, Fuscias," Belisarius said. "All who surrender to us will be treated with leniency. Let it be known among your people that those who lay down their arms will be spared."

"You are most gracious, O General," Fuscias replied, bowing subserviently.

The words were barely out of his mouth when Unigastus came sprinting from the Vandal camp. He was wreathed in smoke and covered in soot.

"Magister, come quickly! It is urgent!" he called out from a distance. He then bolted back into the camp which had by this time degenerated into scene of complete chaos.

Belisarius vaulted from his horse and followed at a run, his mass of bodyguards trailing anxiously behind him. *Dear God, what atrocity awaits me in there?* he wondered.

Inside the palisade wall, be caught sight of Unigastus beckoning him on with waves of his arm, his shouts drowned out by the roar of fire and tumult on every side.

"Magister, it is too dangerous!" Athenodorus urged.

Not heeding him, Belisarius ran ahead until he reached Unigastus, who was now standing before a large pavilion draped with heavy military canvas and displaying the royal insignia of the Vandal king.

"I tried to post guards around it, Magister," Unigastus said, "but the men won't listen to orders once they see what's inside."

With purpose, Belisarius flung up the tent flap and entered the pavilion. What he saw dazzled his eyes. There, dancing before him in the flickering lamp light, was the most fantastic treasure in the world. Heaped up haphazardly in great piles, golden goblets gleamed, silver plate shone, and huge gems sparkled, reflecting the distorted faces of the greedy soldiers whose grasping hands reached for them. Much of the hoard was still packed in heavy coffers, but the men were hard at work breaking these open, so that the ground was already strewn with a cascade of beautiful objects, reliquaries, and jewelry.

Belisarius was thunderstruck, but only for an instant. "No one touches anything here!" he shouted, his commanding voice causing the dozens of renegade soldiers to freeze in fear. "And for those of you who have, if you drop every item you have pilfered and leave here now, your disobedience will be forgotten."

For a moment, the eyes of the imperial soldiers gleamed with avarice and the thought of outright rebellion flamed simultaneously in their hearts. But when they caught sight of the stalwart bodyguards of Belisarius filing into the pavilion in perfect order behind him, each one of them sullenly emptied their pouches on the ground and walked out shamefacedly.

"They may take all they like of the arms, armor, and wealth of the Vandal warriors and nobles," Belisarius said aloud so that all could hear. "But this royal treasure shall be reserved for the emperor alone."

He then turned to his trusted companions. "Guard this treasure well and see that it is not diminished in any way. Do this, and your efforts will be well requited, I promise you."

The men nodded, knowing their master's legendary generosity.

"Set up a perimeter and a watchword," Belisarius commanded Unigastus. "No one enters here without my consent."

✠

The first rays of the morning sun blazed over the horizon to reveal the absolute desolation of the Vandal nation. Sitting in silent circles, distraught women sobbed. Renowned as the most comely in all the world, the one-time wives and daughters of proud Vandal warriors were now the slaves of victorious Roman soldiers.

Not far off, a hundred men picked over the tremendous pile of plundered swords, weapons, and fine armor, looking to upgrade their own kits.

Showing clear signs of fatigue, Belisarius remained in the saddle, issuing orders and barking threats at his soldiers. He strove mightily to restore some semblance of discipline, but by and large, the men refused to heed him in any way, wandering far and wide in search of spoils In frustration, Belisarius gathered his loyalists around him and took his stand atop of a nearby hill, appealing to those who approached to leave off their obsessive quest for booty.

By mid-day, most of his own household guardsmen had come to heel, having secured their own share of the plunder and sent it back to Carthage under the guard.

"Twenty-two hundred is my count, Magister," Armenian John announced, looking haggard but content. "But still no sign of any man from the Fourth."

"Mundilas's men?" Belisarius grunted. "Any sign of him?"

"No," John sighed.

"Never thought he'd go rogue," Belisarius replied, disappointed. "Perhaps he's injured."

"Perhaps."

Belisarius shook his head in frustration. But looking at John, he could not suppress a smile.

John understood. "We have done the impossible, Magister," he enthused, his eyes alight with joy.

"Yes," Belisarius agreed, exhaling a breath with such force that it seemed he had been holding it for the entire campaign. "Yes, by the grace of God, we have done it! And soon—home."

"No," John shook his head. "I can't allow myself to think on it, or I will go mad with anticipation."

"Have you received any more letters from Eudocia?" Belisarius pressed.

"I have a sack of them," John sighed.

"And I assume my sister has a similar sack at home?"

"Yes. Well, unless she discards them," John grinned. "I received her last one before we left Carthage."

"Any news?" Belisarius queried.

John sighed again. "Her letters are generally short on news."

Belisarius nodded sympathetically and remained silent.

"She is a wonderful young woman, your sister," John spoke up, unbidden. "Completely pure of heart, without guile, and with more courage than any soldier I have ever met. Intelligent, she is, and full of insights into life and the world of the spirit. Do you know she is reading St. Jerome's letters? And she has adopted Saint Paula as her patron and model. She has even been studying Hebrew!"

"Hebrew?" Belisarius laughed.

"Yes! So she can make a deeper study of the sacred Scriptures. And my friend, the wedding plans! Your entire family from Thrace is expected, did you know that? Siblings, uncles, aunts, cousins. I think she plans to invite half the province! She is even bringing in most of my family from Armenia."

Belisarius affected shock. "Will I have two follises left to rub together after this wedding?"

"Oh come now," John grinned, his eyes wide. "After this victory and the treasure we have secured for Justinian? You'll be able to tile the Rufinianae with gold solidi if you wanted."

Belisarius scowled at the prospect and his thoughts snapped back to the moment. "But we have secured nothing as yet. And we won't until we get this army back in order. And I have not seen Uliaris since the fight, either. What has become of him?"

"He is a puzzle," John said. "He fought so brilliantly in the battle, and even kept his discipline during the fight for the camp. But then I lost sight of him. I fear he may have gotten caught up in the lust for spoils."

"Let us pray he returns to his senses soon," Belisarius growled.

"Pray who returns to their senses?" a voice boomed out from behind them.

"Ah! There he is!" Belisarius cried out in surprise.

"Uliaris!" John shouted. "Where have you been, you great oaf?"

Uliaris smiled triumphantly. "I was disciplining some of the men. A huge cask of wine was discovered within the Vandal camp. Good stuff, probably for the king, not that filth the soldiers drink. Several of the men had already partaken of it—unwatered I might add—and were behaving in a riotous fashion."

"And you set them straight?" John said, half mockingly.

"I did indeed," Uliaris replied with a self-righteous grin. "And I had the cask secured and placed on a wagon to return it to Carthage where it will be served at the table of our triumphant Magister and his household."

Belisarius raised his eyebrows in delight. "Very thoughtful of you, old friend!"

"Indeed. But other concerns now press urgently upon us," John said in a deadly serious tone.

"That is true," Belisarius added. "For Gelimer remains free and I would have him taken at once if it may be managed—preferably alive. Therefore, assemble a tagma of the swiftest riders and pursue him, John. Follow him night and day. Do not rest until you have him."

"You may count on me, Magister!" John saluted. "And the first man I want at my side is Uliaris."

"An honor, O Strategos!" Uliaris declared, bowing slightly.

"Good. Go now, and may God be with you!"

"Aye, Magister!" the two said in unison as they rode off.

God may be with me, Uliaris thought happily, *but so will you, my darling.* He patted a large skin attached to his saddle, filled with fine wine from Gelimer's cask. *And I promise, I will indulge only sparingly.*

At Carthage

News of the tremendous victory at Tricamarum preceded Belisarius's return to Carthage. The city received the triumphant army with another joyous outburst of celebration. The cause of the barbarian Vandals lay in ruins, and the Roman phoenix had risen miraculously after lying in ashes for a century.

Throughout the city, Vandal fugitives sat nervously in the churches, seeking sanctuary from the frightful all-conquering foe, Belisarius. They now viewed the Roman commander as a God-protected hero who had come upon them like a sudden storm, humbled their mighty king, and wrecked their nation so completely. But if Belisarius was a terror to them, they soon learned that he could be compassionate. He offered them pledges of safety if only they would lay down their arms and agree to enter the emperor's service. Nearly all agreed to these lenient terms.

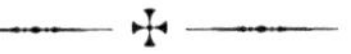

Belisarius spent a day in Carthage putting affairs in order before heading back into the field. He took 2,000 of his biscuit-eaters with him, as well as noble Pharas and his 500 Herulians who had proved their loyalty beyond doubt in the recent battle. There was still the matter of the fugitive Vandal king to deal with, and the last message Belisarius had received indicated that Gelimer had retreated into the depths of Numidia with John close on his heels. Riding at a rapid clip, Belisarius hoped to close the distance and join in the pursuit.

On the second day of the march, under a cloudless blue sky, a single rider was spotted approaching in the distance. As it turned out, he was a dispatch rider from John's force and he insisted upon seeing Belisarius at once.

"What news?" Belisarius asked the man urgently. "Has Gelimer been captured?"

"No indeed, O Magister," the man said gravely. "There is a church some one hundred stades ahead on the road, however, where a man sits as a suppliant waiting for you."

"Speak plainly, soldier!" Belisarius snapped. "Who waits there for me?"

"The dux Uliaris, O Magister," the man replied. "He sent me to bring word to you."

Belisarius shook his head, his eyes wide with horror. "Merciful Heaven! What has he done?" he screamed.

The small white church was perched on a low hill overlooking the road with a round baptistery beside it. It had a sad little stone wall around it that a small child could climb over with no difficulty. Accompanied by twenty men, Belisarius galloped furiously through the front gate, then leaped from his horse and burst in the heavy wooden door.

"Where is he?" he shouted, striding quickly toward the apse.

Uliaris saw him at once and fell on his face before the altar. "Kill me!" he shrieked.

"What have you done? Get on your feet, you wretch!" Belisarius cried, roughly grabbing the man by his shoulders and forcing him to stand.

His face clawed and bleeding, Uliaris sobbed pathetically. "Kill me!" he moaned. "Strike me dead, I deserve no less!"

As he spoke, Belisarius immediately smelled the sickening stench of stale wine and vomit on clothes.

Belisarius punched him hard across the face. "Where did you leave him, you drunken murderer! Where?"

Uliaris crumpled to the ground, whimpering like a child.

"He is two miles from here," an acolyte said, daring to approach Belisarius in his fury. "Deodatus, the presbyter, left two days ago to tend to him, but has not returned."

A fiery wrath gripped Belisarius's heart, like the uncontrollable frenzy of battle. His hand instinctively gripped the hilt of his sword. *I will strike Uliaris down now,* the mad desire surged through his head. *His crime demands it!* But before he could draw, his eyes tarried on the image of Christ above the altar, rendered in brilliant mosaic. Jesus the Pantocrator looked down upon him severely and suddenly the idea of spilling blood in the very sanctuary of a church became unthinkable. His hand recoiled from the sword hilt as if it were a writhing asp.

"Show me where," Belisarius demanded, turning toward the acolyte.

"But I may not leave the church with the presbyter away!"

"You will show me now!" Belisarius shouted, advancing on the much smaller man.

Without another word, the acolyte got up and bolted for the door with Belisarius charging after him.

Uliaris remained in a miserable heap before the altar, banging his head against the marble floor.

✠

A cold wind blew a miserable drizzle into the faces Belisarius's men, who muffled themselves against it in their riding cloaks. Belisarius himself, however, was insensible to any physical discomfort. He rode at the head of the small column bareheaded, soaked and completely crushed in spirit. Not a word escaped his lips and none of his men dared approach him. They only followed.

Beside a tall tree a short distance off the road, Belisarius spotted a forlorn knot of men gathered around a pile of stones. At the sight, he heaved a deep sigh and his shoulders slouched forward. Giving Balan a spur, he trotted ahead of his men.

The presbyter, Deodatus, saw him coming and hurried out to meet him. "Are you Belisarius, the Master of Soldiers?"

"I am, most reverend father," Belisarius said, dismounting. He pushed past the priest never taking his eye of the heap of stones ahead of him.

"Wait!" the priest cried.

Belisarius ignored him.

The men turned toward Belisarius when he approached and he immediately discerned that even the largest and most terrible of them had faces drawn with agony and streaked with tears.

"Magister!" Principius choked. "Forgive...we tried...to save him..."

"How did it happen?" Belisarius pleaded, his eyes fixed with dread on the stone mound before him.

"It was Uliaris, Magister," Athenodorus said solemnly, exhaling a deep breath. "He and John had been inseparable, riding side-by-side each day as we chased after Gelimer. Three days ago, we captured some injured Vandals who told us their king was less than a day's ride ahead. So we rode hard that afternoon and bivouacked right here for the night, expecting to engage the enemy the next morning."

"But Uliaris and John had a disagreement over the provisions," Principius broke in, wiping his eyes with his calloused hand. "Uliaris wanted to send some men to forage for meat. John insisted that we stay together and not waste our arrows with the enemy so close at hand. So Uliaris went off by himself to sulk that night. We didn't know it, but he had gotten hold of a skin of wine and he drank the entire thing. When we woke up in the morning, we found him completely sodden, stumbling around. He said..." Here Principius's voice broke again, and a sob escaped his lips. Unable to continue, he hid his face in his hands.

Athenodorus took up the tale again. "He said he was sick to death of the filth we've been eating and was going to get himself some fresh meat. And behold, at that moment a fat partridge flew into that tree over there—sitting right on that branch—so Uliaris took an arrow...and shot."

"He was so drunk, he didn't even see that John was standing right under the tree, getting into his kit," Principius interjected through his tears. "I was standing next to him. We were talking strategy. I heard a sound...and then he choked...the dart..." Principius forced himself to go on. "The dart took him in the neck. We dared not draw it out, lest he die on the spot. But the wound... there was no hope. He lived out the day and died...early last night."

"So it was pure folly? A stupid drunken blunder?" Belisarius groaned in agony. He fell to his knees beside the burial mound. His mind was a complete blur and tears ran freely down his cheeks into his beard. *It can not be. This must be a dream. For him to die like this, so uselessly!* his mind cried out. *O God! What am I to tell her?*

"You must tell Eudocia, your sister, that he went to God with her name on his lips," a voice in a strange accent rang out behind him. "He was an exceptionally good fellow, this Armenian."

Belisarius got to his feet and turned around. Before him was Deodatus, dressed in the humble robe of a country priest. His hands were folded and his head slightly bowed.

"You were with him, then, reverend Father?" Belisarius asked.

"I was. The poor man could hardly speak. But do not fear. I shrove him. He gave a most poetic account of his sins. Above all, however, he asked me to enjoin you not to punish the man Uliaris who did this."

"Not punish?" Belisarius roared. "The man is a murderer!"

"No. There was no evil intent in what he did," the priest continued, "It was but a tragic mishap—God's way of reminding us that no matter how young, strong and vigorous we are, we may be called before the Eternal Throne at any moment. And John understood that. Though it grieved him to lose his life, his soul was ready to answer the Almighty's call. And, true Christian that he was, his dying wish was that no punishment should fall on his friend Uliaris."

"Indeed, Magister," Athenodorus added. "Uliaris did not act out of malice. We had to restrain him from taking his own life immediately after it happened. And John bound us with oaths to convince you to spare him."

Belisarius turned around, again looking at the stone pile. "Spare him. How can I spare him after what he's done?"

"Your friend John forgave Uliaris completely," the humble presbyter whispered softly. "If he did, certainly you can, too."

"And my sister, his betrothed. How can I face her if I leave his killer unpunished?"

"If she truly loved him and knew his heart, she will understand all," the priest said quietly. "And killing Uliaris, against John's will—do you truly think that will bring her comfort?"

At the priest's words, the rage slowly ebbed out of Belisarius, leaving nothing but a heart shattering emptiness in its place. He had witnessed death thousands of times. Yet now, as he stared at the dismal heap of stones, he felt that a part of himself lay beneath it that he would never reclaim in this world. "I should like to have seen his face one last time," he wept.

"Take courage," the priest said, putting his hand on the general's shoulder. "If you live your life in a fashion worthy of the heavenly kingdom, you will see him again."

✠

The rest of the army came up the next day and the men were shocked when they heard the awful news. John was beloved of the officers and common soldiers alike. The younger men viewed him as a dashing elder brother. To the officers, he was a dependable friend, a wise confidant, and an endless font of enthusiasm. On the field of battle, he was a hero and a born leader who never showed fear in the face of the enemy. The idea that John of Armenia could be killed was unthinkable.

To honor his friend, Belisarius entrusted the care of his grave to the presbyter Deodatus. He also provided a generous endowment for the construction of a proper mausoleum and for the perpetual upkeep of the site.

But Belisarius had no time for extended bereavement. Combining John's men with his own, he entered nearby Hippo Regius, the city made famous as the episcopal see of Saint Augustine and the site of that great saint's death over a century before. There he received word that Gelimer had retreated with a small group of loyalists to the inaccessible environs of Mount Papua. As this area was held by Gelimer's allies, the fierce Moors, Belisarius knew that the Vandal king was now effectively out of reach.

While Belisarius was still considering how to proceed, he was informed that some Romans who had served at the Vandal court were sitting in sanctuary at the cathedral. They claimed to have important information and would surrender it only to him. Without hesitation, Belisarius hurried to the cathedral, nearly as anxious to see the relics of Saint Augustine as to negotiate with his one-time enemies. Long ago he had promised a holy man that he would visit Africa and venerate the relics—he never imagined that he would do so as the conqueror of the Vandals.

The great bronze doors of the cathedral had been thrown wide open, and no one met Belisarius as he entered. He strode directly to the altar, genuflecting as he arrived before the apse.

"It cheers us to see that you are pious, O General," a man called out from beside the altar. He wore the embroidered white tunic and baggy trousers of an official in the Vandal government. Two men stood beside him, similarly attired and looking extremely nervous.

"Before the Lord God who dispenses justice, all men should show piety," Belisarius declared. "And who are you, Romans, who fear your victorious countrymen so much as to seek sanctuary?"

"We are men who served Gelimer while he was king, but who do not bemoan his defeat," the man said. "General, if you will but take an oath to preserve us and our families from harm, I will show you a man who was the very steward of Gelimer and who knows where the Vandal treasury of coin has been secreted."

"I happily take such an oath before God," Belisarius said. "Any Vandal or servant of the Vandals who willingly becomes subject to the emperor shall enjoy his protections to the full."

The man smiled, as did his associates. "Then, come with us down to the crypt and you shall meet the man I spoke of."

"We follow," Belisarius said, "but with caution." He and his bodyguards then drew their swords.

"Your caution is unwarranted, O General," the man said calmly. "There can be no treachery here in a house of God." He led the way to an iron door, behind which was a stone spiral staircase leading down into the darkness. Taking an oil lamp from a bronze stand, the man began to descend. "This place once held the relics of the holy and blessed saint, Augustine. But with the persecution of Catholics by the Vandals, the bishops spirited his bones off to Sardinia many years ago."

Reaching the bottom, the man led them on into the blackness. "So the crypt is now empty of all riches prized by those seeking the City of God."

"Where is this man you spoke of, the steward of Gelimer?" Belisarius asked pointedly, tiring of the man's banter.

"Have you not guessed?" said the man, turning about slowly to face Belisarius. "I am he. My name is Boniface and my lord king ordered me to take his treasury and transport it across the sea to the Visigoths in Spain. And lest you think me faithless to my former master, I attempted to do so three times. But each time, the winds shifted suddenly and forced us back into the harbor. Our last attempt was yesterday. When we failed yet again, and I heard that Belisarius himself had entered the city, I decided that God must want you to have Gelimer's money. So here it is."

The man began lighting lamps which hung from the ceiling. As the light grew, a vault materialized out of the darkness, within which were piled up wooden strongboxes bound with iron chains. Boniface took a large keyring from a hook on the wall and opened one of the boxes. A cascade of gold and silver coins immediately spilled out onto the floor, causing the men behind Belisarius to gasp.

"It is all here," Boniface declared, grabbing a huge fistful. "And it now belongs to you."

As he said this, a rush of voices and footfalls could be heard on the stone steps leading up to the nave of the church. "Magister!" someone shouted. "Is he down there?"

"I am here!" Belisarius replied.

"An urgent message for you!"

"Have this packed up and loaded onto wagons at once," Belisarius barked at Athenodorus gesturing to the strongboxes. "We're taking it with us."

Squinting into the light, Belisarius hurried up the steps and emerged back into the nave.

"An urgent dispatch for you from Carthage," Principius said. "The rider said it was from Procopius—and none but you may see it."

"Oh?" Belisarius grunted. He snatched the dispatch out of Principius's hand, broke the seal and read it:

> The general Solomon and the secretary Procopius, to Belisarius, Master of Soldiers.
>
> We waste no time on greetings, Magister. We say only this: it is imperative that you return to Carthage at once. If we say no more, it is because we fear this missive may fall into the hands of those who would harm your cause.

Belisarius's lips twisted in annoyance. It was very unlike Solomon to send such a cryptic message.

But advice like this from his two most trusted subordinates could not be ignored. "We're moving out," he ordered, handing the dispatch back to

Principius. Behind them, the heavy coffers of coin were already being muscled out of the crypt. "Get some more men down there to assist. I want us on the road to Carthage within the hour."

"But what of Gelimer?" asked Pharas.

"He is out of our reach among the Moors," Principius replied. "Let him rot there."

"No, Pharas is right," Belisarius replied. "Gelimer can not be allowed to reconstitute his army and his hopes. Pharas, take your Herulians to Mount Papua and make sure Gelimer stays there and that no supplies are brought up to him."

"I will do so with pleasure, Magister," Pharas saluted.

Belisarius nodded. "A princely reward will be yours if you can bring him in alive."

XX

AD 534, February
Seventh year of the reign of Justinian, Emperor of the Romans
At Carthage

"He has entered the city," Archelaus announced. "I just received word from the gates."

"So soon? I never expected him back so quickly!" Calonymous cried, jumping up from his desk. A pile of shipping manifests spilled onto the fine mosaic floor. "What are we to do?"

"You worry over nothing," Archelaus scoffed. "Even if he finds out about the letters we have sent to the emperor, what can he do to us?"

"He commands the army!" Calonymous barked back. "He could have us arrested! Impaled!"

"When did you become such a worrying woman, my old friend? It is almost as if you believe the slanders we put in those letters to Justinian about Belisarius acting the tyrant. He has always stayed strictly within the law. And we have broken no law. We have only reported our observations to the emperor."

Calonymous sat back down and took a deep breath. "Yes, you are right. I am agitated over this, I admit it."

"Besides, five duxes of the imperial troops signed the letter. Even if Justinian doesn't believe us, he will trust them. And Belisarius wouldn't dare punish all of them and us besides. If he did, it would prove our accusations true."

"Ah, you are right, you are right!" Calonymous said, smoothing out his dark beard.

"Leon! Wine for your master!" Archelaus shouted, snapping his fingers at the servant standing nearby. "Drink. It will calm you down."

"I have been drinking all day."

"Well, have some more, then."

The servant poured the wine and Calonymous took a deep quaff. "I have filled fifteen ships with plunder so far. I was hoping to sail them out before he came back."

"We'll just have to make sure that the men keep quiet until we can move the ships out without him noticing," Archelaus grunted. "I'll put the word out.

Those who don't hold their tongues will lose them."

"Yes," Calonymous sighed, feeling the unwatered wine go straight to his head. "If we do this right, we'll be rich as caesars."

"And if we can manage to take that insufferable prig and his hideous wife down a few pegs in the process, so much the better," Archelaus whispered with a grin, sipping from his own cup.

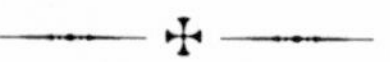

A swarm of litigants greeted Belisarius as he arrived at the royal palace, all shouting at him to hear their cases instantly. In irritation, he announced that he could not do so today but that the law courts would be open for appeals tomorrow at the usual hour. This only made them roar all the louder, so he pressed on through them, entering the palace and ordering his bodyguards to bar the doors behind him.

"Husband!" cried Antonina as she rushed to greet him.

"You are a welcome sight, O wife!" he replied, accepting her embrace warmly.

"I heard about John," she said softly. "How terrible..."

Belisarius put a finger to his lips. "Let us discuss it later in private. The wound is...still raw."

Antonina saw the tears welling up at the corners of his eyes and gave an understanding nod.

"I would speak to Solomon and Procopius at once," Belisarius said, clearing his mind. "Where are they?"

"They are waiting for you in the upper chamber," Antonina replied.

Kissing her on the cheek, he rushed off, climbing a flight of marble stairs three at a time. Inside the council chamber, Solomon and Procopius were alone, sitting at a long table with a pile of parchments scattered before them. When Belisarius burst in, they both stood up in surprise.

"Ah, it is you!" Solomon cried, his voice betraying relief.

"Come in quickly. Close the door," Procopius advised, squinting.

Belisarius did so, then immediately turned to face the two. "Tell me at once what this is about."

"It is bad, very bad," Solomon began. "First, the Moors of Byzacium have revolted and are ravaging the country."

"What? But why? The filthy liars! Did I not meet with their envoys as soon as we took Carthage?"

"You did indeed," Solomon continued. "But apparently, their envoys' true purpose in coming was to see if you wore a beard."

"A beard? What foolishness is this?" Belisarius gasped.

"It seems they had received a prophecy saying that the Moors and Vandals would be destroyed by a host from over the sea, led by a beardless man. However, because you are obviously quite bearded, they assumed that the oracle referred to some other time in the future."

Belisarius chuckled in annoyance. "Had we only known that, we could have told them you were the commander instead of me."

"There is worse news, I'm afraid," Procopius interrupted. "Last month, soon after you left the city, two of Calonymous's ships slipped out of the harbor without permission. We managed to capture one of them at Mandracium, suspecting that it was trying to smuggle stolen loot out of the city. What we found on board the ship was much worse than pirated goods, however." Procopius picked up a folded parchment and tossed it to Belisarius, who picked it up at once.

"We broke the seal," Solomon admitted. "It was too suspicious not to."

"I don't fault you for it," Belisarius replied. Studying the seal, he recognized it right away as that of Calonymous. Unfolding the missive, he began to read:

> To my master, the emperor Cæsar Flavius Justinian, the all-conquering, ever happy, ever pious Augustus, conqueror of the Persians and Vandals from Calonymous, Prefect of the Roman fleet. Greetings.
>
> It is with a regret and trembling that I write to my lord and master this day. For who dares disturb the repose of the emperor unless with matters of supreme urgency? And I dread being the one forced to report such unwelcome news to your most noble ears. But the frightful actions of your commander here in Africa compel me. For Belisarius, whom you have entrusted with the supreme command, is playing the part of the tyrant here in Africa, and it is my concern, and that of many of your other high officers, that this man, who you trusted so entirely, is now seeking to set up a throne for himself here in Carthage...

The note went on at length, but Belisarius had read enough. His hands clenched involuntarily into fists, crumpling the parchment between them.

"It is signed not only by Calonymous, but by Archelaus and several other imperial officers as well," Procopius declared.

"Have you arrested them?" Belisarius growled, trying to keep his voice steady.

Solomon sighed, shaking his head. "No, we can't do that. They have too many supporters; it would be imprudent to arrest them. Plus, to do so might look like an admission of guilt to the emperor."

"What do you mean?" Belisarius said. "If we have the letter, how does this concern the emperor?"

Solomon and Procopius glanced nervously at each other.

"We have *one* of the letters," Procopius said. "The man who carried it confessed that a duplicate had been sent aboard the other ship that slipped out of the harbor—the one we failed to intercept."

"So it is very possible that this filthy calumny is being read by the emperor even now," Belisarius said. He slumped into a chair, exhausted and emotionally drained. "What are we to do?"

Solomon and Procopius again exchanged glances. They had together discussed a wild idea but moments before Belisarius's arrival, but now neither had the courage to broach it.

"Your silence says much, my friends," Belisarius muttered. "It would be best, however, if you remained silent, for your words of advice might cause irreparable harm if you speak them amiss."

Procopius opened his mouth, but said nothing. Solomon just shook his head glumly.

Belisarius stood up. "It seems clear to me that we can do nothing except carry on with our mission for the time being and attempt to settle affairs in Africa as completely as possible. Solomon, you will take a moira of my guardsmen and suppress the Moors of Byzacium. I will keep the rest here and begin to make preparations to return to Constantinople as soon as it may be feasible to do so."

"I shall do as you command, O Magister," Solomon replied.

"I can not allow charges such as these to go unanswered before the emperor," Belisarius snarled, his rage simmering. "Too much has been sacrificed on this campaign to see it all destroyed by wicked lies."

✣

At once, Belisarius and Procopius began to craft a detailed report to Justinian, explaining the achievements of the campaign and the current state of affairs in Africa. They avoided the subject of the calumnious letter of Calonymous all together, choosing instead to focus upon the miraculous feats that had been accomplished in Justinian's name.

They had not quite finished the report when a most amazing thing happened. Some wealthy African landowners summoned Belisarius to a meeting at a suburb of Carthage called Aclas to discuss the unexpected arrival of tax collectors from Constantinople. The conference was held in one of the magnificent villas that had been abandoned by a fugitive Vandal lord, and Belisarius found himself besieged by an angry cohort of nobles, each seeking to know exactly how much he was expected to pay for the privilege of being a Roman citizen.

Belisarius had barely begun to assuage their fears when Pharas and several of his men suddenly burst into the courtyard where they were gathered. "I have come to claim my reward!" he shouted rudely, slamming an empty leather pouch down on the table. Behind him, tied with ropes, were a dozen large Vandal men.

All heads turned in their direction. "It is Gelimer!" someone said in a raised voice. Several gasps went up from the assembled crowd. They couldn't believe their eyes.

Two muscular Heruls pulled the captive Gelimer through the crowd and presented him before Belisarius. A few short months ago, the proud man was the richest king in the world, arrayed in splendor and surrounded by powerful men-at-arms. Now, he stood before his former subjects in a filthy cloak, his beard matted and his blond hair unkempt. His grime-encrusted feet were cracked and bleeding from the long march he had endured. His piercing blue eyes were swollen with infection—rivulets of pus drained down his cheeks like tears.

As soon as Belisarius witnessed the pathetic state of the man, any contempt he had for him vanished. "Untie him," he commanded. "This man, though a one-time enemy of the Romans, is to be treated with respect by virtue of his former office."

"Aye," the Heruls replied as they loosed his bonds.

"You are Gelimer?" Belisarius asked.

The man's lips curled in response.

"Have you nothing to say?"

Gelimer laughed. "One generation cometh, another passeth away."

"What say you?" Belisarius replied, puzzled.

Gelimer opened his mouth to respond, but only a throaty chuckle came forth. This soon escalated into a torrent of cackling laughter which erupted volcanically from the man, shaking him violently.

"He has lost his wits," Pharas explained. "We kept him penned in on Mount Papua, as you commanded, O Magister. Nothing got in or out. Then, after several weeks, he sent down a note asking us to send him up a loaf of bread, a lyre, and a sponge. The bread because he had eaten nothing but horse fodder and rancid goat cheese for nearly a month. The sponge for his swollen eyes, damaged by dust and sun. And the lyre because he had written an ode about his misfortunes and wished to accompany himself on the harp."

"How did you manage to lure him out?" Belisarius asked, shouting so that he could be heard above Gelimer's continuing outbursts.

"I kept reminding him of the pledges that you would extend to him. That he would be given rank and lands by the emperor. That he would be enrolled in the senate, made a Roman patrician, and given great sums of money if only he would agree to surrender. Eventually, his misery got the better of his hopes."

The nobles present looked upon their one-time king with disgust and consternation.

Belisarius felt only pity for the pathetic figure who stood before him, still laughing riotously. "Take him out and give him food and drink," Belisarius commanded. "Perhaps that will quiet him."

As Gelimer was led away, a man stepped forward from among the Vandal captives whom Belisarius immediately recognized. Though thin from privation and covered with dirt, Thrasamund still bore the drooping moustache and scar across his cheek from the wound Belisarius had dealt him during the Nika revolt.

"So you are Belisarius," Thrasamund said with a smug smile. "If only I had killed you in the Hippodrome when I had the chance."

"You!" Belisarius growled as if a foul spectre had risen up before his eyes. Anger welled up within him as he advanced on the man, his fists balled.

Thrasamund didn't move.

Belisarius grabbed him roughly and threw him to the ground. "For your crimes, I will have you put to death, you dog!"

"What, for killing men during a fight?" Thrasamund shouted back gamely. "If that's the case, you are guilty of the same crime many times over."

"No. For treason against the emperor," Belisarius rebutted fiercely.

Thrasamund rose cautiously to his feet. "How could I commit treason when I had no loyalty to Justinian to begin with? For I am Thrasamund, son of Tzazon. I have always been a Vandal, loyal only to my king and uncle—the wreck of a man you saw before you."

"You were in our city, Vandal. You were subject to our laws."

"Was I? Well then tell me, what law is Justinian subject to? He who launches invasions against his neighbors under the flimsiest of pretexts and brings death and destruction to a peaceful country? I say you Romans have done a greater evil here than I ever did."

"Be silent!" Belisarius replied. "You belong to a race of lawless pirates who have sacked Roman cities for a hundred years. And now you seek to lecture us on the law?"

Thrasamund seemed chastened, but he stared Belisarius in the eye nonetheless. "I did not have to surrender with my uncle, Belisarius. I could have continued to raise rebellion against you and believe me, many of the men under my command urged me to do so. But I am here today because I respect you as a warrior and because it is said that you have a reputation for mercy. Was I wrong to trust in that reputation?"

Belisarius shook his head in annoyance as his anger slowly subsided. "No. If you seek mercy, it will be yours."

"I said that I had no loyalty to Justinian," Thrasamund continued. "But now, I am ready to swear my allegience to him." He knelt down and bowed his head in submission. "I do so swear it, by God."

"That is acceptable," Belisarius said tensely.

Thrasamund rose. "And, if I may be so bold, I am used to serving under great war chiefs. I would also swear loyalty to you, assuming you will accept Vandals into your household guards."

Belisarius again advanced on the man who did not shrink before him. His lips tensed as he struggled to hold back the vitriol that was lurking behind them. He clenched his teeth. "Go," he growled. "Be thankful you leave my presence with your head still on your shoulders."

"Aye," the man replied, bowing. "If you can forgive me for the deeds I have done, Belisarius, you have my word that I will repay them a hundred-fold."

"I can forgive," Belisarius said with finality as Thrasamund rejoined the Vandal captives. "But I can not forget."

✠

With the Vandal king his prisoner, Belisarius quickly finished off his report to Justinian, asking for his instructions. It was nearly three months before a ship arrived in Carthage bearing a curt message from the emperor. Justinian gave

Belisarius a choice: return to Constantinople with the Vandal captives, or else remain in Africa to complete the conquest, sending the captives ahead. Though not accusatory in any way, the purpose of the letter was obvious. Belisarius knew he had to return if he wished to stay in the emperor's good graces.

Within two weeks, Belisarius had loaded his household and all his guardsmen aboard ship for the long voyage back to Constantinople. He also embarked nearly three thousand captive Vandals and a staggering amount of treasure, filling up a hundred ships.

His farewell from Carthage was bittersweet. Africa had witnessed his greatest military victory and had established him as a brilliant general. But the campaign had also cost him three of his dearest friends. Dorotheus and John were dead, while Uliaris was so shattered with grief and self-loathing that he seemed as good as dead. For his part, Belisarius had not said one word to the man since he had left him prostrate on the floor of the country church near Hippo.

Belisarius had also decided to place Solomon in command at Carthage and would therefore be returning to Constantinople without his most trusted advisor.

Now as the Hagios Giorgios swung its prow into the open sea toward Sicily, Belisarius's soul remained unsettled. Yes, he had fulfilled the emperor's command magnificently, accomplishing everything he had been tasked to do, and much more besides. But his success had bred vicious enemies who resorted to outright lies to destroy his reputation. Yes, he was full of joy at the thought of returning to his home and the sweet infant daughter he had left behind. But that joy was tinged with anguish at the thought of his sister Eudocia who still waited there patiently for a bridegroom who would never come.

Antonina seemed to sense her husband's anxiety as she came topside to join him. In truth, similar fears plagued her own heart as the image of Theodora's severe visage danced before her mind's eye. With a gentle west wind pushing the ship, the two looked out silently over the calm sea toward the luminous disc of the sun rising in the east, and wondered what sort of reception awaited them in Constantinople.

XXI

AD 534, September
Eighth year of the reign of Justinian, Emperor of the Romans
At Constantinople

The Roman fleet approached the Hellespont on a cloudless day in early September after a voyage of nearly two months. There they were met by a dromon flying Justinian's huge gold and purple pennant.

"The emperor orders you to put in at Hebdomon!" the ship's captain cried. "There, you will be told what to do!"

Belisarius took the news in stride. Hebodomon was a suburb of Constantinople, several miles outside the walls, the site of an imperial palace and military training ground. *Why won't he let us land in the Golden Horn?* he wondered to himself. *Perhaps he doesn't trust me to bring my guardsmen so close to the palace?*

His worries were dispelled, however, as soon as the Hagios Giorgios touched the wharf at Hebdomon and the first person he saw was Marcellinus, the emperor's secretary. Behind him stood a contingent of Excubitors dressed in their ceremonial finery. Also present was the large and obnoxious form of John the Cappadocian, the Praetorian Prefect, surrounded by a few aides. Belisarius knew precisely why he was there.

"Greetings, O General!" Marcellinus said, his short gray beard bristling around his smiling lips. "Our most pious and noble master, Justinian Augustus, sends his greetings to you."

"May he reign!" Belisarius barked back, saluting with fist over chest.

"For many and good years!" the assembled Excubitors chanted.

"General, our most generous emperor has sent me here to welcome you home and to instruct you on how to comport yourself over the next few days."

"I am at the emperor's command," Belisarius replied humbly.

"You and your guardsmen are to remain here to refresh yourselves for two days. Relax. Eat. Get your land legs under you. During that time, I will oversee the accommodations for the captives and our honored guests, the Vandal royalty."

"And I," Cappadocian John broke in, "will take possession of all spoils of war for immediate deposit into the imperial fisc." A logothete beside John thrust a sealed parchment at Belisarius which bore the Imperial insignia.

"As you wish," Belisarius smiled, not bothering to accept the document. "Speak to Rufinus who is acting as fleet purser."

John scowled as Belisarius pushed past him onto dry land, followed by his family and bodyguards.

Antonina caught the rotond Cappadocian's eyes and gave him a look of profound womanly scorn. To her annoyance, John winked at her and blew her a kiss.

"The old tart still likes me," John chuckled, just loud enough for his grinning logothete to hear.

✠

Marcellinus led Belisarius and his household to a comfortable villa in the town of Hebdomon.

"When can we enter the city to see the emperor?" Belisarius asked as soon as he had the man alone.

Marcellinus smiled. "You must be patient, my good man. I know you are anxious to see him. And I tell no lie when I say that he is most anxious to see you as well. But the emperor, as you know, is a man who loves ceremony and he has deemed your victory so glorious and superb that it deserves the type of tribute that has not been seen for nearly five hundred years."

"What do you mean?" Belisarius asked.

"You will see soon enough," Marcellinus replied, smiling.

✠

On the third day, under a brilliant late summer sun, Belisarius stepped out onto the worn cobblestones of the Via Egnatia leading from Hebdomon to Constantinople. Before him stretched a long column of his guardsmen, four abreast. They wore shining new helmets and armor kits supplied by the emperor and were in tremendous high spirits, having spent the past two days eating rich foods and taking their ease.

Next in line were five hundred of the tallest and fairest of the Vandal captives. These men were stripped to the waist to show off their fine physiques and were encumbered with chains. Marching among them were the Vandal nobles, arrayed in fine clothes but also chained and looking unkempt. Gelimer himself was dressed in a purple cloak with a crown on his head. He was also bound with shackles and seemed to be muttering aimlessly to himself.

Behind the captives, forty carts drawn by oxen displayed the magnificent spoils from Africa for all to see—thrones of gold, silver plate, fine ivory carvings, brass decanters, stunning jewelry and finely wrought drinking cups. Even the gilded carriage of the Vandal royal family was on display, drawn by four white stallions. A double line of Scholarians and Excubitors with swords drawn guarded the treasures, which were to be seen, not touched.

Bringing up the rear of the parade column, Belisarius walked. At the request of the emperor, there would be no horses for the soldiers. In ancient times, Rome's main military might resided in her footsoldiers and Justinian was anxious to uphold that tradition, even though it was by this time a complete fiction.

Surrounding Belisarius were thirty of his most able and trusted guardsmen—Principius, Unigastus, Athenodorus, and Boriades among them—all decorated with gold torques, gem-encrusted broaches, and other symbols of imperial favor. On his right hand was his cousin Rufinus, bearing the standard of Belisarius's biscuit-eaters. On his left, walking proudly beside his step-father, was Photius.

Belisarius himself wore his own battle gear, suitably repaired and polished, with a scarlet cloak flowing over his back. On his head he wore a gleaming silver helm trimmed with gold, and around his neck hung a heavy jeweled torque—both gifts of the emperor.

Once all were in place, a trumpet blasted out a few martial notes and the column moved out at a slow march. A short distance from Hebdomon, they crested a low hill and caught sight of Constantinople arrayed before them in all its splendor. The guardsmen of Belisarius cheered. Anxious voices could be heard among the Vandal captives, wondering if they had erred by putting their trust in the promises of Belisarius.

At the two mile marker, they met the first of the jubilant crowds which had spilled out of the city to greet them. Waving banners and chanting accolades, the common folk lined the road on both sides to catch a glimpse of the conquering hero and his mighty men.

There, also, was Marcellinus attired in a patterend tunic and gaudy blue cloak. He merged into the column as Belisarius passed.

"General, I have been tasked with escorting you into the city," he began. "The emperor himself will meet you in the Hippodrome."

Belisarius frowned involuntarily, recalling the last time he had been in that cursed place.

The triumphal procession reached the magnificent Golden Gate just as the sun was approaching its noontime apex. The white marble blocks that made up the structure's triple arches seemed to shimmer in the bright sunlight and the gates themselves, plated with polished gold, were nearly too radiant for mortal eyes to behold. Embroidered silk banners flew amidst the crowd of soldiers massed atop the towering walls, while gold and purple streamers hung from the high archways. Even the four enormous bronze elephants which stood directly above the main gate were festooned gaily with garlands of flowers.

As the procession marched through, a flurry of rose petals descended upon them. Above their heads, a troupe of Green factionists mounted on a balcony half-way up the wall, sang a spirited paean to the soldiers to the tune of a bawdy song.

Once inside the city, the crowd stretched deep into the sidestreets and as far up the Mese as the eye could see. So thick was the mob of curious onlookers that the Excubitors had to force them aside so that the procession could advance.

In the forum of Theodosius, an officially-dressed man with two menacing guardsmen on either side approached Marcellinus wheeling a handcart. Marcellinus chattered quickly with the man and then turned to Belisarius: "Ah yes. General, this is for you."

Belisarius was astonished when Marcellinus opened a chest on the handcart and withdrew a large bag of gold coins.

"What am I meant do with these?"

"Why, scatter them to the crowd, of course!" Marcellinus smiled.

"Truly?" Belisarius asked.

"Let me show you," Marcellinus chirped in excitement. Grabbing a handful of coins, he cast them into the air. The crowd roared and went for them in a mad rush. "Throw more or they'll riot!" he cried exuberantly.

Belisarius reached into the bag and began flinging handfuls of coins to either side. The people roared rapturously, the ones further back pleading for him to throw higher and farther.

"Come, Belisarius! My arthritic old aunt throws better than that!" a young fellow jested from his perch high up on the pedestal of Theodosius's column.

Squinting up at him, Belisarius threw a solidus which reached the lad easily, much to his delight. "Spend some of that on your aunty, wastrel!" Belisarius retorted with a grin. He was starting to enjoy this!

"*Memento mori*," Marcellinus said.

"What?" Belisarius chuckled, turning toward him.

"Remember, thou art mortal," he said again. "You know. That's what a slave is supposed to whisper in the ear of the triumphant general as proceeds."

"I see," Belisarius said. "That puts a bit of a snuffer on things, doesn't it?"

"I suppose it does," Marcellinus said. Then, turning away slightly, he repeated under his breath: "Remember, thou art mortal."

"Stop saying that!" Belisarius chided playfully.

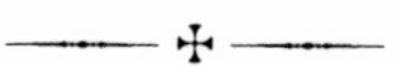

As the procession wound toward the Hippodrome, Belisarius noticed that the district near the palace had changed completely since he had left for Africa. Large areas had been cordoned off with rope and canvas, behind which could be seen the scaffolds and workshops of a sprawling construction site. Rising above the clutter were the truly massive walls of a monumental church. *Hard to believe they built all that in less than two years!* Belisarius mused to himself.

The Hippodrome itself had been completely renovated and showed no trace of the damage it sustained during the Nika riots. Its rows of colonnaded archways soared skyward above the surging crowds which seemed to swell ever larger and more boisterous as the procession advanced. Belisarius could hear loud blasts of organ music emanating from within the Hippodrome, accompanied by the rhythmic chants of the demes. The sound made his heart race as for the first time, the thought entered his mind that all this euphoria was the result of his efforts.

As he stepped onto the track of the Hippodrome, Belisarius was met by a deafening roar. The crowd leapt to its feet with a burst of excitement that shook the massive structure to its foundation. Led by the demes, the crowd began an impromptu doggerel:

Hail Belisarius, Glory of Romans!
Hail Belisarius, Master of dromons,
who sailed with his fleet over storm-tossed waves
to conquer a nation, make kings into slaves.

Hail Belisarius, brave Persian slayer!
Hail Belisarius, Vandal waylayer!
against whom barbarians fall prostrate like dogs,
their corpses in piles like great heaps of logs.

We greet thee, O hero, with fear in our hearts,
Recalling our brush with your sword and your darts.
Have pity on us who acclaim you this day,
and throw us a gold-piece or two on your way!

A burst of jollity followed their last stanza as the crowd erupted into pleas for a donative.

Belsarius shrugged and threw his hands into the air. He had exhausted his supply of coins long before. He was about to walk on when Marcellinus thrust another bag of gold into his hands.

"Last one," he said. "I was saving it for when we got here."

Belisarius reached into the bag and began flinging its contents as far into the crowd as his arm would allow. Fights immediately broke out over the spoils but Belisarius shrugged and kept moving. Expecting factionists not to fight was like expecting a garbage pile not to stink.

The entire procession marched down the track of the hippodrome and passed in front of the imperial seat. There, Justinian and Theodora sat high above in imperial magnificence, arrayed in purple and wearing ornate ceremonial crowns of gold and pearls. Though betraying little external emotion at the spectacle passing before him, Justinian would occasionally press his lips together in the slightest of smiles and nod his head. He lost control of himself only once. As the Menorah and the spoils from Jerusalem went by, he leapt from his throne and leaned over the balustrade to get a closer look.

"Take care, O Augustus, those items are cursed!" a mocking voice from the crowd shouted. "We would hate to see you fall to your death!"

Justinian glared angrily into the laughing crowd, but could not discern the source of the taunt. With a scornful snort, he returned to his throne and his previous dignified posture.

"Serves you right," Theodora muttered, barely moving her lips.

In the tier below the imperial couple sat several of the high palace officials, surveying the loot with a mixture of awe and extreme jealousy.

"Will you look at all that," Narses muttered bitterly.

"It is quite a sight," Cappadocian John replied. "And most of it is going straight from here into the treasury."

"Not the gold, you idiot," Narses retorted, "his men! Look at them! Easily the finest soldiers the empire has seen since the days of Constantine."

"Yes, and the emperor spent an enormous sum outfitting them in that ceremonial junk," John clucked disapprovingly. "Such a pity to waste money on men who don't even appreciate it."

"What I could do with men like that," Narses frowned. "You know, I've heard that his tactics had nothing to do with the victories. It was his men. They fight like lions."

"Really?" Tribonian added. "I hadn't heard that."

"Pah," John said dismissively. "Even if it were true, he selected those men himself, Narses. You can at least give him credit for that." John grinned wickedly, knowing precisely the effect his words would have on the praepositus.

"Credit?" Narses laughed, holding his temper. "Credit is something you have none of after all the debts you've incurred gambling, you fat illiterate dungheap."

John frowned. "I am not illiterate."

"Tell me, John, how much money have you lost since Belisarius returned victorious?"

John's lips twisted into an ugly grimace.

"Ten thousand?" Narses prodded.

John shook his head.

"Twenty thousand?"

John rolled his eyes.

"Fifty thousand?" Narses laughed delightedly.

John stood up suddenly. "You listen here, you little worm," he shouted. "None of that matters, because unlike you money-grubbing paupers, I am a man of means and resources. I can lose fifty thousand like that," John snapped his fingers. He then balled his fist and shook it menacingly at Narses. "Do you think it bothers me, eunuch? Do you?"

Narses didn't flinch in the slightest. "No, of course not," he said mockingly. "You are such a stoic, contemplative man after all, who never blusters or loses his head over anything."

"How dare you…," John's eyes bulged in anger. Beads of sweat formed on his forehead and his heavy fist trembled slightly.

"Sit down, John," Tribonian scolded. "You're blocking my view!"

"Arrogant bastard," the prefect muttered under his breath as he returned to his seat. *Someday they will all tremble before me. By the gods, I swear it.*

✠

By this time, Belisarius and Marcellinus arrived before the Kathisma. Both men immediately prostrated themselves on the ground before Justinian. A hush fell over the crowd as Justinian left them where they were for some minutes.

"You may rise," Justinian finally commanded with a gesture.

In a loud voice, Marcellinus announced: "O most pious and happy Augustus, our master, Justinian, I present to you the general Belisarius who has returned from Africa victorious over the Vandal nation!"

The crowd immediately erupted into a prolonged roar. Belisarius stood his ground, showing no emotion.

"Greetings to you, Belisarius," Justinian said, rising to his feet to better project his voice. "We have received word that you have completed your mission and returned our Africa to the dominion of the Roman Empire."

After a brief pause, Belisarius replied: "Just so have I done, O Master, most noble and illustrious Augustus. By your mandate, I have won back your Africa and thrown off from her citizens the barbarian yoke, through the grace of Almighty God."

Cheers again began from the people, but Justinian stifled them with an upraised arm. "We are also told that you have returned to us with the spoils from this war, including the so-called King of the Vandals, the foul tyrant, Gelimer."

"Just so, O Master," Belisarius replied. "But say the word and I shall present the man before your most exalted throne."

"You may do so."

The vast crowd roiled as Gelimer was brought forward in chains, surrounded by his nobles. Fear gripped the Vandals as they found themselves in the midst of a hundred thousand Romans, all shouting insults and calling for their deaths. From his seat high above them, Justinian looked respendent and terrible all at once to the anxious captives.

Sensing their trepidation, Marcellinus approached Gelimer. "You have nothing to fear," he said softly. "This is all for show, to enhance the prestige of our emperor with the people. You understand, don't you?"

Gelimer smiled at him, showing his yellow teeth. He muttered something under his breath.

"What was that you said?" Marcellinus asked, moving his ear closer.

"Vanity of vanities!" Gelimer said much louder. "All is vanity!"

Marcellinus scowled and moved away.

Justinian's arm went up again, and the people fell silent. "You have brought this usurper before us in the trappings of a king?" the emperor asked, feigning anger.

"A king no longer, O Master," Belisarius replied. "For the Romans have but one king, one emperor, one Augustus: The most noble and pious Justinian, may he reign!"

"For many and good years!" the entire people chanted joyously in unison.

Belisarius stripped Gelimer of his purple cloak and knocked his crown onto the ground. The crowd again erupted in an outburst of cheers and cat-calls. A series of loud blasts from the organ sounded over them.

"Now fall to your knees before the emperor," Belisarius whispered to

Gelimer. "We shall do obeisance to him together."

Gelimer looked at him severely, the spark of sanity returning to his eyes. "I shall do it, though it is nothing but senseless vanity."

Belisarius fell on his face before the throne, as did Gelimer, one-time king of the Vandals.

"Justinian Augustus, you rule!" a mandator cried out.

"Hail the all-conquering emperor!" the people responded in unison.

"God save our most noble and beloved Augustus!"

"May he rule for many and good years!"

"A hundred years to Justinian Augustus!"

"A thousand years to the Roman Empire!"

Chants of this sort continued for a quarter hour or more, during which time neither Belisarius nor Gelimer moved at all. Occasionally, Belisarius could hear the Vandal mutter, "vanity, vanity."

Finally, when the acclamations ended, Justinian raised his hand to speak again: "You may rise."

Both men did so immediately.

"Gelimer, your misdeeds demand the gibbet!" Justinian declared.

The crowd gasped.

"But to inflict such a punishment on you, a defeated man from a crushed people, would be the action of a cruel tyrant. Instead, because you have submitted yourself to us and the Empire of the Romans, I grant you your life! Marcellinus, remove his chains!"

"Hail Justinian the merciful!" a voice rang out.

"Most merciful Augustus, may you reign!" the people responded.

"Yet, more than this," Justinian continued, "in memory of your uncle Hilderic who was a great friend of the Roman people, I will grant you the rank of patrician and an estate in Galatia where you and your family may settle."

"Hail Justinian, the most generous!" the same voice cried out.

"Most generous Augustus, may you reign!"

Gelimer bowed courteously in response. "You are most gracious, your vanity," he muttered under his breath.

Gelimer was then led away by Marcellinus to join the rest of the Vandal captives.

Justinian then turned a fond gaze upon Belisarius. "For your valorous deeds, O Belisarius," the emperor declared, "you are granted the title, *vir illustris*."

"Glory of the Romans!" a loud voice from the crowd shouted, and a cheer went up.

Justinian appeared irked at the interruption, but continued: "And furthermore, we hereby grant you that ancient and most honorable of offices—the Consulship of the Romans for the next year."

At this, a tremendous roar shook the entire Hippodrome. All the people knew that the naming of a consul meant a year of festivals and frequent races. And considering the enormous wealth Belisarius had brought back from Africa, their minds swirled with visions of how opulent such celebrations might be.

"Hail Belisarius, savior of the empire!" the Blue deme chanted.

"Hail Belisarius, conqueror of the Vandals!" the Green deme shouted back louder.

"Hail Belisarius, pride of the army!" the collected soldiers cried.

"Hail Belisarius, glory of the Romans!" the entire mass of people chanted. Again and again they repeated the slogan until Belisarius sensed it had gone on too long. Looking up at the imperial box, he could see the emperor's discomfiture.

Without thinking, Belisarius drew his sword, raised it above his head and pointed it toward Justinian. Seeing this, the people grew perplexed and silence gradually descended.

When they were mostly quiet, Belisarius spoke: "Take care, O Romans, and mind your tongues! You give praise to the servant who was merely doing the bidding of his master. If you wish to laud the success of our campaign in Africa, then laud the man who conceived it, planned it, paid for it, and supported it to the utmost. Who but Justinian, our most pious and God-beloved master dared to envision so bold an enterprise? Who but our most serene and brilliant emperor could have carried forth such a righteous and ambitious campaign against an enemy who was considered insuperable?

"Future generations will say of our most noble emperor, 'men called him mad, but he trusted in the Lord, and the Lord delivered the rich fields of Numidia into his hands.' I ask you, who will remember the servants? It is the master alone who deserves all the glory!"

Belisarius gazed at Justinian high above him. "Justinian Augustus, you conquer!" he screamed, thrusting his sword into the air.

"Hail the all-conquering Augustus!" the people responded.

"Justinian Augustus, ever victorious, you rule!" Belisarius cried out.

"Rule forever, O most pious emperor!"

The acclamations went on. Sitting on his throne in the Kathisma, Justinian soaked it all in, very well satisfied.

XXII

AD 534, October
Eighth year of the reign of Justinian, Emperor of the Romans
At the Rufinianae near Chalcedon

With the euphoria of the triumph behind him, Belisarius returned to the Rufinianae where he would face a task he dreaded with all his heart.

The servants lined the road to the front gate of the estate, waving bright pennants and garlands to welcome their master home. They cheered as Belisarius and Rufinus rode through, followed by Photius and Theodosius. A carriage driven by the surly Eugenius came next, with the exhausted Antonina and Macedonia riding within. Thirty of Belisarius's most trusted guardsmen brought up the rear of the miniature triumphal procession.

Once inside the gate, Belisarius inhaled the sweet fragrence of the acacia trees mingled with the odor of fresh baked bread wafting out from the kitchens. *Home,* he sighed.

"The master is here!" a female voice cried out. Dozens of other servants came running into the courtyard.

From the corner of his eye, Belisarius saw something that astounded him. A tiny girl with ringlets of blond hair falling all around her face toddled before an elderly nurse who sat smiling on a bench.

Joannina!

He lept from his horse and caught the child in his arms, embracing her as she let out a delighted squeal.

"I have missed you so, my girl," he said. "How you have grown!"

Before he knew it, Antonina was embracing both of them.

"Let me see my baby," she cooed urgently.

Belisarius released his daughter and both he and Antonina gazed upon their beautiful child with amazement.

"She looks just like you," Belisarius quipped, overcome with joy. "An angel!"

"You...mama," the girl squawked suddenly in Greek, swatting at Antonina playfully.

"She talks!" the two parents said in unison, laughing.

"She's a precocious child," the nurse broke in. "She's been chatting with me for near on six months now." The old woman stood up and limped forward. She unclasped a large hinged pendant from around her neck and opened it, revealing two tiny portraits inside painted on wood. On the right was the skillful likeness of Antonina; on the left was the bearded face of Belisarius. "Eudocia had this made soon after you left. We've been showing it to little Nina every day."

"Eudocia," Belisarius groaned. "Where is she?"

"In the church," the old woman replied. "She's been in there for a month since she got the letter."

"What letter?" Belisarius said.

Antonina winced. "The letter I sent. After it happened."

"What?" Belisarius barked. "Why did you do such a thing?

"Please don't be angry, husband," Antonina said softly. "She needed to know and it was best coming from my hand."

"Why didn't you tell me?"

"Because you had enough to concern you," Antonina replied gently. "And it is better this way, believe me."

Greatly vexed, Belisarius looked away.

"Go to her now," Antonina said, touching his hand. "I'm sure she's waiting for you."

✠

Belisarius entered the small church with the white dome that stood beside the main house. The inside was silent and brightly lit by the afternoon sun pouring in through the upper windows. A single woman in a black veil was seated on a bench to the left of the altar. Belisarius approached, his footfalls echoing through the space. As he got closer, however, he realized that the woman was not Eudocia.

"You have come a long way," he whispered, sitting next to her.

"As have you," she replied.

"Thank you, mother."

"Antonina sent me a letter about what happened, so I came. She is there." Anna gestured to the form of a young woman curled up in front of the altar asleep. She too was dressed in black.

"How long has she been like that?" Belisarius asked.

"All day. She barely eats unless I force her. She will not leave the church."

"I must speak to her," Belisarius said.

"Come, then, let us wake her."

Slowly, Eudocia opened her eyes, crusted over with dried tears. When she saw her brother sitting before her, she let out a long moan and flung herself on him. A welter of sobs convulsed her.

Belisarius embraced her, appalled at how thin and tense she was. Tears welled up in his eyes. "Forgive me, sister," he murmured quietly, his voice breaking.

After a long time, Eudocia sat up to look at him. Her long curls hung limply around her weary face which now looked much older than her 19 years. "Were you there…when it happened?" she choked.

Belisarius shook his head, his heart utterly crushed. "No. By the time I arrived, he was already gone…and buried."

Eudocia's lower lip trembled as if in anticipation of another torrent of sobs.

"But there was a priest there who told me everything," Belsarius continued.

"So he did have a priest with him…at the end?" Eudocia gasped.

"Yes. He died in God's heavenly grace. And with your name on his lips."

"He did?" Eudocia's sad eyes brightened. She again threw herself into her brother's arms. "Oh, thank you. I was so worried…that he died unshriven." She let out a long sigh and her whole body seemed to relax.

For a long while, the three sat distraught before the altar, saying nothing.

"Eudocia, you must come out," Anna finally said, taking her daughter's hand.

"Yes," Belisarius added. "I loved John more than all others. But death comes to us all, sooner or later. It is the job of those left behind to go on living until it is our time."

"And too much grief is unseemly," Anna added. "It is a sign of pride—that we do not accept God's will."

Eudocia nodded. "You are right, mother. Too much grief is unseemly. But do not think that I spent all my time here in this church merely grieving for John. I loved him. I love him still. But since he has left, I have come to love another man. And I have decided to be with that man from now on."

Both Anna and Belisarius looked at her with distress and astonishment on their faces.

"Why have you never mentioned this other man?" Anna gasped.

"Mother, I mention him every day in my prayers. I have decided to take the veil, for the man I love is the Christ, our Lord. I shall be his bride."

Anna shook her head. "No. A woman must not enter the convent out of grief. Two days ago you said you wanted to die."

"Don't you see?" Eudocia interrupted, steely determination in her voice. "I am already dead. I died to this world when my betrothed was killed. The charms and pleasures of earth hold no joy for me now and never will again."

"You speak too hastily, sister," Belisarius replied softly. "Time will heal your wound. You will see."

"But I don't want this wound to heal," Eudocia said softly. "I will carry it with me to my grave and offer up the pains it gives me for the salvation of souls. Far from a burden, almighty God has given me a great and wonderful gift."

Anna's eyes widened at the girl's words. "Who has taught you this?"

"It was revealed to me," Eudocia replied, "by my bridegroom."

Anna embraced her, tears streaming down her cheeks. "The convent of Saint Euphemia is in Chalcedon. We can go there tomorrow. They will know what to do."

"Yes, please, mother," Eudocia sighed. "Thank you."

The two women walked slowly out of the church, supporting each other as they went. Belisarius watched them go and then turned back to the altar, his face aghast.

John wasn't enough for You? he thought angrily. *You had to take her, too?*

At the Imperial Palace in Constantinople

"You summoned me, O Master?" Narses said, poking his head into the emperor's private library. He rubbed the sleep out of his eyes. It was two hours before dawn.

"Yes, yes, come in!" Justinian replied, squinting up at him. The few oil lamps around the room gave off a feeble light by which the emperor had been poring over a massive old codex. "Sit down. Take your ease," he added.

"What are you reading, O Master, if I may venture to ask?"

"The poems of Gregory Nazianzen," the emperor replied. "I was in the mood for some light reading tonight."

A servant bustled in and poured both men some wine.

"I brought the letter as you requested," Narses said, producing a folded piece of parchment.

Justinian took, unfolded it, and read it, shaking his head. "Do you still think there's merit in it?"

Narses bit his lower lip thoughtfully. "Most likely not, O Master," he opined. "Calonymous is a pirate and Archelaus is his lackey. Belisarius probably made life difficult for them. He is very much a strict legalist, you know."

"Indeed," Justinian smirked. "That's one of the many things I like about the man."

Narses frowned slightly. He had not meant the remark as a compliment. "Furthermore," the praepositus continued, "the imperial officers who co-signed the letter are all commanders of the infantry."

"Yes, that's true. I hadn't noticed that," Justinian interjected. "And Belisarius won his victories with cavalry."

"Just so, O Master. So it is not surprising that the commanders of the footsoldiers would be unhappy. They did little in Africa besides dig ditches."

"The whole thing makes perfect sense, now," Justinian declared. "Belisarius has no ambitions and this letter is nothing but a slander."

"It seems so, O Master," Narses said, a doubt in his voice.

"Seems?" Justinian pressed.

"One can never be too careful with fantastically popular generals," Narses replied, "particularly ones from noble families."

Justinian smiled, though Narses's last words about Belisarius's lineage caused his brow to furrow slightly. "Yes, you're right. All that favor can go to any man's head. Nevertheless, I think we can safely be done with this scandal-mongering missive."

The emperor touched a corner of the letter to the exposed flame of an oil lamp. It flared up quickly and he tossed it onto bronze tray. It was soon reduced to glowing ash.

"Indeed, one can't be too careful with popular generals, no matter how seemingly loyal," Justinian continued. "I think we shall invite Belisarius and his wife to the palace next week for a social call—a private banquet, perhaps—under the pretext of seeing that baby daughter of his. Once the wine is flowing, it will be easier to sound him out."

Narses nodded with a grunt.

"You disapprove?"

"No, Master, certainly not. It's a fine idea." Narses's mind was already on to other matters and he was anxious to change the subject.

"Then what?" Justinian said indulgently. "Come, now. I know what that tone of voice means. Out with it!"

Narses's face reddened slightly. "O Master, forgive me, but may I ask a boon of you?"

"A boon? You?" Justinian replied, amused. "In all your years of service, you've never requested even one favor. Why now?"

Narses frowned slightly. "I have been pondering this request for some time."

"Well, name it," the emperor said with a good-natured smile.

Narses took a breath. "If you think me worthy, O Master, I would like a command of my own."

"What, a military command?" Justinian looked pleasantly bemused. "But you're sixty years old and have never led men in the field before."

"I'm only fifty-five, Master," Narses corrected, "and hale of body."

"But you have a life of comfort and power here in the palace," Justinian replied. "Why in heaven's name would you want to trade that for the cold, damp discomfort of the army?"

"Master, I have been studying military tactics since my childhood," Narses explained. "It's been a passion of mine, as you are aware. And I admit it—the victories achieved by Belisarius have inspired me. I believe that I can perform well if given the chance."

Justinian nodded, gazing at the man as if trying to read his thoughts. "You are more ambitious that I reckoned, Narses."

"Ambitious only to see your cause furthered in whatever ways my feeble efforts may allow, O Master," Narses replied, bowing. "You know my loyalties belong to you and no one else. I am a eunuch. I have no family. The palace is my home and my only family is the imperial family."

"I shall have to think on it," Justinian said. "But for now, you may return to your bed. I have some more reading to do."

"Yes, O Master," Narses said, dejectedly. He prostrated himself, then turned to exit.

"While I consider your request, however, you may begin recruiting," Justinian said, his eyes now scanning St. Gregory's poetry. "One tagma—three hundred men. Good night."

Narses's heart jumped in his chest. "You are most generous and gracious, O Master," the praepositus said serenely with a deep bow, barely repressing the urge to shout for joy.

I am at that, Justinian laughed to himself as Narses's rapid footfalls faded into the night.

✠

Carrying Joannina in his arms, Belisarius led Antonina into the imperial palace through the Chalke Gate. They had been invited there for a purely social function—a private dinner with the imperial couple.

Dressed in a shimmering white tunic with gold embroidery, Justinian greeted them with the utmost warmth and hospitality in the Triklinos—the formal banquet hall at the palace. Belisarius and Antonina did their obeisance, and even little Joannina got down on her hands and knees, as coached, to the delight of Justinian and Theodora.

After exchanging a few pleasantries, Antonina and Joannina were led away to dine in Theodora's private dining room. Though not completely at ease with Theodora, Antonina felt much more confident in the empress's presence now than she had before the Africa campaign. Their banter was light and cordial as they ate. Once the empty plates were removed, Theodora changed her tone.

"It has come to my ear, Antonina, that your husband distributed some of the Vandal treasure to his soldiers in Carthage—against our wishes."

"That is true, O Mistress," Antonina responded, holding her ground. "But it was not coin. It was loot taken from Vandal nobles who had been killed on the battlefield. Fine armor, weapons and the like. Surely, the emperor wouldn't begrudge his soldiers such things?"

Theodora smiled coldly. "Certainly not." She raised a napkin to her lips very slowly, not once taking here eyes off of Antonina. "You know, Antonina," she said at last, "I like you."

"I am flattered, Mistress."

"Really, I do. In many ways, you remind me of myself. We both came from the most sordid of backgrounds and yet managed to marry powerful men. We have much in common, you and I."

"I suppose we do at that, Mistress."

Theodora took a long draught from a slim golden wine goblet. "I must tell you, the reports you sent me from the campaign were excellent—and the information invaluable. As a reward, I have decided to do you a great favor."

Antonina tilted her head slightly in curiosity.

"I have arranged for your daughter, Anastasia, to marry the dux Ildiger," Theodora declared with a smile.

"My…Anastasia?" Antonina stuttered.

"Oh, I know you have kept your illegitimate daughters a well-guarded secret. But few secrets escape my attention, Antonina. I had heard she was as yet unmarried, so I took the liberty of setting up this very advantageous match."

Antonina was speechless.

"Does it not please you?"

"It pleases me very much, Mistress!" Antonina finally burst out. Finding suitable husbands for her two elder daughters had been a serious concern for Antonina and a marriage to a rising young officer like Ildiger was better than she could have hoped.

"Good!" Theodora replied. She suddenly seemed much warmer and more approachable. "Antonina, I want us to be friends. Real friends."

"I would like nothing better, O Mistress."

"But friendship requires trust. It seems you have proven yourself worthy of my trust. Now I will prove myself worthy of yours."

"But certainly I trust you already, Mistress," Antonina protested.

"Don't lie and toady, my dear. It doesn't suit you in the least," Theodora said sternly. "For some time, I have had an agent working in your household. Were you aware of that?"

Antonina shook her head slowly. "No," she gasped, flipping quickly through her servants in her mind, imagining who the spy might be.

"It is Eugenius," the empress said. "He has been in my pay for many years."

Antonina's eyes widened in shock.

"Now that you know this, however, you may not punish him. I want him to serve you as he does me. Keep him in your home and use him to transmit your messages directly to me. Do you understand?"

"Yes, O Mistress," Antonina replied, rapidly trying to recall everything she had ever said to the man, hoping none of it was incriminating.

"Now, I ask you: do you think you can trust me?"

"I was not lying when I said I trusted you before," Antonina replied, gamely.

Theodora nodded. She then turned to one of her serving maids who was sitting off to the side playing dolls with little Joannina. "Bring the child here to me, Constantia." The maid obeyed instantly and Theodora took the girl onto her lap.

Antonina bit her lower lip to prevent it from trembling.

"They are so innocent at this age, aren't they?" Theodora said, petting Joannina's curls.

"When they're not getting into trouble, that is," Antonina replied, keeping her composure.

"Full of sweetness. Not the slightest trace of nastiness or ambition," Theodora smiled benignly. "Would that we could have remained like that."

"Aye," Antonina sighed, suddenly feeling sympathy for the empress.

Theodora let Joannina slide off her lap. "Go ahead, dear. Go to your mother," she said softly.

The small girl toddled over to Antonina and climbed up into her lap.

"Antonina, both of our husbands are brilliant men," Theodora said, her stern face returning. "If they work together, they will achieve great things for the empire. But brilliance engenders jealousy and there are many in the palace who will attempt to drive them apart to further their own careers."

"I understand that perfectly well, O Mistress," Antonina said.

"In that case, let us make a pact," Theodora said, folding her hands in her lap. "I will protect your husband from my husband, if you will protect my husband from your husband."

Antonina couldn't believe what she was hearing. Setting Joannina on the ground, she fell forward and knelt before Theodora, embracing her knees. "You need have no fear of us, O Mistress. My husband will serve Justinian until the day he dies and never betray him. I can say this with the utmost certainty, and may God strike me dead if my words are untrue. And as he serves Justinian, just so will I serve you. I swear it!"

Theodora gave an inscrutable smile and placed her hand on Antonina's head. "You have no idea how glad I am to hear that, my friend. Be assured that as long as you serve me well, you will have an unfailing patroness in me."

✠

"Do you ever wonder what they talk about for all that time?" Justinian asked.

"No, my Lord, it doesn't bear thinking about," Belisarius laughed.

The two men stood on a wide balcony overlooking the sea. The night air was temperate and the sky clear as a great crystal bowl. The moon reflected off the water, illuminating the ships that rocked at anchor in the harbor below.

"I am told that your Antonina is a forthright and resourceful woman," the emperor resumed. "I assume that's why Archaelaus and Calonymous had nothing good to say about her."

"She did not get on well with them, your Piety. That much is true."

"That is because they are small men with small minds," Justinian declared. "Men like that can't abide a strong woman. What they can't grasp is that having a courageous and unfailingly loyal woman behind you makes you twice as strong as a man."

"I can't disagree, my lord."

At that moment, a servant entered and bowed.

"What is it?" Justinian demanded.

"You told me to bring this up as soon as it arrived, O Master," the slave replied, his eyes turned toward the floor.

"Oh, yes!" Justinian cried enthusiastically. "Come bring it here."

The servant handed the emperor a small flat bundle of cloth with something heavy inside. Justinian peeked under the cloth furtively, shielding the item within from Belisarius's view. His eyes then met those of his general and his face cracked into a tremendous smile.

"Would you like to see?" the emperor asked.

"Yes!" Belisarius replied, feeding off the emperor's excitement.

The two men moved to a nearby table and Justinian slowly unwrapped the item.

Belisarius stood agape at the sight. Before him was a solid gold medallion, over a hand-length across. Stamped upon it was a stylized but detailed portrait of Justinian in full military regalia with a plumed helmet and spear. Around the top edge was the inscription: *Dominus Noster Justinianus Perpetuus Augustus.*

"My Lord, it is magnificent!" Belisarius gasped.

"I had a handful of them minted to commemorate your victory," Justinian said happily. "Turn it over. Look at the other side!"

Belisarius took the medallion in his hand and was surprised at how heavy it was. It weighed as much as a brick! On the reverse was an image of the same warlike Justinian, this time on horseback being led by a winged Victory. Above his head was the inscription: *Salus et Gloria Romanorum.*

For a split second, Belisarius's face fell as he gazed upon the image.

"Is it not a thing of beauty?" the emperor asked.

Vanity of vanities, all is vanity. The words ran silently through Belisarius's head, accompanied by the laughing visage of Gelimer. "It is an image worthy of an emperor, my Lord," he replied.

"I'm glad you like it," Justinian said, "because it is yours, in commemoration of your valorous deeds in Africa. May your victory there stand for a thousand years."

"Your Piety is most generous."

"Now, I have more to say to you," Justinian announced, taking Belisarius by the arm and leading him back to the balustrade overlooking the sea. "We have spoken a great deal about the past tonight, but now I wish to speak of the future."

"I am at your service, as always, my Lord."

Justinian gazed out over the sea toward Chrysopolis across the Bosporus. "Belisarius, what do you see as the primary duty of a Roman general?"

"To defend the empire from all who seek to attack it from without, and to uphold the interests of the emperor from all who seek to attack it from within."

"Well said. Now, the empire—let's talk about that. You and I have always lived in a Roman Empire that is only half the size it was in our grandfathers' day. Men have often said that the recovery of the western provinces is an impossibility, that the barbarians are too strong and the Romans too dissipated. But now, with your victory, everything is changed. The door is now open for us to accomplish something that emperors have only dreamed about for sixty years."

"I see what you are saying, my Lord," Belisarius replied catching the emperor's enthusiasm. "What Roman boy hasn't imagined leading the great army that frees the Eternal City from the Gothic yoke?"

"It can happen, Belisarius. I know it can," Justinian said in a raised whisper as if his hope was too fragile to say out loud. "God has put all the levers in my hand that are necessary to make it happen: Africa is ours; the Goths are divided and have a woman on the throne; and there is a dispute over Sicily which we can exploit to provoke a war."

"Provoke, your Piety?"

For an instant, Justinian had forgotten to whom he was speaking. "That was an unfortunate choice of words, my friend. Any war we fight against the Goths, as you must know, would be a just war because we are protecting the Roman citizens who live under their barbarous rule."

Belisarius knew as well as anyone that the Gothic rule in Italy was far from barbaric, but chose to hold his tongue. He was enjoying this prolonged conversation with the emperor too much to anger him with contradiction.

"Regardless," Justinian continued, "we will certainly attempt diplomacy first. I have already dispatched Peter to the court of the Gothic queen. If anyone can convince her to cede her kingdom to us peacefully, he can. But if his mission should fail, it is likely that there will be war between the Romans and Goths. And as my most distinguished general, I would expect you to command our armies."

"Your Piety, I would do so with no hesitation," Belisarius declared. "You know that I am your man. If you command me to go to war against the Goths, I will do so without lacking enthusiasm. And I will take the fight to them until they tremble in fear at the name of Justinian and never dare to rise up against Roman arms again."

"Excellent!" Justinian replied, well pleased with his general's bellicose words. "Imagine it, Belisarius. If we can recover Italy, anything is possible. Gaul. Spain. Even Britain. Together, you and I could restore the world!"

Belisarius's heart swelled at the bold ambition of the emperor. How closely it mirrored his own hopes! To win great victories and restore the Roman imperium throughout the world—what Roman boy hadn't dreamed of such things?

In his hand, however, the false warlike image of Justinian on the golden medallion glared up at him enigmatically.

Epilogue

AD 534, DECEMBER
Eighth year of the reign of Justinian, Emperor of the Romans
At Constantinople

All of Constantinople anxiously awaited the beginning of Belisarius's term as consul on January 1. Though the office no longer carried any political power, its prestige as a vestige of Roman republican tradition was immense. Those nominated to the office were considered the most brilliant and highly favored men of the empire. They were also expected to spend enormous amounts of money on shows, races, and festivals to entertain the populace.

While appreciating the emperor's favor, Belisarius found the preparations for his consulship to be tedious in the extreme. Beginning in November, he met daily with officials in the palace in charge of the various ceremonies, feasts, and celebrations that were to accompany his inauguration. He was spared having to deal with the Blue and Green factions in planning the dozen races and wild beast shows that he was expected to sponsor. Antonina, who was much better suited to managing these sorts of affairs, relieved him of this gehenna.

So Belisarius found himself spending most of his time at his house in Constantinople, escaping to the Rufinianae only rarely to visit his family or train with his biscuit-eaters.

Each day as he walked from his house to the palace, he was greeted by all manner of people on the street. Some lauded him. Others asked him for favors. A few taunted him. But all wanted to be able to tell their friends and family that they had spoken to the great Belisarius. For his part, Belisarius was usually willing to give a friendly ear to any who approached him.

One day, as the festival of Christmas approached, Belisarius took a more circuitous route home from the palace, hoping to avoid the crowds on the Mese. This path took him by the shrine of the Hodegetria—a place he had studiously avoided since returning from Africa. As he walked the cobblestone street, a force outside his own will made him pause before the entrance to the shrine.

It beckoned to him.

He resisted.

The last time he had been in there, Armenian John had been with him.

The time before that, Florentius. Now, both were dead.

This place is cursed, a voice seemed to whisper in his ear.

But the pull proved too strong. Without thinking, he strode cautiously into the shrine.

He was met by an acolyte. The man recognized him, and said merely, "Come."

By the time he reached the covered balcony where the icon resided above its bubbling font, Belisarius felt annoyed. *Why am I wasting my time here?* he sighed silently in his heart. He knelt down before the image of the Virgin and Christ Child and tried to pray.

Nothing. His soul was completely barren, wilted, dried up.

A million earthly thoughts and cares seemed to crowd out his prayers. The consulship. Rome. Antonina. A disobedient slave. Photius. Solomon. A destitute comrade. His mother. His siblings. His training regimen. Justinian. A tenant who couldn't pay his rent. Joannina. A letter from Constantinus. Theodora. Calonymous. Each worry shouted at him, demanding his attention.

Even thinking about his departed friends didn't help clear his mind. He could muster no more tears for John or Dorotheus. As for Florentius, it had been so long that he could barely remember his face. Time had healed his wounds and the scars no longer pained him.

He lifted his eyes to the icon, illuminated by oil lamps that hung nearby. He was at once surprised at how fresh and vibrant the image appeared. *They say Saint Luke painted this,* his mind mused. *And yet, it looks to me as if some monk could have painted it last week.*

"She is beautiful, is she not?" a voice crackled from behind him. "She points to her Son. Always to her Son."

Belisarius didn't move. *I know that voice....*

"You are the only one left, *Strategos,* of the three."

"Yes," Belisarius said aloud, not turning around. "The other two have perished, Antiochus."

"Not perished," the holy man corrected. "They live."

"No, they both died most miserably and before their time."

"Indeed not," Antiochus retorted, slowly but clearly. "They were both called up to God at precisely their appointed times. For oftentimes, young men are summoned to Heaven before they can sully their souls, while old men are allowed to live long lives in hopes they repent of their wickedness before they die."

Belisarius stood up and wheeled around. His eyes searched for the source of the voice but he could see no one at first.

"I am here, *Strategos.*"

A slight movement caught Belisarius's attention. Sitting on a bench carved from living stone was a bearded man in a long gray cloak. A deep shadow covered him and a heavy woolen hood concealed what features the darkness did not.

"Why are you here?" Belisarius asked.

"I am performing my devotions," Antiochus responded. "I have been abiding with the sleepless ones of the Studion Monastery, but I was told to come here on the third day past the nones of December to venerate Our Lady. When the Lord calls, I obey."

"Will you come into the light so that I may see you?"

"As you wish," Antiochus said. He rose to his feet and shambled slowly toward Belisarius.

As he entered the glow of the oil lamps around the icon, Belisarius at once noticed his feet were bare and ulcerated. "I am sorry," Belisarius said. "Had I known about your feet..."

"Do not concern yourself," Antiochus chided with a smile. "For me every step is penance. And that is a good thing."

"Will you sit?" Belisarius said, gesturing to the edge of the font.

"I will not," Antiochus replied with a smile. His weatherbeaten face was alive with a joyful radiance.

"I have gone to Africa, as you said I would," Belisarius said.

"I know it," Antiochus replied. "Did you venerate the holy places?"

"In Carthage, yes. In Hippo Regius, I could not because Augustine's bones have been moved."

Antiochus nodded. "But at least you saw his crypt."

"Indeed I did. It was filled with Vandal gold."

"Ah, a worldly treasure replaces a heavenly one," Antiochus lamented.

Belisarius shook his head and looked again toward the Hodegetria icon.

"You are troubled, my son," Antiochus observed.

"I am," Belisarius replied with a sigh. "God has given me success beyond anything I thought I could achieve. And yet..." He paused to collect his thoughts. "Why has He stripped me of those friends who were my chief supports in matters of the spirit? When Florentius was alive, he used to drag me to the Divine Liturgy—every day if I let him. And John never tired of reminding me of my devotions and was always ready to accompany me. But now they are gone. And I have no one..."

"They are gone, but you are not abandoned, my son," Antiochus said. "They pray for you in Heaven."

"Yes, but I don't hear them!" Belisarius interjected. "I no longer feel their presence here on earth where I need them."

"God will provide what you need here on earth as well. You must trust Him in all things."

Belisarius took a deep breath.

"Trust Him," Antiochus repeated.

"You are right. And I spoke too hastily. I am blessed with fine people around me still. My wife, Antonina, is a rare woman who eases my burdens and makes my life a joy. And just recently, my childhood friend Constantinus wrote to me wanting to reconcile. So even though the Lord has taken away some of my dear ones, He sends others to replace them."

Antiochus smiled sadly. "You have been blessed, indeed, my son. Only, take care when trying to interpret the actions of Providence."

But Belisarius didn't hear his warning. His mind had already strayed back to the long list of cares clamoring for his attention. "I must go, Antiochus. Will you give me your blessing?"

"It is my pleasure to do so," the just man replied.

Belisarius knelt down before him, casting his eyes to the ground.

Antiochus placed his hand on his head and intoned solemnly: "May the blessing of Our Lord Jesus Christ descend upon you and remain with you always. May your enemies be confused and your friends be loyal. May you be clear-eyed and courageous. May you always trust in God and be wary of the desires of your heart which often deceive. May God send his angels to defend you in battle and may he grant you the mercy of a good death in His own time. Amen."

"You are most gracious, Antiochus," Belisarius said, regaining his feet. He embraced the man, then turned on his heel. "God calls me to do even greater deeds for the emperor. I am certain of it. So you must pray for me without ceasing."

"Do not doubt that I shall," Antiochus replied.

"And for the imperial cause," Belisarius added.

Antiochus blinked and put up his hand, half in blessing, half in salute. "Farewell, O *Strategos*,"

"Farewell," Belisarius replied, bowing his head slightly. He then walked briskly out of the shrine.

Heaving a deep sigh, Antiochus shuffled painfully back to his bench to resume his devotions.

"Have mercy on him, O Lord," the old man said in a raised whisper.

End of Book II

Glossary

Ahura Mazda – The benevolent spirit of the Zoroastrian religion of Persia.

Angra Mainyu – The hostile spirit of the Zoroastrian religion of Persia.

Arianism – A heresy which held that God the Son, Christ, was unlike the Father and had been created by the Father. Condemned at the Council of Nicaea (AD 325) and at the Council of Constantinople (AD 381).

Atrium – An open-air room at the entrance of a Roman house, usually containing a pool for catching rain-water.

Bandifer – A Roman standard-bearer.

Bucellarii – *lit.* "Biscuit-eaters." Mercenaries in the pay of private individuals.

Byzantium – Ancient name of the city of Constantinople, capital of the eastern Roman Empire.

Candidatus – A bodyguard of the Roman emperor.

Centenaria – One hundred pounds of gold.

Chalcedonian – A supporter of the decisions of the Council of Chalcedon (AD 451), particularly with regard to the dual natures of Christ.

Chanaranges – Persian term for general.

Consul – A Roman office dating back to the founding of the Republic. By late Imperial times, the office was entirely ceremonial and would be abolished completely in the mid-6th century AD.

Corselet – A mail-shirt.

Cubicularius – An imperial chamberlain or manservant.

Cursores – An open formation of soldiers used to pursue a fleeing enemy.

Daphne – The private quarters of the emperor in the imperial palace.

Defensores – A formation of soldiers in close order which follows up the *cursores* in case they should fall back.

Dekarch – Roman army rank. Leader of 10 men.

Delphax – The great audience hall in the imperial palace.

Demes – The Green and Blue factions of the Hippodrome.

Dromon – A late Roman warship powered by sail and oar and noted for speed.

Dux (alternately **Moirarch**) – *lit.* Duke. An officer of the Roman army in charge of a *moira.*

Eutychianism – A heresy similar to monophysitism which was condemned at the Council of Chalcedon (AD 451).

Euxine Sea – The Black Sea.

Excubitors – The palace guards of the Roman Emperor in the 6th century AD.

Fisc – The public treasury of the Roman Empire.

Flagrum – A whip with multiple thongs attached to a handle, usually with barbs of bone or metal knotted into the thongs.

Follis – A large Roman bronze coin equal to 40 *nummi* or 1/420 of a *solidus*. Justinian changed the ratio to 1/180 of a *solidus* in AD 539.

Hekatontarch – Roman army rank. Officer in command of 100 men.

Hodegetria – *lit.* "She who shows the way." A title for the Blessed Virgin Mary and also the name of a famous icon of the Virgin and Christ Child brought to Constantinople in the mid-5th century AD by the empress Pulcheria. The icon, along with the fountain in its shrine, was thought to possess miraculous healing powers.

Ilarch – Roman army rank. The first in rank among the hekatontarchs. Second in command of a *tagma*.

Immortals – The Persian elite armored cavalry.

Ister River – Another name for the river Danube. A frontier river that separated the Romans to the south from the various barbarian peoples that lived beyond it to the north.

Logothete – Officials of the Roman government who served within the Praetorian Prefecture and were responsible for the tax collectors in the provinces.

Magister Militum – *lit.* "Master of Soldiers." A commanding general responsible for a large regional field army. In the Roman Empire of the early 6th century AD, there were five such armies: Two in the vicinity of Constantinople (*in Praesentalis*), one each in Thrace (*per Thracias*), Illyricum (*per Illyricum*) and the East (*per Orientem*).

Magister Officiorum – *lit.* "Master of Offices." A senior official in the Roman government with a function similar to that of a prime minister.

Mandator – A herald or spokesman.

Meros – A late Roman formation of soldiers made up of three *moiras* or approximately 6,000 men.

Moira – A late Roman formation of soldiers usually made up of three or more tagmas or approximately 2,000 men.

Monophysitism – A heresy which held that Christ had a single nature rather than the two natures as affirmed at the Council of Chalcedon (AD 451).

Nika – *lit.* "Victory" in Greek.

Nomisma – *pl.* Nomismata. See *Solidus*.

Nummus – The smallest unit of Roman bronze currency in the 6th century AD.

Optio – A trusted assistant to the commanding officer in the Roman army.

Orthros – The eastern Christian equivalent of Matins or early morning prayers.

Pantocrator – *lit.* "Ruler of all." A title for Jesus as depicted in icons as the ruler of Heaven and Earth, bestowing a blessing on mankind.

Praepositus Sacri Cubiculi – *lit.* "Overseer of the Sacred Bedchamber." The High Chamberlain of the Roman emperor.

Praetorian Prefect – A senior official in the Roman government, primarily responsible for the collection of taxes.

Prefect of the City – A high official responsible for the administration of the city of Constantinople.

Primicerius – Department heads in the Roman imperial bureaucracy.

Prison of Oblivion – A prison for Persians of high rank. Once sentenced, a person sent to this prison could never be spoken of again by anyone on the outside under pain of death.

Scholarians – Ceremonial soldiers of the Roman imperial court, who served an honorary function and were completely unsuited for combat.

Silentiary – A Roman courtier responsible for keeping order during imperial audiences.

Solidus (alternately **Nomisma**)– Standard unit of Roman gold currency in the 6th century AD.

Spathar – *lit.* "Swordsman." A guardian of the imperial bedchamber.

Sphendone – The curved end of the Hippodrome in Constantinople.

Spina – The central axis of the Hippodrome around which the chariots raced.

Stade – A unit of measure roughly equivalent to 1/7 of a mile.

Strategos – *lit.* "General." Commander of a Roman army.

Tagma – A late Roman formation of soldiers usually made up of approximately 300 men. Also called a bandon or numerus.

Tribune (alternately **Comes**) – *lit.* "Count." An officer of the Roman army in charge of a tagma.

Theotokos – *lit.* "God-bearer." A title for the Blessed Virgin Mary, officially affirmed as orthodox at the Council of Ephesus in AD 431.

Via Egnatia – One of the main roads of the eastern Roman Empire, stretching from Dyrrachium on the Adriatic Sea through Thessalonica to Constantinople.

Vir Illustris – *lit.* "Illustrious man." A title denoting the highest rank within the late Roman senate.

Dramatis Personae

(All mentioned below were figures known to history unless otherwise noted)

Achates – Manservant of the usurper, Hypatius (fictional).

Agricola – One of the brothers of Belisarius (fictional).

Aigan – A Hunnic captain and a member of Belisarius's household guard.

Alamoundaras – A brutal Arab kinglet who is allied to the Persians and the scourge of the Roman towns of the Eastern frontier.

Amantius – Praepositus Sacri Cubiculi under the emperor Anastasius.

Ammatas – A Vandal prince and brother of the Vandal king, Gelimer.

Anastasia – Daughter of Antonina born years before her marriage to Belisarius (fictional).

Anastasius – Emperor of the Romans AD 491–518. Uncle of Hypatius, Pompeius, and Probus.

Anna – Mother of Belisarius (fictional).

Antipater – A logothete from Egypt, killed during the Nika Rebellion.

Antonina – Wife of Belisarius.

Archelaus – Fleet purser and quartermaster of Belisarius's African army.

Arethas – An Arab kinglet who was an unreliable ally of the Romans.

Aristo – A physician in the Roman army (fictional).

Ascan – A captain of the Hunnic mercenaries serving under Justinian. Killed at the Battle of Callinicus, AD 531.

Athenodorus – A tribune in Belisarius's household guard.

Azarethas – The Persian commander at the Battle of Callinicus.

Balas – A captain of the Hun mercenaries serving under Belisarius.

Barbatus – A Roman cavalry officer who served under Belisarius in Africa.

Basilides – Magister Officiorum under Justinian.

Belisarius – Magister Militum and Justinian's right-hand man.

Bessas – A Gothic general serving the Romans.

Boniface of Carthage – The Catholic bishop of Carthage during the reign of Gelimer.

Boniface – The steward of the Vandal king, Gelimer.

Boriades – A member of Belisarius's household guard.

Bouzes – A Roman general commanding troops from Libanus who fought alongside Belisarius at Daras and Callinicus.

Cabades – King of the Persians. Father of Chosroes the Great.

Calonymous – An Alexandrian Roman and commander of Belisarius's African invasion fleet.

Caoses – Eldest son of King Cabades of Persia.

Celer – Commander of the Scholarians at the beginning of Justinian's reign.

Chosroes (the Great) – Youngest son of King Cabades of Persia. Subsequent King of Persia in his own right.

Cleon – A leader of the Green faction in Constantinople (fictional).

Constantinus – A Roman general and comrade of Belisarius.

Constantiolus – A Roman general who served under Justinian.

Decius – see *Theodosius.*

Delphios – A leader of the Blue faction in Constantinople (fictional).

Diogenes – A bodyguard of Belisarius.

Dorotheus – A Roman general who fought alongside Belisarius while he was Magister Militum of the East.

Elithios – A Blue factionist criminal who helped instigate the Nika Rebellion (fictional).

Ephraim – An imperial bodyguard who supported the usurper Hypatius.

Epiphanius – Patriarch of Constantinople at the beginning of Justinian's reign.

Euagees – A courtier of Hilderic, the deposed king of the Vandals.

Eudaimon – The Prefect of the City of Constantinople under Justinian.

Eudocia – Youngest sister of Belisarius (fictional).

Eugenius – A slave of the household of Belisarius.

Florentius – A Roman tribune, killed at the Battle of Satala in AD 530.

Fulvia – The head lady-in-waiting to the empress Theodora (fictional).

Fuscias – Prime minister of the Vandal king, Gelimer.

Gaiseric – King of the Vandals who conquered Roman Africa in AD 439. He later achieved infamy by sacking Rome in AD 455.

Gelimer – Arian King of the Vandals who was hostile to the Romans.

Germanus – A Roman general and nephew of Justinian.

Gibamundus – A nephew of Gelimer, King of the Vandals.

Gildo – A Vandal courier (fictional).

Godas – The Vandal governor of Sardinia who rebelled against Gelimer.

Gothaeus – A courtier of the Vandal king, Gelimer.

Gregorius – A soldier in Belisarius's household guard (fictional).

Hermogenes – The Magister Officiorum during the early part of Justinian's reign, and a diplomat to the court of the Persian King.

Hilderic – King of the Vandals who was friendly to the Romans. He was deposed by his nephew, Gelimer, who usurped his throne.

Hypatius – Nephew of the deceased emperor, Anastasius. Brother of Probus and Pompeius.

Hypatius of Ephesus – Bishop of Ephesus and an orthodox theologian.

Ildiger – An officer in the Roman army. Husband of Antonina's daughter, Anastasia.

Joannina – Daughter of Belisarius and Antonina.

John of Armenia – A Roman general and comrade of Belisarius.

John of Cappadocia – Praetorian Prefect under Justinian.

John the Nephew of Vitalian (also called Bloody John) – A Roman general.

Justin – Emperor of the Romans, AD 518– 527. Uncle of Justinian.

Justinian – Emperor of the Romans, AD 527– 565.

Macedonia – A slave of the household of Belisarius.

Marcellinus – Secretary to the emperor Justinian.

Marcellus – A Roman officer and comrade of Belisarius.

Martinus – A Roman officer who served with Belisarius in Africa.

Mauricius – A Gepid officer. Son of Mundus.

Mebodes – Persian Master of Soldiers under Cabades and later Chosroes.

Mundilas – A tribune in Belisarius's household guard.

Mundus – A Gepid noble who became Magister Militum of Illyricum. He fought for Justinian during the Nika Rebellion and subsequently was given command of the campaign against the Goths in Dalmatia.

Narses – Praepositus Sacri Cubiculi of Justinian and a chief advisor.

Optatus – Steward of Sergius the merchant in Syracuse (fictional).

Pappas – A Roman army officer who served under Belisarius in Africa.

Peter – A general of Justinian's imperial household guard.

Peter the Patrician – A Roman diplomat under Justinian. Later he was Justinian's Magister Officiorum for over 25 years.

Pharas – A prince of the Heruls who fought under Belisarius at Daras and in Africa.

Phaulos – A Green factionist criminal who helped instigate the Nika Rebellion (fictional).

Photius – Son of Antonina and step-son of Belisarius.

Pompeius – Nephew of the deceased Emperor Anastasius. Brother of Hypatius and Probus.

Principius – A tribune in Belisarius's household guard.

Probus – Nephew of the emperor Anastasius. Brother of Hypatius and Pompeius.

Procopius – The secretary of Belisarius and the most important historian of the Justinianic period.

Pudentius – A Roman who rebelled against the Vandals in Tripolis.

Pulcheria – Daughter of Antonina born years before her marriage to Belisarius (fictional).

Rufinus – A Roman patrician and diplomat to the court of the Persian King. Son of Silvanus.

Rufinus the Younger – Son of Rufinus. Cousin of Belisarius and his standard-bearer.

Rufus – A logothete serving under John the Cappadocian (fictional).

Sabbatius – The father of Justinian.

Sergius – A merchant in Syracuse (fictional).

Silvanus – A Roman patrician and the father of Rufinus.

Sinnion – A captain of the Hun mercenaries serving under Belisarius.

Sittas – Magister Militum and brother-in-law of the Empress Theodora who was Belisarius's colleague early in their careers.

Solomon – The steward of Belisarius who later became a general and the governor of Roman Africa.

Stotzas – A Roman tribune serving under Martinus. Later a rebel commander in Roman Africa.

Tattimuth – A Roman military officer sent to aid the rebellion against the Vandals in Tripolis.

Theocritus – A failed candidate for emperor put forth by Amantius after the death of Anastasius.

Theodora – Empress of the Romans and wife of Justinian.

Theodosius – Adopted son of Belisarius and Antonina. Originally called Decius in this novel.

Thomas – A silentiary who was also Justinian's personal physician.

Thrasamund – Son of the Vandal prince, Tzazon. Nephew of Gelimer, the Vandal king (fictional).

Tribonian – Roman Quaestor and Justinian's chief legal expert who was the prime mover behind Justinian's reform of Roman law.

Trajan – A Roman military officer and comrade of Belisarius who served under him in the East.

Tzazon – A Vandal prince and brother of King Gelimer.

Uliaris – A Roman officer and comrade of Belisarius.

Unigastus – A tribune and member of Belisarius's household guard.

Valerian – A Roman cavalry officer who served under Belisarius in Africa.

Vidimundus – A Gothic tribune serving in the Roman army and a comrade of Belisarius (fictional).

Vitalian – A Roman general who rebelled multiple times against the emperor Anastasius. He was later assassinated during the reign of Justin.

Zames – Second son of the Persian king, Cabades.

If you enjoyed this book, you might also be interested in these other high-quality works from Arx Publishing...

Belisarius: The First Shall Be Last by Paolo A. Belzoni
"The book strikes one as a conservative rallying cry to the 'Christian West' today....Not that the book deliberately carries a political message. On its own terms, it is an ambitious tale, filled with action, spectacle, and intrigues of all kinds....Painstakingly authentic in its historical, military, and religious detail, assiduously researched and replete with facts."

—John J. Desjarlais, CatholicFiction.net

Leave If You Can by Luise Rinser
"One sentence on the book's back cover describes the novel as exploring 'the challenge of God's mystical call versus the overpowering allure of the world.' I'd add that it not only takes on the challenge to heed God's call when the world is pulling us in other directions, but also how someone might feel the draw to religious life....Overall, this was a book that provided an excellent example of someone answering God's call to pursue the vocation He has laid before them."

—Day by Day in Our World blog

Angels in Iron by Nicholas C. Prata
"The novel's principal strength is its attention to historical detail and the unrelenting realism with which the battle scenes—and there are many—are described....In addition to being an exciting action/adventure yarn and quite a page-turner, *Angels in Iron* is valuable as a miniature history lesson....This is a book that belongs on the bookshelf of every Catholic man, should be read by every Catholic boy (11 or older, I would say), and stocked by every Catholic school library."

—Latin Mass Magazine

Crown of the World: Knight of the Temple by Nathan Sadasivan
"*Knight of the Temple* is written in a style of historical fiction that was prevalent in American Catholic literature several decades ago and follows in the footsteps of such Catholic classics as *The Outlaws of Ravenhurst* and the novels of Louis de Wohl, but with greater intensity. *Knight of the Temple* is a really excellent work, fraught with tension, that hooks us for part two."

—Phillip D. Campbell III, *Saint Austin Review*

The Laviniad: An Epic Poem by Claudio R. Salvucci
"The author successfully writes in the style of the ancient epic in modern English. Lovers of classic tales will really appreciate the poetry and the plot. The poem reads easily and naturally with the flow and flavor of the ancient epics."

—Favorite Resources for Catholic Homeschoolers

For further information on these titles, or to order, visit:
www.arxpub.com

CPSIA information can be obtained at www.ICGtesting.com
Printed in the USA
BVOW072327301011

274814BV00001B/1/P